# The Red Chair

*Book One in the*
*Grace Simms Trilogy*

# The Red Chair

a
# DÄNNA WILBERG
novel

Pretty Road Press
FOLSOM CALIFORNIA

**The Red Chair**

Book One in the Grace Simms Trilogy
by Dänna Wilberg

Literary Edition (with book-group discussion questions)

Published by
Pretty Road Press
P.O. Box 273
Folsom, California 95763
www.PrettyRoadPress.com

Cover Painting by Jim Marxen (www.MarxenArt.com)

This book is a work of fiction. The names, characters, businesses, organizations, places, events, and incidents are the product of the author's imagination or are used fictitiously. The author intends no resemblance to actual persons, living or dead.

Printed in the United States of America

ISBN 978-0-9826014-8-8

19 18 17 16 15    5 4 3 2 1

*To the one whose love held no boundaries:*
*my mother, my friend, my inspiration,*
*and my biggest fan, Sonia Dennis*

*Her story lived November 12, 1927 to February 8, 2011*

# Acknowledgments

This story was inspired by *love*, a foundation that launches us to soar to great heights. Without the help of a dedicated teacher and devoted friend, Donna Benedict, *The Red Chair* would still be in my head, ruminating and collecting dust. Donna retaught me the basic fundamentals of grammar and sentence structure after I suffered injuries in a car accident. She reminded me how to differentiate between a verb and a noun, knowledge I had lost due to closed head trauma. I can never be grateful enough for her time, energy, and love.

And thank you Evie Turner at KVIE television for reminding me that writing is what I loved to do.

Ten years is a long time to wait for meals, to side-step messes, and stand outside the door. I am grateful to my husband, Don, who allowed a writer her space. I am thankful to him for picking up the slack, carrying the load, and being so damn patient. I promised I would buy him dinner when the book got published. He thought that was fair.

Having five beautiful daughters gives a writer plenty of fodder for content and characterization when it comes to dating, starting a career, and growing up. Thank you my lovelies—Dawn, Elia, Ashleigh, Erika, and Olivia—for your encouragement and for giving me tips on how to keep my characters fresh, and interesting. Sorry about the sex and violence; you know better, right? Right?

I always felt this story was meant to be told by the synchronistic events preceding its publication. Compelled to pick up a newspaper in a doctor's office one day, I stumbled upon an ad for the El Dorado Writers Guild, the most amazing critique group a novice could ask for. I remember driving down the freeway the next day, oblivious to make-up and dirty hair because I had a story to share! Nick, Kirk, Pat, Lizanne, Dena, Sammie, Lisa, Donna, Marsha, Duncan, Ellen, Bill, and all of the members who spent years sharing their expertise, I can't thank you enough. I couldn't have grown without you

Thank you to my Saturday critique group, Cathy, Suzanne, and Donna who paid attention to the right stuff and gave me awesome edits. Also thanks to Noreen, Linda, and Tina for listening to me go on and on about murder plots on our way to spiritual expos. And more acknowledgments go to my professional friends, Mark Yankauer, M.A., M.F.T. and Jenyn Darnell, M.A.,M.F.T., for answering all my *what if* questions.

I am grateful to Robin Burcell and Penny Warner, as well, for their endorsements.

My sister Kathy's passion for my success has been unrelenting. Even when she was busy or had other things on her plate, she stopped to listen. And to my mother Sonia, to whom I dedicate this submission, thank you for being my biggest fan! Although you are no longer with us, your input and encouragement supersedes all boundaries.

Oh, and thank you FEAR, for daring me to write this book. What were you thinking??...I'm an Aries!

# Prologue

James Freeman, mesmerized by the face in half shadow and the body shimmering in crimson jewels, secretly wished the pole she straddled was his. Candy, head thrown back and legs spread wide, descended slowly to the ground. Ginger-colored hair swept the floor as she cat-crawled to the edge of the stage and rose to a hypnotic beat. On the last note, she ripped off her bra unveiling perfect breasts tipped in glittering peaks.

"Holy shit!" James dug in his tattered wallet for a five-dollar bill.

The dark-haired man sitting next to James dipped one manicured hand into his cashmere coat pocket, extracted a wad of money, and said, "If you want her attention, I suggest a twenty."

James winced. "A twenty?"

"A lap dance will set you back a C-note," the man said. "But hey, you're a decent looking guy. A twenty might get you a peek." The man winked and extended his hand. "The name's Jess Bartell."

"James," he replied, shifting in his seat. While his eyes roamed Candy's curves, James imagined the pleasures her luscious lips could perform. "Damn, she's hot."

"Watch this." Jess waved a hundred-dollar bill. Candy, drawn like a magnet, crouched down and jiggled her breasts inches from his face. He deposited his money inside her bejeweled thong.

"Thanks, Counselor," she purred.

She winked at James and blew him a kiss. Her perfume sweetened the air, the fragrance exotic, distinctive, expensive—like the woman wearing it. "Jesus Christ, she's amazing," he said. James drained his glass and set it on the bar. He turned to his new friend. "I haven't been to a strip club in years."

Jess threw back a shot. "How about another drink?" he asked. "My treat." He tossed a fifty on the bar, ordered two more shots of Black Maple Hill, and turned to James. "You must be married."

"Past tense," James chuckled bitterly. "Took me two years to get my kids back. You?"

"I keep the little woman tied up at home." Jess leaned closer. "A man needs a little excitement now and then, don't you agree?"

"Hell yeah, especially after the day I had: thirty-two emergencies. Can you imagine?"

"You're a doctor?"

James shook his head. "I wish! No, triage nurse. Huge wreck on Highway 50 this morning. What's your gig?"

"I'm a litigator. Civil, criminal, a few estate battles. Nothing exciting. But I expect that to change now that I'm back in Sacramento." He held up another hundred. Candy instantly appeared, and he pulled the tiny triangle away from her privates to slip the cash inside. James craned his neck to catch that peek Jess mentioned.

"Hey Sugar, save some money for later." Candy pried Jess's hand from her flimsy fabric while her eyes fixed on James. "Maybe we can all go someplace later, have a little fun?"

"I'd love to take a bite out of your sweet ass again," Jess growled, clutching her behind.

Her smile faded. She dipped and twisted her hips, breaking his grasp. "Still got a mark from last time, bad boy."

James watched her writhe across the bar, collecting bills as she went. His tight jeans strangled his manhood. He considered spending his last twenty for one touch of her velvety skin, but his conscience intervened. *Can't keep a babysitter if you show up empty handed.* He stuffed the bill back in his pocket. *Playboy* was the closest he'd been to a woman since Sheryl left. The bitch had started taking the starch out of his libido after the birth of their first daughter, Charming. He went months without sex, and after baby Jetta had come along, he felt like he was married to a nun. Come to find out, her reason for avoiding sex had nothing to do with her lack of desire and more to do with her lack of desire to have sex with *him*.

She preferred his good buddy, Kevin. Since the divorce, he'd been too bitter to think about women or sex. Until now, until Candy.

Jess nudged James's shoulder. "You want to meet her?"

"Meet her? I wanna eat her up."

"I suggest you meet her first."

"And how do you propose I do that?"

"Let's just say, I have an *in* with her." The lawyer motioned over his shoulder "C'mon, let's grab a booth. We'll have more privacy."

"Thanks, man. Must be my lucky night," James said.

"Mine too. I plan to reunite with the girl of my dreams—the one that got away."

"Got away?"

"We met in college. She's amazing, smart, witty, and has a body that won't quit. Funny the mistakes we make in life." His expression soured, "I should've married her. But all that's going to change." His hazel eyes turned to pitch. A smile stretched across his face. "I have a plan. First, I call her, remind her how good we were together, and suggest we get together for ol' time's sake. Then I wait awhile. Let the memories simmer before I call her again." He leaned closer to James. "Believe me, it won't take long before she's mine."

"Doesn't being married complicate things?"

Jess relaxed against the back of the booth. "Are you kidding? Jenna's happy when I'm gone." He rolled his eyes. "Living with me can be torture."

James disapproved of the man's plan. He knew the result of being on the wrong side of a love triangle, but who was he to judge? *Let it go, man; have a good time.*

When Candy's shift ended, the lawyer kept his word and made the introduction. She latched on to James instantly, interested in his line of work and his single status. They were so engrossed in their new connection neither noticed the lawyer had moved across the room to grope a brunette wearing a skimpy cowgirl outfit.

"Wanna lap dance?" Candy snuggled closer.

"No, that's okay," James said.

"Your buddy paid me already." Her fingertips inched toward his crotch. "*A lot.*"

"Keep the money; it'll be our secret," he said, deflecting her move.

"Don't you like me?"

"What's not to like? You're gorgeous. It's just— It's been a long day." James had already tallied the babysitter's hours in his head. The twenty burning a hole in his wallet would barely cover what he owed her. "I just stopped in for a beer. I didn't plan on—"

"Right. A few beers. Get your rocks off. I get it." Candy slid to the edge of the booth. James grabbed her hand.

"I'm not like that." James thought about his little girls, school in the morning. He had lunches to pack, clothes in the dryer. "How about dinner sometime?"

"Dinner? As in date?"

"Flowers, the whole bit," he said, glancing at his watch. "How are you getting home?"

"I walk. I'm just a couple of blocks from here."

"It's late. I can take you."

"I shouldn't but, okay. I'll get changed. Wait here."

James never imagined having someone sit in the car beside him other than Sheryl. *She's history, dude. Get over it.* He glanced Candy's way, and she smiled. He cleared his throat, hoping to chase away his nerves. Small talk wasn't his strong suit. "So, how do you know Jess?"

Her smile morphed into a sneer. "He's a lawyer. He helped me out of a scrape. No big deal," she said, turning her attention out the window. "He comes in the club occasionally. He plays rough, but he's one helluva tipper."

"What's *occasionally*?"

Her voice became flat and dry. "I have bills to pay."

James rested his hand on hers. They drove the rest of the way to her house in silence.

"This is it,' she said, "Home sweet home." He walked her to her door and leaned in to kiss her cheek goodnight when she pulled him close. "You're not getting away that easily," she said, placing his hands on her buttocks. "My peaches ripe enough for you, baby?" She planted tiny kisses on his chin, inching toward his lips. Her pelvis gyrated against his aching groin. Her breasts pressed into his chest.

He kneaded handfuls of spandex, working his way up her ribcage to her breasts. His thumbs circled her nipples into hard knots as she filled his hands with pliable flesh. Rock hard, he was ready to explode, but he knew if he overextended his time with the babysitter, he'd have to stop at the ATM. *Two days 'til payday.* "I'd better go."

She slid her hand between his legs and gave him a wicked look. "I think you should come inside."

He backed away.

"I'll call you."

And he did. Twenty minutes later.

"I wanted to tell you how much I enjoyed meeting you."

"Too bad you had to rush off," she complained.

"I'd like to be honest. I have kids. Two…girls: Charming's six; Jetta's four and a half. Babysitters get expensive."

"I feel better knowing you weren't running home to your wife or girlfriend. And for the record, I love kids."

When payday rolled around, he invited Candy to dinner. At the end of the evening, she insisted they go back to her place. "For dessert," she said. Her lips turned out to be even sweeter than he had experienced at her door. When it came to ways of using her mouth, she was a pro.

"Did I please you?" She cuddled close, massaging him into oblivion. He answered with a kiss. Sheryl was the only woman he'd known sexually, with the exception of a chubby girl he felt up in sixth grade.

He could've lived a lifetime without ever experiencing such gratifying orgasms. Candy proved to be a generous lover, focused on *his* needs. He knew it wouldn't take much to spoil him. But when she hinted about making room in his closet for a few of her things, he got nervous.

"Let's take it slow," he said. "We hardly know each other. I have my kids. There's ballet and soccer. They've been through a lot."

"Don't you like what we have, James? Don't I treat you good?"

He had to admit, it had been a long time since he felt happy. "You know my history. Let me talk to my therapist and see what she has to say."

"Therapist? You see a therapist? I thought you were a man who knew his mind, or does your decision making only go as far as your dick?"

"Seeing as I just got screwed over by one woman, thinking

with my dick for a while doesn't seem like such a bad idea, now does it?"

He saw the hurt look in Candy's eyes and folded her in his arms, but his thoughts were elsewhere. He could hardly swallow. His therapist, so fine, made the gorgeous Candy look like an ugly duckling. His therapist, sexy without trying, exuded confidence. She had the allure and sophistication of a movie star in the lime-light. Yet with a mere exchange of words, she could crawl inside his soul and make all his troubles melt.

As if sensing her catch drifting, Candy pulled away. "Is your therapist a man or a woman?"

"A woman."

She reclaimed her position and held him close. "I hate her already."

# CHAPTER 1

# Trepidation

Damn!" Grace pounded the steering wheel. The stamped ticket she pulled from the machine at the parking lot entrance read 9:04. Her client was scheduled at nine. She glanced at her dash clock in disbelief. *I'm never late to work.* When she rounded the corner, the last thing she expected to see was a green sedan occupying her assigned space. She slammed on her brakes, barely missing the bumper. *What the—!*

Trolling the aisles for a place to park added to her frustration. Her temper flared as she futilely climbed higher levels to no avail. Finally, on the fourth floor, she swung into a tight spot next to a cement post, nearly shearing off her side-view mirror.

She caught her harried reflection in the mirror. *Breathe.* The call she had received from her college crush the night before pulsed in her brain like a bad hangover. Eight years without a word, and now— *He's here.* The mere sound of his voice gave her butterflies. How would she react to seeing him again? *Why Sacramento, Jess? Why now?*

She jammed the gearshift into park, flung her purse over her shoulder and stuffed the remainder of a glazed donut into her mouth. She grabbed her coffee in one hand, car keys in the other, and opened the door. She squeezed through the narrow opening unable to avoid her skirt from riding up around her thighs and exposing her ivory lace. While licking sticky glaze from her fingers, a prickle skittered along the nape of her neck. Her throat constricted. She swallowed hard. *Someone is watching.*

She turned quick, ready to throw her coffee. *No one there.* She scanned her surroundings, paying close attention to shadows, expecting one of them to move. *It's nothing,* the practical voice inside her head mocked. *You're a grown woman now, a trained professional for christsakes!* And yet her pulse quickened. Her cheeks flushed.

"Hello? Anybody there?" Her words echoed in the concrete structure. No one answered.

More chills raced along her spine.

She slammed her car door and looked around one last time. *Someone is watching. I know it.* Adrenaline flooded her nervous system. *Why are you standing here? Run!* Her spiked heels hit concrete, resounding like firecrackers popping on the fourth of July. The sound chased her across the parking lot. She looked over her shoulder twice, expecting to see a gunman, but all she saw were rows and rows of cars. *Not again,* she prayed.

She charged into the elevator, colliding with an old woman.

The woman yowled and rubbed her foot.

"Sorry! Are you hurt?" Grace attempted to slow the stampede in her chest. *Years ago,* she reminded herself. *That stalking happened years ago.*

The old woman's loud protest stopped mid-sentence. The elevator doors stuttered.

Grace froze. Her eyelids squeezed tight, fearing any moment she'd be snatched, her throat slit, and her body dumped on the stained concrete. Horror flashed behind her eyes: images of lying in a pool of blood, oil, and antifreeze.

"Are you okay?" the woman asked.

"I'm fine," Grace muttered.

The old woman continued to stare. "Go like this," she said and brushed her nose.

Grace discovered crunchy icing stuck between her nose and upper lip. "Thanks," she said, unclenching her jaw and forcing a laugh. "Breakfast. I was in a hurry."

*No one there…let it go.*

\*\*\*

*A shadowy figure watched Grace's long legs emerge from her car. Blonde hair spilled across the swell of her breasts and the curve of her spine. Her skirt hiked above her thighs.* Not your typical psychotherapist. *When Grace's cool voice called out, the figure wanted to rush to her…say things. Bad things.* Not yet. Be silent. For now, revel in her fear.

*>Bang!<*

The car door? *The figure listened until the clicking heels darting across the parking lot faded.* Safe to come out now. *The beauty scurrying toward the elevator put nasty ideas in the figure's head:* sharp objects, so much blood. *Ugly thoughts continued to brew. The figure envisioned trembling lips pressed against the beauty's ear.* She'll plead for her life.

*When the door closed and the elevator began its decent, the figure peered through Grace's car windows and spotted a manila envelope on the passenger seat. On the label:* Grace's home address. *A smile followed the discovery. After committing the delightful tidbit to memory, the figure sang a little tune and headed for the stairs,* "I know where you live."

\*\*\*

The elevator came to a halt on the second floor. Grace stayed back and let the old woman exit first, mindful of minutes ticking away. When her path cleared, she raced down the hall to her suite. She smoothed her black pencil skirt over slim hips and fluffed trapped heat from her heavy curls. Shoulders squared, she entered the office as if it were any other day.

"Morning, Sal," she said to the petite woman minding the front desk.

"Good morning," the woman chirped. "You're late. Everything okay?" Aside from being Grace's office manager, Sal was her friend, her very intuitive friend.

"Am I?" How could she justify lazing in the mirror this morning, inspecting her face for signs of aging? The clothes strewed from one end of her bedroom to the other? Her shoes, usually organized neatly in boxes, piled in a heap on her closet floor?

"Your face is flushed."

How did she explain getting spooked in the parking garage? "I was running— This creepy— It felt like— Never mind; I'm sure it's nothing. Do you have my first appointment ready to go?"

"Breathe. James hasn't arrived yet. Here: today's mail." Sal studied Grace carefully. "Goin' somewhere after work?"

"What's with the questions?" Grace tugged the fabric clinging to her hips.

"Your outfit for starters."

"What's wrong with my outfit?" Grace adjusted the scooped neckline on her red-knit sweater.

"Nothing," Sal smirked. "Make-up looks nice, too."

"A little lipstick and mascara. Not a big deal."

"That eye shadow brings out your pretty brown eyes." Sal said, peering over her glasses. "Sure you don't have a date?"

"No! I don't have a date." Grace snapped up her mail, shuffled through the envelopes, and tossed the bundle back on the counter. *Gave up my search for Mr. Right a long time ago.*

"Then what is it?" Sal drummed her fingers.

"What's what? I didn't feel like wearing a suit today, that's all."

"How many times did you change this morning?" Sal persisted, removing her glasses to monitor Grace's reaction.

"Three...okay? I felt frumpy."

"Ah- hah!" Sal flipped the page on the calendar. "I almost forgot. You have a *little* birthday coming up."

"*Little* birthday? I'm going to be thirty-one."

"Aw, that's nothing. You're good until at least...*fifty*. Sal peered over her thin frames. "Trust me. One day you'll wish you were thirty-nine."

"No, I won't." Grace regarded her spiked heels. She had rummaged through the closet on her hands and knees and dug in boxes to find them. She admired the teardrop cut-out above her pinky toe. *Sexy.* She had splurged on the shoes for her last date. *I was twenty-six then. What a loser that guy was!* She cleared her throat. "I'd better get to work."

"You might want to get your eyebrows out from the middle of your forehead. You look...uh...desperate."

"What do you mean, *des*—" Just then, one hundred-seventy-five pounds of molten male walked through the door. "Hi, James."

"Morning ladies, did I interrupt something?"

"Not at all," Grace said sweetly. "Take a seat. I'll be right with you."

James nodded and headed toward the waiting room. Sal nudged Grace, and they both watched his broad shoulders, muscular arms, and tight tush disappear from view.

"Don't say a word," Grace hissed.

# CHAPTER 2
## James Freeman

James followed Grace's orders and filled one of the vanilla faux-suede chairs that lined the waiting room's clay-colored walls. Nerves piqued and palms sweaty, he nibbled the cuticle on his left thumb. Candy had nagged him to make the appointment with Grace. Candy wanted to move forward with their relationship. She felt Grace was the key. Candy's persistence echoed in his brain: "The sooner you talk to her, the sooner we can be together."

His heart beat to the rhythm of Grace's hips as she approached the waiting room. He scanned her body, critiquing her long legs, tight skirt, and hint of cleavage. *Gorgeous.* Her voice carried a melody to his ears when she said, "Give me a moment James, and then we can get started."

The recollection of Candy's comment about therapists and orthopedic shoes tickled him inside. *If she only knew.*

\*\*\*

Grace unlocked the door to her familiar, eclectic space. Morning sun illuminated the walls in a soft, warm glow. Black, crimson, and sage pillows rested against an off-white sofa. A black-lacquered table divided her angled, matching chairs. Nestled between the overstuffed ensemble stood the crown jewel, her soft, supple, red-leather chair. It embraced her body each time she sat down. For Grace, the chair symbolized sacrifice, passion, success. She worked hard to get where she was; *no regrets*. Across from the grouping, tall multi-paned windows filled one wall, the view sublime. Her world.

Each item in the room meticulously chosen to make a client feel not only special and worthy, but also empowered, comfortable and secure.

She walked toward the back of the room past a black-lacquered bookcase, taking her place behind the mahogany desk that once belonged to her great-grandfather. She fluffed her hair to let the heat escape. Hormones? Or nerves? *Focus.*

James hadn't booked an appointment in a while. She began skimming through his file. *We have a lot of catching up to do.*

James, an ER triage nurse had gone through a messy divorce more than a year and a half ago. With the help of a man James considered a friend, his ex-wife Sheryl purloined their two daughters and moved out while James was at work one night. Sheryl had manipulated the *friend* into believing James had molested the couple's eldest daughter, Charming. She showed him pictures of James kissing little Charming while she was in the bathtub and naked on their bed. Sheryl neglected to reveal that she coaxed James into posing with Charming in the photos. Despite James's protests, she convinced him that Charming would find the photos endearing additions to her baby book when she grew up. Sheryl insisted she loved similar *innocent* photos her parents took of her naked when she was little.

When Sheryl left, James immediately filed for divorce and petitioned the court to get his kids back. Unfortunately, the pictures were used against him during the custody hearing. A court battle ensued. The trial dragged on. Vicious gossip and mistrust among James's family and friends continued to grow. For James, being without his kids by far constituted the climax of his nightmare.

Sheryl's ugly accusations provoked an anger James never knew could exist inside. He began to suffer bouts of severe depression. Grace treated him every two weeks for almost a year. When Sheryl's drug abuse was discovered and her allegations against James disproved, his lawyer started getting results. James became more positive. His anger diminished, and so did his need for counseling. When he was awarded full custody of his kids, life began to go well, and James decided to see Grace only as needed. In the last year he had been in to see her only once. When he called to book the session, he expressed his desire to date again. *This should be interesting,* Grace thought. She closed the file and went to retrieve her client.

"C'mon back, James." Grace followed behind him, enjoying the aftershave he wore. "Come in," she said, squeezing past him. "Sit. Get comfortable." Once he entered, Grace closed the door, sat down, and crossed her legs. "Tell me what's been going on."

Even before James began to speak, she noted the change in his appearance. His light-brown, wavy hair appeared longer, professionally cut and highlighted. He'd traded in his "Will Work for Beer" T-shirt and holey jeans for a black-silk pullover and khaki pants. She sensed a new influence in his life.

"I'm doin' pretty good," he said. "Charming turned seven last week. She started ballet classes and loves to pirouette around the house. Jetta's five now. Mimics everything her big sister does. She's a lot better. Sleeps through the night in this new place we moved into." He stared at the floor.

"Where did you move to?"

"The foothills, Shingle Springs. Too many memories with Sheryl in Rancho."

"Nice…a fresh start."

"It's closer to work. The schools are better. It's something I needed to do."

"Good. What else is going on?" Grace smiled, happy that things turned out well for James. He was a great father, but his new look didn't totally convince her that he was on solid ground. For one, he lacked the confident attitude that went along with his designer clothes. Two, his cuticles were ragged—evidence from a prior admission that he worried. He chewed them down to the quick thinking about the kids, money, or *a woman*. And three, he had to think too long to come up with an answer to her question.

"The hospital's been shorthanded lately," he finally said. "I've been working extra shifts and taking care of the kids."

"What have you been doing for yourself?"

"I met someone." Grace observed the way the corner of his lip quivered when he smiled.

"Tell me about her." She urged James to continue with a smile of her own. He scooted forward to adjust his pants. *Too tight all of a sudden?* She had an inkling the couple had passed first base.

"She's great with the kids," he said, looking at his shoes. "I like her, but I don't know, she's not exactly the motherly type."

"What is she like?" Grace leaned back in her chair.

"Well, she's about five-nine, long hair, nice body, energetic—" He looked up to find Grace's poker face. "She's nice," he continued. "We've gotten together about four or five times. I took her to dinner. We went to her place. We met for lunch. She's come over a couple of times after the kids were in bed."

When his body began to slouch, Grace sensed something wrong. "Where did you meet her?"

"A bar," he stammered. "She dances there." His posture stiffened. "I stopped in for a beer… met this guy. He introduced us." He nibbled another ragged cuticle.

"What kind of dancing does she do?" Grace asked, exploring his discomfort.

"She's uh…you know…one of those exotic dancers."

"Exotic? Like a belly dancer? I'm not sure I know what you mean."

"She's a stripper! A pole dancer. She takes off her clothes and shakes her ass for tips."

"Oh, I see," said Grace. "And this is a problem?"

"Yeah, I don't want the kids exposed to…*that*." He lowered his voice. "They've met her; they like her. She's funny. We have fun. But man, I don't know." He bit his thumbnail down to the quick until it bled. "I'm not good at this girlfriend stuff."

"It's a big change for you, James. You and Sheryl were together for sixteen years."

"Yeah, fucking bitch!" He swiped his hand across his face. "Sorry. It's just that she complicated my life so much. I need a partner. I feel like I'm raising those kids by myself, even though Sheryl has, you know, some limited visitation."

"Oh? When did visitations start?"

"Last month. She's out of rehab." His hands balled into a fist. "When I see her, I feel screwed all over again." He took a deep breath, exhaled, and pushed his sleeves up over tanned forearms. "The bitch still gets to me some days, I guess."

"You're bound to have bad days, James. Anger is normal; you've been through a lot."

James made a grunting sound and started chewing his other thumbnail. He listened intently to her words as she went on to say, "Suppressing anger is unhealthy; letting it get out of control is unproductive. What Sheryl did was unacceptable. It hurt you, but it's important to realize that desperation led her to create the mess she put you in. She couldn't find a healthier way to get her needs fulfilled. Had she come to you and communicated those needs, it would've been a whole different scenario. She wasn't strong enough to face her demons, so she unleashed them on you."

"Yeah, I should have seen it coming."

"You didn't cause her to do what she did, James. You don't have to punish yourself." Grace wanted to move on to his new interest. "You feel ready to start dating. That's healthy. You have choices. If this girl isn't right for you, don't settle. You have just begun to get back into the world. Be good to yourself. Be selective. Get to know what you want."

"I'm horny, okay?" A blush pooled in his cheeks. He covered his face with his hand and shook his head. "Did I just say that?"

"Getting aroused is healthy, James. Keep it in perspective. Sex is not love, although it can be loving when it's right. It's like the anger issue. Find ways to be healthy about your sexuality."

"She acts like we should be in a relationship because I slept with her," he revealed.

"Do you see that as a red flag?"

"Yeah, but at least she wants to be with me."

"I'm sure there are others who enjoy sex that aren't interested in flinging themselves into a relationship."

"You're right. Candy isn't right for me." He scrubbed his thighs with his palms. "Whew, she's somethin' else though…fuck!"

Grace simply observed and waited for him to continue.

He talked about his sexual relationship with his ex-wife and how he hadn't felt comfortable with women. He married young. Because the sex was good at the time, he assumed it was love.

"I wish I had given it more thought then."

"Knowing the difference between lust and love takes time to discover," Grace said. "Do you feel that if you become sexual with someone, marriage is the next step?"

"I did. I don't think that's true anymore."

"Sometimes people don't give themselves a chance to discover the difference because of their upbringing. This establishes a shaky foundation for marriage, and it's not surprising that many couples can't withstand the discoveries that take place within a marriage once they know each other better. Maturity plays a big part, too."

"I hear what you're saying. Sheryl and I were fifteen when we started dating. She was raised Catholic. We were always going to hell for wanting each other," he snickered. "Maybe if I had let her spread her wings a little—"

"She had choices, James. That guy she met—"

"My *friend?*" he sniped.

"Plotting against you gave her an excuse to find comfort in his bed."

"Yeah, I guess."

"She took it to the extreme. Her accusations were damaging. *She* made that choice."

"Some choice. She went from being a wife and mother to a crack whore. Her teeth are messed up. She's barely ninety pounds," he said. "He introduced her to some pretty nasty shit."

"Give yourself time to get over the hurt."

"Maybe if I hung around the library I would've met a girl like you."

"Good place to stop, James," Grace said, trying to sound indifferent to his flirting. "When would you like to set up our next appointment?"

"Two weeks? I guess I should have a talk with Candy and think about my anger issues."

"Sounds like a plan," Grace said. "Check with Sal on the way out; she'll get you set up. Take care, James."

Grace closed her door and mentally began her summation. *James Freeman cleans up very nicely.* She tried to imagine what Candy looked like from the description James had given. Her mind backtracked to the statement she made about finding a person looking for just sex. Perhaps she needed to take her own advice. *Would I be satisfied with a one-night stand?* She already knew the answer.

# CHAPTER 3
## Becky Jensen

Becky would never rival the model posed on the fashion magazine she held in her lap. She lacked beauty and sophistication, her most attractive feature being her childlike innocence. She wasn't homely. She wasn't pretty. She was Becky.

"Hi, Becky," Grace poked her head into the waiting room. "Sorry for the delay. I'll be with you in a moment."

Grace opened Becky's chart for a quick review, beginning with the transcript of the call Grace received from her dear family friend and mentor, Dr. Meltz. He had described Becky's case, explaining the need for restraints and meds. "She's calm now…lucid; I can't keep her here," he said. "There are no beds available, and I don't want to transfer her to County." He sighed, and his tone softened. "She told me about some guy; says he's her angel. Will you talk to her?"

Dr. Meltz sensed her indecisiveness. He was good at that. "I held you the day you were born; do an old man a favor, will you?"

How could she refuse? Her dad and Dr. Meltz were med-school buddies, best friends at one time. She adored Dr. Meltz, maybe even worshiped him a little. She didn't want to disappoint.

She flipped through notes from previous sessions, determined to unlock the mystery of the man her client claimed to be her angel. Becky was twenty-three, intelligent, but emotionally stunted. Her voice and behavior leaned toward adolescence, as if she were stuck there. Grace knew that when pain became the result of trusting and loving, the unconscious mind dealt with the instinctive needs of the id, and another coping mechanism developed in its place. Traumatized children often created imaginary friends or became fixated with super heroes. Grace pondered the possibilities. Was Becky's angel someone she created to make her feel safe? Loved? Was it possible the girl managed to hide an atrocity she experienced as a child by splitting from reality and fixating on this savior? If this coping mechanism served her well until that day at the mall, what changed? And why did her psychological crutch take on a physical form?

***

Becky was used to waiting. From the time she was a child, she had lived her life one day at a time, always expecting the worst, secretly hoping for the best. Waiting gave her time to think and reflect.

Her job at Nordstrom, for instance, surpassed all her expectations. She started out in the dress department doing alterations, solitary work. She didn't think her supervisor knew she existed other than reprimanding her once for her unorthodox appearance. Evidently the woman didn't *get* that Becky's multiple piercings signified she was able to *do the pain*. Therefore, Becky was shocked when the woman approached her and asked her to work counter sales.

It was her second week manning a register on her own, and she looked forward to the Mother's Day rush. Staying busy kept her demons cloaked behind a smile. When she arrived for her shift, the store was teeming with shoppers. She still remembered the mélange of perfume scents wafting through the air that day. Girls giggled, trying on hats and modeling for each other.

She was busy helping a customer with accessories when she heard, "May I see that scarf?" She instantly spun around to face him. Her heart beat a staccato rhythm. Her throat went dry; she couldn't swallow. She struggled to force the words, "It's you. You're here." She walked up behind him and threw her arms around his waist, never expecting him to react the way he did.

He spun around so fast that he sent her flying toward the glass counter. Her mind reeled in confusion as he reached out just in time to break her fall. "I'm sorry," he said. "You caught me off guard. Did I hurt you?" His apology sounded sincere, but his eyes were dark pools. *Fathomless.*

The words floated from her lips: "It's you."

"You must have me confused with someone else," he said and hurried away.

A crowd gathered. People surrounded her, pummeling her with questions. "Are you okay, miss? Do you want me to call security?" The faces around her grew distorted and blurry. She searched the crowd. He was gone. At that moment, it felt as though her mind snapped, and she began to scream.

Suddenly, she was surrounded by men in blue uniforms. She remembered a prick burned in her arm, and her thoughts quickly turned soggy and grey. A host of facial features swam before her eyes. She recognized no one. The sound of sirens melded with flashing lights. Everything became surreal. She remembered thinking, *where am I?* She felt as if she were submerged in oatmeal, her arms and legs immobile. Kind eyes hovered above her. Someone else was speaking, but all she heard were kittens crying. She closed her eyes and watched her stepfather Dan drown them one by one.

"I'm Dr. Meltz," said the man bent over her body. He lifted her eyelid, then the other, each time blinding her with a tiny light. "Do you know where you are, Miss Jensen?"

"It was him," she said.

"Who, Miss Jensen?"

"My angel." Her body hovered above the table. Her words were strung on a cord and pulled from her brain.

"You're at Mercy Hospital. You experienced a traumatic episode at Nordstrom. Do you remember what happened?"

"He pushed me away."

"Who pushed you away?" the doctor asked.

Her tongue felt too thick to explain; it felt as though she was being submerged in thick goo. *I'll never eat oatmeal again.* Her eyes fought against the light; her lids weighted down.

Dr. Meltz patted her hand. "The sedative will wear off in an hour or so. Perhaps we can talk then."

Becky let go, falling into a deep sleep. Her angel was there to catch her. "We'll get through this together," he whispered. His words filled her head like a swarm of bees.

*Stop!*

Once again cognitive of her surroundings—*therapist's waiting room*—she opened a magazine, determined to quiet the voice in her head. *What do they know about love?*

\*\*\*

"Becky?" Grace tapped the girl's shoulder, and she jumped. "I didn't mean to startle you. Ready?"

Becky tossed the magazine on the table. "How long have you been standing there?"

"Only a moment. Come. This way."

\*\*\*

Grace opened the manila folder and dated a fresh page. Pen poised in hand, Grace began the session. "The last time we met, you shared what you remembered about the incident in the mall, about the man you saw, any more thoughts?"

"He's all I think about," Becky said. "I think about his eyes. I think about the way he looks at me." The young girl leaned back into soft cushions. One leg slid sensuously over the other. A sly grin played upon her face. Her haunting voice continued. "His eyes are so beautiful, sexy…compassionate. He affects me like no other." Becky closed her eyes. Smoky lids fringed in dark lashes began to flutter. "His eyes reach into my soul, seeking a part of me I haven't even dared to explore."

Grace recognized desire when she saw it: *Jess Bartell.* His handsome face loomed in her vision. Why did he call last night? *What does he expect from me?* Eight years had gone by. *I did what had to be done. I moved on.* She pushed her quandary to the back of her mind. *Not now. Focus.*

"Does this man have a name?" She watched Becky's fingertips flutter across her collarbone, but thoughts channeled deep in the dark chasm of Grace's mind. Jess's eyes connected with hers, stroking her most sensitive emotions, her most secretive yearnings, and her impure thoughts. *Focus!*

Becky leaned forward, rested her elbows on her tanned knees and spoke through her splayed fingers. "When he looks at me a certain way, I fall under a spell or something. He holds me in his gaze until my heart beats like a captured bird, and I can't breathe."

Grace noted Becky's dramatic response. *Possibly held her against her will?* "What then?"

"He smiles, and he lets me go *slowly*."

"Sounds cruel—"

"It's not like that."

"No?"

"He's my angel."

"Angels don't toy with people's emotions," Grace said.

Becky's body stiffened. "You don't understand Dr. Grace; he's not a monster!"

Grace begged to differ. She knew the hold a man could have on a woman's heart. A small shiver traveled her spine. *He can't wrap you around his finger again...unless you let him.*

The clock ticked away minutes.

"Do you want to tell me more?"

"No." Becky's smile flickered. Her jade eyes blurred into watercolor seascapes. "You just want to make me believe he doesn't exist. He does! He's gentle and kind."

"I believe he exists. What I'm trying to understand is his relation to you. Is this man a friend? Relative? How do you know him."

The girl stifled her tears. Turning away, she seemed to withdraw her trust, and she wouldn't say.

Grace leaned closer. "Can you describe him to me?"

Becky's expression chilled. She rose, sauntered across the room and stared at the Picasso print. She ran her finger along the edge of the frame and said, "I knew it was him. I knew the moment I heard his voice...I told you that!" She spun around, her cold eyes flashing, "Remember?"

Grace remained cool, deflecting the hateful look directed her way. She could only imagine her client's frustration. "Yes, I remember."

Becky began to brood. They had discussed the incident in their first session two weeks prior. Becky told Grace when she heard his voice, it signaled her brain to track the source. She said her heart accelerated when she saw him; she couldn't breathe. "My skin burned like fire."

What Becky described were symptoms of a panic attack: heart palpitations, shortness of breath, and flushing. Grace knew the signs. She needed more information about the scintillating voice the girl had heard. Where did his voice originate? Did it stem from fear? *What about her anger?* "As I recall," she prompted, "you said his voice was familiar."

"How many times do I have to tell you, it was *him*! His voice has been stuck in my head for so long, how could I not recognize it?"

"How long have you been hearing his voice?"

Becky flopped back down on the sofa with such force the cushions practically swallowed her whole. "If you spoke to someone on the phone for years and then heard them speak in person, wouldn't you recognize them?"

"Go on. I'm listening."

Becky's eyes glistened with tears. Grace softened her tone, seeing the girl's distress.

"Something is hurting you," Grace said. "What is it?"

"He *pushed* me. I tried to hug him, and he pushed me away."

"Then what happened?"

"I must've appeared stunned because he apologized. I told him he didn't hurt me. I said, 'You just saved my life.'"

"How did he respond?"

"He said, 'You must have me confused with someone else.'"

"You said he saved your life. What did you mean by that?"

Becky dried her tears and sat up straight. "Is that what I said?"

"Yes. How did he save your life?"

"He stopped me from falling, didn't he?"

The two sat in silence, reflecting. Grace worked to piece together the facts. Things weren't adding up. She would have to dig deeper.

Grace came back to the moment. "What do you like about this man?"

"I love his hair." The girl's buoyancy returned as if she were indulging in a gooey treat. Head tilted back, eyes closed, she pictured the man in her mind.

Grace shared the girl's reverie. She wanted to rake her own hands through Jess's dark hair, feel the silky waves slide between her fingers and unearth feelings kept hidden from everyone except *him*. Grace cleared her throat, trying to stay professional. "Can you tell me what you're feeling, Becky?"

"I don't know. He has great hair."

In her notes, Grace had written and circled the word *compassionate*. Becky had used this word to describe the man's eyes. Compassionate eyes and great hair weren't much to go on; she smiled to encourage her client. "Go on. I'd like to hear more."

Becky placed two fingers on her parted lips, timidly exploring their moist flesh, and then traced her way down to the opening of her blouse. "When I close my eyes, I can feel the warmth of his breath on top of my head. His hand—it's so strong—slides the length of my arm, and he whispers, 'It's okay. We can do this together. You're going to be fine. I'll see to that.'" A single tear splashed on the top of Becky's hand.

Grace sensed the girl's despair. She didn't want her slipping away. "What other thoughts do you have?"

Becky tilted her head. "Thoughts I shouldn't be having."

"Like what?"

"I have thoughts about...about his body. "

"His body?" Grace's ears perked. "Go on."

Becky's voice lowered an octave. "I picture him standing before me. I unbutton his shirt, slide my hands around his waist. He feels so good! His stomach is firm. Hmmm. He has a mature physique. He's kind of—" She lowered her eyes and looked away. "Anyways, I love his body." She placed her hands in her lap and refrained from further explanation.

Grace noted Becky's description of the man's body. Possible transference? Father? Uncle, perhaps? She took advantage of Becky's introspection to question further. "Is he okay with you touching him in such a personal manner?" Grace wondered if, in fact, this man were forbidden fruit. "Does he resist you?"

Becky pressed a wrinkle in her plaid skirt with her palm. "Not in my mind. In my mind...he surrenders." Rueful, she added, "Only in my mind, though."

Graces wondered if she was dealing with post-traumatic stress disorder. "What happens after you unbutton his shirt?"

Grace flinched at the girl's sudden change. Becky's head snapped up. She squared her shoulders. Her eyes flashed.

"First, I kiss his stomach," she said. "I have tasted him over and over again...in my mind." Becky lifted herself up an inch or so, shifted her weight, and squeezed her knees together. Her slight blush indicated she had stirred up some heat; she caressed her arms and continued her fantasy: "I move up toward his chest, unbuttoning as I go." She closed her eyes, and her body quivered.

A searing thought penetrated Grace's concentration. She did

her best to ignore the tingle and doodled the name "J-E-S-S" beside the notes on Becky's chart. *No. Not again.*

Becky was not done: "I can feel the wetness from my mouth on my chin as I kiss his warm, salty skin. He's so delicious. I want the texture of his skin against mine." She took a deep breath and continued, "*Mmmm*, he smells like ocean air. Dark hair feathers a trail from his navel to his chest, and I can't resist rubbing my cheek against it. He excites me like no one else." Becky's brows knitted together. "I have imagined this so many times," she said, opening her eyes. "Yet I've never seen him undressed. Don't you find that strange?"

"Well," Grace replied, "certain body types can lend themselves to certain characteristics, I suppose. Continue," she urged. Grace added the supposition to her notes.

"I um, I finish unbuttoning his shirt, exposing his chest." Becky's face flushed as she tried to describe her mystery man's physical attributes. "He is— He has—" She stumbled, unable to find the right words. "I wanted to— *Oooooh*, I can't do this, Grace!"

"Perhaps this is a good place to stop then. Are you okay?"

"We didn't get very far, did we?"

"Actually, I think you did a great job. You shared more of what you've been storing in your head. That's a good thing. And you managed to describe your feelings with less hesitation. I think we made progress. What do you think?"

"Yes," Becky said. "Progress."

Grace's always tried to empower her clients with their own conclusions before she ended a session. The girl's smile was hopeful. She had moxie. Natural survival instincts made her strong like steel, but emotionally she was fragile, like hand-blown glass. In order for them to build a solid foundation, Grace would have to be the hammer before she could be the glue.

***

With Becky gone, Sal turned to Grace. "Watch your heart. I know how you get too involved with your patients." Sal's face filled with concern.

"You're right. Where's that spray can of Teflon when I need it?" A few years ago, when Grace began her private practice, she made herself too available to her clients and left little reserve for herself. She became run-down, emotionally and physically. Grace devoted herself to her clients, and Sal looked out for her.

Sal hummed as she watered the ivy next to a dish filled with butterscotch candy. "You're going to need Botox if you don't get that look off your face." Sal mimicked Grace's scowl.

"That bad, huh?"

"You seem bothered."

"Lot on my mind. That's all. By the way, were there any messages?"

"Nope."

Grace's heart sank. *Surely he would have called by now.*

Sal pinched a few leaves. "Wanna talk about it?"

"No."

Sal cocked her hip, "This is about a man."

"It's an adjustment to an uncontrollable situation, that's all." Grace thumbed through the pages of a fashion magazine.

"Sure it is. Okay if I leave a few minutes early today?"

"No problem."

"Buns has a dentist appointment."

"And how is Buns these days?" Grace asked.

Buns was the youngest—and Grace's favorite—of Sal's five boys. His full name was Brunswick; John, Sal's husband, had a passion for bowling and a reputation for warped humor.

"We're finally getting that front tooth of his fixed. Can you believe he's giving me static about getting it bonded? He says the chip gives him character."

"Uh huh," Grace agreed, half listening. Her mind probed elsewhere: "By the way, I meant to ask you where you parked this morning."

"Where I always park—second floor on the end. Why?"

"My spot was taken. I had to park on four."

"That's because you were late. Two and three fill up after eight-thirty." Sal paused. "Something's wrong. What is it?"

"Why do you always assume something is wrong?"

"Because you're making that face again."

"I have a ton of work," Grace said, relaxing her brow.

The last thing she wanted to do was worry her friend. Sal's happy-go-lucky spirit had been threatened four years earlier when she found a lump in her breast. Grace counseled women who had survived cancer, but struggled with the trauma of losing their breasts. Sal refused to have a mastectomy. She was convinced she could beat the disease. She and John went on a second honeymoon to Fiji. She learned to parasail and took up bridge. For six months she lived in denial, believing nothing could go wrong with her body and that no problem existed she and God couldn't mend. In the end, the cancer failed to progress. Her surgeon agreed a lumpectomy would suffice. The doctor removed her lymph nodes, leaving her breast intact.

It seemed Grace and Sal always had each other's backs. Starting out as neighbors in Southern California, Sal came to Grace's rescue when Grace started her period. Grace, two days shy of her thirteenth birthday, called her mother at work in a panic, complaining about the pain. Her mother told Grace to suck it up; there were worse things in life to come. Sal, who had stopped by to drop off tomatoes from her garden, saw Grace's distress. Sal stayed until she felt comfortable enough to talk. After Grace told her what was wrong, Sal rushed home and returned armed with pads, ginger tea, a bottle of Midol, and a candy bar. Not another word was said about it, but when Grace turned twenty-one, Sal sent her a bottle of amaretto and a little note: "For your cramps."

Sal was the reason Grace relocated to Sacramento after she finished grad school and her psych rotation. During Sal's cancer crisis, John worked long hours. Five young boys proved to be a handful even for a healthy mom. Grace moved in to help. After Sal recovered, she offered Grace permanent residency. "Start your own practice,"she said. "Live here as long as you like. Save some money. Buy a house. Be your own person." Sal's offer was irresistible.

Sal knew Grace's parents were controlling. Being an only child had its disadvantages. Sal, on the other hand, brought balance to Grace's life. Eventually, she accepted Sal's offer. Grace worked two jobs, saved her money, and bought a house. The day she put a deposit on her office, she called Sal to ask if she would be her secretary. Sal conferenced John on three-way. They both said yes." And so it began...

Grace returned to her office, leaned against the door, and closed her eyes. *What's wrong with me?* She placed her hand to her heart. The beat was not her norm. *Same trepidation you experienced freshman year of college when you thought you were being stalked.* She never saw the person in Chicago, but she heard footsteps and felt a strong, ominous presence on several occasions. She was certain she was being watched. She recalled the baseball bat near her bed—and the mace. Frightened, she went to police, but they advised, without proof, there was nothing they could do. Luckily, Jess came along, *a knight in shining armor,* and he was the counter threat that finally intimidated her pursuer into cowardly retreat.

She stared out the window, thinking about Jess. *What's the big deal? You didn't really expect him to follow up right away, did you? There's a reason things didn't work out.* Their attempt at a long-distance friendship fizzled long ago. First, the phone calls got shorter, and then the frequency decreased. Before long Grace was forced to accept their fate. He belonged to another, and she…she convinced her heart things worked out for the best. *I wonder if Jess is happy in his marriage.* Part of her wanted to imagine he wasn't. *And if that were true?*

"Stop torturing yourself. You have work to do." She checked the time. *Marilyn is late.*

# CHAPTER 4
# Marilyn Beauchamp

Dave's car sat parked on the side of the house. *Why is he home?* Marilyn glanced at the list of errands still clipped to the sun visor as she lumbered out of her car. *He said he was swamped at work and wouldn't have time to run around getting paint.* She couldn't tell him she'd booked a therapy appointment for eleven. She didn't have time to buy paint either.

For some reason the front door was locked. Marilyn rang the bell, but heard no steps. He'd sneer at her empty hands, ask her why she didn't stop at the hardware store or get his beer. He'd never understand she wasn't in the mood to stand in lines or to wander the grocery isles aimlessly, trying to resist her craving for chocolate moon pies. She almost hyperventilated every time she thought of picking out paint for Nevada's room. *He could care less it takes me hours to make those kinds of decisions. He should be grateful I picked up his prescription and stamps.*

*Darn litterbugs. No respect*, she thought, removing the empty gum package from her azalea bush. The sun began to warm things up outside. She rang the bell again. *Broken?* She dug through her purse for the key Dave insisted she keep separate from her car keys. He treated her like a dumb-ass. "If you lose your goddamn key, I'll have to change the locks," he complained. She only misplaced her house key once in the entire time they were married. The key had fallen out of her pants pocket. Later she had found it at the bottom of the hamper. She couldn't figure out why he was so fussy about the dang locks.

Her hand shook when she tried to insert the key. *Look at you. You're a nervous wreck.* She felt nauseous. The key wouldn't go in. Upside down? *Stupid, stupid, stupid.* On the second try, she heard giggling. *Strange.* Nevada's car wasn't parked on the street. She put her ear to the door and listened. Her fist clenched. She turned the key, grabbed the handle, and charged into the house.

Dave knelt on their living room floor in front of the couch, his pants puddled around his ankles. A young woman, half his age, froze with her legs in the air. Her clothes littered the floor next to Dave. She quickly covered globular mounds of flesh with her hands.

"That ain't gonna protect your virtue, honey!" Marilyn seethed. *Beer cans everywhere.*

"What the fuck are you doin' home?" Dave yelled.

Marilyn didn't respond. His question seized her brain. She felt cold. *This must be what it feels like to die.*

Dave didn't have the decency to pull up his pants. At least his sex kitten closed her legs and tried to cover herself in long blonde hair. Her large eyes widened with fear.

Marilyn wanted to jam a thumb into each brown orb. She hated brown eyes. She hated blondes. She hated being old. Most of all, she hated Dave. "Get your *dirty* feet off my couch."

The young woman obeyed. Marilyn wouldn't give Dave the satisfaction of making a scene. No, this time he wasn't going turn things around, make it her fault. Her calm voice sounded foreign to her. "Dave, how many times have I asked you to use the coasters? Rings!" She pointed at the milky circles. "Cans leave those nasty rings." She walked away.

***

Marilyn hung her floral muumuu on a crocheted hanger. She wiggled into polyester pants and shimmied into a loose top. With time to kill before her appointment, she picked up a paperback from her nightstand and propped herself against the headboard. She shed no tear when Dave's engine rumbled outside the house. The crunching gravel beneath the truck's tires resembled the sound of her gnashing teeth. Hate simmered in her chest and rose in her throat. She tasted the bitterness. "All I need is a plan," she said.

***

The minute hand on the clock crawled from twelve to four. Grace had difficulty concentrating on Marilyn's chart. She scanned her notes: "Marilyn Beauchamp. Victim of loveless marriage. Now one year in therapy."

When Marilyn turned fifty, her life had become a whirlwind of transitions. Her youngest daughter graduated from high school and moved out before the ink dried on her diploma. Marilyn's twenty-year-old son impregnated his seventeen-year-old girlfriend. They decided an abortion was the solution and broke up afterward. Her son sank into a deep depression. Marilyn felt helpless.

Grace's mind wandered from her client's predicament to her own. What would it be like to be married to Jess? Was he a kind and loving husband? *Surely he must be. I can't imagine him any other way.* Maybe if she had tried a little harder to win his heart back then…

*He didn't mention his wife or children.*

Her soul-searching was interrupted by the familiar timbre of her client barging through the door, apologizing for her tardiness. *Marilyn.*

"Hi Grace. Sorry, I'm late. Traffic, you know. How are you?"

"I'm fine. More important, how are you?" Grace glanced up and down her client, performing her routine visual check, but remaining nonchalant. Any changes in appearance gave Grace an indication of how her clients were feeling about themselves. Marilyn's attire varied between homespun and "who cares." Her relaxed shape, grey hair, and stray facial whiskers shouted pre-menopause. She appeared older than fifty, but when she smiled, her dimples took ten years away.

Grace wondered how her own mother had survived *the change* with such dignity. Her mother remained fit and youthful at sixty three.

Marilyn settled in an overstuffed chair across from Grace and began, "Nathan is attending sessions at New Day. He's on Zoloft for his depression. He seems to be doing better."

"Fantastic…glad to hear it. Now, how are you?"

"Well, I guess I'm relieved now that Nathan's getting some help."

"Last time we met," Grace said, "we discussed you doing

more for yourself, getting out, having fun."

"I've been busy getting Nathan situated, and I've been cleaning out Nevada's room. She took the major stuff, but left the crap behind when she moved. Thought I'd paint, build some shelves, and make myself a craft room. Dave isn't home much, and when he is, well you know…"

In a previous session Marilyn revealed the discovery her husband was having sex with her friend. The woman was fifteen years younger and a size two. "Is Dave still involved with that woman?" Grace asked.

"He says he's not. I don't believe him…or should I say, I don't believe that he is not seeing someone." Marilyn was too embarrassed to mention the latest sex-tot. She crossed thick ankles and tucked a chunk of salt-streaked hair behind one ear. "I ran into my so-called friend, Alise, at the store the other day. Bitch had the nerve to ask me how I was doing."

"Must've been uncomfortable for you," Grace consoled, tuning into her client's word choice. *Bitch* wasn't a word normally used by this woman, born and raised in the Bible belt. "Want to talk about what happened?"

"You know, I think I felt worse for her than I did for myself," Marilyn said.

"How so?"

"She disappointed her family big time. Her husband left, and according to rumor…"

Her client's tone became smug.

"…the kids won't talk to her or have anything to do with her. Shame really—Dave wasn't worth it."

"What's Dave been up to?" Grace jotted the incident on her pad, penciled in the date, and circled the word *bitch*.

"You know how it is," Marilyn sniffled. She dug in her pocket for a tissue to dab her cornflower blue eyes. "Everywhere I turn I'm reminded of what I'm not. Used to be a woman kept her privates private. Dave used to be happy with a pin-up of Farrah Fawcett in the garage. Now he's got some bitch stripping on the screen saver of our computer. Half the icons he's saved on the desktop are for those kinds of web sites." Marilyn grunted and stretched faded-orange cotton over her bulging waistline.

Grace penciled a checkmark next to the circled word in her

notes. "Sounds to me like Dave spends a lot of time on the computer."

"Shoot, he practically slobbers all over himself when we watch TV, too. Makes all kinds of moaning sounds. It makes me sick. I feel like a troll." Marilyn gave her therapist the once over. "Hell… how would you know, Grace?"

The therapist adjusted herself in her red chair. She knew many women felt threatened by changes in society. They felt threatened by internet porn, strip joints, plastic surgery, reality shows, and even hamburger commercials. *Temptation everywhere.* For years Grace counseled women who were in deceptive marriages. Today, blatant sexuality seemed to be epidemic. Rampant sleaze seemed to penetrate the average household.

Understanding Marilyn's pain wasn't enough to shield the therapist from her client's contemptuous glare. Marilyn's disparaging remarks arose from her need to vent her inadequacy.

"What does Dave have to say about his behavior?" Grace asked.

"He blames it on a mid-life crisis!"

"Yes, well, he needs to blame someone or something."

"He says he was always too busy working…never had time to play. What about me?"

Marilyn jammed her thumb into her breastbone. "I gave up my youth, too! Just because I put on a few pounds and have a few wrinkles. Does that mean I don't like sex? Does that mean I don't need affection? Should I go out and get myself a college jock?"

Grace didn't comment. For some women nothing was worse for their self-esteem than their changing shapes and empty households. Sexy models prancing across the television, taunting viewers with their perfection, made these women feel inadequate and obsolete. Add to that an ignorant husband who thought being a man entitled him to every *Barbie* half his age.

"I'm sure getting a guy isn't a problem for you," said Marilyn, as her eyes raked over Grace's body like sharp claws. Grace remained indifferent, hoping to diffuse the anger directed at her. "Besides," Marilyn's voice lowered to a lethal level, "Dave says guys can get young, hot babes anytime they want, so what would they want with *me*?"

"It's not about you," Grace replied calmly, watching the contempt in her client's eyes liquefy. "Dave acts out because of the way he feels about his own sexuality, not yours."

"Hard to believe it's not about me," she whimpered, "when it's me he acts so mean to."

"How's his drinking been?"

"He still maintains status quo." Marilyn sniffed, catching a tear with one chipped fuchsia thumbnail, a color she most likely found among her daughter's things.

"Dave's drinking contributes to his behavior," said Grace. "He drinks…lashes out at you, tries to make you responsible for his internal struggle."

"The problem is— Um, he thinks his behavior is perfectly normal! He thinks he behaves like any ordinary man. He says if I took better care of myself, he wouldn't have to look elsewhere!" Marilyn tugged at the polyester pant leg, snug around her thigh.

"Well, that mind-set certainly works in his favor! 'It's your fault I went out and had a fling with your friend! Your fault I act like a jerk when we watch TV.' Is that the way you see things?"

"No. No, I don't!" Marilyn blotted her eyes and straightened her posture.

"Our time is about up here today, but I'd like to give you some homework. I'd like you to take a look at this book. It's about codependency. I know we've talked about it before. The author has gone through a similar situation. If you think the information doesn't pertain to your situation, bring the book back next time, and we'll go from there. If you find it helpful, try the exercises in the back of the book." When she reached out to give Marilyn's hand a slight squeeze, the woman pulled away. "Same time next week?"

"Sure," Marilyn replied, her voice brittle. She brushed past Grace without a goodbye. She seemed livid.

***

Once outside, Marilyn's body began to shake. She hated feeling this way. She hated Dave. She hated her life. She hated Grace for being pretty—and for being right about being codependent. *Oh Grace, you're such a smarty pants, aren't you?*

Marilyn shoved her car key into the ignition. She looked long and hard into the rear view mirror. The eyes looking back scared her to death. She didn't want to live. She wanted to kill. *Things need to change.* Satisfied with her conviction, she put her car in reverse. "*You'll be sorry,*" she whispered.

She grabbed dark glasses to protect her swollen eyes from the bright sun and pulled into traffic. The corners of her mouth quivered as they drew into a smile. She knew what needed to be done. *No other way.*

# CHAPTER 5
# Bruce Tessler

Bruce Tessler, a computer programmer for a packaging company, presented himself as a quiet man. Those who knew him described him as unobtrusive, even dim.

Deep-set eyes, confined to thick glasses, offset his fair complexion and blended with his beige attire. The only shine emitting from his forty-five years of life radiated from the bare spot on the top of his head.

His gambling problem started when he won a hundred dollars on a scratch-off lottery ticket, a birthday gift. The next day he invested his winnings into more scratch-off tickets. When the payout cut his profit in half, he went to a nearby casino to increase his odds. When he won a little money back, he felt better, but he wanted more. He began frequenting a nearby casino on Fridays after work. Then he went on both Fridays and Wednesdays. Determined to prove his luck would change, he rationalized three days a week and dipped into his life savings.

Months later, while indulging himself on one of his weekly jaunts, he fed a twenty into his favorite Zeus II penny slot machine. Once his money was counted and recorded, a blast of fire and the sound of heralding trumpets brought the screen to life. He pulled the handle. Five reels began to spin, teasing Bruce with colorful symbols in winning combinations. *Nothing.* Another pull. *Nothing.* He increased his one-dollar bet to the maximum, two-fifty. Three wreaths lined up on the top row, paying him seventy-five cents. *Cheap mother-fucker.* He dropped his bet down to fifty cents.

After three spins he hit the max button by mistake. The first reel slowed, stopping on four Zeuses and a wild symbol. The second reel slowed, lining up five more Zeuses.

"C'mon," Bruce yelled, encouraging the third reel to follow suit. "Yes!" Five more Zeus icons tumbled into place. "C'mon, baby, five more." The reel stopped with two wild symbols and three Zeuses. "Yeah, that's it, five more!" The reel slowed, this time, Pegasus, a bunch of grapes, a cloud impaled by a thunderbolt, and a jeweled goblet rolled into place. *Damn!* Gold coins erupted onscreen like fireworks. Bruce watched the counter go up and up. *Not the big one, but sweet.* The counter stopped with seven-hundred-fifty dollars added to his credits. *That's more like it.* He pulled again. *Nothing.*

Determined to repeat his good fortune, Bruce gave back his seven-hundred and fifty dollars. Elation turned to disappointment, then depression, then self-loathing. He prayed that God would show His mercy, bringing luck to the fifty cents remaining in his credits. *Last chance.* He pulled the lever. *Nothing.*

He drove home, kicking himself for his lack of self-control. "Next time," he whispered.

As soon as he walked in the door, Debra, his wife, said, "I tried to cash a check at the grocery store today. The clerk said I'd been cut off. Said the last three checks I'd written for groceries had bounced. Why would our account be short?"

"Use the damn credit card," Bruce said.

"It's not the registers; *you're* the problem, and I blame my brother for giving you those damn lottery tickets."

"Don't you dare say a word to him," Bruce ordered. "I don't need everyone on my back for having a little fun."

"Your *fun* is costing us. You know what's coming next, don't you? We're gonna lose this house and everything we've ever worked for."

"*We've* worked for? I don't recall you getting your fat ass up every morning to go to work."

"You're right. My fat ass was home raising your children."

"What about the last ten years? You're not breastfeeding a twenty-two and twenty-six-year old."

"So taking care of your mother and making sure your alcoholic father doesn't beat the crap out of her doesn't count?"

"Get off my case. I'll get the money back."

"I've been hearing that for months. I don't believe you. Get some professional help, or I'm gone."

When Bruce heard the door slam, he breathed a sigh of relief. *Let her go to her sister's and cool off. She'll come to her senses.*

\*\*\*

Two days later, when things had cooled down with Debra, Bruce drove to Thunder Valley Casino Resort in Lincoln, determined to change his luck. *I need a change of scenery, that's all.* He slipped a hundred into the bill changer and waited for the breakdown. He changed the twenties into fives. *Not taking any chances today.*

When the hundred was gone, he headed for the ATM machine. He pulled three hundred dollars from an ATM. The receipt showed a balance of $39.83. *Cutting it close.*

He straddled a stool at a dollar machine and risked it all. He watched the cherries, eagles, and dollar signs spin: matching, spinning, aligning, realigning. They came to rest with three eagles in a row. Suddenly lights flashed and an exuberant alarm whooped. He'd beaten the odds. One hundred in, seven hundred out. *That's more like it.*

"Cocktail?" The young cocktail waitress leaned over, offering a tray of drinks and an inspiring view.

"How 'bout a beer?" Bruce suggested with a thank-you.

After three beers and more cleavage, he was down to three hundred. *Time to move on.* He shifted to another bank of machines. *Debra's going to be pissed.* But if he felt like blowing his paycheck, so what?

An hour later he had seventy cents in his pocket. The cocktail waitress had disappeared, taking with her the tray of drinks and her distractions. "Next time."

The house was dark when he got home. *Bitch, there better be some dinner left.* He was starving. The beers churned in his stomach. "Debra?" He flipped on the light in the kitchen. "Debra? I'm home."

Bruce turned on the bedroom light and found the closet door wide open. All of Debra's clothes were gone.

The Gambler's Hotline referred him to Grace.

\*\*\*

"How are things going for you Bruce?" Grace began.

"Pretty shitty."

"Let's hear it. What's so shitty?"

"My life."

"What's been going on since the last time we met?"

"Debra said she's not coming back. I received a foreclosure notice on the house. The kids won't take my calls and won't return my messages." Bruce licked his lips and swallowed. "I was always there for those kids, and they can't even pick up the goddamn phone? Lend their ol' man a few bucks? Invite me for dinner once and awhile? They know Debra left me!" Bruce hammered his leg with his fist. "I'll bet the bitch is turning everyone against me."

Since their first session, Bruce had displayed an assortment of emotions—hurt, anger and betrayal. Today Grace let him simmer in his feelings before speaking. It took a moment to analyze whether he was on another one of his pity trips or if he had begun to realize the seriousness of his predicament. If the latter were true, he might be ready to work on fixing his problem. She proceeded with a little commiseration.

"People are reluctant to be pulled into someone else's problems. It may not be necessary to take their reaction so personally."

"How can I not take it personal?" he grumbled.

At times it was difficult for Grace to remain unbiased. The air changed with Bruce in the room. *Sour.* "Situations become difficult when children, friends, or family members feel they need to take sides in a divorce. Maybe Debra is getting the same treatment as you. All things considered, she may be in a more favorable position because of your gambling, but that isn't to say everyone likes her better." Grace leaned forward, "Bruce, how others feel about you isn't the issue right now. How do you feel about yourself? Who do you see when you look in the proverbial mirror?"

Bruce didn't answer right away. One meaty hand rubbed his furrowed brow.

Grace held her ground. She wanted him to open up and to realize that playing the "blame game" didn't do him much good. She wanted him to move on.

"I see a guy who really messed up, I suppose. But I can't help myself." His hand settled on his hairless dome. "I want to win! I want to win big...so I can tell everyone to go scratch!"

"What would you do if you won?"

"I'd buy a yacht or— Or a sail boat. I'd buy myself an expensive cigar and sit on my big boat and smoke my cigar. Maybe watch the sunset."

"Let me get this straight. Winning removes the family from the picture?"

"It would be nice to have Debra next to me, but she would probably be a bitch, go on and on about the stink or...or how her hair was getting messed up or some shit like that!"

They replayed this and similar scenarios. Grace noted that Bruce felt suppressed by his choice of partner, his choice of career, and his friends. There was always something to feel discontented about. Winning a hundred dollars gave him a high; losing left him low. Either way was better than the hum-drum lifestyle he had been leading. Bruce attended a few Gamblers Anonymous meetings, but his stubbornness deemed the meetings less than beneficial. Grace suspected his oxytocin and dopamine levels were low, but Bruce poo-pooed the idea of taking medication. Certain conditions could leave a person with a habit waiting to happen, but without proper testing she was speculating. Besides, his insurance had lapsed.

"I'm curious, Bruce. When you gamble, do you drink?"

"What's that got...I..." he sputtered defensively. He acted as if Grace had caught him doing something naughty. "Why?"

*Bingo.* She hit a tender spot. She would not let him off the hook, nor would she be baited into answering a question with a question. It would be best to wait. Eventually he would run out of line. She waited.

"Okay, yeah. I stopped at Thunder Valley before coming here. I had a drink. Those broads in those little outfits can be so persuasive. There's a new one there. She's a tall brunette with big—" He held wide-spread fingers inches from his chest. "Yeah," he said with a sigh. "Most of the time I refuse or maybe just have one to be polite. You know: tip a buck or two. But this new gal is something else. I think I had three. I didn't want to take a chance on a DUI."

"I imagine those pretty girls are hired to be a distraction,"

Grace said. "The more they loosen you up, the looser your wallet becomes." Grace got the impression he resented her observation. She watched him dig dirt from his fingernails while he considered the implications. His lips became white and taut. Color wicked up his neck. Anger simmered below the surface. Grace fought the urge to open a window; she suddenly needed fresh air.

"What's going on, Bruce? Talk to me."

"I know they hit on guys like me."

"Guys like you? What does that mean?"

"You know. The geeks, the suckers, the guys women think they can use."

"Users are attracted to easy targets. What do you think makes a person an easy target?"

"I'm not stupid, Grace!"

"Never said you were." Grace closed his folder seeing he wasn't ready to answer. "It's time for us to quit. We can continue this discussion in our next session. Any plans for the weekend?"

"My neighbor's kid is in a band. He invited me to go hear them play at the Purple Place in El Dorado Hills. He says they play a lot of my kind of tunes, so maybe I'll go. I'm not into the bar scene. Women are bitches…but with Debra gone, I do get lonely."

"Sounds like fun. I hope you enjoy yourself." As Bruce rose to leave, something struck Grace as peculiar. She couldn't quite put her finger on what it was. She decided to walk him to the front desk. "Do you dance?" she asked, pondering his height. *He seems taller.* She glanced at his shoes and noticed their thick rubber soles. Odd, she hadn't noticed earlier.

"Yeah, I love to dance. Debra and I danced all the time when we were in college. Man, what the hell happened?" he said, wiping his brow.

"We can talk about that next time we meet."

"That's what they all say." His sneer gave her chills.

Grace let Sal deal with Bruce on his way out. She went back to her office and closed the door. "I don't have to take to everyone," she mumbled under her breath.

She remembered the "Bruce types" who attended some of the parties her folks hosted when she was a little girl. One man in particular came to mind, Jack Reardon. Her dad intercepted any attempt Jack made to talk to Grace. Grace hated the smell of his sour breath and the way he licked his lips when he talked. By the end of the evening, Jack's hair, strategically placed across his freckled pate when the evening began, resembled a sweater sleeve dangling from a dresser drawer. He staggered around the room crashing into furniture. His wife apologetically steered him toward the door, enduring his ass-grabbing and the amorous slobber he smacked on her cheek.

There were men Grace hadn't thought of in many years. Some were her dad's colleagues, his golf buddies. They were men who were the epitome of up-standing citizens, heroes in the medical community, devoted fathers and grandfathers, but behind closed doors, many of these men were drunken louts and womanizers.

It was unethical of Grace to judge Bruce, but she couldn't help herself. He brought to mind unpleasantness, sour breath, and *a person who hides his true self so well.*

# CHAPTER 6

# Meet-Up

From the moment Jess Bartell called to announce he had moved back to town, Grace struggled to keep her emotions tethered. Mixed emotions over seeing him again plagued her all week. When he asked if they could get together to catch up, she knew she was flirting with the possibility of another broken heart. Worse yet—*breaking rule number one*. She vowed never to get involved with a married man, but curiosity got the best of her when Jess called back to make the arrangements. She agreed to have one drink. After all, they were friends, right? *Eight years is a long time*. Would she even recognize him, let alone be attracted to him? While searching the crowd with anticipation, she felt someone come up close behind her. Suddenly, the din of voices became a blur of loud clatter. Shrill laughter penetrated her head. Her cheeks burned. Her palms felt sweaty. *My God, what's happening to me? Am I losing control?*

"You've grown more beautiful, I see." As soon as Jess spoke, the spell was broken.

Grace spun around to face hazel eyes that could melt snow. "Jess, how nice to see you," she stammered as he placed a kiss on her cheek. She caught herself staring. *He's even more handsome than I remember*. Eight years faded fast.

After another quick hug, Jess rerouted his charm to the young lady who held the menus. "Two please," he said, placing his hand on the small of Grace's back. He dignified his move with a little push as they moved through the crowd of patrons celebrating the week's end. Glasses clinked. Merriment filled the room, but all Grace heard were little *pings* vibrating from her heart strings. She couldn't deny being with Jess made her world feel so right.

As they walked up the short stairway to the upper part of the bar, Grace's radar picked up Jess's stare. She twisted. Her eyes followed where his were directed. "I always knew you were an ass man."

"Wha— I—" Jess's eyes darted away. His face reddened. His boyish grin stole her heart.

"Up here okay with you?" She pointed to the waitress waiting patiently by their table.

"Uh-huh." His answer was barely audible.

Grace felt a bit naughty, aware of the cool silk gliding across her warm skin when she moved. *Is it my imagination? Or did I just hear him catch his breath?* The thought was delightful.

Once they were seated, Jess leaned forward and planted a light kiss on her lips. "Wow, it's been too long." He turned to address their server. "I'll have a microbrew. Grace, what would you like?"

Without warning, a feeling grabbed her with such intensity she didn't hear Jess's question. She combed the lower level of the restaurant, expecting to hone in on the eyes she felt raking over her body. She didn't connect with anyone. *Strange.*

"Grace?" Jess repeated his question.

"A glass of Zin will be fine," she replied, casting one last glance around the room.

"Do you have Perry Creek Zin Man?" he asked the waiter. "She likes the fruit forward."

"You remembered," she said, impressed by more than his memory. "I can't get over it."

"I can't get over how beautiful you are," he said. "I think about you and how good we were for each other."

His sugar-sweet words satisfied a hunger she had long denied, his soulful expression irresistible. *Don't let him get the better of you.* Mental chastising mingled among quick recollections of the torment her clients experienced in mending their shattered hearts. *Jess is married; we have no future. We're just friends.* "How long have you and Jenna been back in Sacramento?"

"We finalized our move from LA two weeks ago." Her question diffused his charm a tad. "We bought a house in Fair Oaks. It's nice, much bigger than the one we owned in LA." He picked up his napkin and began shredding it in tiny pieces.

*He's not happy,* she thought.

"The firm I'm with now is great. I'm glad to be independent from Jake, my father-in-law.

"I thought he was your mentor."

"He didn't do me any favors. I worked my ass off, but he never let me get too far ahead."

"Tight leash?" she asked.

"Yes, very tight." He made a choking sound to illustrate.

"What a jerk!" Grace concurred. She didn't know Jake, but she knew his daughter Jenna was spoiled rotten and had little regard for those not in her league. Grace imagined the silver spoon between her thin lips. *Like father, like daughter.*

"Ah, it was a good learning experience."

Grace noticed the flush around his collar. She sensed *stuff* got in the way of a *perfect* life. "Tell me more. What are you into now?"

"Do you remember when I came back to Chicago for a couple of months after I passed the bar in LA?"

"Right before you married Jenna?" The sharp tone in her voice caught them both by surprise. She watched him gather the torn pieces of napkin into his hand. *Did he have regrets?* He squeezed the paper and opened his fist like he was performing a magic trick. But the pieces didn't magically become whole again; they were still pieces.

"Yes." Their eyes engaged. For a moment they shared his anguish, and then he returned to the scattered paper on the table and his story. "I worked on my first family case with a good buddy of Jake's, Everett Stein, who practiced in Illinois."

"I thought you could only take cases in the state where you took the bar?"

"I worked with him as a friend of the court. It was a horrible, sad case. Very complicated, but great experience. Everett gave Jake a good report and said he was lucky to have me."

Grace caught another flicker of pain in Jess's eyes. As he spoke, she sipped her drink and assessed his body language.

"So…nine years later Everett flies to LA for his annual visit with Jake, and we drive over to Palm Springs for a little golf. Everett gets ready to putt. He stops, turns around, and says, "I've always wanted to grow grapes. I'm moving to Sacramento. You coming with me, son?"

Grace tried to picture the scene.

"Jake almost choked. He says, 'Hey Ev, I thought we were friends? Jess is *my* boy!'"

Grace nodded, waiting for the big finish.

"Everett putts. The ball rolls in the hole. He turns to my father-in-law and says, 'Yes, we are friends, but this is business, Jake…and Jess is nobody's *boy*.' Jess pushed the pieces of napkin into a neat pile. "So, here I am!"

Grace sensed his pride when he told his stories. It was as if he were telling them for the first time.

"Okay, another time," Jess starts another story. "This guy comes home after searching for his wife and daughter all night. They have been gone less than twenty-four hours, so he can't file a missing persons report yet. When he gets home, the sheriff pulls up with a couple of other cop cars."

Grace watched Jess's luscious lips command the words in his stories. His flawless skin began to need a shave. Tiny laugh lines creased the corners of his eyes. *We were kids back then…*

Jess continued, "My client rushes toward them to hear the news, but the cops were there with a warrant to remove him from the premises!"

Grace wasn't listening as intently as she let on. She could smell his clean scent from across the table. An onlooker might think she were in a drunken stupor or suffering from asthma with all the short breaths she needed to inhale him.

He didn't notice. He kept talking.

"Now, my client's confused," he said. "His wife and daughter are God-knows-where. He's been pleading with police to help find them. Now the cops are planted on his front lawn with their weapons drawn and pointed at his head! The guy is freaking out!"

"How horrible!" Grace interjected, but she hadn't comprehended a word he said.

"And this whole big fiasco begins! The neighbors start coming out to see what all the brouhaha is about, and the guy is so embarrassed he surrenders. The sheriff cuffs him, and they take him off to the station."

Grace studied his hands. Long fingers tapped on the table.

They rolled into his palm. They pointed, lay still side by side, and then tapped some more. She put her own hands on the table, tempted to slide them under his, craving their warmth. He rambled on, oblivious to her lusts. She smiled to herself. *He's here. I can't believe it. He's here with me.*

"Now get this," Jess continued. Grace pushed her desires from her mind long enough to catch up with his story. "For years the woman deposited just enough money into their checking account to cover bills and stashed the rest. So my client goes to the bank and discovers all his money is gone."

"How could he not know?" Grace inquired, trying to fill in the details she missed. "Didn't he check the bank statements?"

"He worked out of town. The wife took care of their finances. All of their bills were paid and up to date. He never had a reason to question her activities. Besides, he was busy working his ass off."

"So what happened to the money?" she asked.

"Who knows? They went to court. The wife came out the winner! The witnesses she produced— girlfriends, her sister—all testified under oath that he was violent. They never saw him hit her, but she always had bruises."

"Okay, so where did the bruises come from? Were they self-inflicted?" Grace opposed. She worked with women all the time who came from violent households. Many of them lied and said their husbands or boyfriends weren't responsible for their bruises, not the other way around.

"This woman was very clever," he said. "She was into building stuff. My client bought her a jigsaw for Christmas, so she could make wooden lawn ornaments. He said she worked with large sheets of plywood; she was always bruised and banged up."

Grace's mind wandered again. Jess didn't dwell in the past like she did. He kept current with stories like this one.

"When he got here, he contacted me," Jess boasted.

"Well, at least he got the best lawyer in town," Grace said, lifting her glass to toast. "Salute."

He raised his glass. When he returned his gaze to Grace, a shy smile spread across his handsome face.

"Enough shop talk," he said. He took a deep breath. Grace felt the warmth in his eyes as he brought his face inches from hers. "How's my Grace?" When he stroked her forearm with his fingertips, tiny shivers raced through her body. She loved the way his eyes sparkled when he got fired up. *It's not his eyes you're reacting to; it's his touch.*

"I'm fine," she answered. "Hungry." She hoped he didn't suspect the effect he was bestowing on her. *Stop it!* Her mind debated. *Enjoy it for what it's worth. It's been years; you don't really know him anymore.* But the truth was inescapable. *You still want him.* She formulated her final, clinical summation: *You're in trouble.*

They ordered a brick of onion rings to share while they drank. Grace relaxed and let her thoughts have free reign. They talked about the way Sacramento planned to change downtown's aesthetics and whether it would bring more revenue for the local businesses. She told him about her week without divulging any personal information about her clients. She generalized about the precarious situations people got themselves into. They laughed about how crazy people could be.

"Speaking of crazies, how's your mom and dad?" he asked.

"Certifiably nuts," she giggled. "They take turns. What about your family?" She noticed his features turned dark and brooding at the question. He was about to change the subject when, as quickly as the glint in his eyes left, it returned.

"What is it they say about *out of sight?*" He burst into nervous laughter. "C'mon, you've met them." He rolled his eyes and shook his head.

She didn't over analyze the situation. It felt good to laugh. In the past, she could always count on having a good time with Jess. *Things are different now.*

When their server came by announcing, "Last call," they both snapped back to reality. Jess checked his watch.

"Damn," he muttered. "I'll be right back."

Grace watched as he hurried toward the doorway, cell phone in hand. *Dialing his wife with an excuse why he's late? Oh, his luscious lips.* Reality hit home. When he returned, she rose. "It's late," she said, placing her cash on the table. "I need to be going."

Moods changed. The moment became awkward, their exit thick with silent reflection. Once outside the bar, Jess pulled Grace toward him, cupped her face, and placed a tender kiss on her lips. "I had a great time. I missed this. I missed *us.* It was so good to see you, laugh with you."

Her body reacted to the pucker of his lips. Fire burned below. "We'll have to do this again," she said, mindless of the consequences.

"Can I call you?" He kicked a stone with the side of his shoe.

"Sure," she stammered. "That would be fine."

Jess seemed overjoyed with her response. His smile returned and his steps seemed light. She watched for his wave goodbye as he drove off.

She started her ignition. Her brain was too preoccupied sorting through her conflicting emotions to notice the beams that pulled away from the curb seconds after she did. Grace sank so deep into self-absorption she failed to notice the car following her home.

*** 

*You're in trouble, girl!* She turned into her drive, pulled into her garage, and shifted into park. "This is all wrong!" she admonished herself aloud, pressing the button above her visor. The garage door had closed half-way by the time the dark-green car drove past the house.

Inside Grace flicked on the light switch, kicked off her shoes, and walked into the living room. She picked up the mail, which had been stuffed through the metal slot in the front door. Nothing too exciting: bills, junk mail, and a thank-you note from her neighbor, Judy, for watering her flowers while she cared for her sister in Ohio.

All was quiet: no open arms or sleepy greetings from little ones in super-hero pajamas. No dog, jumping or panting, all happy to see her. Not even a cat sauntering around her ankles, purring, and *meowing* to be fed. She came home to her little beta fish, Alpha, who had retreated to his late-night, stone fortress to dream of *angel* fish or finding Nemo.

Grace looked in the fridge out of habit, hoping the cake fairy had come, but as usual she was disappointed. After a visual sweep of her kitchen, now filled with dark shadows, she checked the back door to make sure it was locked. When she stopped to inhale the sweetness of the lime geraniums lining her windowsill, she saw movement out of the corner of her eye. Her skin prickled.

She backed away from the window to investigate the long shadow that spilled across the back yard. The pulse in her neck throbbed from strain and fear. She watched. Nothing moved. *There's something out there.* She could feel it waiting, watching.

When the neighbor's cat howled, Grace jumped and did a scaredy-cat dance on the kitchen floor. "Damn!" she gasped in relief. *That explains it.*

Upstairs she turned on a Luther Vandross CD, calming her nerves while she ritually washed her face and applied *anti-* this, and *anti-* that creams. When she finished she studied the full-length mirror behind the bathroom door, critiquing her body as she swayed to the music. She visualized herself back at the restaurant when she walked in front of Jess. She moved her hips from side to side. *Your butt isn't too bad for almost thirty-one.* She admired her sexy black-silk panties while she stripped out of the matching bra. She massaged her full breasts and imagined her college crush watching her trace the firm peaks with her fingertips. *Jess.*

Her imagination provoked another thought. She visualized her client Becky's vignette with her own imaginary lover. Grace closed her eyes and mentally moved toward Jess, unbuttoning his shirt and slipping her hands inside to feel his warm body. Her breath quickened as the fantasy progressed. Her hand slipped down her flat stomach past the black lace to her sweet spot. She continued exploring his chest with her mouth, tasting his skin, and sucking his nipples. Her mind flowed to the scenario Becky described in their last session, replacing Becky's mystery man with Jess—*my dark-haired, imaginary lover.*

Fully aroused, she found it hard not to climax at that very moment. *I want more.* One option rested in her nightstand drawer. She sat on the bed, ready to be satisfied. Jess reappeared behind her closed her eyes as she listened to Luther's sensuous tone. She imagined moving down to Jess's navel with her hot kisses. She undid his pants and eased them to the floor. She grabbed his backside and kneaded gently, tracing the crevice below his muscular back with her fingertips. Jess's moans encouraged her to move on with her mouth, while he caressed her face and touched her hair. He tilted her chin. His eyes fixed on hers. The passion and burning desire expressed in his eyes caused something to well inside, a connection she had never felt before. As she brought his body back to her mouth and began to descend his perfectly shaped high-rise, deep-seated emotions rose to the surface. *I have always desired this man.*

In her fantasy she was intimate with Jess's body. She knew what pleased him. In return, he knew how to touch her—body and soul. While she enjoyed the taste of him, he confessed how much he loved what she was doing. His whiskey-tenor voice drove her wild. He wrestled her to the bed as he slipped off her panties and kissed his way back up her body. When he positioned his weight on top of her, she felt his heart beat with anticipation. His tender kisses teased her parted lips. Brushing strands of hair from her face, he caressed her cheek with his fingertips. The passion brewing in his hazel eyes intensified as he reached down, spread her legs, and prepared for his entry. Pleased with her readiness, he smiled. His kisses became more urgent. Their tongues and lips found a perfect exchange of taunting and tasting. Their bodies found a perfect rhythm for making love. His sexual prowess took Grace to places unknown. Their bodies rocked in unison as their pleasure grew into a plethora of sensational explosions. Her uncontrollable spasms encouraged Jess to climax with her. "You are so beautiful," he whispered. His words teemed with emotion as he pushed inside her and spilled his seed.

When her fantasy reached its crescendo, tremors overtook her body, bringing her to a delicious, fulfilling orgasm. Gasping, she let her legs collapse while the last pulsating sensation drained her energy. Once her breathing slowed, she opened her eyes and returned to her surroundings.

Thoughts of Jess, her imaginary lover, waned. Her naked body adjusted to the temperature of the room. Cold, she smoothed her sheets and pulled the comforter to her chin. When was the last time she shared a bed with anyone? Or held a man? How long had it been since she felt the warmth of another human next to her body? She didn't want a relationship. She was a free spirit, determined to live her life without depending on anyone else to fill her days with complexity. So why did she feel so lonely?

Grace couldn't control the rush of sorrow that crumbled her reserve. She hadn't cried in so long. She thought of Becky and the pain Becky endured daily, wanting someone either imaginary or unattainable. Perhaps her own perfect mate and lover resided in a world of make-believe, the only place she could go to escape pain. Grace didn't want to be in that place. She didn't want a man she couldn't have. She wanted to be content with what she did have—

Jess as her friend. "I can't imagine it any other way," she said aloud. *Huh, what a lie!* mocked the voice inside her head. *You just did.*

*** 

Saturday morning started out in a fog. Grace retrieved the paper from her front porch, intending to catch up on the local news with her first cup of coffee. She couldn't concentrate. Her thoughts were still tangled in the sheets with Jess, the ache for him persistent. She rationalized her emotions, recapping their date the night before. She enjoyed his company. They laughed a lot. They were catching up, closing an eight-year gap over drinks. However, she couldn't blame her amorous mood on the alcohol. *No,* she had nursed the two glasses of wine. *This is about sex, he makes you weak.* Although her fantasy was physically satisfying, mentally…it was exhausting. She hadn't thought of Jess sexually in years. *Liar.*

They met in Chicago, *freshman year in college.* She attended Northwestern. He studied law at Loyola University. At first, they passed each on their way to and from the bus stop, making casual eye contact. Then, one chilly evening she remembered being unnerved. Certain that someone was following her, she ducked into the No Exit Café on the corner of Lunt and Greenwood, for a cup of hot cider. They served the best cider in town, and she loved the charming ambience. The interior of the café was shaped like a cracker box. *My safe-haven.* She smiled to herself remembering small, round, wooden tables aged by time and scarred with lover's initials and the doodles of bored patrons. A raised floor ran the length of one wall with beautiful inlaid wood and marble chess tables lined eye-level with the tinted windows. Brass railings kept spectators from getting too close during chess tournaments, but they gave others a place to lean during more social times of the day. Grace loved the ornate wood bar and the antique brass urns that held the delicious coffee they served. She loved the shoosh of the espresso machine releasing steamy froth for lattes and hot water for their interesting assortment of imported teas. The food menu wasn't extensive, but what they served was decadent.

She decided to treat herself to ham on bakery rye that evening, and she waited anxiously for her food to be prepared. The girl behind the counter scooped homemade potato salad, plunked a kosher dill pickle on the side of the plate next to the sandwich, and filled a tall glass mug with cider. The aroma made Grace salivate. After she paid for her food, she put a tip in the wench jar and picked up her plate. She grabbed the handle of the mug and turned, oblivious to her surroundings. She accidentally hit Jess's elbow with her mug.

Despite Jess's effort to move away, Grace spilled hot cider all over his shoes. Grace's reflexes kicked in at the same time, reeling her backwards. Her shoulder hit the bar. Her arm jerked forward, and the sandwich flew through the air. Rye bread went in one direction, ham in the other. Potato salad plopped between them. How the pickle survived the wreck, she didn't know. *Fate?*

"Are you all right?" Jess stared at the surviving pickle.

"Your shoes, they're going to be sticky!"

"Don't worry. At least they'll smell divine," he said, laughing. "I prefer cider to the pickle smell any day!" He reached for napkins, getting close enough for Grace to enjoy his fresh, clean scent.

"Boy, I just had these polished, too," he joked, wiping his well-worn, leather boots. When he lifted his head, their eyes fused together.

The waitress came from behind the counter with a damp rag to pick up the mess splattered on the planked floor. "Hi, Jess," she cooed while shaking her auburn hair to one side. Grace hadn't noticed her beauty until that moment. The petite form bent over, revealing ample breasts, a tiny waist, and a round bottom. Grace suddenly felt awkward, looking from one to the other, waiting for his response to the girl's flirtation.

"Hi, Marilee," he said, nonchalant. "Would you mind getting this young lady another sandwich, and let us have two of those ciders. I planned on coffee, but I've changed my mind."

When he finished cleaning his shoes, he rose to face Grace. His eyes held her captive. "We'll be right over there," he told Marilee. "That's if you'll join me?" he leaned in with a whisper to Grace. "If you eat slow, I won't be tempted to leave here before my shoes dry." Stepping back, he added, "You wouldn't want me to catch a cold, would you?"

Grace couldn't recall what her reply was at the time, but she never forgot that evening. She remembered his eyes, his sense of humor, his voice, and how self-assured he was about how she would respond. She remembered following him to a table. Looking back at Marilee, she caught the girl's cold stare before she returned to her work. For one instant Grace thought, *uh, oh, broken heart alert*. But soon she was swept away by Jess's enchanting smile and ignored her instincts. *You are hooked.*

She extended her hand. "Grace Simms," she remembered introducing herself. "Believe it or not, my name is Grace."

"Burgess Bartell. *Jess* to my friends," he said, taking her hand in both of his. "I've seen you around—"

"The bus stop," she interjected.

He casually took half of her sandwich and began to ask her questions.

Just when she thought she began to bore him, he surprised her. "Excuse me, Marilee. Can we have another sandwich and two more ciders?" Grace recalled the strange look she threw him and what Jess said: "I'm sorry, that was presumptuous. Would you rather have coffee?"

They talked for hours and laughed while they shared stories of why they had chosen schools in Chicago. Coincidently, both hailed from Southern California, expediting a quick bond. Toward the end of the evening, when the conversation turned a bit more serious, Jess divulged his future intentions. "After I finish school and pass the bar, I'm going to marry the girl back home. It's part of 'the plan'."

Reared with an open mind and a disciplined heart, Grace didn't react to Jess's unavailability. In fact, she was relieved. Just a little. *You were in pursuit of a career. Adamant to go to school without being scathed by failed relationships. No drama transcending from teenager to adult.* Conflict in high school made Grace determined to get a good education. She intended to get to know herself. She wanted to figure out her strengths and weaknesses and what made her tick. *No need for distractions or regrets.* Then why did their meeting seem so perfect? Why did she feel she needed him then? One very good reason: *You were scared. Someone was stalking you.*

Jess graduated two years before Grace. Afterward, their paths barely crossed. He went to live in LA. He called when he passed the bar. All according to plan, he married Jenna a year later.

Grace didn't attend the wedding, even though she was home that summer. Her dad's illness gave her an excuse, but, truth be known, she wasn't crazy about Jenna. All information about Jenna pointed to her quest for possessions. Grace never understood Jess's attraction to her. They appeared to be opposites. He was warm, giving, and compassionate. Jenna was cold, shallow, and self-centered. Grace was in no position to judge. She didn't have first-hand, intimate knowledge of Jenna like Jess did. He didn't reveal much about her, which seemed odd. He kept personal details to himself, and Grace didn't pry. Jess was happy with Jenna, so Grace was happy for him.

Grace stayed in Chicago until graduation and missed Jess terribly. She dated with more interest in acquiring friends than love. When a guy came along Grace was attracted to, she wasn't shy about having her needs met; she enjoyed sex. But she didn't get involved. None of them measured up to Jess. *He's so sensual,* she thought. She loved his dark, curly hair, his beautiful hazel eyes, and thick black lashes. She adored his square jaw and the little dimples on each side of his mouth that appeared when he flashed his contagious smiles. Jess was kind. He didn't work at it; it was just the way he was, a quality Grace found attractive. Many of the guys that she dated were nice, but they lacked magnetism. *Nothing you can do about it now. He's married to Jenna. You moved on with your life.*

The phone rang, interrupting Grace's angst. "Sal—"

"John wants to know if you want to go bowling with us tonight." Grace heard John in the background feeding Sal dialogue. "He says he has a friend he wants you to meet."

"What's he saying about bowling skills? Grace asked. "Tell John, no, I'm not interested in the size of the guy's equipment."

>slap<

"Sal, don't hit your husband."

"He's being funny," Sal said.

Grace didn't appreciate the humor. "Sorry. I'm not in the mood."

"C'mon, Grace, have some fun."

"I like fun. Do you want to go for a bike ride with me tomorrow?"

Sal responded with an audible sigh, "Can't. Grocery shopping to do. Where are you biking to?"

"Not sure yet."

"Watch out for mountain lions," Sal warned. "I don't own a black dress, and you know how I feel about funerals."

"Of course."

"What's wrong?" Sal asked, her antenna up again.

"Nothing," said Grace.

"Nothing?"

"Nothing I can't handle. I have a lot to do today. I'd better go."

"Call me later if you want to talk about *nothing*."

"I will. Thanks." Grace hung up, feeling low. *A husband, kids, bowling, grocery shopping.* She yearned for the life Sal led.

*The radio… to drown out the quiet.* Music motivated her to do house-cleaning, but couldn't sustain her through dusk. After a microwave dinner, two candy bars, and a few short stories in *Capitol Crimes*, Grace fell asleep on the sofa. She awoke at three, turned off the TV, and proceeded to switch on every light in the house while she checked the locks. *When did you become afraid of the dark?* her sleepy mind wanted to know.

***

Sunday morning Grace rode her bicycle along the American River Parkway, attempting to enjoy her solitude. Unfortunately, she couldn't relax. Everywhere she went, an ominous presence compelled her to look over her shoulder. *Why are you paranoid?* Was she becoming hypersensitive with her birthday coming up? Afraid to be alone? *Perfect timing: Jess showing up when you're feeling unnerved, vulnerable.* Flirting with him would be flirting with danger. If she didn't put their relationship back into perspective and put him out of her mind, she would drive herself mad. The scar on her heart began to throb. *Keep busy—*

When she returned home from her bike ride, she began trimming the bushes in her front yard.

Her neighbor Eli stopped by to chat late Sunday afternoon and broke the monotony. Helping others made Eli feel useful. Grace welcomed the diversion. While they tossed around ideas about installing wrought-iron curtain rods in Grace's kitchen, Eli pointed out some needed repairs: a small leak in the ceiling, a crack in the wall above the door frame leading into the dining area, and screws missing on the plate behind the deadbolt on the back door—all flaws she hadn't noticed before.

"I can fix this baby up in no time, Gracie. I jus' need a little plaster. Did you get the roof checked like I?"

Her eyes were drawn to the kitchen window. *No shadows out*

*there now; nothing moving.* A chill ran up her spine nevertheless. "No, Eli, I haven't had a chance to get someone out here." *It was just a cat.*

"That's okay, baby; we ain't gonna get much mo' rain for now. But I suggest you get someone out here before the summer be over." Eli moved toward the door to leave.

"I know. I know…I will Eli. I promise. Do you have to leave?" She didn't want to sound desperate, but right now she didn't want to be alone. "How about some dinner?"

"I guess I could stay a bit," he agreed. "Make me feel like a teenager again, havin' a date with the prettiest girl in town." His flattery lightened her mood. She got a kick out of how spry he was for eighty-two. She was grateful for his company. Yet, that nagging feeling wouldn't let up. *It was just a cat, Grace.*

The couple shared a pizza, watched a movie, and called it an evening about eight o'clock. After starting a load of wash, Grace headed upstairs to prepare her clothes for the next morning. She felt better and less edgy. The day had turned out nice. She took a long, leisurely shower, and then settled into bed with a hot cup of tea and a book on transcendental meditation. She fell asleep before her tea got cold. Hours later, the phone woke her up.

"Hello?"

>click<

***

Monday morning came in haste, piling anxiety upon a sleepless night. The hang-up disturbed Grace. *Why?* It wasn't like she never had a hang-up before? *Kids.* They prank-called all the time. *It was a Sunday, after midnight, not your typical kid-prank scenario.*

Reaching for the doughnut box, she snuck a peek out the kitchen window.

"You're being ridiculous!" she cried out loud to herself. But once she stuck a doughnut into her mouth, she checked the lock on the window. Everything was secure—nothing to fear. *Then why is your heart pounding?* If she didn't stop this nonsense, she would drive herself nuts. She snatched her keys from the counter and slammed the door. Still annoyed with herself, she threw her briefcase in the back seat and started her engine—twice. She switched radio stations until she found a funny morning show to squelch her crazy notions.

\*\*\*

Becky Jensen wasn't due in the office until ten o'clock, giving Sal and Grace more than an hour to kibitz and rearrange files. When the girl arrived, Grace let Sal finish the files while she escorted Becky into her office.

"How are things going for you, Becky?" Grace asked. "Did you have a nice weekend?"

"It was okay. I didn't do much." Becky scraped the chipped, blue polish from her short, stubby nails. Grace remembered when Becky first came to see her; the girl's nails were long and French-manicured.

"That's pretty, blue polish," Grace took Becky's hand for a closer look. "I haven't worn that color since I was a little girl."

"I haven't been able to get my nails done since—" She looked at Grace wide-eyed and tucked her hands beneath her legs. "They're awful."

Their conversation always became strained when Grace tried to coax Becky into talking about her past. The girl drifted off when the discussion got too serious. She preferred to talk about her mystery man and abstract things like the color of flower pots. She hated terracotta and wondered why it was so popular. Fortunately, time passed *tout de suite*. When their session was over, Becky made a swift exit.

Grace returned to her office to update Becky's file. After noting highlights from their session, she placed her face in her hands, welcoming their coolness. She massaged her aching temples with her thumbs to relieve some of the pressure. She closed her eyes, allowing her thoughts to flow. She recalled her initial meetings with Becky, piecing together notes along with fragments of conversation and visual imprints. She fast forwarded to today's session, stopping at significant places to ponder.

"His eyes control me," Becky said.

"Control you in what way?"

"When he looks at me, all I want to do is please him."

"Please him how?"

"You know," Becky said shyly.

"No, I don't know. Tell me."

"I want to make him happy."

"Make him happy how?" Grace had caught herself stroking the smooth red-lambskin leather on the arm of her chair. "What would you do to make him happy?"

Becky ignored the question. "I thought he would know that."

"When is the last time you saw this man?"

"I see him every time I close my eyes. He is with me, always."

Grace opened her eyes to stop her own images. "Damn," she swore under her breath. Frustrated, she leaned back in her red chair and stared into space. Contemplating Becky's admission of wanting to please her mystery man triggered her own desire—*Jess*. Powerless, she succumbed to this weakness, and it bothered her. Craving the feelings he imposed on her was too distracting. She had worked too hard to get where she was today to go backwards. It took years of self- exploration to complete her studies and get her head on straight so she could treat others. *You got over him a long time ago.* Why the battle? *You're not an ottoman; you're human.*

"We love the familiar," someone once told her. Could that be true? Perhaps she and Jess were connected on a spiritual plane, bound by some unforeseeable force. Was it a life-cord that couldn't be severed? Or was she simply drawn like a moth to a flame? Her gut told her their love would end in disaster. *Love? Who said anything about love? Physical attraction; nothing more!* The tingle in her pelvis confirmed the thought. But did the ache in her heart corroborate the need to believe she was capable of love? Did it put to rest her mother's persistent nagging: "I'm sure someday you'll bless me with grandchildren."

***

*Nearby the figure sat alone, envisioning Grace: beautiful, desirable. But— If things didn't change…*

*Drawing a small tool from its leather pouch, the figure turned it this way and that, pondering it as a potential solution to the problem.*

# CHAPTER 7
# Chris and Yolanda

A young couple, Chris and Yolanda suffered the loss of their first baby during its birth. When their attempt at grief counseling failed, they sought Grace's help on how to heal without alienating one another. Grace initially observed the young couple had a close relationship, one of the most important keys to dealing with any kind of trauma and moving forward.

The couple dated each other exclusively through high school and married after attending two years of junior college. Yolanda worked for a pediatric cardiologist. Chris worked in his dad's auto body shop as the financial and advertisement manager.

Yolanda came from a large, Texas family she dearly loved, but rarely saw, therefore relying on Chris as a surrogate for her family's love and support.

Both had stability going for them. Grace felt that the unfortunate death of their baby might even strengthen their bond if they could share their grief and not suppress their feelings. Losing a child was a devastating experience, perhaps more difficult for them because of the late-stage gestation.

Yolanda had carried full term, but in the last days before the birth, the baby had not moved. This originally hadn't alarmed her obstetrician. Experiencing her first pregnancy, Yolanda didn't quite know what to expect. She had taken maternity leave a week prior to her due date to get some rest and to finish painting the nursery. When she stopped by the office where she worked to pick up her paycheck, she was corralled by her employer, Dr.

Fitz, who wanted an update on her condition.

Grace thumbed through her notes absorbing information. She closed her eyes to visualize their first session.

"When I mentioned the lack of activity," Yolanda said, "Dr. Fitz stooped down and talked directly to my belly." It was clear to Grace that Yolanda admired the doctor and trusted him completely. She went on to explain how he ushered her into an examining room.

"He had his stethoscope in hand, and he ordered me up on the table," she said, describing a doctor who had a vested interest in the baby. "He was flattered that we were naming our baby May, after his mother, despite the fact he thought it was a boy. He listened and decided he didn't like what he was hearing and made a call to the hospital. The next thing I knew," she said, "I was in the OR having an emergency cesarean."

"When she came to," Chris said, tears streaming down his face, "we found out our little May was stillborn. The umbilical cord had wrapped around her neck."

The outer office door opened; Grace opened her eyes. She checked her watch. She gave the couple a minute to sign in and then got up to welcome them.

"Hi, Chris. Yolanda, pretty dress."

It was the first time Grace had seen Yolanda dressed in something low cut. She always wore high necklines, and her hair was down today, not clipped back or in a ponytail.

"How are you guys doing?" Grace asked while noting the changes in the couples' chart.

Chris seemed eager to get the session started. "Yolanda," he said, "finally learned how to cook a steak on the grill without burning it!" He recoiled from the playful slap he received from Yolanda and rubbed his hand up and down her knee. "I'm kidding, Babe," he assured. They both giggled.

"Well, Yolanda, that's a secret you'll have to share with me. When I cook a steak, it's either raw, charred, or both." Grace watched the body language between the couple, noting their intimacy. *Good sign.* "So were you the 'grill' instructor, Chris?" Grace asked, making mental note of the way Yolanda was glowing when she looked up at him. Desire burned in her eyes.

"Yeah, she's a great cook. I like to tease her."

"So, what was for dessert?" Grace was correct in her assumption. The two of them couldn't keep a straight face. It was obvious that Yolanda was hot for Chris—his muscular build and golden brown skin. A touch of Polynesian heritage had fashioned exotic eyes, a small nose, and square jaw. Full lips spread wide, displaying gleaming teeth. He laughed, exposing a pierced tongue.

Grace figured most young women would find Chris irresistible. She, however, sensed a strong character flaw embedded within his attractive package. *A cruel streak.* At the moment Yolanda seemed oblivious to it. Perhaps it was a feature he didn't often display.

"Want to share what all the giggling is about?" Grace leaned back in her chair and waited for her clients to respond.

"I'll go first," Chris volunteered. "When I came home from work last night, Yolanda had made this beautiful dinner: flowers, candles—the whole bit. Normally I do the barbecuing, so I'm checking out these steaks. And they're perfect!" Chris's hands helped tell the story. "So, I'm like, 'Yo, did you cook these?'" Chris shuffled his feet. "Dumb question, I know, but when I stopped and thought about it, I never let her barbecue before. I guess I do that a lot—take control. Anyways, I told her what I thought, and we went from there."

His admission showed progress. Grace made a notation.

"Great. Sounds like it paid off," Grace commended, "Yolanda, how did it feel to get validation from Chris?"

Chris pulled a butterscotch candy from his breast pocket, put the candy in Yolanda's hand, and kissed her on the cheek. He reached in his pocket to pull out another piece for himself. His eyes never left Yolanda's. Grace attempted to read the interaction. *He's taking control.*

Although Grace complimented the couple on their progress, after an hour had gone by, she felt they had barely scratched the surface of what was really going on. Experience and intuition claimed there was more to the picture than the loss of a child. She glanced at the clock; the session had gone by quickly. *No time to dig further.*

She wrapped up the session and rose to open the door. From the corner of her eye, she happened to see Yolanda pull her hair back, revealing discoloration at the base of her neck. Grace's blood ran cold. *Ligature marks?*

"Yolanda, what happened to your neck?"

Chris's eyes followed Grace's stare. "Yolanda has been keeping me up nights, scratching. A reaction to one of her medications, we think."

"Yeah, I'm not sure which one," Yolanda agreed, nervously. She tossed her hair to cover the marks, but her eyes couldn't hide the lie.

Chris grabbed hold of Yolanda's arm, making her flinch. "Let's go."

Yolanda obeyed. "It's nothing, really," she turned to Grace, forcing a smile. "See you in two weeks."

*Medication my ass! Those are ligature marks.* The hair stood up on the nape of Grace's neck. She didn't buy Chris's little innocent act. Hard as she tried to remain impartial, unease overcame her. She didn't trust him. *They're both lying.*

* * *

Outside the office, Yolanda pulled away from her husband's tight grip and hissed, "She didn't believe us, Chris. How are we going to go back to her?"

"We don't," he replied nonchalantly. "Besides, our private life is none of her business. We pay her to listen, not to judge."

Chris unlocked the car door, and Yolanda slid into the passenger seat. "Told you not to wear that dress."

She winced when he slammed the door and watched him wipe finger smudges off the car's green paint with the bottom of his T-shirt. Tears welled in her eyes, and her cervix twitched, knowing what was in store once they reached home.

# CHAPTER 8
# Tim Ashton

S al? Did Dr. Alameda call?"

"Nope, I'm waiting on the fax. Mr. Ashton is scheduled for three."

Many of the referrals Grace received were for clients who experienced depression, post-traumatic stress disorder, anxiety, and bi-polar disorder—conditions controllable with medication and talk therapy. Mr. Ashton's referral came from a doctor unfamiliar to Grace. Although she had tried several times, she was unable to reach the referring doctor to get more information.

"Go to lunch," Grace directed. "I'll be here until one thirty. I'm sure his office will respond before three."

"Wish I could join you at Bandera's for a birthday lunch," Sal said regretfully, "but I have —"

"Kids! A family! No worries. I get it. Will you be back by three?"

"That's my goal. You know how appointments go."

Grace nodded, "Unpredictable."

For the next half hour, Grace updated files and waited, but no fax. At one thirty, she gave up and locked the door.

When she arrived at Bandera's, the restaurant was crowded. A couple sitting at the bar got up, and Grace took a seat. She placed her order and a request: "Smile, Krissy. Makes the food taste better."

Krissy had no sooner walked away when Grace sensed a hand on the back of her chair and warm breath near the side of her face. She turned and almost bumped noses with the man squeezing onto the stool next to hers.

Geez, is it always this crowded?" he asked, pulling his jacket out from under his tall frame.

"Sac State is down the street. Must be finals week."

"So, what are we having today?" The man perused the menu while he stole glances at Grace. His grin, full of mischief, matched the sparkle in his eyes. He seemed amused by everything around him.

"We? I'm having the house salad and cornbread," Grace said. "What you order is entirely up to you."

"Well then, how 'bout a recommendation?" His gaze dropped to her lips before his eyes imprisoned hers in sapphire blue.

She turned away before he affected her better judgment. "I'm sure you'll manage."

He wasn't dissuaded.

"Ever had the salmon? Wow, they have meatloaf? The steak sounds good. Ever try the steak?"

Grace ignored his questions until he leaned closer, speaking to her in hushed tones.

"How about the blackened sea bass?"

"I've never ordered it," she conspired in a whisper.

His chuckle grew into hearty laughter. Grace enjoyed his merriment, but she hadn't a clue what prompted his giddiness. "Did I say something funny?"

"I apologize. I should be asking the waitress these questions. Thanks for being a good sport." He nudged her shoulder playfully.

Her intuition along with years of active duty dealing with assorted personalities warned her against any further conversation with this character, yet...she found him charming and interesting. He had a way about him, a *distraction, nothing more*. She zoned in on generous, vermilion-lined flesh spewing words he carefully chose. Imagining his kiss induced a twinge of excitement. The corners of her mouth lifted when he spoke and wove his magic spell.

Her day began with eyes reflecting remorse, anger, and sadness.

His are *flirtatious, passionate, and just plain full of hell*. The man's infectious laughter put Grace in a glorious mood, and the hour flew by rapidly. She couldn't recall the last time she enjoyed a meal with a man—*besides Jess?* "I need to get back to work." She grabbed her check and deposited a twenty in the pocket of the leather folder. The man's wide grin showed his appreciation when she slid off the bar stool and gave him a titillating show of her legs. She thanked him for his pleasantries and rushed for the exit. Halfway to the door, the man cried out, causing customer's heads to turn.

"Lady, you can't just leave me like this. I'm in love!"

"You'll get over it!" she called over her shoulder. Then, donning her sunglasses with a dramatic sweep, she walked out of Bandera's into the blinding sunlight. She didn't look back.

\*\*\*

*Eyes filled with smoldering hatred watched
Grace dig through her purse for keys.*

*The eyes scrutinized the way her skirt crept up her long legs
as she slid behind the wheel of her car. When Grace pulled out
of the parking space, the figure turned away—unnoticed.*

\*\*\*

At two forty-five, the psychotherapist unlocked the door to her suite and flipped the light switch. She gathered the fax she finally received from Dr. Alameda. She hummed on the way into her office to prepare a folder for Mr. Ashton.

She took her time assessing new clients, believing personalities were anything but typical. Everyone who walked through her door was an original painting, a unique genre.

She learned life's challenges filled a person's palette with color. How a person dealt with life experiences gave each color its own distinctive hue. Some of her clients needed coddling; others needed their space. From an early age she was taught when encountering an injured animal to stay calm, gain their trust, do what you can to help with love, and set them free. People were no different, and those words flashed in her mind like a mantra before she greeted each client.

In her office, she contemplated the view from her window. She usually kept the blinds closed during the heat of the day. However, the sun had reached a point where it passed through the prisms displayed on the window sill. She turned the wand to part the slats, and rainbows splashed on the wall.

The outer door opened at five minutes to three. Grace put her thoughts aside to listen. When she didn't hear Sal's keys clunk on the front desk, she rose from her chair.

"Mr. Ashton?" She rushed down the hall, extending her hand in propriety. However, when the man lowered the magazine and stood to the sound of her greeting, she went slack-jawed.

They spied each other with instant recognition, but before Grace had the chance to rescind the offer of her hand, Mr. Ashton took hold and squeezed.

"You are a vision, he said. "Am I in heaven?"

"Mr. Ashton, this is highly unusual, I assure you." Grace wasn't easily thrown off kilter, but when he didn't budge or wipe the fat grin off his face, she suggested in her best professional tone, "Come this way."

Once the man sat down, Grace tilted the blinds and flipped a switch bathing the room in harsh artificial light. She pushed back in her chair to embrace the familiar heady scent of leather. *Focus.*

Opening the new manila folder made a cracking sound, penetrating thick silence. On the blank, yellow tablet before her, she penciled the date. She crossed her legs and cleared her voice.

"Mr. Ashton—"

"If you had told me your name at Bandera's, I would've canceled," the new client said.

"You still have the option," Grace called his bluff. He had waited months for this appointment.

"I was flirting with you," he said.

"You didn't know…if you're uncomfortable—"

"I thought we were getting to know each other."

"You thought wrong," she said. "All that you know about me is what I ate for lunch." Her words had no effect. His amusement didn't waver. "Shall we begin?"

"Does that mean you're not interested?"

"My interest in you is strictly professional, Mr. Ashton."

"I declared my love for you."

"Bygones."

"Tim, I prefer *Tim.*"

"All right, Tim." His eyes drew her in. She blinked to deflect his attempt to control. "In the note I received from Dr. Alameda, he recommended counseling on a regular basis. He couldn't accommodate you, correct?"

"My insurance doesn't pay for top-dog professionals, Miss— It is *Miss*, isn't it?"

"Yes." Redirecting the conversation, she said, "It must be frustrating. Psychiatrists are in high demand and short supply. Few do therapy anymore. They diagnose, prescribe medication, and then refer you to a therapist for further treatment."

"I guess I shouldn't complain." His expression turned wicked. He eased back in the chair.

Grace unclipped a form from his folder. "I would like you to fill out this short questionnaire before we get started."

He reached for the paper, honing in on the way Grace's skirt slid upwards as she leaned forward. His eyes danced around her ankles before they settled on the space between her legs.

"Do you need a pen?" Grace didn't wait for his answer. She crossed the room to fetch one from her desk drawer. "Here you go," she said, wrapping her skirt tight under her knees as she sat. "When you finish, we'll go over a few things."

While Tim filled out the questionnaire, Grace reviewed Dr. Alameda's fax. She had little time to read Tim's assessments before he arrived, and found it difficult to decipher the doctor's handwritten notes. She didn't want to miss anything she needed to know about this man. By the third page of the file, her blood chilled. In tiny scribble with underlines in the margin, Dr. Alameda wrote, "Aggressive, violent behavior." Tim never would have guessed the quickening inside her. Every nerve ending stood in full alert. *He doesn't appear to be dangerous.* She repeated that mantra in her head, inhaling confidence and exhaling fear.

"All done?" Her voice remained even toned. "Great." Her smile appearing cordial, she reached for the finished form. "Let's just go over a few things. Stop me if you have any questions."

"I'll do that," he said with a roguish grin.

"Let's start with a little background, shall we?" Her eyes held his steadfast. His playful fleer began to fade.

Composure was something all therapists worked at. Flirtations came with the territory; *it is not acceptable to respond—no matter how tempting. End of story.*

"Where would you like me to start?" he asked.

"Where did you grow up?"

"Midwest. Southern Illinois."

"Oh? Country or college town?" Grace thought back to Bandera's when they'd spoken earlier. She could tell by the way Tim climbed into the bar stool that he had experience. She would've said *city* as the place of origin. He lacked restaurant finesse, indicating he probably came from a lower, middle-class family, one that didn't spend much time at the dinner table.

"Galesburg. Ever hear of Galesburg?"

"Of course, home of Carl Sandburg...Knox College." Grace's perception was correct. She remembered touring the town one weekend while attending college in Chicago. Galesburg was a railroad town, originally established to foster religious education in the late 1800s. *Perfect climate for dysfunction. Dad works long hours on the railroad. Stops at the local tavern each day on his way home. Meanwhile, mom's at home trying to remedy his alcoholism and indiscretions with strong doses of fire and brimstone.* "Did you attend all four years at the same high school?"

"Yes."

"Friends? Were you popular?" She saw Tim was blessed with classic good looks, similar to a young Mel Gibson. He would've been able to adjust in many social environments.

"Not really. I mingled in all the circles at school, but I would say on the average I kept pretty much to myself. I remember one good buddy, John Swink. I think he put up with me because no one dared to mess with him as long as we were friends." Tim stopped there. Grace picked up the lead.

"How was dating for you?"

"I went out a little. Girls thought I was obnoxious." His smile deepened. "I always ended up pissing them off after a couple of dates."

"Oh?"

His smile evaporated. "I guess I had anger issues."

"Were you abusive?"

"No," he said, shaking his head.

She felt relieved and waited for him to arrange his memories into an explanation.

"There was one girl–Melanie. We were on again, off again, all through high school. She'd try to prove she could do better than me. I'd try to prove she couldn't."

"And?"

Tim chuckled, "She ended up pregnant by our class valedictorian the summer after graduation."

"How did you feel about that?"

"I felt sorry for her," he said in disgust. "At least I respected her enough to use protection. The bitch tried to get me to sleep with her after he dumped her." He began to chuckle again as if the memory amused him. "That was one time I had the good sense to say no."

"Were you in the habit of saying yes to everything?"

"I didn't mean to imply— Geez, you just met me."

Grace remained apathetic. She sensed the chemical change in his brain, as if a cog had been removed, unleashing something ugly he had kept imprisoned for years. *Now he's not sure therapy's such a good idea.* She ignored his indignation and moved on.

She redirected his thoughts. "Play sports in school?" She could picture him playing baseball, maybe some football. He had an athletic build, but she sensed he lacked the discipline required to be a serious athlete.

"A little baseball, some hockey, football in high school." His mood seemed to darken, His focus settled on Grace's exposed knees.

Grace wrote comments in the margin of the questionnaire, aware of the energy shift and his eyes on her knees.

"Tell me about your parents. What was it like growing up in the Ashton household?"

"You're digging, aren't you?" Tim's features changed. One brow arched. The other stiffened. His pupils grew until his irises were thin, blue rings. His lips hugged his teeth tightly. "What is it that you're looking for, Miss Simms?" The happy-go-lucky person from Bandera's was gone. "I assure you, nothing earth-shattering happened to me as a child or a teenager. I happen to have a chemical imbalance exacerbated by the stress of my job."

"Why don't you tell me about your job?"

Grace noted Tim's discomfort when he talked about his childhood. She sensed it could be a borderline disorder stemming from an attempt to cope with internal anguish, usually in early stages of development. High functioning borderlines were able to act completely normal for the most part, hiding their illness until they became strangers unto themselves. Some borderlines only let those close to them see the side of their personality the illness created. Others lived from crisis to crisis. It would take more sessions to determine the severity of this man's illness. She knew one thing for certain: *he's keeping a secret.*

\* \* \*

Sal, busy inputting Tim Ashton's information, noticed Grace standing in the doorway with her back to the wall and gazing at the ceiling.

"Wow! That bad, huh? Do you think the universe is plotting against you?"

"What?"

"You know, all the cute ones are either damaged or married?"

Grace countered the remark with a glare.

"Oh, excuse me. Was that an insensitive thing to say?"

Grace returned to wall gazing.

Sal rose to close the distance between them. "What's goin' on? Anything to do with the Adonis that just left?"

"I ran into him at Bandera's. He sat next to me and flirted a little."

"Uh oh." Sal's mouth moved in many directions, struggling to maintain a neutral position. "Of course, you set him straight before his ass met the chair, right?"

"Of course!" Grace didn't divulge her initial interest in the man.

"Sometimes I think you're part squirrel, the way you attract nuts!"

Grace jutted her bottom lip to pout. Sal jutted hers further. Grace conceded, "You're priceless." Sal could take any situation and make a joke out of it. With a heart as big as the sky and compassion as deep as the sea, she had a knack for poking fun at the shoes you wore if you were walking toward disaster. "I know …if I would get out more, I might meet someone normal, right?"

"I didn't say anything!"

"You didn't have to. You made your point. Who's next?"

"You're clear for the rest of the day."

"Good, I certainly can use the time to catch up on my charting."

Once her notes were complete, she went to her bookshelf in search of information for one of her clients. She opened a book on local support groups, but she couldn't concentrate. Her eyes kept sliding to the phone in anticipation of a call. When the phone's red light finally flashed, she stared at it, willing the call to be from the person she desired. In the next moment there was a light knock on the door.

"Jess Bartell is on the phone. Ya busy?"

Sal had a way of extracting information from people with few words. That simple little question caused Grace to react. Sal read her like a book. "You missed your calling, Sal. You should've been a private investigator!"

Sal smiled with satisfaction and waited for an answer.

"I'll take it, but maybe you should go sharpen pencils or shred paper—something distracting. You know, so you won't be tempted to eavesdrop."

Sal returned the barb with an exaggerated, wounded look and closed the door.

Grace took a deep breath, fluffed her hair, and picked up the phone. Before she pressed the button, she cleared her throat. "Grace Simms speaking."

"Grace! Hi, it's Jess. Is it a good time to talk?"

She closed her eyes and quietly stamped her feet up and down in a victory dance.

"I'm two blocks from your office. My hearing was postponed and I'm starved. Can I talk you into running away with me for the afternoon?"

"Sure!" Did she sound too eager? His next question gave her butterflies.

"What about for the rest of your life?" He played with her, and she loved it.

"I won't commit to that," she countered, "but if there's chocolate cake involved, we may be able to negotiate." She twirled her hair and slipped out of one shoe.

"Hmmm, you do strike a hard bargain. How soon can we discuss the terms?"

"Give me twenty minutes, Counselor," she said, looking at the clock. "I'll meet you at the Crab Shack. If you have a "Sex on the

Beach" and a basket of fried calamari waiting, you may earn your-self extra points for the evening."

"Oh baby, your wish is my command!" he laughed. "See you soon."

Grace held the phone to her breast and closed her eyes. "Please God," she whispered, "don't let me be stupid. We're friends; just friends." She wondered if he remembered today was her birthday.

Grace emerged from her office glowing. "I have birthday plans!"

"My, my! All of a sudden thirty-one doesn't seem so bad."

Grace felt radiant. She floated toward the door, fanned her face and shook her booty. Sal let out a hardy laugh, "I take it some-one's sexy voice melted your butter again, naughty girl!"

Grace stopped dancing, feigning innocence, "I have no idea what you're talking about!"

"Liar."

"All right," she purred. "We're having dinner…lunch…din-ner…dessert? Drinks! Two adults getting together for social pur-poses!"

Sal stood her ground. "Liar."

When Grace sank into one of the waiting room chairs, Sal joined her. "I don't want to be a noodge, but he's married, isn't he? Isn't that a bit dangerous in your weakened condition? I see the way you salivate when good-looking guys come in here. You need attention, affection, and a good uh…uh–" Sal thrust her pelvis back and forth in the chair. "Ya know?" she said, her phony New York accent prominent. "Just– Just be careful, 'kay?"

Grace stood and gave the woman a warm hug. Sal knew Grace's needs better than she did herself. The woman could be darn-right spooky. *She's right.* Grace was lonely and vulnerable. "Fine. We'll just have dinner. I won't run away with him or sleep with him, okay?"

"Deal," Sal agreed, her smile warm.

"God…if I can't manage to behave," Grace warned, "I'm fir-ing you tomorrow. I wouldn't be able to live with the guilt!"

She heard her friend mumble "Yeah, yeah, yeah," as she walked out the door.

\*\*\*

It was a gorgeous day. Grace checked her watch. If she walked at a brisk pace, she'd make it to the Crab Shack in time for calamari. While rethinking her conversation, she realized that Jess hadn't actually asked her on a date *per se*. He said eat, talk, have a few laughs, *and go home*. That's all she wanted. *Who are you kidding?*

She knew Sal was right. *You WILL behave*. But her body betrayed her good sense.

*Damn! Being a trained professional doesn't make you any less human*. When it came to matters of the heart, it was just as difficult for her to sort things out as anyone else. *You want him—simple*.

Suddenly a wolf whistle interrupted her revelation. She turned in the direction of a honking horn to see Jess waving madly and making cat calls while hanging out of his car window like a wild teenager.

"Great!" she said aloud. "There are no grown-ups present today!" She hurried to catch up.

While crossing the train tracks, she caught her heel between the rail and the plank. Seemingly in slow motion, her body went reeling, the ground coming closer into view. But before she met the asphalt with her face, she was grabbed from behind and hoisted into the air. Her first reaction was to grab her skirt and pull it down. The lace thong she had chosen that morning wasn't appropriate for someone involved in a fall.

"Man, oh man, Grace!" Jess screeched, placing her back on her feet. Unable to control his laughter, he managed, "Did I rattle you that much?"

Embarrassed, Grace began slinging obscenities at her captor, making him laugh even harder.

"Wow, a *thank you* would be nice!" he said. "You know, you'd still be cute with a bruise on your nose, but I don't know how good it would feel! His laughter subsided; he wiped tears from his eyes.

Grace lifted her foot to assess the damage to her heel. "These are my favorite shoes," she groaned. Deep-red Italian leather formed her idea of the perfect pump. The toes weren't too pointed, too round, nor too square. The red leather plunged deep, showing toe cleavage. The space between the front of the shoe and the back exposed her arch. A delicate strap accentuated where her shapely ankle met her foot, making them sexier than a shoe with a strap that crossed the instep. The three-inch heel formed a narrow square peg, tapering to a little gold band at the bottom that had bent when it wedged between the tracks. The leather was shredded on one side, and the outer top of the heel was scraped and scuffed.

Thankfully, the shoe remained intact, and she hadn't twisted her ankle—or worse. "My dad bought me these shoes for my birthday, Jess. They're the first personal gift he ever gave me. Look, they're ruined!"

"I'm sorry. I didn't realize. C'mere."

Jess wrapped his arms around Grace and held her close as he rested his chin on the top of her head. The couple stood still for a few moments. For Grace it seemed like an eternity. She nuzzled in the crook of his arm, inhaling his fresh, clean scent. She took a deep breath, held it, and committed the moment to memory. The city noise blended into a pulsating rhythm that accompanied the beat of his heart. Somewhere off in the distance a bass boomed, adding to the song of life. She was about to drift off until he murmured, "It's okay, Grace. You can't help that you're such a klutz."

She exploded from his grip, gasping, her eyes flashing, speechless. Jess gave her a commiserating look that would've won an Academy Award. She socked his arm in retribution. He laughed so hard it made her rethink the seriousness of his remark, and she chimed in, feeling much better.

He pulled her back into his arms and squeezed, then held her at arm's length. He crouched down and looked her in the eye. "That's my Grace. Now…can we go eat? I'm starving!" He grabbed her and flung her over his shoulder without giving her a chance to protest.

*Neither one noticed the figure across the street watching them play.*

"Don't you dare kick or scream," he said. "I'll let you down when it's safe."

Laughter swelled as she pummeled his shoulders.

"Jess, please—"

When she slithered from his arms, their eyes connected long enough to ignite her fire. She wondered if he were aware of her heat mingling with his. *I want him.*

He took her hand and led her to the door, walking very close. *Pheromones, Grace. Normal, natural. No big deal.* She needed logic to override her conflicting feelings. She let go of Jess's hand to adjust the purse strap on her shoulder, her excuse to take a deep breath.

"You okay?" he asked.

"I think you just knocked the wind out of me a little. I'm fine." *Liar.* Her heart slowed, the heat in her cheeks diminished. *Is this what Becky has been trying to convey? Or is it what falling in love feels like?*

\* \* \*

The crowd had picked up inside the Crab Shack leaving the couple with a choice of being added to a wait list for a table or sitting at the bar. Jess decided they would do both.

Climbing onto bar stools, their knees bumped together. Jess reached down to absorb the shock, holding Grace's leg with a firm grip. "Gosh, Grace, you are an accident waiting to happen!"

"Do you mind?" she said, flicking his hand away. She found it hard enough to control her libido. Suspecting the effect he was having on her, he withdrew his hand from her knee, mocking her with hazel eyes. His lips spread into a wide grin, creating crevices on each side of his mouth, enhancing his handsome face.

*I'm doomed.*

"Stop it," he said in a Falsetto voice.

"Bite me," she retorted.

"Be right back." Jess flung himself off the stool and gave her the one-minute signal. In his absence she made contact with the bartender, ordering a beer, and a "Sex on the Beach." By the time the drinks arrived, Jess was back with a small, paper bag.

"Here. This is perfect for you!" he said.

She took the bag and started to dig through her purse for her wallet to pay for the drinks, but Jess grabbed her wrist, thwarting her effort.

"Open the bag," he insisted.

Grace peeked inside the bag and pulled out a T-shirt. She examined the words as she held it in front of her. "BITE ME!" it read, advertising the Crab Shack below.

"I'm touched. Thank you," she smiled and held the shirt against her chest. "You are such a goof." A warm glow betrayed her better sense when she kissed him lightly on the cheek in thanks. She knew it was to be an evening of torturous restraint when he smiled affectionately.

"It's you."

Minutes evaporated. They joked, verbally sparred and enjoyed each other's company. Once they were seated at a table, the distance between them didn't end the intimacy they shared at the bar. When their food arrived, however, their flirtatious banter turned to commentary about their ravenous appetites and then to Jess's work.

Grace had difficulty concentrating on their conversation, instead, focusing on the way his mouth moved in a sensual motion as he chewed his food. Her eyes roamed from his mouth to his throat as he swallowed and back again. *Funny, how an ordinary function can transform into a fantasy when you feel an attraction for someone.* She envisioned herself nibbling on Jess's neck, kissing the corner of his mouth, and licking his salty taste from her lips.

Suddenly, Jess stopped talking and waved his hand in front of her face. "Grace! Earth to Grace! Are you okay?"

Grace popped out of her dreamlike state, pinched a calamari ring with her fingers, and tossed it into her mouth. She began to chew, avoiding his question. She gestured for him to continue what he was saying. *Good save,* she thought. Jess started to launch back into his story, but stopped again.

"What's on your mind Grace?" he asked. "You seem—"

"Why is it," she interrupted, "when I am with you, we always eat fried food?"

"So we can drink more and remain responsible adults." His seriousness grew. "Alcohol on an empty stomach can get you buzzed too fast. You need grease to line your stomach. Nothing gets past the grease!" He added, "I always ate bacon before I went out drinking, didn't you?"

"I never did those things. I was an angel, remember?" she blushed. "This is silly…talking about greasy food," she chided, holding his gaze. Grace knew that a basic function like eating stimulated the brain's reward circuits, releasing dopamine, the chemical responsible for feeling intense pleasure. *Sex does the same thing.* She didn't know what she needed more. *Food or sex?* All she knew was she had developed a ferocious appetite. *A little of both would do nicely.*

Just as the moment seemed to linger, they were invaded by a group of servers who arrived at the table with a pink feather boa, a pair of fairy wings, a wand, and a plastic rhinestone tiara. Sure they had the wrong table, Grace began her protest until she caught Jess's big grin. "Oh you!" she cried as the servers decked her out in the birthday get-up and pulled her to her feet. She sprinkled "fairy dust" around the room while more servers gathered to sing *Happy Birthday*. Other patrons joined in, and soon the chorus sounded full and festive. No one had ever sung to her in public before. When the song was finished, she was presented with a beautiful cake decked out in thirty-one flaming candles. Embarrassed, but secretly delighted, she conjured her wish and blew out the candles.

"I know you hate birthdays," Jess confessed, "but I remembered what you said about negotiating." His grin turned wicked. "And I do like cake." He nibbled a piece as if it were a delicate flower, deliberately driving her wild.

"I'll get you for this," she taunted, digging her spoon into the chocolate treat. She licked the frosting in circular motions and watched him squirm. He scooped up a spoonful and began to lick the chocolate with tiny flicks. When she dipped her finger in the whipped cream and smeared it across her lips, he held up his spoon in surrender.

After dessert, they sat back, groaning delightfully. "There goes that twenty pounds I lost before I came back to Sacramento," he complained. She never thought of him as overweight, although he obsessed about it now and then. She thought his physique was solid, *tempting*.

"Do you want another drink?" he asked.

"No, thank you. I'm about to burst!"

He reached for his wallet and pulled out a generous amount for their waiter. She tingled when he smiled and asked, "Are you ready to go?"

Being with Jess tonight was different. He hadn't said a word about Jenna, and truth be told, she didn't want to share his attention with *his wife*. But now she had to place Jenna in the picture or risk her emotions getting out of hand. Jenna was the flashing red light in her head, the virtual braking system that stopped her from unleashing her feminine wiles on Jess. He picked up on the sudden mood change.

"Something wrong?" he asked, steering her out of the restaurant. He placed his hand on the small of her back, sending shivers up her spine.

"No, I'm great, Jess," she replied, hoping to sound convincing. "That was fun. I enjoyed myself. Thank you."

"The night is still young. What about a night cap? We could take a walk. Oh wait– I forgot. You're in heels." His sarcasm prepared him for rejection.

"Oh!" she gasped. "Where's my T-shirt?" She intended to pull it out of the bag to remind him what it said, but discovered it wasn't in her purse.

"Wait here. I'll go get it." He ran off.

While Grace stood alone in the parking lot, the weight of someone's stare prompted her to pivot on her heels. She spotted a figure in the shadows, thirty feet away. *Could be a homeless person or a jogger stopping to rest,* she reasoned. From her position, she couldn't tell if the figure wearing baggy sweats was male or female. The face was hidden beneath the brim of a ball cap. Approximately five-feet-ten, medium build, was the only information gathered before the figure bolted away.

Jess came toward her swinging the bag, but she didn't notice. Her attention stuck on the direction of the figure.

"Someone you know?" his voice gave her a start.

"No," she said, smoothing bumps that crawled up her arms.

"What's wrong?"

"Got a creepy feeling, that's all."

"C'mon," he said, "It's probably nothing."

He handed her the bag, and they walked in the opposite direction. Jess looked back, pretending to get his bearings.

Grace wasn't convinced. *He's being protective.* "I'm parked up the street." The incident caused a shift in their moods. "Maybe we should call it a night."

"Sure," he said, trying to hide his disappointment. "No problem."

"I had a great time, but to be honest, it's been a long day. I'm beat." *Just as well.*

If they continued their playfulness, things might've gotten out of hand. "Can I take a rain-check on the nightcap?"

"Of course."

Grace turned right. Jess followed.

"Must be the carbs in the cake making me sluggish. I couldn't help myself though, it was so delicious. This has been the best birthday. Thanks, Jess." She pulled him into the elevator, but once inside, the sodium lights stole the last glimmer of romance out of the evening. By the time they had reached her car and she had dug for her keys, any spark between them diminished to wishful thinking.

"Let's do this more often," he said, closing Grace's car door. "Be careful going home and call me! I'm in court all day tomorrow, but leave a message."

"Jess, I—"

"You're busy too, right. Okay, that won't work. How about if we meet on Friday? There's this great place in El Dorado Hills I want to take you to. It's called Reunion Night Club. They have great music, dancing, killer food. I can pick you up at eight o'clock. Sound good?

"Jess, what are you doing?"

"Collecting my rain check. What's the big deal? Do you have a date or something?"

"No, I don't have a husband either." She lifted one brow to make her point. He frowned, taking it to heart.

"I see. You…uh…you got me there." He banged his hand on the roof of her car, giving her the all-clear signal. As her car rolled backwards, their eyes caught and held one last time. His eyes filled with disappointment, but his sigh indicated he understood.

As Grace approached the garage exit, she noticed the green car parked in the last row, by itself. When she passed by, she saw a hooded figure seated inside, but couldn't see the person's face. She looked in her rear-view mirror and handed the attendant her parking pass. One last look before pulling into traffic, she noticed the car was still there.

*Maybe it's someone waiting for the young ,pretty, parking attendant to finish her shift?* She checked her mirrors once again. No one followed. *Let it go.*

On her way home, Grace processed the evening in its entirety, starting with her unladylike spill and how Jess caught her around the waist and pulled her close to his body. Next, she recalled his excitement when the servers brought out the birthday cake. It was obvious he wanted to please her, but why? "Why does he do these special things," she questioned aloud, "things he should be doing for his wife?" Deep down, she already knew the answer.

"Come on, Grace. You're the professional! You know better! This is a quagmire!" But even as she scolded herself, her mind multitasked how to safely resume their relationship without complications.

God had a funny way of intercepting her thoughts and drawing attention to what he had to say about a situation. Grace turned up the radio and sang along:

"Only fools rush in…"

"I should find myself a single doctor. Settle down," she grumbled aloud. "Maybe have a few kids."

To distract her mind from further argumentative thoughts, she channel-surfed the radio. She had difficulty finding a station with clear reception, but stopped when she reached one without static. Gwen Stefani sang:

"You really love me underneath it all; you really want me underneath it all. I'm really lucky, underneath it all…"

The lyrics reminded Grace of a night when she and Jess were in college. It was late April then, too. They had gone to Uno's for pizza. The place was packed. They drank a couple pitchers of beer while they waited for a table. During their meal, they drank a couple more. By the end of the evening, they were undeniably wasted. The memory was bittersweet. It was Jess's bright idea to walk to the lake to sober up.

When they reached the beach, it was deserted. He dared her to go into the water, wagering he'd do her laundry for two weeks if she did. Grace not only loved a dare, she hated doing laundry. Pictures formed in her mind's eye.

She took off her shoes and T-shirt. She slipped out of her shorts. Drunk and determined to win the bet, she unhooked her bra and flung it at him. Once her panties were off, she bolted for the water. When Jess got over his shock at her impulsiveness, he chased after her. He laughed so hard he lost his balance and fell into the water fully clothed. She paused at the part where she helped him to his feet. Wet, sandy fabric clung to his body. Grit stung her nipples as he held her tight against his chest. His warm groin pressed against her shivering body. A little moan escaped his lips before he attempted to kiss her. *We were drunk*, she reminded herself. It would've been a mistake. No matter how bad she wanted to let go—to let her body surrender to his—logic ruled. *His plan was to marry Jenna.* Besides, she had plans of her own. And if they had given into their sexual urges…*what then?* She dismissed one thought, making room for another—the stranger across the street from the restaurant, the parked car. *Jess made you feel safe back then. Is that what this is all about? He makes you feel safe?*

Once inside the garage, she immediately closed the overhead door, hurried inside the house, and turned the lock. After the kitchen was lit, she moved to the windows and drew the shades. *Better.* One habit led to another. She retrieved her mail beneath the slot in the front door and went back into the kitchen to sort through it. She weeded out her bills and tossed the rest into the trash. During her routine refrigerator check, she tingled from her recollection of the delicious cake she shared earlier with Jess. *Bad girl,* she laughed. *What would Sal think about their tantalizing escapade?*

Grace cooed to her fish, dropped food into the tank, and headed upstairs for bed. Once she completed her nightly regime, she slipped into short, silk pajamas. The material soothed her skin; the happy faces fulfilled her need to feel grounded.

Sleep came easy, but she awoke hours later with a dreadful feeling. There was no nightmare or strange dream to quantify her discomfort. She couldn't reason away the heaviness she felt in her chest. She glanced at her alarm clock. *It's two a.m.*

*Outside, a car cruised by slowly, back and forth like a shark.*

# CHAPTER 9

## Garret Weston

The next morning Grace woke on the edge of a dream—nothing prophetic, an elusive image of her red chair. Could it be symbolic? *Like you need to get up, get ready for work?* She didn't remember falling asleep.

After a quick shower, she dressed and fought the urge to spend more time in front of the mirror. Focusing on her day helped alleviate temptation.

She grabbed a cup of coffee before the pot finished brewing. She sipped while she jotted reminders on sticky notes. The last doughnut in the package called to her. "Sorry, my love," she said, resisting the sweet seduction. "Time to leave."

The garage door lifted, revealing a fabulous day. Despite the early hour, the sun had already begun warming the crisp, fresh air. Grace smelled verbena and heard cicadas sing in the trees, a glimpse of an early summer. Humming to herself, she backed out of the garage and stopped at the end of her drive to wait for traffic to clear. When she checked to her left, an acrid taste caught in her throat. On the left side of the street, a few houses down, sat the car she had seen the night before. Although her neighbor's trash cans partially concealed the car, there was no mistaking the dark-green sedan's tinted windows. She was too far away to identify the slouched figure occupying the driver's seat.

She squeezed the steering wheel to stop her hands from shaking. Backing into the street, Grace aimed her car in the direction of the green one. She glanced nonchalantly into the green car's window, not looking directly at the driver as she passed. She relied on her peripheral vision to gather as many details she could. Half-way down the block, she checked her rear-view mirror to see if the car followed. It didn't matter. The person already knew where she worked...*where she lived*...and was either tracking her activities or getting satisfaction by *stalking* her. The realization of the latter hit Grace like a lightning bolt. Her whole body began to tremble. Running her hands through her hair, she heard her voice of reason speak. *Get a grip.* She took deep breaths, exhaling her fear. *Think.* She recalled consulting for the DA's office and having counseled several police officers who worked downtown at the Twenty-Second Precinct. She had contacts. A man she worked with last year on a rape case stuck out in her mind—*Garret Weston.* Grace recalled the night she met Garret Weston. It was last October. A nine-teen-year old girl had been brutally beaten and raped near a local college campus. College campuses were high profile. They called Grace to help. When she arrived at the hospital, a group of young officers stood outside the curtained area where the victim was be-ing treated. They laughed and flirted with the nurses. She was on her way to break up the crowd when another officer came from behind. Having the advantage of a longer stride, he passed her by. He spoke to the men quietly, but point-blank. The hallway cleared immediately. *Garret Weston: impressive, polite, and gentle, but not a man to mess with. He didn't impose his authority; he gained respect.* He was the one to call when she got to her office.

Grace parked facing the street on the second level of her of-fice building. She would have preferred to park where foot traffic passed. *No.* The stranger might wonder why she veered from her normal routine. *Don't let fear cloud your judgment.*

She walked briskly, fluffing her hair and checking her watch, hoping no one noticed that she hadn't taken a breath since she got out of the car. Two flights of stairs, two steps, and a landing separated the garage from the doorway that led to the office suites. Once inside, she faced an atrium with a large seating area. It was still early. *No one around.* She looked over her shoulder as she in-serted her key and pushed through the door. The room was dark. Sal hadn't arrived yet. After she relocked the door, she flipped on the lights and headed for the phone in her office to dial the police station. Watching the door, she listened to the rings. After the second ring, a recording informed Grace, "If you have an emergency dial 911. If not, regular office hours are 8:30 a.m. until 4:30 p.m. If you know your party's extension, dial it now." Her next option was to leave a message after the beep. She paced the floor ready to state her business until the option was cut short by a loud, piercing shrill.

"Damn!" she swore, banging down the phone. Suddenly her outburst was interrupted by a noise coming from the outer office. She froze. Blood rushed in her ears. Her heart began to pound. A metallic taste filled her mouth. *The door.*

Her senses heightened. She was relieved to smell her secretary's familiar scent, Windsong. *Nobody wears that scent like Sal.* Grace rushed to greet the woman with a hug, making her jump.

"Goddamn, Grace! You scared the bajeezies out of me!"

"I'm so sorry, Sal! I didn't mean to scare you. I'm glad to see you!"

"What are you doing here so early? What's wrong?"

"I have Becky at nine. I needed to look up a few things. Come, sit down. I have something to tell you."

"Uh oh, this sounds serious. Can I put on some coffee first?"

"No, I'll get the coffee. You sit."

"Now I'm scared! Do you even know how to make coffee?" Sal teased.

"I make lousy coffee, but you're my friend, so you're going to humor me and let me do this."

"Why are your hands shaking? The pot goes on the burner, under the basket."

"I have a stalker, Sal. I saw this green car parked here in the garage last night, and then this morning it was parked on my street!"

"Shut up! Are you sure? Did you call the cops? Why didn't you call me?"

"Because—"

"Grace! You need to put water in the machine before you turn it on. Please sit down. Let me get the coffee ready."

"I had a strange feeling someone was watching me outside the Crab Shack last night. When I turned to see if my suspicion was warranted, I saw this figure…in the distance, hurrying away. It was creepy, you know? Then—"

"Are you sure it wasn't—"

"My imagination? No, there's more. After Jess walked me to my car, I was pulling out of the parking garage, and right before I reached the booth, I noticed a green car with someone sitting inside. Again, I got that creepy feeling, but I sloughed it off."

"Did you—?"

"I took precautions, Sal, so put those eyebrows back where they belong!" Grace rubbed her temples. "When I got home, I closed the garage door before I got out of my car, like you had suggested once before, and I relocked my door right away. Everything seemed fine. Besides, I had other things on my mind, and I forgot about it. And then this morning, I backed out of the garage, and when I stopped at the end of my drive, I saw the same car parked down the street!"

"You gotta call the police!"

"I already did. The office doesn't open until eight thirty," she said, checking the clock. "I have twelve minutes."

"How you doin'?" Sal asked in her mothering tone.

"I'm fine. We're going to nip this in the bud. I refuse to have to look over my shoulder every minute of the day."

"Right. Let's get this creep and be done with it." With that said, Sal went into the little kitchenette area to rescue her coffee pot. She dumped the grounds back into the can and rinsed the basket. She reached for a new filter, caught Grace's eye, and smiled. "So, how was Prince Charming?"

"He embarrassed the living daylights out of me." Grace's face brightened. "He told the waiter it was my birthday." Her eyes twinkled; color tinted her cheeks. "When we finished eating, a group of servers came to our table with a tiara and a feather boa. They gave me a mason jar full of glittery confetti to sprinkle around the room while they sang *Happy Birthday* to me. Can you imagine?"

"Oh my," Sal said. "You must've railed into him good for that one."

"That was my first reaction, but the kids were so enthusiastic, and then I saw everyone's smiling faces, and I thought, *this is fun*. These people are sharing a happy moment with me. Why spoil it? Besides, Crab Shack's cake is so delicious; I would've stood on my head for a piece."

"You're a jewel, Grace. I would've loved to have been a fly on the wall for that one!"

"Yeah, it was nice." She sighed. "Best birthday I've ever had."

"So did you—?" Sal's brows danced up and down.

"Ah, it's eight-thirty," Grace dodged Sal's curiosity. "Let me get this call over with." She rushed to her office, and slammed the door behind her. She hit redial, connected with the dispatcher at the Twenty-Second Precinct, and asked to speak with Sergeant Garret Weston. Once she identified herself, she was put on hold. When Garret picked up, she almost felt silly. Was she overreacting? Would he even remember her?

"Hello, Miss Simms," he said. "It's been awhile. Is it still *Miss?*"

"Yes. You can call me *Grace.*" *He remembers me.*

"What can I do for you, Grace?"

Upon retelling her story, she gave him as much information as she could about the car and a description of the person lurking near the Crab Shack.

"Do you know of anyone with a grudge? Jilted lover? Jealous girlfriend? Disgruntled patient?" The barrage of questions lasted for fifteen minutes. Garret took Grace's personal information, including the make and model of her car, license plate number, and a list of her daily activities.

"In your line of work, Miss Simms, you're a target for all kinds of lunatics. This could be a cake walk, or it could be a nightmare."

"I like cake, Sergeant."

"Good! Let's get this guy! Meanwhile, try and keep your normal routine. Safety in numbers: key advice here. And you know the drill. Lock your doors and windows. Do you have a dog?" he asked.

"No, I have a fish," she replied, trying not to sound glib.

"Great! I hope you named it Jaws!" He chuckled. "Seriously, Grace, if you don't have a dog, get one. A mean one. Let me give you a friend's number. She volunteers at the Animal Rescue Center in Placerville. She'll fix you up with a good dog."

Grace took down the information and thanked the sergeant for his time. As she hung up the phone, she heard the outer door open and close. When she heard Sal greet her client, she checked the time. It was Becky.

*Becky is never early.*

\* \* \*

Garret pushed back in his chair. *Remember you?* He smiled. *How could I forget?* His day had been for shit. Every nut case in Sacramento had come forward that morning to confess to the multiple rapes headlining the Sacramento Bee for more than a month. His feet were killing him. His stomach screamed to be fed, and his left molar ached like hell. To top it off, he received another call—a college student, raped on campus.

When he stormed into the ER that October night, he was tempted to put someone's ass in a sling.

But then he saw Grace walking down the hall in front of him, and he fell in love before he even saw her face. Maybe it was the way she walked with her head held high or the little wiggle in her hips. He couldn't say. All he remembered was he wanted to rescue her from his swarm of testosterone-driven officers who had stopped flirting with the nurses and banded together like a pack of hungry wolves. When he passed by her in the hall, he caught a whiff of her sweetness. It affected him like a drug.

It had been years since he felt that way about anyone. When he lost his high school sweetheart to a drunk driver, he lost interest in love. He poured himself into his work, putting drunk drivers behind bars. He earned a law degree and promotion after promotion. He conjured Grace's warm smile. *No one will hurt you, I promise.*

He examined the palm of his hand, following tiny lines with his index finger. *Grandma said someday I would meet the girl of my dreams.* He thought her predictions were rubbish—until he met Grace. Unfortunately the timing of their first encounter wasn't right. And now? *How can fate be so cruel?*

\*\*\*

"Becky?" Grace called from the doorway. As Becky approached, Grace pressed her lips together and placed her gaze elsewhere. *Oh, my Lord,* she thought, *what on earth is she wearing?* Becky passed by with total disregard, but Grace took the opportunity to get a better look at the atrocious outfit. Becky's skirt looked as though dingy rags were sewn together in a small semi-circle, banded with scraps of leather, and finished with a short train made of fuchsia-sequined fabric. Her breasts were squeezed into a lemon-colored bandeaux top and a patchwork leather vest, leaving her midriff bare. Teal, mesh stockings met black, engineer boots half-way between her ankle and her calf. When she first met Becky, Grace did notice that the girl had some holes for piercings. Now that the holes were filled with studs, rings and spikes, Grace wondered what else the girl was hiding about her true self. *Okay, you have my attention.*

When Becky plopped into the overstuffed chair, Grace took her seat without a mention of Becky's outrageous look. "So, what's new, Becky?" she asked, dangling a pen loose between her fingers.

"Nothin'."

"What would you like to talk about?" Grace waited for Becky's response, trying to figure out her sudden change in wardrobe choices. Becky usually dressed conservatively. *Why the change?*

"He's all I think about," she said. "He's so beautiful to me."

"Does he have a name?" Grace knew naming this man would bring him to the forefront and encourage reality, rather than quixotic behavior.

"You keep asking me that question. His name doesn't matter to me!" Becky yanked a loose thread from the edge of her makeshift hem.

"I'm simply trying to understand. Tell me more."

"I keep thinking about that day at the mall," Becky lamented, pulling tufts of black hair fringed in blonde away from her slender neck. "I was so happy—happy to see him after all these years."

"When is the last time you saw him?"

Becky glared. "I don't remember."

Grace could tell Becky was unwilling to cooperate. The girl wanted her to believe this man existed. Providing any information made Becky uncomfortable. *Why?*

Time for another approach. "Have you returned to work?" Grace asked.

"No. I don't want to go back there. People are going to think I'm a freak."

"Did you have a good working relationship with these people before you left?"

"No, not really. I talked to a couple of the girls, but we weren't buddy-buddy or anything."

"What kind of work would you like to do?" Grace asked.

"I don't know. I like plants. I'm not qualified to do much. I designed this outfit myself. Do you like it?"

Grace didn't have the heart to tell her she looked like a cross between a clown and a hooker. "It's interesting. What did you want to be when you were a little girl, Becky?"

Becky hesitated, as if trying to censor her emotions.

"I wanted to be a dancer, like the girls in *Saturday Night Fever* and *Grease*."

"What did you like about them?"

"They were pretty. I liked the way they swished their skirts. My brother Georgie liked to watch them because he could see their underpants." Becky made a face.

"I wasn't aware that you had a brother," Grace said, stunned. She had spent hours with this girl. Not once had Becky mentioned a brother. In fact, she had offered little about her family history on the information sheet.

Since the beginning of their sessions, they had focused primarily on her mishap at the mall. Grace remained hopeful that Becky would divulge something that would be useful to her progress. "Tell me about Georgie."

"Georgie was a punk. He was always tattling on me. He took my dolls all the time and wrote his name on their faces with ink pens."

"Uh-oh." Grace appeared sympathetic.

"Yeah, once the ink soaked in, you couldn't wipe it off. He thought that was funny. Then, when I'd punch him he'd cry super loud, like I was murdering him or something. My mom or dad would come in and beat the crap out of me for hitting him. He could do no wrong."

"It sounds like he is younger than you."

"Yeah, Mom had him when I was three. He was my half-brother."

"So, your mom remarried when you were two or three?"

"I was two. My real dad never married my mom. She married Dan when I was two. Yeah, two." Becky looked down at the floor; her voice faded. The memory seemed painful, but Grace continued to question. No pain, no gain.

"Was Dan a good dad to you?"

Looking up at the ceiling, Becky's expression changed to a hard, flat stare. The ceiling became her focus as she spoke.

"I was his property. I don't think he liked me very much. I wasn't smart like Georgie."

"Maybe because he was younger—"

"Georgie was sneaky," she snapped. "He acted nice to Dad's face; Mom's too. He was so *perfect*." Her features softened. She looked at Grace, as if challenging her to make sense of it all.

"Where is Georgie now?" Grace asked.

"He's— I don't know. I haven't talked to my family in a while."

"How long is *a while*?"

"Seems like forever. I was emancipated when I was pretty young."

"Wow, how did you manage that?"

"I worked for this lady sewing," she said with a smirk. "She let me live in her house, in the basement. I was used to that. The lady sewed wedding dresses. She got a lot of money for doing it. I sewed on the pearls, beads, sequins. Stuff like that. In between I worked for the neighbor in her beauty shop." Becky's posture began to relax.

"How ambitious. What did you do in the beauty shop?" Grace asked.

"I swept up, shampooed hair, and did a manicure now and then. I have steady hands. Must've been all that sewing."

Goosebumps gathered on Grace's skin. She knew of the house Becky referred to. It was a low-income boarding house set up by a non-profit group to transition women from hostile environments back into society. The criteria to get accepted into this home was pretty extensive. Its residents needed to have a background of substantiated violence. The women were recommended by the courts, and there was a long waiting list. Only the most severe cases were placed as a priority, providing there was a vacancy. The overseer of the house was a retired seamstress from England.

"The lady I sewed for—she didn't want to do it anymore. She had a friend who worked at Nordstrom. They do a lot of mending and hemming at the store. That's what I did most of the time—alterations." Becky's beautiful eyes flickered as they scanned back and forth to search for information that connected her to the memory. She shared a few more details about her job, allowing Grace to see a different side of her.

"I learned a lot there," Becky said. "I learned how to run the cash register and do charges. Most of the girls needed to use calculators, but I didn't. I never realized I was good at math. I mean…not that I am super good at math. I just don't need a calculator, that's all."

"Did you make friends with any of your co-workers?"

"I've gone to lunch with Pat, this lady— She's older than me, but she's nice. And this other girl that just started, Blanca, I think her name is. We're not best buds or anything; we just didn't like eating alone."

Grace rerouted the conversation in attempt to get back to some of the family background. "Must be nice getting an employee discount around the holidays?"

"I never gave it much thought." The girl leaned forward to close the space between them. "Do you want to know something *specific*, Dr. Grace?" Her eyes flashed.

"I would like to talk a little bit more about your family background," Grace spoke softly. Her eyes never wavered from Becky's.

When the girl pursed her lips and tilted her head, Grace perceived the injustice that had taken place in her past.

"You want to hear how horrible my family life was, don't you? When we were little kids, my mom and Dan fought a lot. When Dan knocked my mom around, he locked us downstairs.

It was hard for Georgie because there was no bathroom down there, and Georgie would wet his pants and cry. When the coast was clear—when Mom and Dan stopped *fighting*—Mom would unlock the door, so I could take Georgie to the bathroom and clean him up. One night Dan barged in and saw me washing George and spanked *me*. I still can't figure out why *I* got spanked, but that's pretty much the way it went."

"Did your dad, Dan, hit you a lot?"

"We spent a lot of time in the basement."

"That must have been horrible for you, Becky."

"Yeah, I guess."

There were no tears. Her expression remained stoic, but her leg pumped up and down.

"It's hard for children to understand the injustices they endure as children. Even when we become adults, it's hard to look rationally at another *adult's* behavior, when the scars that were left were those left on a *child's* mind."

Becky chewed on her thumb while Grace continued to explain.

"It is perfectly normal for a child to seek solace of some sort. In your case, this man—your angel—perhaps he manifested in your mind as a coping mechanism. Perhaps he made life endurable for you. Typically, children seek something to soothe them, nurture them. It is instinctive to want to be loved. Do you remember when this *man* came into your mind?"

Becky's eyes welled up with tears. "So, I was just put into a neat little box and labeled *damaged*. Wow, Dr. Grace."

"That was an explanation, not a label." Grace moved closer to reassure the girl of her good intent and made eye contact to show the compassion she felt toward her. "Unfortunately, Becky, there's a lot of abuse that goes on in this world. Some cases are more severe physically, some more severe emotionally, some both. Some children get through the abuse with minimal scarring. Some are scarred for life. Everyone is different in how they process their experiences. *But*...the bottom line is that it's *all* horrific. We need to sort out how *you*, how Becky the child, has processed her experiences. How is Becky, the *adult,* dealing with these issues now? Repressed emotions can erupt inside and beg to surface. For instance, this man you envision may be a manifestation of your deep need to be loved."

"He's *real*, Dr. Grace, I *told* you that!" Becky seethed with anger. Grace needed to return her to a safe place within the next few minutes.

"Yes, Becky, the *man* you saw, *he's* real. You saw him at the mall. But who he is to you is why we need to dig deep. Tell me more about Georgie."

Grace waited for Becky to resume. She felt they had made a little progress. Their time was about up, and Grace didn't want Becky to launch into a dark place only to cut her off. She thought she would let Becky take the lead and assess from there.

Becky sat still for a moment and then began to laugh.

"What's funny?" Grace asked.

"No one saved Georgie from coming unglued."

Graced smiled, trying to share the levity, but inside she thought of how sociopaths developed from this kind of environment. Years of cruelty were stored in this girl's head. Her brother had to have his own set of problems, but right now *Becky* was her concern, so she said nothing.

"Time's up for today, Becky. How about if we talk again in a couple of days?" Grace rose from her chair.

"Dr. Grace?"

"Yeah?"

"Do you think I'll ever get better?"

Grace saw the tears well up in Becky's eyes again and felt her pain. She couldn't help herself. She threw her arms around the girl and gave her a hug. Grace felt as though she held a sparrow. Becky felt so frail in her arms. The girl clung for a moment, then let go.

"Sorry." Becky sniffed.

Grace handed her a tissue. "I'll see you in a couple of days. And by the way, I like your boots."

Once Becky was gone, Grace approached the front desk.

Sal shook her head. "What the hell was she wearing?"

"Long story. Any calls?"

"No." Sal placed her hands on her hips. "Things are getting crazy around here. What did the police say?"

"I talked to Sergeant Weston. He told me to get a dog."

"Great!" Sal's brow disappeared beneath her bangs. "Is this dog gonna carry a gun?"

"He said he would check things out. He will. Don't worry."

"Okay, you're being stalked by some maniac," Sal complained. "Your clients are dressing like its Halloween." She slammed a file drawer closed. "And I'm not supposed to worry?"

"Don't. I'll be fine."

"Fine!" Sal punched buttons on her keyboard until her screen went to the underwater scene. "James isn't due in for a few minutes. Coffee?" She held up a cup. "So what's with Becky?"

Grace held up her hand.

Sal groused, "I know how you are about privacy and all, but—"

"Coffee sounds good." Grace's reply fell flat.

Sal retreated.

Patients were off limits. When it came to patient privacy, there were no exceptions.

Although Sal typed up the notes for each session, the information remained confidential, as long as it wasn't discussed.

"That outfit...I mean, it was ...," Sal hesitated. "It just isn't the kind of thing that she normally wears..." She poured coffee into the cup, pulled two sweeteners from the sugar bowl, and handed them to Grace along with the steaming brew and continued "... that's all."

"Yeah, Becky sure can wear bright colors." She accepted the cup. "Any cream back there?"

Grace drank her coffee black, but when Sal made it, she loaded it with cream and sugar to enhance the rich flavor. She hoped changing the subject would let them move on from the awkward situation. It was difficult sometimes not to talk about what went on behind closed doors, even casually. Grace was adamant about protecting the privacy of people who trusted her with personal information. She knew Sal felt concern for Becky; it was hard not to, but discussing her case was a definite no-no.

"How about some hazelnut creamer?" Sal suggested, pulling the bottle from the fridge.

"Mmmm, thanks." Grace took the bottle, poured a generous amount of the creamer into her cup, opened the sweetener packets, and added them to her coffee. Sal handed her a spoon and waited for Grace to finish stirring to hand it back. No one spoke.

When the phone rang, Sal turned her attention back to her job. Grace picked up her coffee and went back to her office. She sat down in her chair to enjoy the warmth of the cup in her hands. As she sipped, she replayed the images from the morning in her head. She started to dwell on the parked car and tried to imagine who the person could be. When her heart rate increased, she let it go and switched her thoughts to Becky. The outfit Becky wore— *wild.* What would cause her to change her appearance?

Grace thought about the attention the girl would call to herself and then questioned the pay-off.

Becky wasn't a here-I-am kind of girl. If anything, she was the kind of girl who blended in with the scenery. She didn't perceive herself as striking or beautiful. Her black hair, thick and shiny, her complexion resembled ivory bisque. Grace couldn't tell if her teeth were straight. *She never smiles like that.* She opened Becky's folder and wrote: "Childhood:" *What are you trying to tell me Becky?* The crack in the glass was getting larger.

\* \* \*

Grace peeked outside to see if anyone skulked across the street. A chill zipped down her spine. The sun broke through a white fluffy cloud perched in an asphalt sky. The contrast was ominous. *Breathtaking.* Rain wasn't forecast—or was it? She couldn't remember the last time she watched the news, checked the weather in the newspaper, or listened to the radio. She enjoyed the beauty for another moment and let her thoughts drift. *You're lonely. You're feeling vulnerable. Someone is trying to scare the wits out of you. You have no big, strong man to protect you.*

She leaned back in her chair, scooped up a handful of hair and twisted. She let it go, smoothed it out, and scooped it up again. *Forty minutes until Tim Ashton arrives.* Like James, he kept her on her toes. *I'm not in the mood for two in one day.* She had to measure her words carefully with both men, so as not to give them the impression her boundaries could be crossed or manipulated. Tim's sadistic smile hovered in her mind.

She took a book off the shelf and began to read. She couldn't concentrate. Her mind wanted to conjure images of her stiff body, lying on a metal slab in the morgue beneath a sheet barely covering her breasts. She shivered. *Don't let this creep get to you. Focus.* To quiet the little voice inside her head, she opened her top desk drawer and began sorting pens from paperclips. Forty minutes went by.

# CHAPTER 10
# The Letter

Hello, Mr. Ashton." Grace greeted her client from the doorway and waited for him to approach. *If looks could kill.* She moved out of his way, creating a comfortable distance between her body and his negative vibes. She observed the man's height as he walked past. Sergeant Weston had asked if she had any enemies. *Do I?* she wondered, comparing Tim's frame to the person she saw fleeing from the Crab Shack the other night. Tim Ashton seemed larger. *The person was in the distance…it was getting dark. How can you be sure?*

"It's Tim— I asked that you call me *Tim*. It makes me feel less like a…*sicko*." Tim sat down, choosing the sofa. He moved the puffy pillows out of his way, sat back, and crossed his legs. Grace saw a spark and heard a loud snap—an electrical shock when Tim touched his knee. He didn't flinch. "May I call you Grace? Grace is such a pretty name."

"That's right, I remember. You prefer *Tim. Grace* is fine." As she spoke, his eyes broke from her stare to roam her body. *Good thing I'm wearing slacks.* She opened his folder and placed it in her lap, obstructing his view. "The last time we met, you said you had plans to visit your Mom in Galesburg. How did that go?"

"Great!" He redirected his eyes from her crotch to her breasts. "We attended the Rutabaga Festival. It was nice."

Grace tipped the folder so it covered her breasts and her crotch. Her eyes beckoned his attention and won. He went on to explain that his mother was a generous contributor to the

Orpheum Theatre and that this year the event featured the Knox Jazz Ensemble, along with Jim Rotundi and the Eric Alexander Quintet.

"It was nice," he repeated, "if you like jazz."

Grace wasn't sure if he was questioning her taste in music or not. She waited for him to continue, his alert eyes contradicting his relaxed demeanor.

"The theater is beautiful. Have you ever been to Galesburg, Miss Simms?"

"I'm familiar with it. I went to school in Chicago."

"Northwestern?" Tim's smirk indicated he was pleased, having tricked Grace into sharing personal information. This guy was clever. He wanted to get to know her, whether she wanted him to or not.

"Let's get back to you," she said matter-of-factly.

Tim's smile spread across his lips. His eyes never wavered from hers. It was his way of challenging her professional position, and he seemed amused by her no-nonsense demeanor. She could tell he was used to this game of cat and mouse. He had been playing it all of his life. She observed how he brought his finger to his lips to control them from collapsing into laughter. She remained stoic. Moments passed. He retreated.

"It was an enjoyable trip, I guess you could say. My mother is seventy nine. She's holding up well, I suppose. My aunt, who is sixty three, looks in on Mom. Aunt Edith was raised as Mom's sister, but I believe she's the illegitimate daughter of my mother's older sister Dora. She's a peach… and not hell bent on propriety like my mother."

Grace picked up on the bitterness that crept into his tone. "How so?"

"My mother is 'Ms. Manners.' She makes Martha Stewart look like an amateur. Don't get me wrong. I have nothing against Martha Stewart. But I can take just so much of 'mommy dearest'."

He's baiting me, she thought. *Okay, let's go fishing.* She took the bait and threw back the hook. "Oh? Did you have problems with your mom growing up?"

She watched color rise from his neck to his cheeks.

"She's not my problem, Grace. *I'm* my problem. Right now? I could care less about my mother…or anyone else for that matter!"

His expression made Grace flash on the movie scene from Peter Benchley's *Jaws:* the shark grabs a barrel full of gun powder in his mouth and takes off, pulling the boat with him..

"However, tomorrow," he spluttered, sitting up straight, and appearing larger, "I may find that I don't know anyone who *isn't* my best friend. I take my meds; I exercise; I meditate. I even got myself a kitten! Nothing helps. The screaming starts in my head, and it won't stop. I berate myself. I loathe myself, and then I can do no wrong. My relationships are fucked up. Is that okay to say?" He didn't wait for an answer. "I like what I do, but I hate my job, granted. I lose my temper now and then. So what! People can be so fucking stupid. I want to ring their fucking necks! I can't believe the stupid fucking things that I have put up with! A guy has just so much patience!"

He took a breath and began to rant again.

"I guess I'm fucking sick of everything and everyone. They all can take a flying fuck through a donut hole for all I care."

"Who are *they,* Tim? Anyone in particular?"

"No! Today I'm including the fucking mailman!"

Grace noted Tim's abrupt mood change. He was acting out. Those who suffer with BPD, Borderline Personality Disorder, make attempts to alleviate their pain by dumping it onto someone else. She contemplated how rage, blaming, criticizing, and physical violence were characteristic of high functioning borderlines. They could act perfectly normal most of the time and be successful, outgoing and well liked, until stress or a particular issue triggered their dysfunctional coping mechanisms. Grace needed to find the source of his anguish and address it. She, too, sat up straight, letting him know she was not intimidated by his outburst. Her voice filled with concern. "What's upsetting you today, Tim?" she asked.

"I think I liked talking about my mother more than I do about my job." His mood changed once more.

Another calm before the tornado rips? *I didn't mention his job.* "I'm hearing a lot of anger about your work situation, Tim. Let it out. Tell me what's wrong." She held eye contact to show him she had no intention of dismissing the issue. The ticking sound of the clock on her desk grew louder while she waited for him to break the silence. His growing tension seemed to suck the air out of the room.

"I got passed up for the promotion I worked my ass off to get. I've been with the company seventeen fucking years! He gave *my* promotion to some asshole that's been with the company less than a year! Can you believe that?" Tim's face started to turn red again. "I wanted to punch his fucking face in!" he said in a low, seething tone.

She glanced down. Spittle escaped his lips and landed on her shoe. He was too busy reliving the torment and rejection he had experienced with his boss to notice. She wanted badly to reach for a tissue.

"He told me there'd be other opportunities," Tim continued. "I told him to shove the job up his ass! I don't need to work for a company that has no fucking loyalty!"

When Tim finished spewing, he shielded his eyes with his hand, but it was too late; Grace had already witnessed tears in his eyes. He remained still, staring at his knees. The color began to drain from his face; his flash of anger subsided. *Time for me to interject.*

"When did this happen?" Grace wanted more details. "Did your boss give you a reason why you weren't chosen for the position?" She hoped he would open up about his feelings. When he looked up, she caught the chill in his stare.

"I didn't ask." His eyes locked onto to hers like a steel trap.

Grace conceded, before the game begun. *He's trying to regain his power by using a visual stronghold on mine.* She wanted him to regain his power on his own volition, not by trying to take hers away or anyone else's. Without a contest there was no winner or loser.

"I realize it's been a short time since this happened, but have you given any thought to what you're going to do now that you've quit your job? Do you have something else lined up?" She hoped to engage him in a more positive thought, so she added, "I can't imagine you having any problem finding other employment." She hoped to infuse sunshine to his dilemma. She would settle for partly cloudy. Their session had run over by ten minutes, and she needed to relieve her bladder desperately.

"Yeah, I guess you're right. I should have quit years ago. Now I don't have any excuse."

The storm was over. His body relaxed. He ran his hand through his hair, blowing out tension through his lips.

Grace couldn't help noticing how nicely his mouth puckered up. She tried to remember the last time she had been kissed by nice lips. *Besides Jess?* She shifted in her seat, diffusing the heat heading for her loins. "We've run out of time today, Tim. If you like, we can set up another appointment."

Grace turned to look at the calendar on her desk.

"How about next week?" he suggested. "If I get an interview with St. Peter to guard the Pearly Gates, I'll call you."

"With today's gas prices, I'd suggest something closer to home."

They laughed, dissipating a few more clouds before they said their goodbyes. He got up and let himself out.

After Grace finished charting a quick synopsis of Tim's episode, including his subtle hint pertaining to suicide, she headed for the ladies room.

***

The tenants on each floor shared a large bathroom with four regular and two handicapped stalls. A bank of four sinks lined a mirrored wall on the left side of the room. To the right, was a little conversation area consisting of two poppy-colored barrel chairs and a round coffee table piled high with old magazines. The rectangular skylight, lined with greenery, gave the room a cozy ambience. Many of the tenants would relax there on their breaks. The toilet area was situated in the back of the room partitioned by a freestanding wall for privacy.

Grace hurried, barely making it into the stall in time. After she finished and flushed, she heard the outer door open. Whoever came in didn't enter one of the empty stalls. Grace didn't hear the lock engage, the rattle of a paper seat cover, or tissue rolling. She didn't hear anything.

While she buttoned her pants and straightened her pockets, she peered through the crack in the door. When she saw a shadow stretch across the tile floor, she expected a person to come into view. When the shadow didn't move, she froze. She watched and listened. *Too quiet.* The shadow remained still. After a minute passed, she began to feel silly. *The door probably stuck open, casting a shadow.* But, just as she was about to look away, the shadow moved. She held her breath. The voice inside her head protested. *Do you intend to stay trapped in here?* She inched her way out of the stall. One hand balled into a fist by her side. Her heart pounded. Her finger nails dug deep grooves into her palm. Her knees weakened.

"Hello? Is someone there?" she called out, her voice shaky. No one answered. She heard the outer door shut and crept around the partition. When she realized she was alone, she exhaled and headed toward the sink to wash her hands. Reaching for the soap dispenser, she caught her image in the mirror. A pale woman with dark circles and wild eyes stared back at her. *Fear is taking its toll.* "It could've been anyone," she whispered, regaining her composure. She surveyed the area for signs of activity. *C'mon Miss Therapist, think logically.* She hadn't heard water. *Maybe the person came in for a paper towel?* Hadn't she done that before when Sal forgot to pick up napkins? She shook the water from her hands and reached for a paper towel. The towel holder was automatic; *I would've heard the motor.* Next theory? *Someone came in to grab a magazine? That makes more sense.* She confronted the frightened image in the mirror. *Let it go. You're on the verge of driving yourself crazy.*

On her way out, she checked the area one more time. Nothing out of the ordinary—except for a letter-size envelope propped up in one of the barrel chairs. *That wasn't there before.* Her breath caught in her throat. She picked up the envelope with the paper toweling she intended to deposit in the trashcan next to the door. Her hand shook. Her blood ran cold as she read the words written on the front of the envelope in bold print: "Die Bitch."

***

Sal was on the phone with a client when Grace rushed through the door of her office carrying a paper towel like it was a bomb. She turned and watched her boss until her head could turn no further.

"Hold on, please," she said, pressing the hold button. "Grace? Are you all right?" she yelled down the hall. "Grace?" No answer. When she saw the button for Grace's private line was lit, she finished taking the message and answered the next call.

"Hi, John. Yeah, I'm feeling a little better, but hey…something's up. Grace just ran through here holding something in a paper towel!" She paused to listen. "No, John, Grace doesn't panic like that. If it were a spider, she would've taken the damn thing outside and let it go. You know how she is about stuff like that."

Sal was still chatting with John when Grace came out of her office with an ashen face. "Hey honey, she's right here; call ya back later." Sal hung up the phone and came around the desk. "Grace? What's wrong?"

"Sergeant Weston is on his way up here. Buzz me when he comes in."

Grace's shaken demeanor gave Sal chills. She hadn't made eye contact with Sal when she spoke; she'd looked through her.

"Are you going to tell me what's up? Or do I have to beat it out of you?" she demanded, giving Grace a hard look reserved for her boys when she meant business.

"I'll tell you later, Sal, after I talk to the sergeant. I feel sick. Do you have any Pepto-Bismol? Who's up— Damn, I need to sit down."

"Arlene Pratt," Sal answered, deciding not to press the issue further. "Her appointment is at five. You have half an hour. Let me get you a glass of water. I may have antacids in my purse."

Sal didn't wait for Grace's permission to act. She filled a paper cup with water and rummaged through her purse, feeling victorious when she pulled out a blister pack of chewable Tums. "Here, take these." She handed Grace the Tums and then the cup.

"This day needs to end soon," said Grace. "I need to lie down." Grace put her head on Sal's shoulder and began to cry. Sal didn't say a word. She put her arm around Grace, kneading the knots in her friend's shoulder while she listened to her purge her pent-up anguish.

***

The emotional meltdown cut short when the door opened to a tall man in a police uniform. Grace dug a tissue from her pocket and dabbed her eyes before advancing toward the door with her hand extended to Sergeant Garret Weston.

"Thanks for coming so soon. Come on. Let's go into my office," she said, forcing her steely reserve to the surface once again. She stopped mid-stride, remembering that Sal and the sergeant hadn't been introduced. Intuition told her that the two would be seeing more of each other.

"Sergeant Weston, this is my friend and office manager, Sal La Porta. Sal, Sergeant Garret Weston."

"Sal," he said, shaking the woman's hand. Sal nodded politely.

"Would you please hold my calls for now?" Grace didn't wait for an answer. She flashed Sal a grateful smile, led the officer down the hall to her office and closed the door.

\* \* \*

"I didn't open it," she said, handing him the paper towel. "I wasn't sure what to do. All I know is that it wasn't there when I went into the ladies room. I heard someone come in, but never saw anyone."

"Do you know of any other *Bitch* this could have been intended for?" he asked. She must have looked horrified, he rephrased his question. "I'm sorry, I didn't mean– I feel like an oaf! I was– I thought a little humor– I have such bad timing." He cleared his throat and shuffled his feet. "I remembered what a beaut– Class– Uh, intelligent and kind person you were to work with, I can't imagine someone calling you a– There I go again. I apologize, Ms. Simms. In my twelve years on the force, I think that had to be the stupidest question I have ever– Please forgive me."

"It's Grace…and you're forgiven. I guess I'm rattled to say the least. In all my years of being in this profession, I have never encountered a threat from anyone."

He believed that to be true. *Who would want to harm a beautiful woman like Grace?*

"Think back to when you entered the ladies room," he suggested. "Did you notice anyone in the hallway or across the atrium?"

"No, to be honest with you, I was in such a hurry that I was oblivious. I only became aware of my surroundings once I was inside. Habit, I guess. I like privacy."

"Well, I'll get this to our lab. By the way, it was smart of you to wrap the envelope in a paper towel. Let's hope whoever delivered it left us fingerprints. I'll contact you as soon as we get something. How about that dog? Did you call Pam yet?" The guilt on Grace's face gave her away. "Give her a call, Grace. She'll hook you up with a good dog." He tried to convince her by cocking his head and giving her a sweet smile. He had hoped she'd be more receptive to this approach rather than his sense of humor.

"Okay, you win," she conceded.

He decided she liked his sweet side. "Good." He reached in his pocket and pulled out a small leather pouch. "My business card. Call me anytime." Her fingertips brushed his when she took the card, sending little chills up his spine. He couldn't remember a woman affecting him the way Grace did. *Is that why you act like a buffoon around her?* Perhaps changing subjects would help reduce the blood flooding capillaries in his cheeks. "Bigger isn't necessarily better," he said.

"What?" Her face warmed to a rosy pink.

*This isn't the time or place to be making a love connection.* He couldn't believe he was hitting on her. What an awkward moment. *I feel like a teenager.* "Great Danes are huge," he said, attempting to redeem his dignity. "Dobermans are smaller, but meaner. Shepherds are good protectors, and they don't bark all the time." He gauged her reaction by her nod. "I'd like to stop by and take a look at your house, if I may. You know, just to, uh, check the windows, check out the neighborhood; that sort of thing."

He began to heat up. Words poured out of his mouth before he was able to stop them. Luckily, his notorious poker face helped him to recover from another blundering statement. He was getting ridiculous! He would need a cold shower if he didn't get away from this enchantress. He checked his watch. "I better get back to the station before the lab guys leave for the day." He slipped the envelope into his breast pocket, careful not to disturb the paper towel wrapper, and he started for the door.

"Thanks, Sergeant. I'll look forward to hearing from you then." She followed him to the outer office, wanting to grab his hand and take him home with her. *He's sweet, but you don't want a pet. You want someone you can cuddle on the couch with.*

Suddenly, he stopped short, and she almost bumped her nose on the police radio hanging from the loop on his shoulder.

"*Garret,*" he said. His smile revealed perfect white teeth and a pair of deep dimples.

"Yes. *Garret*, sure," she said. "Thank you." Once he was out the door, she slapped her forehead with the palm of her hand. "Geez!"

"Well?" Sal stood behind the counter waiting for Grace to give her the scoop. "Am I canceling your appointments? You need to take some time for yourself."

"I'm fine, Sal. Thanks. I'm just rattled. I found a note in the ladies room, and it wasn't friendly. Garret...I mean Sergeant Weston is going to check it out for me. I'm sure it's harmless. Just someone trying to freak me out. I'm fine, and I'm tougher than I look. Right?"

"Right," Sal replied.

"I'll be in my office," Grace said nonchalantly. Inside, she felt like Jell-O.

# CHAPTER 11
# Arlene Pratt

Arlene Pratt arrived a few minutes before her appointment. She was busy picking lint off her socks when Grace called her into the office.

"Arlene, hi. Come on back."

Grace escorted her client into the room and shut the door. She could smell alcohol despite the woman's efforts to cover her fumes with cheap cologne and breath mints.

"Hi, Grace. I'm early; did you notice?"

"I did, Arlene. Great job!"

"I wasn't going to come at all. I didn't want to get dressed today. I'm tired of coming here."

"I'm glad you made it, Arlene," Grace said, groaning inwardly. "How are things going for you?"

Arlene dug through her purse, placed it beside her, changed her mind, and put it back on her lap. "My son steals from me. He denies it, but I know he is."

"What has he stolen?"

"He steals my cigarettes, my books, my Pop Tarts. I had a whole box of them hidden under my bed, and now they're gone! I'm gonna kill 'im if he don't quit takin' my stuff."

"Does your son live with you now?"

"No."

"He steals your things when he comes to visit?"

"No."

"I'm sorry, I don't understand," Grace confessed.

An explanation would not compute in Arlene's brain. She skipped to another subject.

"My dog pissed all over the bed the other night. I was so mad!"

"That must have been awful."

"Nobody would clean it up, but me."

"Was somebody else there?"

"No. I had to use bleach. I had to wash my bedspread three times with bleach."

"Is the dog a puppy?"

"No. The cats don't like her. That's why she pisses all over my bed."

"How many cats do you have?"

"Six," she replied, after doing the arithmetic on her fingers.

"Let's get back to your son, shall we?"

"He don't live with me."

"That's what you said. How often does he visit?"

"He comes when I'm at work and steals my stuff."

"How does he get in? Does he have a key?"

"He— I never gave him a key."

"How does he get in?"

"He just does."

Grace waited until Arlene unclenched her fists. The woman rummaged through her purse again to make sure nothing was missing before she placed it beside her.

"How is work?"

"This broad I work with makes me mad. I'm gonna kill 'er."

"Why would you want to do that?"

"She makes me mad. She talks behind my back; she takes my pens. I'm gonna kill 'er."

"How is the new medication working for you, Arlene?"

Grace noted that Arlene had been switched to Seroquel, a medication used to treat bi-polar depression.

"It's not good. It makes me sleepy."

"Did you tell your doctor?"

"Yeah, he's stupid."

"Why do you feel he's stupid?"

"He told me I can't have my martinis anymore! He's stupid!"

"If you're taking medication, the two might not get along very well. He doesn't want you to have a drug interaction."

"That's what *he* said. He's stupid!"

"It sounds to me like you don't care much for your doctor."

"He gives me a bad time. I wanna kill 'im!"

The woman crossed her arms and propped them on her protruding belly. Her jaw jutted forward, balancing the corners of her mouth. Arlene always wanted to kill someone, figuratively speaking. Alcohol provoked her anger and paranoia.

Arlene's demons surfaced at fifteen when her family had fallen victim to a home invasion robbery. She watched her parents brutally beaten to death by four young men hopped up on methamphetamines. After the intruders had gathered the goods they wanted, they helped themselves to Arlene and her twelve-year-old sister, Adele.

Adele never got over the horror and hanged herself. Two days later Arlene gave birth to her unknown rapist's son. The baby was immediately put into foster care while Arlene was put on antipsychotic medication. Her mind left her that day, never to return.

"What have you been doing for fun, Arlene?"

Grace wasn't expecting the woman to produce any cheery recounts, but it was worth a stab.

"I went to the movies with Misty."

"Who's Misty?"

"My neighbor."

"Great! How was the movie?"

"Lousy."

"That's too bad." Grace glanced at the clock, the minute hand tormenting her. "Tell me about your neighbor."

"She chews too loud, and she smells like old meat."

"There must be something you like about her."

"I like her car."

"What else?"

"She brings me cupcakes. She has lots of money."

"Do you see her often?"

"Every day."

"It sounds like you've made a friend."

"She's not my friend. She smacks her lips. It pisses me off. I wanna kill 'er."

"What are your plans for the week?"

"I'm not coming here. I hate this place." Her pout became a glare. "I only like your red chair."

Grace understood Arlene's illness. It was her job to do so, but today, the woman's behavior made her skin crawl. She was ready to go home.

# CHAPTER 12

# The Button

When Grace arrived home, the first thing she did before closing the garage's overhead door was to check the area for potential places a person could hide. Once satisfied with her safety, she entered the house and took off her shoes. She walked through the kitchen to the front door and bent down to picked up her mail. A chill ran through her while sorting through the envelopes. *Anticipating another threatening message?* She forced herself to remain calm. *I will not succumb to fear.* Yet…she went from room to room parting drapes and checking window locks, just to be sure.

Upstairs she found her opera glasses and surveyed the backyard from her bedroom window. The shrubbery, thinner in some spots than others, might not serve as the best hiding place during the day. *But after dark, the greenery would be a haven to anyone.* The very thought sent her heart racing.

Suddenly the phone rang and she jumped.

"Hello," she said, sucking in air.

"Ms. Simms? Sergeant Weston here. Are you all right?"

"I'm fine. The phone…it…I was just checking the window locks." She took a deep breath and exhaled, calming herself before she continued. "Any word yet from the lab on the envelope?"

"Sorry. Nothing conclusive." He paused, and she sensed his frustration. "It takes time. They checked for prints. There weren't any, so now they have to break things down. It's going to be a few days before we get results."

"Whoever left the note didn't intend to make it easy for us, did they?"

"No. The purpose, as you well know, is to terrify the person they've targeted."

Grace remained silent.

"Actually," he said, "I'm down the street, checking out the area where you said you saw the car parked this morning. Mind if I stop by?"

"No, not at all."

"Great. Be there in a couple of minutes."

Grace hung up and hurried to the bathroom to splash water on her face. She grabbed her jeans and T-shirt from the closet and started to change. An object fell out of her pocket. She barely noticed it until she reached for her shoes. She picked it up before her mind registered what it was.

Her stomach clenched. A sharp pain stabbed her temple. *This can't be happening.* Yet, she couldn't take her eyes away from the red, lambskin-leather button she held in her hand. The quarter-sized object seemed too surreal.

The doorbell rang, causing her to jump again. She dropped the button, ran downstairs, and flung open the door. She expected Garret, but no one was there.

A small squeaky sound escaped from her throat.

"Grace, I'm over here. Just a sec," Garret called from the corner of the house.

Relief washed over her. She took several deep breaths while Garret finished checking the perimeter of the house. He appeared from the other side and ran up the stairs. His smile disappeared when he saw her distress.

"What's wrong? What happened?"

"Someone's been in my pants."

"What?"

Grace pulled him into the house and locked the door.

"Up here," she said. "A button. It fell out of my jeans."

"Ohhhhh," Garret said, his cheeks flowering pink.

Garret followed Grace up the stairs, appreciating the way her jeans hugged every delicious curve. He followed her close, cursing their timing once again. He shouldn't be looking, and he definitely couldn't touch. But the message his heart proclaimed outweighed his better sense. *I want her.*

He wanted to scoop her up in his arms and ravish her on the stairway. Everything about her seemed right: *Right size, right weight, the color of her hair, the sound of her voice.* He smiled. *She's elegant even when she's upset.* He watched her arms swing gracefully. Her hips sway from side to side. They reached the top of the stairs too soon.

Her sweet scent lingered in the air as she led him through a maze of black-lacquer furniture to her master bath. He followed, absorbing every detail. Chagall prints brightened off-white walls. Black pillows accented a soft, cream comforter. Lacy green plants lined the ledge above the window seat. A sloped ceiling separated by a wide beam added to the charming ambience. The Casablanca fan pushed her scent in his direction.

He wondered if she shared her bed with anyone. He had no right thinking such thoughts, yet he pictured her stretched out on the bed, the cool air causing tiny bumps to rise on her velvety skin. He wanted to warm her with kisses, massage her tense muscles, and drown in her eyes. He imagined listening to her ramble on about her day, her dreams. He'd turn her over, his lips tasting the back of her knees. *Maybe someday, when the time is right.*

He followed through the dove-white, tiled bath to a large walk-in closet where Grace pointed to a small, red object, as if it were something distasteful.

"There!" she said. Her eyes couldn't conceal her emotion.

What Garret knew about loving a woman would fit into a gum wrapper, but his expertise for reading fear could fill a book. "It looks like a button from a chair. Do you recognize it?"

"Yes, it's exactly like the buttons on the chair in my office."

"Did you notice one missing?"

"No, that's what's unnerving, I was just there! I was sitting in my chair not thirty, forty minutes ago. I would've noticed if there was a button missing, for Christ's sake!" Suddenly, her face puzzled, and it seemed as though she were not sure of anything.

"Show me where you found it." He pulled out his phone and punched in a number. "Hey, Jack? Garret here. Spider still around? Good, let me talk to him, would you? Thanks."

He extracted a pair of latex gloves out of his back pocket and pulled one on. His eyes never left Grace while he waited for Spider to pick up the phone. *She's unraveling, one thread at a time.*

She rubbed her furrowed brow. Her eyes were glassy, her lips pale.

"Spider, do me a favor. I need a crime kit." He gave Spider the address and wrapped up the call. "Thanks, buddy." Garret lifted Grace's chin with his ungloved hand. "Hang in there, kiddo. We'll get this freak."

He squatted down to get a better look at the closet floor while Grace sat on the edge of the bathtub rubbing her temples.

"Were all the doors and windows locked when you came home?"

"Yes. I double-checked them right before you came over."

"Do you remember the last time you wore those jeans?"

"I'm not sure. Last week maybe?"

"Is there a possibility that the button was in the pocket before today?"

"I don't think so; I would've felt it." He watched as she patted the denim stretched across her hips. "And anyways, I would've noticed a button missing from my chair." She rubbed her brow. "At least I think I would have."

The nagging self-doubt returned. When *did* she wear the jeans last? She closed her eyes. "It was last Saturday." The memory returned in a flash. "I wore them to the market. I came home and put groceries away. I didn't change my clothes. I went to the bank, then Nordstrom— I grabbed a sandwich at Togos and came home. I wore them again on Sunday. My friend Eli came over in the morning. We hung out most of the day…at hardware stores, Home Depot—that sort of thing. We were searching for curtain rods for my kitchen."

"Is he a close friend?"

"He lives close by. We've known each other many years. He does work for me on occasion."

"Don't mean to pry, Grace, but I need to ask."

"No problem." Grace felt his twinge of curiosity from across the room. She was trained to pick up on voice inflection and body language. When he asked about Eli, his voice rose with more inflection in his tone? *Interest?* She examined her own defensive answer. That little push, that invisible shield she tended to put up when she felt someone getting too close. She liked him, but this was not the time to be thinking about romance. She had her plate full figuring out who wanted to scare her. *Who wants to see you harmed?*

Her thoughts were interrupted by the doorbell. When she

rose to answer the door, Garret took charge.

"Sit. I'll get it. Probably Spider." He stopped mid-stride. "You weren't expecting anyone, were you?"

"No," she said. Her smile more than confirmed her answer.

"Be right back," he said. His smile confirmed his relief.

Spider and Garret talked for a short while outside before they came back into the house. They lumbered up the stairs, talking shop while equipment clattered.

"Grace Simms, this is Spider. He's our crime lab guru. He's going to see if he can get some prints. He'll be dusting your windows, door jambs, your closet door, and whatever else he can find that needs dusting."

"I don't do dishes though," Spider joked, extending his hand to Grace.

"Good thing my cleaning lady came this week!"

Spider's ears perked. "Housekeeper?"

"Yes, she comes once a month to do the deep cleaning. She's in her late fifties. I've known her for years."

"Does she work alone?" Spider asked. The men exchanged a glance.

"Yes, I'm not a messy person."

"I was just thinking maybe—"

"Sergeant Weston, Tina is as honest as the day is long. As I said, I've employed her for years. I trust her implicitly."

"Of course," Garret replied. "How many rooms do you have in this house, Ms. Simms? It'll help determine how many sound devices to install."

"Two bedrooms upstairs, two baths—including this one— my office downstairs, another half-bath, living room, and kitchen. There's also a sub-level with a little laundry room. And a pantry off the kitchen, which, by the way, is available to you and Mr. Spider if you're hungry. I just realized it's past your dinner time. I have some deli meats and cheeses if you two would like me to make you a sandwich. There's juice and spring water in the fridge, if you'd like to help yourself."

"Thanks, we're fine for now. How about you? Are you hungry?"

She wanted to answer yes. *Hungry for a good kiss and whatever follows, but that thought will have to wait.* "I'm fine, thank you. I had a late lunch." She turned to go. "I'll be downstairs if you need me."

While the men went to work upstairs, Grace sat in her office, writing down activities she remembered doing while wearing the jeans. She listed places she had been, becoming unnerved at the prospect of someone getting close enough to slip the button into her pocket without her knowledge. Worse yet—*were they in my home?*

She closed her eyes, reliving the sequence of events. She saw herself at the market, the deli, and then home. She put away groceries and left for Nordstrom where she returned a blouse and tried on a couple dresses. The only time she was away from the dressing room, where her pants hung on a hook, was when she was critiquing the way the dresses fit in the tri-view mirror. The store was busy. Women had been bustling in and out with arms full of clothing the whole time she was there.

Her mind's eye surveyed the construction of the dressing room. The room was filled with partitioned stalls with curtain closures. Grace tried to conclude whether it would be possible to reach over the side of the partition. *Perhaps if one were tall enough.* And the curtain closures... could someone slip in and out without being noticed? Possibly, but that didn't explain why she didn't feel the button in her pocket. Surely she would've noticed the button missing from her chair! *Really? You have been rather distracted lately— with thoughts of Jess.*

Grace was running up the stairs to share the new information with Garret when they collided mid-way.

"Oh, sorry! Excuse me," he said, grabbing her arm to correct her balance. "I was on my way down to ask you something."

"I was on my way up to tell you something," she said, chuckling. When their eyes met, she caught another glimmer of interest in more than just her situation.

"Okay, up or down?" he asked.

"Down is fine. Would you like coffee?" She led him to the kitchen, motioning for him to sit on one of the bar stools while she made her way around the counter. She held up the pot and repeated her question. "Fresh brewed okay?"

"Yes, that would be great. Spider's a caffeine freak. He likes it a little too strong for my taste. Must be his European blood," he said a notch above a whisper. His smile was warm and engaging. "So, what did you want to tell me?"

"I remembered, last week I tried on dresses at Nordstrom. It's the only place I can think of where anyone would have had access to my jeans. I hung them on a hook in the dressing room. I went out to the full-length mirrors for, um, a minute, maybe two. I know there were others in the adjoining dressing rooms. The curtain was closed, but the sides of the cubicle only come up to here." She raised her hand above her shoulder. "If a person were tall enough, they could've slipped the button inside my pocket while I was out by the mirror."

"What a coincidence," Garret said. "Just so happens, Spider, being very good at what he does, concluded the carpet fibers he found on the button don't match the carpet in your bedroom. The fiber on the button is dark grey, commercial grade. Do you have cream?"

"Yes. Sugar?"

"Mmmm. Blonde *and* sweet."

"You *are* referring to your coffee?" she intimated, slipping out of one shoe.

"Yes! Of course. I like my coffee blonde and sweet." He dropped his gaze to the floor and shuffled his feet like a twelve-year-old who just had just been busted for staring at the neighbor's beautiful wife.

Grace noticed his composure slip when he was around her, and she wondered if he had this problem around all women—*or just me?*

He dumped a spoonful of sugar in his cup. "I'm sorry, what store did you say you were shopping at again?"

"Nordstrom. Second floor. I used the dressing room closest to the Jones of New York collection." She closed her eyes and turned, "East side of the store."

"You navigate with your eyes closed?" he laughed heartily. "I'm impressed!"

Grace didn't expect to see this side of Sergeant Weston. *Garret.* He was serious about his work. She had witnessed that first hand, but they seemed to share conviviality between them. The laughter helped dispel her fear.

When she reached for two more mugs in one of the top cabinets, her T-shirt crept up, exposing her mid-section. She hurried to pull it down.

"Need some help?" Grace felt his eyes follow her movement. She heard his sigh.

"I think I'm good now, but thank you for asking," she said, throwing him a playful jab.

She poured coffee in the remaining cups and pulled another spoon from the drawer. When she turned, she caught him staring. She leaned across the counter, and he shied away.

"About Spider, is that his real name?" she whispered.

"No, it's…uh…Frank Spiderelli," he sputtered. "Everyone calls him Spider for short. I forget it's not his real name when I introduce him. Sorry."

"How does he take his coffee?"

"Black."

"Shall I?" she raised the cup in a question. "Or would you like to bring it to him?"

She held out the mug waiting for him to decide, keeping her eye contact firm. His green eyes grew large, and he swallowed. He squirmed in his seat.

"Do you mind?" he asked, his voice weak.

"Not at all," she smiled, releasing him from her spell.

Garret followed Grace up the stairs, keeping his distance to enjoy the view, catching a whiff of her sweetness and watching the way her hair swished across her shoulders as she walked. He knew he would have to let go of this infatuation and focus on business at hand: find the moron and stop him. Maybe he'd ask her to dinner or something once the creep was apprehended.

Spider and Garret finished their coffee, packed up the equipment, and headed for Nordstrom.

"I'll be back if that's okay, Grace. We shouldn't be long. I'll let you know what we find. And, I plan to get over to your office to see if the button matches your chair. Do you have a key?"

"Yes, I do." Checking her watch, she added, "The cleaning crew is usually there at this time. I'm sure they'll let you in."

"Great. I'll stop on my way back from Nordstrom. I'll call you when I finish."

Grace no sooner closed the door and turned the lock when she heard a knock. It was Garret.

"I'll call Pam Stublonski," Garret said. "We'll see about getting you a dog. Any requests?"

"Please don't get one that's taller than me, okay?"

"Deal." He gave her a reassuring wink and waved goodbye.

Once the door was relocked, Grace headed upstairs for two aspirin. Her head ached and stomach acid churned—all signs of stress. She swallowed the tablets and headed back downstairs. *Turn on the radio.* Music relaxed her. She waltzed over to the refrigerator and pulled out the makings for a salad. She diced up a piece of French bread she had saved from a previous meal and tossed the pieces into a frying pan with a blend of oil and butter. She hummed along to a Dave Matthews tune while she stirred. Once the croutons were browned, she scooped them on top of crumbled bacon bits and chopped romaine lettuce. After drizzling balsamic vinegar over the ingredients, she heaped a large portion of salad onto a plate, turned off the radio, and went into her office. She turned on the small portable TV. She munched on her dinner watching an old rerun of *I Love Lucy.* Lucy and Ethel were working in a candy factory. Grace giggled as Lucy stuffed chocolates into her pockets and her mouth while attempting to keep up with the speed of the assembly line.

*People's expressions say so much,* she thought, reviewing the encounter she had with Garret on the stairway. *He's so attractive.* He liked her too. His body language said it all. What to do? Their public service vocations had brought them together originally, but this time *you're the "victim,"* she thought. She detested that term. She had a *situation*—one that would be rectified shortly. Once her *situation* was over, *we'll be on the same playing field.*

She finished her salad, cleaned up the dishes, and returned to work. She pored over James's file. His appointment drew near. It was time to review her notes as well as to interpret her illegible writing for Sal. While she read, she thought of their last session and how he had indicated that he felt unworthy of finding someone with any intelligence or class. He would've had to have something on the ball to become a triage nurse. Education took perseverance, especially while supporting a household and raising two kids.

"Okay, buddy boy. Who stole your power? You have smarts, looks. Who made you feel worthless: a) ex-wife Sheryl, b) daddy ,or c) mom?" Grace had originally evaluated him as suffering from stress and anxiety with underlying anger issues. James took a four-week, anger-management course during the time Sheryl had custody of their children. Grace remembered a time when he was out for blood, but he knew if he lost control, he would lose the kids. His medication hadn't changed since their first session. He was still on thirty milligrams of Zoloft, plus over-the-counter meds for the arthritis he developed from an old football injury to his knee. Grace thought about Candy. *It will be a quite a blow when he tells her he doesn't want her coming around anymore.*

Grace frequently treated females suffering from low self-esteem. They gave their bodies to anyone who paid the least bit of attention to them. Many girls stripped for the power they felt having men as captive audiences. Drugs were a motivator for that line of work, and young women lacking skills to get a decent paying job stripped as a way to support their children. Some even stripped to finance their college education. Grace wasn't sure where Candy fit into the mix, but she was sure of one thing: James wasn't finished with her.

When Grace heard the phone, she grabbed it on the second ring.

"Hello?"

>click<

The phone rang again. Her hand shook as she picked it up. She didn't speak; she listened. At first all she heard was a crackling sound, but then a voice broke through the static.

"Hello? Hello? Damn it!"

"Garret? Is that you?"

"Yeah, my phone keeps cutting out," he said. "I couldn't hear you. Can you hear me okay?"

"I can now." She closed her eyes and waited for her anxiety to pass. "I thought someone hung up on me."

"Oh? I didn't frighten you, did I?"

"No, I just thought— Never mind. Where are you?"

"I just left your office. The cleaning crew let us in. Spider had to scoot. I'm headed back to your house. Is that okay? If you're tired, we can talk tomorrow."

"No, it's fine. What about you? Would you rather we talk tomorrow?"

"I am beat. It's been a long day, but a sandwich sounds mighty good right now. Does the offer still stand?"

"Mustard? Mayo? Or both?"

"Both. Be there in ten minutes," he said.

"See you then." She was secretly relieved he was coming over. *You don't want to be alone.* Grace closed the folder. She didn't notice the wrapper that floated to the floor and slid under her desk.

She went to the kitchen to prepare Garret's sandwich and start a fresh pot of coffee. As promised, the bell rang in ten minutes.

"Hi, come on in," Grace said. "I'm almost finished with your sandwich. How about a salad to go with it? I make a pretty decent spinach salad."

"Aw, Grace, you don't have to go to all that trouble. A sandwich is fine."

"You don't know what you're missing," she teased.

"Yes I do: spinach caught in my teeth. It happens every time," he teased back.

"I'm sure it *is* delicious and it sounds so…so healthy, but no thanks."

She placed the plate before him at the breakfast bar and leaned nearby watching him eat. When the coffee finished brewing, she fixed him a cup with enough cream to make the color blonde, and one teaspoon of sugar, just as she had watched him do earlier.

"A quick study. Wow! Come and work for me!" He sounded more touched than impressed but tried to hide it with a bit of sarcasm.

"No," she said, arching a brow.

"I'm crushed." He stuck out his bottom lip and pretended to pout. When she wasn't moved by his performance or by his suggestion, he held up his hands to surrender. "You're the first person to fix my coffee the way I like it." A rosy glow colored his face.

"You're welcome."

Their fencing resulted in a long moment of silence. Garret retreated; Grace softened. Both learned something new about each other.

Grace put Garret's plate in the sink. He was fed. It was time to talk.

"What did you and Spider find out?" she asked.

"We stopped by Nordstrom. Spider took a sample of their carpet. *No bueno.* It wasn't a match. Then I went by your office."

Grace stiffened. "And?"

"The button *is* from your chair," he said, "and the grey fiber matches *your* carpet. This means someone either removed the button and dropped it or laid the tool on the floor before they removed the button. If it's any consolation, it's hard to tell a button is missing. It was removed near the lower back."

"Really? She sat down hard and felt her jaw tighten.

"We had to kneel on the floor to see it. Those buttons are set deep, with pre-tied nylon loops. It felt like the retaining clip was still inside the chair."

Their eyes met.

His voice softened like butter. "Talk to me," he said. "What are you thinking?"

"Someone removed a button from my chair…but when? I didn't notice it was missing. How long has it been gone?"

Garret didn't comment. He listened as she thought out loud.

"I wore those jeans last weekend." She paced the kitchen floor. "I didn't notice the button in my pocket then. I think I would be able to feel a button in my pocket," she surmised. "It's not a tiny object." She grabbed a hunk of her hair and twisted it into a lock while she paced. "This whole situation is unnerving."

"We'll figure it out, Grace. Spider took everything back to the lab. We'll see what he comes up with."

"I'm sure you've done all that you can." Grace rubbed her forehead.

"Don't get discouraged. We'll find out what's going on here and get it resolved." He reached over and took her hand.

For one fleeting moment, she imagined him bringing her fingers to his lips and kissing them one by one—kissing the little wrinkle that had formed between her brow…then maybe the tip of her nose, lingering long enough for her lips to part. Grace withdrew her hand. She noticed him staring at her mouth.

"What about the envelope?" she asked, sounding a little too throaty. "Was there anything inside of it?"

"Don't know yet. It's still being analyzed. Report should be back soon. Believe me, you'll know when I know."

"Thanks."

"*And*, I talked to Pam Stublonski about getting you a dog. She said there may be a German shepherd at the pound, a female. Still a youngster, but Pam says she's smart as a whip. She wasn't sure if the dog was still there or not. She said to call her in the morning.

She'll take a ride up there with you if you want.

"I'll call Sal tonight at home and have her rearrange my schedule. I've never owned a dog, Garret. They intimidate me. I'm not sure I'm going to be a good pet parent."

"Sure you will. And who knows? You may even fall in love."

"That's highly unlikely."

"You never know."

He gave her a wink and her arm a gentle squeeze. "It's late. I should be going. You have my number at the station, but I don't think I gave you my cell." He reached in his back pocket for a business card and took the pen from his shirt pocket. He scribbled his number on the backside of the card. "Call me anytime. Understand? I don't care if it's three in the morning. You call me!"

Grace nodded. She didn't like being vulnerable.

"Uh, huh, I can see *rebellion* in those beautiful eyes already," he teased. "Let me do my job, Grace, *please*. Let me protect you."

"You're so perceptive." She gave him a little nudge with her elbow and walked him to the front door. He stopped to examine her dead bolt.

"Guess this will have to do for now," he said, pulling on the locked door. "Bye, Grace. I'll call you if I get anything new, and you call me if you need me. I mean it!" His stern look melted into a warm smile as he unlocked the deadbolt. "Keep the door locked... and get some rest."

"I'll do that." She went to close the door, but he stopped it with his foot.

"Oh, and thanks for the sandwich," he said, taking a step backwards. "Best I ever had." His smile grew. The tips of his ears turned crimson. His eyes sparkled. "Okay, bye."

Grace closed the door, locked it, and went into the kitchen to check the lock on the back door. Then she did the same with the garage entry. She flipped off the lights on her way upstairs.

She twisted the tub faucets. A hot bath would relax her nerves. She went to her closet to get a robe, and her eyes were drawn to the spot where she'd found the button. A chill ran up her spine and gave her goose bumps. She caught her reflection in the mirror. *You're crumbling.* Dark circles were forming under her eyes, a red flag that all was not well in her world. *Why would someone want to hurt you? Why would someone want to scare you?* She helped people. She didn't have clients capable of such behavior, did she? *Resentment. Vengeance.* The stalker left her a note that said "Die Bitch."

Her body trembled. She slipped into the tub. The hot water didn't warm the chill in her soul. *Who?* Tim Ashton came to mind. She had ruled him out because of his height. *Maybe the person you saw fleeing by the Crab Shack was jogging. Maybe the person in the car was taller?* Tim had a temper, but was he the stalking type?

Tim was attracted to her at the restaurant. He flirted a little during their sessions, but he seemed to respect the boundary line drawn between them. *The note doesn't seem his style.* However, in retrospect, he *was* aware of how much she loved her chair. She remembered the brief conversation they'd had about it:

"Nice chair." He slid his hand across the leather to satisfy his curiosity, clearly enjoying its texture. "Looks expensive. Red. Nice color, too." Grace didn't take the gesture to be any more than an observation, although, in the beginning, he had made a comment about the exorbitant prices that therapists charged. He acquired a creepy look when he said, "It's a beauty. Must have cost a pretty penny."

She recalled defending herself, something she didn't normally do. "Yes, very pricey, but, I saved up for almost a year. I fell in love with it the first time I sat in it." He seemed satisfied with her answer. He even apologized for being presumptuous.

*No, this person has a gripe, not an attraction or status envy,* she thought. This stalker wanted to create fear by strategically making her doubt her sanity and by infiltrating her personal space. This person took risks.

The warm water began to work its magic. She leaned back, closed her eyes, and let the lavender-scented bath salts soothe her tension. Her brain switched gears, taking her back to when she was twelve years old:

Her father had volunteered her to do some yard work for the elderly lady next door. Grace was happy to help; she loved the way the old women smelled, sweet like honeysuckle and Camay soap. Her name was Leola White, but everyone called her Sugar.

One time, the woman promised Grace a homemade lemon bar when she finished the list of chores. Grace looked forward to the reward.

She was trimming bushes and cleaning up the flower bed that

overflowed onto the driveway when the sound of the electrical trimmer startled a hummingbird that was feeding nearby. The bird flew into the garage and tangled itself in one of the thick spider webs lining the rafters. Grace promptly fetched a ladder and climbed to the top to rescue the small creature. But before she was able to capture the bird, it had battered itself up against the window in the peak of the wooden structure and fell to one of the sills below. While she untangled the bird's feet, she could feel its heart beat in its tiny chest. Its eyes kept closing. Its wings fluttered weakly. Pretty soon, the bird was motionless. Grace opened her cupped hands revealing the limp body. She didn't panic. She closed her eyes and talked to God.

God answered with rushes of energy and a feeling she couldn't describe. When she opened her eyes, she was amazed to find the hummingbird's tiny eyes looked back. Life had miraculously returned in the tiny creature. Gently, she removed the rest of the webs restricting the bird's movement while she reassured the creature there was nothing to fear. The bird relaxed in her hands until she finished untangling the tiny feet and never broke eye contact.

The moment the bird flew from her open hands she realized her calling. *Help release those tangled up in fear and set them free.*

The change in the water temperature brought Grace back to her present surroundings. She turned on the tap, added hot water, and mixed it with her hands, letting droplets trickle over her raised knees. Satisfied, she turned off the water and leaned back, closing her eyes to continue reminiscing.

"You make the best lemon bars in the world, Sugar. Can I have another one?"

"Yes, but you take it home for later. I don't want to spoil your supper. Finish up now. I have one more thing I'd like you to do. Cut me some of those Birds of Paradise out front. They don't last long in the heat, and I'd like to enjoy them a bit longer."

"You grow the prettiest flowers, Sugar. Maybe someday I can help you plant some."

"One day you'll be planting seeds of your own. There's something special about you; you were born with a gift." She leaned her forehead on Grace's so they were eye to eye, "You use that gift to benefit others and leave the flowers to us old ladies." That was all she said. She mussed Grace's hair, pinched her nose affectionately, and left the room.

Grace finished her lemon bar and went back outside. She clipped the freshest flowers and set them down on the grass. When she stooped down to collect the bouquet, a hummingbird hovered inches from her face. She remembered asking, "Hello, is that you? Are you all better?" The bird landed on her hand momentarily as if to say thank you and zoomed off. Grace was elated for some time afterwards. It was one of the most rewarding and memorable experiences in her life.

The memory faded as Grace became aware of the chill in the bath water. The clock on her vanity read 11:02. She must have fallen asleep. When she rose out of the water, she got an eerie feeling. She dried herself quickly, donned the robe that hung from the same hook as her jeans. She tightened the sash. Feeling compelled, she checked the pockets to make sure nothing had been slipped into them without her knowledge.

*Empty.* Sweet relief.

Suddenly she realized Alpha, her fish, hadn't been fed, and she headed downstairs. When she flipped on the kitchen switch, the light didn't go on, so she repeated the motion. Nothing.

Adrenaline rushed through her veins. She reached for the switch on the opposite wall. She held her breath and flipped it up. When the hallway lit up, she exhaled. Her anxiety quickly alleviated once she was out of the darkness. She looked up to see the black edging on the bulb in the kitchen fixture.

"Geez, Grace! Don't give yourself a heart attack! You're only thirty-one!"

Her fear dispelled. She reached into the cabinet over the stove and pulled out a packet of light bulbs. She fetched the step stool from the laundry area and set about changing the light. When she finished, she flipped the switch, successfully lighting the room.

"Okay. Next time think first, panic later." She fed her fish and opened the refrigerator out of habit. Seeing nothing of interest, she closed the door, turned off the light, and went upstairs to bed. She was just about to fall asleep when the phone rang.

"Hello?"

No answer.

"Hello? Garret?"

She checked the clock on her nightstand, noting the time,

11:19. She repeated the greeting once more. Heavy silence hung on the other end of the line.

"Hello?"

>click<

# CHAPTER 13

# The Wrapper

Grace didn't change her routine the next morning except to call Pam Stublonski, the dog trainer Garret suggested. She couldn't believe she now considered becoming a pet owner. She loved animals–*from a distance*. She knew nothing about dogs.

"If you're nervous, a dog will sense that," Pam said.

"I don't know how to change that part of me," Grace admitted. "I've never owned anything bigger than a fish."

Pam's knowledge put Grace's fears to rest. The woman told her that dogs could detect emotions better than people, and if a person's intent were to do harm, a dog would pick up on their vibes immediately. They discussed different breeds, and Pam was kind enough to address Grace's questions and concerns. By the end of the conversation, Grace was more optimistic about getting a dog.

"You'll do fine. You just need to connect with the right one," Pam said.

"I feel better about it already."

Grace sat in her kitchen and imagined what it would be like to have the empty space filled with more than her own thoughts. She spied a small area near the laundry room. That would be an ideal spot for the dog's dishes. She pictured an animal snoozing on the rug in front of her kitchen sink and wondered if divine intervention had played a part in her new attitude. Pam turned out to be a godsend. So was Garret.

She locked her door, rechecked it, and left for work.

\* \* \*

Sal arrived in the office shortly after Grace. "Good morning, Sal," Grace said, "How are you?"

"I'm fine. John took the boys to school this morning, so I got a chance to sleep in. Sorry, I didn't get your call until a little while ago. What's going on?"

"When I finish with Marilyn and Bruce this morning, I'm going to meet a woman Garr— Sergeant Weston knows to go look at dogs."

"Garret, eh?"

"Don't start."

"Now there's a catch," Sal said, ignoring Grace's warning. "He reminds me of my John when he was that age."

"Really?"

"Big strappin' guy—"

Marilyn came through the door and interrupted their conversation.

"Hi Marilyn, come on back." Grace turned to Sal. "We'll talk more later."

Grace led Marilyn to her office, but before she closed the door behind her, Marilyn was seated at the edge of her chair bubbling with excitement.

"Guess what, Grace!"

"From the enthusiasm in your voice, it sounds like good news."

"I did it!"

"Did what?"

"I signed up for school."

Her client was beaming. After months of Grace's advocating, Marilyn had registered for dental hygienist school and was looking very proud of herself.

"That's great news!"

"Yeah, I thought you would be happy for me. No one at home is."

"No one? How do you feel about that?"

Marilyn thought for a moment.

"For the last twenty-five years I've been devoted to my family, putting my hopes and dreams on the back burner. I felt it was my duty…sacrificing my needs for everyone else's made me a better wife and mother. I never stopped to notice that while I held everyone up, there was no one there for me."

Grace observed the handful of shirt Marilyn had bunched in her hand. She twisted it as she talked.

"They think I'm crazy for trying to go back to school." She blinked back tears. "Nevada said I was too old."

At fifty-two, Marilyn felt she was no longer needed by her family, which was painful for her to digest. It was as though she were trying to scoop up her life with a slotted spoon. Grace handed Marilyn the box of tissues.

"Of course, they're not going to like it," Grace said. "They might have to take care of themselves."

Grace could see that her comment cut deep, so she explained. "Your family depends on you to do things for them that they are capable of doing for themselves. You've been *doing* for everyone for twenty-five years! And while you were cleaning up after everyone, making sure there was food in the fridge, the laundry was done, the johns were clean and stocked, they were out there living their lives. They're going to feel inconvenienced now, like they would if their favorite restaurant closed or the dry cleaners moved to another location. They'll get used to you being unavailable and begin to handle things for themselves. They'll survive…and who knows, this experience may empower them as well."

"You're right, Grace. I do need to do this for myself, and if they can't adjust, well, too bad! I'm done wipin' asses. Let them wipe their own! I want to get through school, get a job, and get the hell out!"

By the time their session was over, Marilyn had filled the room with boisterous laughter.

"I'll see you in a couple of weeks." Grace rose to open the door.

"No, Grace, I'll call you. I'm not sure what my schedule is going to be like. Once I get started in school, I'll let you know." Marilyn turned and gave Grace a bear hug that felt strong and self-assured.

"You go, girl." Without becoming overly emotional, Grace said, "I'm here if you need me. Good luck!" Grace meant every word. The woman had worked hard and deserved to be happy. And although Grace didn't expect it would be the last time she would see Marilyn, she wanted to make her feel that if it was the last time, it was okay.

Grace tidied her desk and jotted down bits of her session with Marilyn. She smiled to herself. Marilyn would make a wonderful hygienist. She pictured the woman in a colorful smock, hovering over a patient, a mask covering her face, leaving only her eyes exposed. Marilyn had a gleam in her eyes that would make people feel at ease. That thought prompted another.

She imagined Garret's eyes. They smiled before his mouth did. They expressed emotion, leaving little need for words—more so than Jess's. Jess had beautiful eyes; his lashes were thick and black. Dark flecks gave his hazel irises character, and their color changed hue depending on the color he wore. Garret's eyes were clear, defined by the dark ring that circled the green pools. He, too, had dark lashes that complimented his brown, sun-kissed hair and olive complexion. She thought about their encounter on her stairway the other night when their eyes briefly melted into one another's. Little shivers traveled up her spine. Unable to contain her smile once it started, she bit her lower lip.

The possibility of Garret being in tune with her thoughts didn't cross Grace's mind until Sal buzzed to let her know he was holding on line one. Grace fluffed her hair and cleared her throat.

"Hello, Grace Simms."

"Hi. Good morning. It's Garret. I wanted to check in with you. How did you sleep?"

"I'm a bit water logged this morning; I fell asleep in the bathtub."

"Oh? I *see...*"

She didn't intend for him to get a provocative image from what she said, so she quickly changed the subject.

"I got a hang-up. It was probably nothing, but I wrote down the time; it was 11:19 p.m."

His sigh was audible and his voice sharp. "Tell me about the hang-up."

"Like I said, the phone rang at 11:19. I answered it, said hello three times and then...click."

"Why didn't you call me?"

"I didn't think there was anything you could do about it. Besides, it may have been nothing. I was sleepy; I didn't want to dwell on it." She could feel his disapproval on the other end of the line. "That's what this person wants me to do, Garret! Be scared, lose sleep, look over my shoulder. I won't give in to that."

"That's great. I'm glad you feel in control, Grace, but I can't do my job unless I know what's going on."

"You sound upset."

"Frustrated." His tone changed. "Not to worry. We'll get this resolved. I'm glad you got a good night's sleep."

"How about you?"

"What about me?" he asked.

"Did you get a good night's sleep?" Secretly, she wanted him to confess he was up half the night thinking about her, to admit she had been on his mind since the day she called the station. Not only did he want to protect her, he had developed a crush on her. The switch on his emotions had short-circuited, and he was no longer in command of his heart.

"Grace, uh, Ms. Simms, I'm going to send one of my guys over to your house to put a tracer on your phone, if that's okay with you?"

She slipped her foot back into her shoe, feeling silly for her delusions of grandeur.

"What will that entail?" she asked.

"It's no big deal," he said. "We put a little device into the receiver, hook up a few gadgets."

"Okay, let's do it. Will four-thirty work for you?"

"Perfect." He was about to hang up. "Oh! Wait…I almost forgot to tell you. We got the envelope back from the lab."

"And?"

"The envelope contained a candy wrapper."

Silence.

"Grace?"

"I'm here."

"It's a yellow cellophane candy wrapper…from a butterscotch candy."

"Garret, that's the kind of candy we have here in the office… on the counter!"

"Well, good news, bad news: at least we know more than we did. What's your take on this, Grace? Do you think you have a loose cannon in your midst?"

"You know I can't divulge client information, Sergeant. Maybe it's just a coincidence."

"Denial? *Coming* from you, Ms. Simms? Tsk, tsk. I'll see you at four-thirty. Oh, and one more thing..." Her heart leapt, praying she wasn't wrong about him, that she wasn't misreading his signals, until he said, "I'm sending one of my men to pick up your red chair. We need it for evidence."

# CHAPTER 14

# The Red Chair

W hen Sal had taken the call from Sergeant Weston, she buzzed Grace's office immediately. "Hold one minute please while I transfer the call."

Once the call was put through, Sal chewed her bottom lip, a habit developed from sitting in emergency rooms, waiting for a doctor to appear with a diagnosis of the latest football injury. Sam, her oldest of five boys, was a senior in high school and worked towards earning a football scholarship to NYU. Oakland, her second son, a junior, expected the same honor if he continued to play as well as his older brother. Justice and Mack were identical twins. Neither of them had a desire to play football; their passion was swimming. Buns, her youngest, was her wild seed. He loved to dabble in everything that could be taken apart and put back together again. He was also the cutest. Twelve years old and already the girls were chasing him.

Grace was the daughter Sal never had. *Whatever happens to her affects me, too.* Sal ran her fingertip across her lower lip. Grace's situation brought her great concern. The lip biting confirmed it. She only drew blood when she was afraid for her children.

The red light on the phone blinked off, and Grace came out of her office in a huff.

"Can you believe they have to take my chair? Damn! Damn, damn, damn! They're going to ruin it, Sal. Damn!"

Her hissy fit was cut short by the burly officer who walked through the door pushing a hand-cart, his walkie-talkie busy with chatter.

"Ms. Simms?" the officer addressed both women.

"I'm Grace Simms," she offered, along with her hand.

"Detective Daniel McCarthy, Twenty-Second Precinct. I've been sent here to pick up a red leather chair."

"This way. Sergeant Weston just now informed me you were coming. I'm not happy."

"He gave me strict instructions to deliver your chair unharmed, or it will cost me my head!" He chuckled and then reassured Grace. "I promise I will treat it like I treat my baby girl, Melody, gently, but firm." His laugh came from his belly, melting Grace's ire.

"Wow! She's a beauty. Love the color. The wife bought me a La-Z-Boy last Christmas." With gloved hands, Officer McCarthy placed a plastic tarp over the chair before he pushed it on its hind legs and hoisted it onto a cart lined with moving blankets. "Yeah, she said she's sorry she settled for the brown one they had on display. She's a *red* kinda girl too." He wrapped the padded, quilted fabric around the chair and secured it with a bungee cord. "There we go. Cinchy."

Officer McCarthy patted Grace's arm. "Not to worry. She's in good hands."

"Thank you, Officer. And please thank Sergeant Weston for the special handling."

"Oh, he'd probably like his thanks coming directly from you." He winked. "The sarge is single, you know."

"I'm not sure that has anything to do with my chair, do you?"

"You're right, sorry. I'm a born matchmaker. He's a hell of a guy. I'd like to see him take more time out to live a little. Take a pretty woman, such as yourself, out to dinner…pardon my saying."

"Please thank him for me, Detective McCarthy." Grace slipped a wad of tissues underneath the bungee cord for extra cushioning. "Be careful, that's my ba— My favorite chair."

"Will do. Have a great day now, you hear?"

"Yes, you do the same." Grace winced as she watched the man maneuver the chair through the door. *You better be careful, mister!* A lump formed in her throat.

As soon as the door closed, Sal popped out of her seat and confronted Grace like the Spanish Inquisition. "Would you please tell me what the heck is going on here, Grace Simms?"

"Sal, you're my friend. I love you dearly, but I can't share the details of this investigation with anyone. Please don't be upset."

"Upset? I'm not upset. I'm scared!"

"C'mon, let's sit down," Grace said. They sat in the waiting area, both at the edge of their seats. "This little incident, the stalking, has developed a bit further. Someone is doing their damnedest to scare me. I'm sorry I didn't take into consideration how you may feel about this. I've been selfish. I apologize. What's happening does affect you, and I'm sorry you're scared. Would you like to take time off until we get the matter resolved?"

"No! Of course not! I just want to know what it is we're dealing with, that's all. Have there been threats?" Sal didn't wait for an answer. "There have been, haven't there?"

"Not exactly."

"What's that supposed to mean? *Not exactly*?"

"That means there haven't been any direct threats. This person leaves things for me to find, creating a fear factor. I'm unnerved, to say the least, but I refuse to give into this game. *And* I certainly don't want to jeopardize your safety if it gets any worse."

Sal responded with a hug. Grace welcomed the warmth of her friend and tightened the hold. Tears formed in her eyes. Her chin trembled, and suddenly she felt vulnerable. She lingered in her friend's embrace a moment longer and then wiped her tear-stained cheeks with the back of her hand and pulled away. She grasped Sal's forearms and spoke with confidence. "We are not going to let this person intimidate us. Garret Weston is the *best;* he will find out who is doing this. He'll lock the guy's sorry ass up, and we will remain unscathed. Do you understand me, Salome?"

"You call me that again and you'll see what real trouble is all about!" They hugged quickly; laughter relieved their pressure.

"Who's coming in next? What day is it? Have we eaten lunch yet?"

"Bruce at eleven and it's only ten forty-five. And to answer your last question, we don't eat lunch often enough to remember."

"Sal, did I ever tell you how fascinated I am with the way you are able to move your eyebrows?"

"Did I ever tell you what a smarty pants you are?"

"Yes, many times. Let's have a quick cup of your delicious coffee. Sound good?"

"You're on." Sal set to the task at once. She poured the coffee and placed the cups on a tray along with creamer, spoons, and sweetener. When she set the tray on the table, the cups clinked together, bringing Grace back from her reverie.

"What else is on your mind?" Sal leaned forward. "And don't tell me *nothin'*. You forget: you may be the expert, but I'm a mom. I'm clairvoyant."

"What would I do without you?" Grace asked.

"I don't know, but I'm not going to be much help if you don't give me the green light to stick my two cents in."

"You win. I've been thinking about how nice it would be to have a strong hand to hold right now. This sergeant, *Garret Weston,* is very attractive, personable, and warm. It would be nice to have a man like him in my life. When I go out with Jess, we have fun, but there's no 'afterwards,' there's no 'next morning', no 'breakfast in bed.' We see each other on *his* terms, which I have allowed to be my terms all these years because what we have *is* special. I guess what I'm hedging at is that I want more."

Sal applauded. "Honey, that's great! I am so happy to hear you finally admit it. Everyone needs their space, but they also need to love and be loved. I'm sure you have preached that sermon a hundred times. You're included in the word *everyone,* you know. It's not a term used to mean everybody *but* you."

"You're right, Sal." Grace clasped her hands behind her head. "I've been so busy being satisfied with my life, I forgot there was a piece missing. Jess was close enough to a relationship to make me think that was enough. I could have fun without all the strings."

"So this sergeant—this Garret Weston—changed your mind?"

Grace unclasped her hands and crossed them over her chest. "Actually, I've realized it for a while. When I made Garret a sandwich the other night, it hit me. I *enjoyed* doing that for him, taking care of that one small need. I cook for Eli on occasion and that keeps the domestic side of me fulfilled, but this was different. It was...*intimate.*"

"You're blushing, girlfriend."

Grace put her hands to her face to hide the glow. There was no way to stop the heat radiating from her cheeks.

When Bruce walked in for his appointment with her, she was tempted to tell him he was in the wrong offices so she could continue her 'girl' talk with Sal. Instead, she took her cup and client and went into her office. Closing the door behind her, she quickly rechecked the heat coming from her face. *Yes*, she thought, mentally hugging herself. *I want more.*

# CHAPTER 15

# Sneaky

So, Bruce, the last time we met, you planned to go to Placerville to see a neighbor's son's band perform. How did that go?"

"Never made it. My son stopped by to see me and have a man-to-man. I'm sure his mother put him up to it. It was rather amusing to see him talking in *his* voice with her words spewing from his mouth."

"What did he have to say?"

"Basically, that I'm a screw-up, an embarrassment, and if I don't change my behavior, I stand to lose everything."

"Yeah, that's a possibility, but not a sermon you want coming from your son. How did you handle yourself?"

"Huh! I told him I lost what was important to me a long time ago." Bruce pinched his upper lip between his thumb and forefinger to choke back tears. An emotional revelation surfaced. Grace took the opportunity to seize the moment.

"What did you lose, Bruce?"

"Shit, Grace, don't make me cry. I'm humiliated enough as it is."

"It is not my intention to humiliate you, Bruce. I would like to know your thoughts, so we can work on what's bothering you. And for what it's worth, tears are very healthy, so we're off to a great start. Can you tell me what you lost?"

"My dignity!" He spat the word like it tasted rotten, and then he put his face in his hands, sobbing.

Grace let him be. She would pursue the matter when he finished releasing his pent-up emotions.

After a few minutes had passed, Bruce collected himself and grabbed a tissue. He blew his nose and began to laugh. "Shit, I can't remember the last time I cried. I think it was when Carrie Mitchell broke up with me senior year in high school. Yeah, right before the prom. I was devastated. Not just because she broke up with me, but because my ol' man said she would."

Grace listened patiently as she wrote on Bruce's chart. When he stopped talking, she stopped writing. "Why did he think that would happen?"

"My dad knew her dad. I guess her dad didn't like my dad and told my dad he didn't think I was good enough to take Carrie to the prom. Hell, we had been dating for about four months already. Anyways, they had money, and Carrie's dad thought she should go in style, you know, the limo—the works. I thought it would be neat, but my dad was resistant to the idea. He said it was frivolous, but looking back, I think he didn't want us going in a limo because he didn't want Carrie's dad to get his way. He finally caved, but shit, he made me clean my grandma's house from top to bottom before he would make a reservation. It took me two weeks. I worked every day after school, even weekends. That's how bad it was, and when it came time to make the reservation, the local limo company was booked. So was every other limo company in Sacramento County! I couldn't imagine how every single limo could be reserved, but my dad said they were, and I believed him."

Bruce wiped his face with his hand.

"What did you end up doing?"

"Well, I told Carrie that I couldn't get a limo. At first she was cool with it. We asked some of the other kids we knew if they had room in theirs, but no one did. Then Carrie changed her tune." Bruce stopped to piece together the breakup in his mind before he was able to relay it to Grace. "Everyone told Carrie she should go with this guy, Kelly Farnsworth. He was a jock; his family was loaded. The guy had a reputation of being a lover boy, and for some reason, his date backed out at the last minute."

Bruce chuckled sardonically and continued, "Funny, how our better judgment goes out the window when we become shallow. Carrie told me this incident proved to her I wasn't a take-charge kind of guy and that she needed someone she could rely on. Can you believe that shit? Anyways, she broke it off, went to the prom with Kelly. When I saw her later that summer, her belly stuck out like a watermelon. I guess it was some limo ride."

Grace shifted in her seat. *That explains his animosity toward women.* "So what happened with your dad?"

"I found a business card on the counter for one of the local limo companies. I don't why, but I had to hear it first-hand that I screwed up and missed out, so I called them. Come to find out, they had three limos that weren't booked that night. The guy on the phone told me they plan on kids procrastinating and always have a few extras available just in case."

"Did you talk to your dad about it?"

"No. I turned off all the lights in the living room and sat there. I wanted to kill myself. I wanted to kill him," Bruce sneered.

Grace felt a tingle in her spine. "It's easy to see why you're angry. What would you have said to your dad?"

"What do you mean?"

"If you could tell your dad how he made you feel, what would you say?"

"Thanks for fucking up my life!"

"Your whole life? Or was it that particular time in your life? Was he a bad father?"

"Not really. I mean, he did stupid stuff. He cheated on my mom once. He'd come home drunk every now, and then. Hell, it was the seventies. Everyone smoked, drank, and cheated, but on the whole he was decent."

"Did he allow you to make your own decisions?"

"As soon as I graduated, I moved out. Before then? His house, his rules."

Grace began to see another side to Bruce.

"Okay. Let's stop for today and pick it up here next time. This is a pivotal point we can discuss further, but I want to leave you with this thought. When our parents control our decision-making process, they stunt our growth. You had no control over getting the limousine for the prom. As a result, you paid dearly. You lost your date, and you found out that you had been deceived. From what you said, the reason was selfish. Your dad's ego was at stake."

"Yeah," Bruce sighed.

"He didn't want Carrie's dad to have a say in the matter, which sounds to me like he had his own control issues," Grace said. "When this happens—when kids or young adults, model their behavior after their parents and the parents' behavior is inappropriate or unhealthy—what do you think happens?"

"That's the way he was, Grace."

"No, that's the way he was taught to be, like you were taught that you had no control over your life. Do you understand what I'm saying?" Grace gave him a smile, hoping the realization hit home.

A light went on in his face. "Yes, I understand *exactly* what you mean. Wow, I never would have thought about it that way."

"Well, give it some more thought, and as I said, we'll talk more about it next time, okay?"

"You always give me something to ponder, that's for sure," said Bruce.

"You're doing the work. The changes have to come from you."

Bruce was in no hurry to leave. Normally, Grace would've stuck it out for a few more minutes, but she had an appointment to meet Pam to go dog shopping. She picked up his file and waited by the open door for him to leave.

Once Grace finished her notations in Bruce's file, she dialed Pam, who suggested they ride together to the animal shelter. Unfamiliar with the Placerville area, Grace was happy to oblige. "So when I get off Fifty at Missouri Flat Road, which way do I turn?"

Pam's voice sounded sweet, and crisp. "Turn right, go to the first light. There's a Wal-Mart on that corner. Go through the light and turn in. I'll be parked by the garden section. You have my cell; call me."

Grace couldn't believe she looked forward to getting a dog. Why hadn't she thought of getting one before? She liked dogs—some dogs, that is, dogs that didn't jump and sniff. She would have to remember to tell Pam: no jumpers or sniffers.

"I'll be back by two o'clock, Sal. You can page me if you need to. Wish me luck."

"Of course I wish you luck. You're gonna connect with a good dog, I just know it. I feel it in my bones. Be sure to look in their eyes," she said pointing to her own. "They'll tell ya if they're the one."

"Thanks, I'll do that. And speaking of bones, I'm bringing

back lunch. What do you want?"

"Aw Grace, I don't know. My appetite has been pretty lousy lately. Must be the *change*."

"You've lost a lot of weight, Sal. You can't afford to lose any more," Grace said, patting her hip, "so don't give me a bad time, okay?

"You win. I want a burger, a single with everything…and fries."

"You got it. How about a shake?"

Sal didn't reply. Instead, she shot a rubber band at her boss. Grace got the message and left before Sal picked up the stapler.

On the way to the elevator, Grace stopped short. *Are those footsteps behind me?* She turned around. *No one is there.* She dug in her purse as an excuse to kill time, trying to listen more intently. She heard a faint noise in the distance, but after a minute or two, she heard silence. *You're being paranoid,* she told herself.

She decided the open stairway was a better option, but when she passed the elevator, the doors opened. A stunning redhead emerged, looking in both directions as if she were indecisive about which way to go.

"Are you lost?" Grace asked her.

"I'm not sure. Do the numbers run up this way," she pointed, "or that way?" Her voice was sultry.

Grace detected a bit of a southern accent. *Virginia perhaps?*

"What number are you looking for?" Grace was curious. She wanted the woman to speak again so she could determine her origin.

"Oh, never mind," the woman mumbled. She seemed to have figured it out for herself.

Grace changed her mind about using the elevator since it was empty, but pushed the "Door Close" button more times than necessary. "I am not going to be paranoid," she said aloud inside the small enclosure. "I am going to stop you, whoever you are!"

She felt better once the door opened and she exited, finally able to breathe. She hurried to her car, the unlock button ready to be triggered within ten feet of her door. Once she was in her car, she relocked immediately and checked her surroundings. "No, you're not getting paranoid; you're already there!"

Maneuvering through traffic onto the freeway ramp distracted her. She merged into traffic before turning on the radio. Music helped her focus. She sang all the way to Placerville.

When Grace arrived at her destination, she gave Pam a call. "I'm pulling into the lot as we speak. How will I recognize you?"

"Don't worry, I see you. Garret told me to look for a blonde driving a black Acura."

Grace pulled into a space and turned off the ignition. Before Grace opened her door, a short, freckled-faced woman with squinty eyes and blonde hair tucked behind her ears peered through the window.

Grace jumped.

"Wanna take my truck?" the woman asked.

"Sure," Grace replied, and once her heart was no longer in her throat, she thrust out her hand. "I'm Grace by the way, which is redundant, I know, but under the circumstances, a formal introduction is imperative, don't you think?"

"What circumstance is that?"

"Well, if I happen to adopt today, it will be my very first time. I wouldn't want to share the experience with someone I hadn't introduced myself to."

"Wow, first-timer. *Poor dog*," the woman grinned.

"Excuse me?"

"You're not going to talk *baby talk* to it are you?" she teased. "Dogs don't like that."

"And you know that how?"

Pam leaned toward Grace as if to share a secret.

"They just don't, *okay*?" Pam rolled her eyes.

"I'll remember that."

When they arrived at the pound, Grace was saddened by how many animals had either been abandoned or had wandered away from home. She walked slowly, investigating each cage with her radar on for just the right animal. When she reached the end of the aisle, she turned and started over. It wasn't until she dropped down to get a better look at an Irish setter that she noticed another pair of sad brown eyes staring from the rear of the cage.

"Hey, what are you doing way back there?" Grace asked. "C'mere." Rising with a stretch, the dog came forward. Black with tan markings, the dog's brows danced around melancholy eyes. Pam came up alongside.

"That one's Sneaky. She makes you think she's submissive, but she's a pistol! She's a runt. Looks like someone tried to breed her with a Tervueren. Long-haired Shepherds aren't considered show material. Illegal breeders dump these beauties all the time…can't sell them for a premium. We usually get them when they're pups though. I'm not sure where this one came from, but long-haired sheps are supposed to be more affectionate." Pam unlatched the pen and grabbed hold of the dog's collar. She clipped a leash to the ring and gave a handful of dog biscuits to Grace. "Here, take these. Bribery works wonders," she said, popping a small, green speckled bone in the dog's mouth. She turned to Grace. "Take the leash; walk her around. Talk to her. I'll be inside." Pam turned to go, but then added, "I think she's the one, but remember: no baby talk!" Laughing, she jogged back to the office.

"Sneaky, I'm Grace, and I have a problem. Well, not a problem *per se*, it's more of a *situation*, and I need a furry friend to scare this creep. Are you up for the job? It doesn't pay much, but the accommodations are comfortable. Of course, there is *no way* you will ever be allowed on my bed. That's forbidden; are we clear?" Grace squatted, meeting eye to eye with the shepherd. "I like to get up early except for Sundays. On Sundays I sleep 'til I wake up, so you would have to be patient. No whining and whimpering, understand? I don't have male sleep-overs, so you won't have to worry about someone monopolizing your place on the sofa." Grace stopped talking and listened to her heartstrings. "That's not to say there won't *ever* be a man in my bed or next to me on the sofa–just not right now."

The dog gave a short bark and wagged her tail.

"Oh and one more thing: I don't like jumpers, lickers, or sniffers. Are we clear about that?"

When Sneaky grinned, her tongue hung from her stretched jaw. A small whimper preceded a loud bark. Her eyes pleaded with Grace.

As if having a sixth sense, Pam appeared with a clipboard and paperwork for Grace to sign.

"How did you know I wanted to adopt Sneaky?"

"She adopted you. Sneaky hasn't responded to anyone for the last three weeks. Garret has been paying her upkeep; she was scheduled to be put down if she wasn't adopted soon."

Sneaky responded with a low cry followed by a hardy bark. Grace patted her head, surprised at the bond that had developed in a few short minutes. *This is the one.*

Once they were finished with the amenities, Pam drove Grace back to her car. Heading back to Sacramento, Grace kept glancing at Sneaky, who occupied the passenger's seat and seemed to be enjoying the scenery. "We live in a small house," Grace said. "I think you'll find it cozy. I hope you're not a shoe carnivore; I didn't think about *that*. We'll get you some toys later. First, I want to introduce you to Sal. You're going to love her."

When they pulled forward to the In 'n Out drive-through, Sneaky watched intently as the employees fried burgers and packed them in bags. Grace laughed while the dog sniffed the air with a dreamy look on her face.

"You and I will get along just fine," she said, stroking the dog's long fur. She didn't notice the car that pulled into the lot behind her. She wasn't aware of the person behind the wheel, watching her. *Seething.*

* * *

When Grace arrived back at the office, Sal was primed.

"Hey? Who do we have here?"

"Sal, I'd like you to meet Sneaky."

"You've got to be joking. *Sneaky?*"

"The name suits her, believe me."

"Hi, Sneaky. I'm Auntie Sal. I'm the one who will spoil you rotten and send you home to Mommy."

"You better not spoil my dog!"

"I've been waiting for this chance." Sal reached behind the counter and pulled out a gift bag covered in paw prints. "Here, this is for you both."

"Gosh, Sal, you didn't have to—" Once again, Grace's heart-strings felt a tug. *What if this is as close to having children as I get?* Her eyes misted over.

"Just say thank you, Grace. It's not a big deal."

"Thank you. Let's look, Sneaky. C'mere girl." She led the dog into the waiting area, where they all sat while Grace opened the bag.

"Wow, look at this, Sneaky–a leather bone."

"It's *rawhide*, Grace."

"And a squeaky toy!"

Sneaky's hefty bark made the women laugh.

"Go on; there's more."

Grace reached back in and pulled out a small, glass jar filled with doggy treats from the "Pooch Palace," a dog brush, and a pewter picture frame with "My Doggy and Me" spelled out in rhinestone studded letters. "How cute!"

"Dig deeper. There's one more thing in there."

Grace rustled through tissue and pulled out a disposable camera.

"Boy, Sal, I don't know what to say!"

"Good. Just be quiet and let me take a picture of you two before my burger gets cold."

Grace knelt down to pose with her dog. They both smiled.

\*\*\*

*>plink<*

*The loud sound broke the silence on the second floor of the parking garage when the surveillance camera lens shattered. The figure behind the dark-tinted windows unscrewed the silencer from the gun and laid it next to a six-inch blade.*

*"I wonder what your pretty face will look like slashed into small, pie-shaped pieces."*

# CHAPTER 16
# Carlos

Garret was parked in front of Grace's house waiting when she pulled up the drive. Another person sat in the car with him. By the time Grace got Sneaky back on her leash, Garret was already near the garage door with a short man carrying a toolbox.

"Hi, Miss Simms," Garret said. "Meet Carlos Munoz, listening-device expert extraordinaire."

"Nice to meet you, Miss Simms," Carlos said, extending his hand. "We should only be a minute or two. And who is this?" His hand reached out to the dog.

"Sneaky," Grace answered. "I adopted her today. We're still getting acquainted." As soon as Garret held out his hand, the dog was there to give it a lick. Grace intervened. "I'm sorry; remember what we talked about—no licking!"

"What?" asked Garret.

"I'm talking to Sneaky." Grace moved out of the way of the wagging tail. The dog was happy to see Garret and vice versa.

"You two are old friends, I see."

"Yeah, she's my buddy."

"It was nice of you to pay for her upkeep until she got adopted, said Grace. "Why didn't you take her yourself?"

"I can't have pets where I live." The dog responded with a bark.

Carlos reached out for his lick, too. "Looks like you got yourself a honey there, Miss Simms."

"Thanks, Mr. Munoz," she said. "I think we'll be *buddies* in no time." Grace turned to Garret. "So, was this a set-up? Pam said the dog didn't take to anyone."

"She did?" Garret looked surprised. "Huh, she took to me," he said. "Maybe that's why they called her *Sneaky*, right?" Garret smoothed the dog's silky coat. "You're one smart lady, aren't you?"

"Thank you, Sergeant."

"I was talking to—"

"Uh, huh."

Their brief flirtation ended at the front door. Garret insisted he enter the premises before Grace. He put his hand alongside his hip, ready to draw his gun. Carlos followed, also ready to draw. Sneaky stood perfectly still, ears perked, until she heard Garret's whistle. She darted through the door, ripping the leash out of Grace's hand. Once Garret established there were no intruders, he let Grace enter her domain.

Carlos went to work dismantling her phone in the kitchen. He inserted a tiny button-shaped device and reassembled the phone.

"One down. Next?"

"Upstairs," said Grace. "I'll show you."

Garret shortened the leash around his hand as Sneaky sniffed her way through the living room.

"You can take her leash off; it's okay," Grace said with authority.

"She's *working*." Garret placed his hand on the dog's backside; the dog sat.

"I'm not touching that one!" Carlos laughed.

"Good!" Grace and Garret answered simultaneously.

"Please explain how she *works*," Grace asked. "I've never owned a dog before."

"Well, we touch to familiarize ourselves with things; they smell."

"And then what?"

"This little girl here has her own tracking device built into her DNA. Whatever she smells here, she'll stick into her computer and compare it with the other data stored in her brain."

"And that's when I'll wish she could talk?"

"Oh, but she can," said Garret. "Ask her what she found, and she'll tell you. And being the perceptive person you are, in time you'll know what she's saying. It's in the eyes, the body language. You just have to pay attention. She'll tell you what you want to know."

"She's already scammed me once," Grace joked, "How can I trust her?"

Garret shook with laughter. "Aw, Grace, I'm sorry, but you do make me laugh."

Sneaky feigned innocence, dusting the hardwood floor with her tail.

"All done," Carlos announced. "We'll be able to track any phone numbers coming in. Unfortunately, things don't work like they do in the movies. We don't have the manpower to sit and watch for calls twenty-four-seven, so what *you* will do when a call comes in is check this little box. The phone number will be displayed, and next to it will be a description. Say, for instance, your girlfriend calls, it will display her name next to the number, like on a cell phone. If a number comes in from a telemarketer, it should come up with a company name. Now, if our buddy calls from a blocked phone number, here's what will happen. A signal goes to our dispatcher, kind of like a silent alarm. She'll call you on *this one here*," he said, handing her a cell phone. "She'll ask you if everything is okay. Say the number *one*, the call will then be traced, and we'll take care of it. If something is wrong, you're going to say the number *nine*. If by some chance you cannot *say* the number *nine*, you have another option; you can press a key, any key. That will then alert the dispatcher there's a problem, and we'll have a car here pronto. Any questions?"

"Wow."

"Yeah, blows your mind what techno geeks are coming up with, huh?"

"What if I press the wrong button by mistake?"

"This system is designed to be panic proof," said Carlos. "That's why for an 'all-clear' your only option is to speak. You don't have to remember which is which. And for help, you say 'nine.' It's easy to remember, like 911. If, for instance, someone has a gun to your head or you can't remember the number, press anything. To hang up the phone, you flip it closed, which will disconnect it. You don't ever have to press a key to turn it off. Cool, huh?"

"Very."

Garret had taken Sneaky back downstairs. Grace could tell how much he liked the dog and almost felt sorry that he wasn't able to keep Sneaky for himself.

"I need to get her some food, a dish. I have treats, thanks to *Auntie* Sal."

"Oh, one sec," said Garret. "I'll be right back."

When he returned, he produced every item a new pet parent needed to start out life with a dog, including a twenty-pound bag of kibble.

Together they set up an area near the laundry room for the dog to eat. Grace ran upstairs to get a blanket, but by the time she returned, Garret had retrieved a dog bed out of the trunk of his car.

"I'm not sure if she'll like this. Most dogs like to sleep on the floor…or on their owner's bed."

"We have a deal, right, Sneaky? My bed is off limits." Grace couldn't tell who was more wounded by her remark, the dog or Garret. "Will I hurt her feelings if I have you put her bed in the hallway upstairs?"

Garret shrugged his shoulders. "Ask her."

"As a trained professional, I can tell you right now, you're giving this animal way too much power." Grace wondered if he would spoil his children.

"I'm sure you're right; she's not even my dog!"

Grace caught the wink he gave Sneaky before he took the bed upstairs. *Probably spoil them rotten,* she thought, *but he'd be a good dad.*

"Well, our job is finished. I guess we should go. You may want to walk her. They do have their needs. I'm sure Pam told you that this sweetie is in tip-top condition." He pet the dog's head and further procrastinated by asking, "Do you plan to take her for a walk? I could go with you to make sure she behaves."

"Why wouldn't she behave?" Grace asked innocently.

"Just a suggestion." He felt the oaf inside him surface. Suddenly his shoes needed re-tying.

"I could use some tips, but I do need to change and make a few phone calls."

"Perfect. I'll take Carlos back to the station and come back."

"Fine. Where did he go anyway? I wanted to thank him."

"Ah, he went outside to smoke."

"Well, I will see you later then. Tell him thank you for me."

"You bet. I'll be sure to do that. Bye."

Garret tried to wipe the grin off his face. The dog was a great diversion; he took advantage. He gave her ears a scratch and headed for the backdoor.

"See ya later," Grace said.

"Bye," he called. She heard the back door slam.

* * *

"Carlos?"

When Carlos didn't answer after three shouts, Garret experienced a surge of energy in his step as he headed toward the street. Carlos had a nicotine call about every half-hour. Garret expected to find him leaning against the front of the squad car, one foot perched on the bumper, sucking on one of his poison sticks, as he called them, blowing perfect smoke rings. But Carlos wasn't there.

"Carlos?" Garret's voice raised a notch. "Hey man, where are you?" Garret stood on the street curb, scoping out each direction. No luck. His friend was nowhere in sight. *Odd*, he thought walking past the back door and toward the back yard. The sun had set long ago. Garret couldn't see a thing. *Carlos hates the dark.* It was not an area Carlos would choose for a smoke break. Garret was about to call Carlos on his cell phone when he stepped into the shadows and stopped. He spotted something a few feet in front of him that didn't make sense. A high-pitch sound rang in his ears. His heart skipped several beats. Adrenaline pumped into his nervous system as his brain interpreted what his eyes struggled to see. "Carlos?" He rushed towards the twisted feet sticking out from behind the trash can.

"Carlos!" he shouted. Carlos didn't move.

Garret threw the can aside to reveal the man's body. "Carlos, nooooo!" He cried in disbelief.

His heart sank when he saw the slash in Carlos's neck, pumping blood into the dark pool on the sidewalk. He feared he was too late, but he tried to stop the bleeding, nevertheless.

Grace was in the kitchen when she heard yelling outside, the tone in Garret's voice chilling. She flung open the door and saw Garret bent over Carlos. The sight confused her. *Was Garret choking him?* He held his neck so tight. *Was Carlos having a heart attack?* She saw Garret put his ear to the man's chest. *No*, she thought, there's too much…*blood*. Bile rose in her throat as she realized what had happened.

"I called 911," Garret said faintly. He leaned back on his heels, but he didn't remove his bloody hand from the gaping flesh, still trying unsuccessfully to save his friend's life.

Carlos died, holding an unlit cigarette between two fingers and clutching a lighter in his other hand.

# CHAPTER 17

# Jealousy

Grace's fear tasted like a tarnished silver spoon when she unlocked the door to her office. Surveillance cameras blinked in each corner of the room. Sal's desk was empty and would remain that way until the murderer was caught.

"I can take it from here, officer. Thank you," Grace said.

"I'm in no hurry. Take your time." The young officer seemed eager to chat. "I've only been on the job for eight months, but in that short time, I got to know Carlos Munoz quite well."

The officer blocked the doorway. He continued to talk. Grace continued to listen. According to the officer, Carlos had two beautiful daughters—Isabella, sixteen, and Janine, whose twenty-first birthday was coming up next week. "Carlos planned to take her to Las Vegas," he said. "Too bad he won't be around to see his baby turn twenty-one. He adored his girls. They were all he ever talked about."

"That's too bad." Grace lowered her gaze. "Could you please excuse me? I have some work to do." She pushed past the officer. She didn't want him to witness the tears welling in her eyes.

Grace didn't turn on any lights when she entered her office. What was the point? It was bright enough for her to see the red chair was gone, bright enough for her to pull the information she needed from her desk drawer, and bright enough to keep the bogeyman at bay. She sat back on the sofa and tried to imagine what her clients saw when they poured their hearts out or raged about the injustices in their world. *Why would anyone want to kill Carlos?*

*Why choose your house?* The question seemed irrelevant now. *You're one of them. Something terrible happened, and for the first time in your life, you can't cope.* She slipped off her shoes, curled up on the couch, and wept.

Her meltdown was cut short by the vibrating noise coming from her purse. She checked the number on her pager. It was Becky. The message was flagged urgent.

Grace immediately dialed the message center.

"Grace? *Please* call me," she cried. "I need to see you! P*leeeeez.*"

Grace hit replay and listened to the message one more time. The metallic taste in her mouth returned. She pressed the button to call the girl back and realized, she'd bitten her lip. *Again.* She blotted blood from her lip with a tissue and waited for Becky to pick up.

"Hello?"

"Becky, it's Grace Simms. I got your message."

"I saw him, Grace. I saw him again. He's real!"

"Calm down. You saw *him*, your angel?"

"I was on the light rail going to Folsom. My dentist is there. I saw him going into a Starbucks near 65th Street."

"Was the train moving when you saw him, Becky? It's possible—"

"I saw him. He's real! Dammit, why won't you believe me?"

"It's not that I don't believe you," said Grace. "I'm just trying to recreate the scenario in my mind so we're on the same page. That's all." Grace couldn't afford to slip up. She needed more information. "Okay, I'm waiting," she teased. "Tell me, was he the same as when you *last* saw him? Was his hair longer? Was he dressed nice? Details. I know this is *exciting* for you."

"I *knew* you'd understand," Becky said. "Yes, he looked the same. I couldn't believe it when I first saw him. I was just thinking about him, and there he was...walking into Starbucks!"

"Did he see you?"

"No, I was too far away."

"I'm really curious, Becky. What does he look like?"

"I've told you, Grace. He has dark curly hair, hazel eyes. He's lost weight, I think. I remember him being more...meaty, stocky."

"Has he aged any?"

"It wasn't that long ago. I know what you're doing! *He's real,*" she insisted.

>click<

Grace interpreted the hang up as Becky's way of saying that she wasn't ready to talk. "Damn!" She banged the phone on the hook, inhaled, and redialed. Becky's phone rang. When it stopped ringing, there was a heavy silence on the other end. "Becky, I know you're there. Let's talk. Can you come in right now? I'll wait."

"He's *real* Grace," the girl whispered.

"I'll be waiting. See you soon."

Grace didn't move off the couch while she waited for Becky. She stared at the empty space across from her, conjuring an image of her red chair with one button missing. Becky didn't tell her she had a brother. What else was she holding back? Who is this man? She needed to find out and solve the mystery. She wanted to make things right for her client.

Then her thoughts reversed. She reflected on the memorial service that morning: Carlos's daughters sitting in the front pew, beautiful shells with the life sucked out of them by the tragedy of their murdered father. They didn't cry. They didn't make eye contact. They merely floated through the crowd, nodding and hugging those paying their respects. Carlos came from a large family. The sound of their weeping carried by the morning breeze reminded Grace of a pod of whales she heard singing in Bodega Bay. It was heart wrenching.

"Miss Simms? There's a Becky Jensen here to see you."

"Thanks, officer."

"*What's going on, Grace?* Why did you call the police? I didn't do anything! What *is* this? Did you tell me to come here so you could arrest me?" Becky tried to push her way past the officer. The young man held his arm out to stop her.

The voice that came from Becky was not that of a twenty-three year old, but that of a defiant adolescent.

"The policeman's not here for you, Becky. Calm down. There's been an incident. He's here to watch over things."

"Why? What happened?"

"Nothing you need to be concerned with. We need to concentrate on *you* right now. Come and sit." Grace nodded to the officer and shut the door. She sat in the overstuffed chair, giving Becky room to stretch on the sofa. "Tell me again what you saw."

"Where's your chair?"

"Long story. What did you see?"

Becky's eyes swept the room. "I told you, I was on the train. We were passing a Starbucks. I saw him go in. Why is it so dark in here?"

"Becky, do you want to know who he is?"

"What kind of question is *that?*"

"You saw him. Describe him to me."

"I told you, he has dark curly hair, hazel eyes."

"How tall is he?"

"I don't know."

"Estimate. Five feet, ten inches? Six feet?"

"I don't know."

"How old does he look?"

"I told you, it doesn't matter!"

"It does matter. The officer that escorted you in is about twenty-five years old. Do you think the man you saw was older? Or younger?"

"I don't know."

"Becky, this is what makes it hard. You tell me you saw him, yet you can't describe the physical attributes that make him *real.* Age, height—these are details you should be able to recall. If someone were to ask you what your brother looks like, how would you describe him?"

"Georgie is short. He's got dirty blond hair."

"How old is he?"

"Eleven."

"This is exactly what I'm talking about. You can give me details about your brother, so why can't you give me details about this man?"

"I don't know, Grace!"

"Would you consider hypnosis? See what we can come up with?"

"No!"

"Okay."

"I know he's real. That's all that matters."

Quiet minutes ticked by while Grace figured out how to proceed. "What matters, Becky, is how this man, *real* or *not,* affects you emotionally. Let's go back, shall we?"

"Go back where?"

"To the beginning. Before you saw this man at the mall, what were you doing? You were working. You had occasional lunches with coworkers. You had a life. What are you doing now?"

"I have a life."

"Doing what? I'm painting this picture because I want you to see the emotional disruption this man has caused in your life."

"He's real."

"Working keeps us productive and self-fulfilled. Friends keep us fulfilled. Doing fun things keeps us fulfilled. Even if this man lived down the street, he wasn't interested in having a relationship with you. He walked away."

"He cares. I know he does," Becky whimpered.

"How so?"

"He said, '*It's okay; we can do this together*.'" Becky closed her eyes. Tears streamed down her cheeks.

"Becky, I'm trying to help you untangle these thoughts you're having. Can you tell me when he said that?" Grace felt impatient. She was weary, and it was affecting her work. She needed to take a deep breath.

"I can't remember. I just remember him holding me, smoothing my hair with his hand... whispering those words to me, "*It's okay; we'll get through this togeth–*" Her words dropped off. Tears landed on her small hands.

Grace put her hand over the girl's, patting reassurance. This was a mystery. Without putting the girl under hypnosis, there was little chance to find out who this man was.

"I'm curious," Grace said. "You seemed dead set against hypnotherapy. Have you ever been hypnotized before?"

Becky wiped her face clear of emotion and stared at her lap.

"Becky, it's okay. Tell me. Did someone hypnotize you? Was that an uncomfortable experience for you?"

"No. It's pretty funny actually." Her laugh was sardonic. "I used to try and hypnotize Georgie. We had a lot of time to kill in the basement. Me and Georgie were looking for dirty pictures that my stepdad hid inside the pages of some hardcover books he kept in a box. Anyways, we found this book on hypnotism. It was my mom's. Me and Georgie practiced hypnotizing each other. I tried to get him to cluck like a chicken, but that didn't work. Eventually, I got him to do things."

"Like what?" Grace kept her tone light.

"God, I think the worse thing I made him do was cut himself with a Swiss army knife." Becky's leg bounced nonchalantly over the other. Her face was void of remorse.

"How old were you?" Grace gave no indication that the girl had struck a nerve.

"I don't know. Twelve. Maybe thirteen."

"So was Georgie able to put you under as well?"

"Heck no." Her leg bounced harder.

"Let's get back to this man. You remember him holding you. You remember his voice, his eyes, hair—" Grace paused until Becky conjured the image. "You've described his body to me. Is that from memory? Or from when you saw him at the mall?"

"I'm not sure I know what you mean."

"You mentioned he looked like he'd lost weight since you last saw him."

"Yes, he did." A rose tint blossomed in her cheeks.

"Did he lose the weight since the time you remember him holding you? Or from the time you saw him at the mall?"

"From…from the time he held me," the girl said, looking puzzled by her own recollection.

"Good. That's good, Becky."

\* \* \*

The officer stood guard near the outer doorway to Grace's office, needing to relieve himself in the worst way. He contemplated poking his head in the door to see if the therapist was going to be much longer. If so, he would advise her to lock herself in until he returned, but when he got close to the door, he didn't hear anything and decided he'd better wait. He spotted the candy dish on the counter and decided to help himself to a piece, hoping it would take his mind off his full bladder. Once the butterscotch was unwrapped, he went around to the other side of the counter in search of a place to deposit the wrapper. He reached down to put the paper in the basket and noticed another wrapper on the floor. He muttered to himself as he picked it up and put it in the trash along with his.

\* \* \*

Garret filed through his day aimlessly. He was guilt ridden

about Carlos's death. He suppressed the pragmatic voice that emerged and told himself he wasn't to blame. He had witnessed many gruesome scenarios in his career, but none that hit as hard as seeing a fellow officer and friend lying in the dirt with his throat slit, flies gathering in a frenzy.

His determination to catch this killer surpassed his need to eat, sleep, or function as a human being. His demeanor changed with Grace. Gone was the buffoon, the oaf that dreamed of getting close enough to smell her hair without stepping on her foot. Gone were the butterflies that he felt in her presence. All he held on to was his need to protect her. He slammed the drawer with his foot and leaned as far back in his chair as the springs would allow.

Grace's red-leather chair occupied a corner in the evidence room. It looked lonely and out of place against the dirty, faux brick. His men found nothing conclusive to speed up the investigation. The button had been removed with a small instrument, possibly a suture remover or a seam ripper. He visualized Carlos, lying in blood, his throat slashed. "Or a switchblade?"

\* \* \*

Grace walked Becky to the desk out front and gave an excuse for Sal's absence. Once they agreed on a date and time for the next appointment, Becky was escorted out by the officer. Grace returned to her desk.

The officer's light knock startled her. "Excuse me, Miss Simms. I need to take a minute. Nature calls. Can you lock the door behind me?"

"No problem." Grace followed the man to the door and locked it. The phone at the front desk rang, startling her a second time. She answered it after checking the number on the caller ID. "Jess?"

"Grace, I've been worried sick about you. Are you okay?"

"I'm fine, Jess," she said sharply, falling silent.

"You're talking to *me*, Grace."

Silence held the moment.

"No, I'm not fine."

"Talk to me."

"I can't tell you much."

"I'm not looking for an inside scoop. I read the papers. I know that cop was murdered at your house. What happened was tragic," he sighed. "Grace, I know you well enough to know your heart is bleeding right now. What can I do to ease your suffering? That's all I want to know."

Grace's lip began to quiver. Jess always knew what to say to bust down her walls.

"Can you come and get me?" Grace sobbed into the phone.

"Yes, I can. We'll get through this Grace."

\* \* \*

The young officer picked up mail left outside the office door. He knocked to let Grace know that he had returned. "Miss Simms? It's Officer DeMarco."

She unlocked the door and made a mental note to have a chain lock installed. If she were to be there by herself, it would serve its purpose. She couldn't depend on a deputy watching over her every day. Her clients were important to her. She intended to keep her appointments.

"I'll be leaving, Grace said. "If you could walk me to my car, that would be great."

"No problem. Oh, here's your mail. It was left outside the door. Must've come while I was indisposed."

Grace sorted through the stack of mail, separated junk from bills, and set aside the envelope shaped like a greeting card until she finished with business. She missed Sal, her cheery disposition, and her office skills. Grace fumbled through the best she could, but she wanted the nightmare to end. She wanted her life back.

She looked for a return address on the card before she inserted the letter opener. There wasn't one on either the front or the back. Her spine tingled. Her nerve endings magnified her response.

"Officer DeMarco, I think you'd better take a look at this one. There isn't a return address. I don't want to open it."

"I'll see that Sergeant Weston receives it promptly. Are you all right, Miss? You look a little pale. Can I get you some water?"

"I'll be fine. I—"

"Grace?" Jess appeared in the doorway, startling them both.

"God, Jess! You scared the—"

"Sorry. What's wrong? You look pale."

"I just got something suspicious in the mail."

"Damn, Grace! This guy doesn't let up," he said.

"Miss Simms?" The young officer stepped closer, his hand positioned close to his revolver. "Everything all right here?"

"Officer, this is my friend, Jess Bartell. He's going to take me to— Where?"

Jess brushed a hair from Grace's cheek. "When's the last time you ate?"

"I don't remember, but I'm not hungry."

He tilted her chin and captured her attention with his stern look. "Greasy food always helps at a time like this."

"You've got to be kidding."

"No, I'm dead serious. It coats your stomach, so it takes longer for the alcohol to catch up with you."

"This is why I love you, Jess. You're a mind reader. A nice greasy plate of nachos and a pitcher of margaritas sound good to me."

"Knock, knock. Am I interrupting anything?" Garret stood in the doorway, still dressed in his sergeant's uniform, his face drawn, the sparkle missing from his sea-green eyes.

"No, we were about to leave," Grace said. She moved between the two men.

"Sergeant Garret Weston, Jess Bartell."

The men shook hands, sizing each other up.

Grace could tell that Garret felt awkward and something else that could be construed as *jealousy* if he were not so pragmatic.

"Excuse me, Sergeant," the young officer interrupted. "Miss Simms received this, a short time ago," he said, handing the envelope to his superior with a gloved hand.

Garret pulled a glove from his pocket and diverted his eyes from his polished adversary to examine the envelope. He took it from the officer and held it to the light. A slow whistle escaped his pursed lips. "Eventually, our boy will get sloppy. Let's hope today's the day."

Jess asked, "Sergeant, why do you assume it's a male?"

Grace sensed underlying hostility in Jess's question.

"Do you know something I don't, Mr. Bartell?" Garret moved into Jess's space. His voice cracked with emotion when he spoke. "If you do, please share. I buried a fellow officer this morning. He was also my friend." He took another step forward and said, "I'm listening."

"I'm sorry, Sergeant, truly I am," Jess said dryly, stepping closer to Grace. "I was just curious. I'm sure Grace mentioned the person she saw watching her at the Crab Shack?"

"Yes. Yes, she did. And?"

"To me, the person's sex was questionable."

"How so?"

"The person we saw was about five-foot-nine or ten. The clothes were baggy, unrevealing. It was about eighty-five degrees outside. My impression was that he or she was way overdressed for such a warm day, that's all."

"Did you make a statement yet, Mr. Bartell?"

"No, I haven't, but I would be happy to. Anything to help Grace, Sergeant," he said, wrapping his arm around Grace's shoulder.

Grace observed the interaction between the two men. Garret looked pointedly at Jess's wedding ring, his shoes, and his Brooks Brothers slacks. Jess was unaffected by the man's open hostility. He didn't back down.

"Yes, Sergeant, I'm a lawyer, and yes, I am married. Is there anything else you want to know?"

"Yes. Yes, I do. Perhaps you could come down to the station. We can get that report filled out."

"Can it wait? Grace and I were about to have lunch. She hasn't eaten since yesterday."

"Sure. No problem." Garret squared his shoulders and directed his question to Grace. "How's Sneaky?"

"Seems to be doing great. I'll be home soon to check on her. Thank you, Gar— I mean, Sergeant Weston." Grace ran her hand down his arm as she passed by.

He didn't respond. He looked through her.

# CHAPTER 18

# No Regrets

When they arrived at The Park Lounge, they chose a table for two near the window. The waitress brought them their drinks and menus. Grace pushed hers aside; Jess ordered food for them both. He couldn't remember her sitting this still. More than grief caused her moodiness. He was almost positive his presence in her office disturbed Sergeant Weston.

"Do you want to talk about it? You know you can tell me anything," he said, reaching for her hand, "You're my Grace."

She pulled her hand away. "Why did you marry her?"

"Jenna?" Jess stiffened. "Why are you asking me that now? We're talking about you?"

Grace took a quick swig from her glass. "The question *is* about me. Why did you marry Jenna?"

Jess held his glass with both hands, searching for his answer in the amber liquid. He sipped slowly as he tried to put together words in his head that would make sense once they came out of his mouth. His pained expression didn't soften the hard look in her eyes. When he didn't answer, she stared out the window. The day turned cloudy. She wandered away from the question, leaving him stuck in a void.

The afternoon crowd began filling tables around them, narrowing his window of opportunity by the second. He needed to tell her how he felt. She deserved to know. When he finally spoke, she looked him square in the eye.

"When I met Jenna, I had no direction. I knew what I wanted

to do. I wanted to go to college and become a lawyer. I lacked drive and ambition. I felt empty. Jenna gave me purpose. She wanted things. I thought being able to provide those things for her would make me happy. You know, live out the American dream. The wife, the house, kids…the whole enchilada." He paused to take a drink as if to choke down his admission with another sip of whiskey.

"When I met you, I wandered off course. I laughed for no reason. All of my senses were heightened to a level I never imagined possible. Food tasted better when I was with you. People were more interesting. The sky had more stars. I hugged my pillow at night, pretending it was you. Can you believe that?"

Tears rolled down Grace's face. "Why did you marry her then?"

"Because she needed me, Grace. She was making plans for *us*. You were making plans for *you*."

"You told me the day I met you that you planned to marry her, Jess. I never saw you waver once."

"That's not true. That night we got drunk at Uno's, remember? We went to the beach. You took off your clothes and jumped in the water. I followed you in not caring about anything except catching you, holding you…making love to you. Do you remember?" Jess paused. Before he could proceed convincingly, he needed her response. When a smile tugged at the corners of her mouth, he said, "Aha! You do remember, don't you? Don't try to hide it. I can see it on your face!"

"Yes, I remember," she chuckled softly, breaking some of the tension. The memory brought her back to a time when life was simple. "Not having to do laundry for two weeks was like winning the lottery to me back then." She did remember him holding her. Her heart trembled, reminding her of the pain those memories caused on lonely nights when she played the what-if game. "God we were drunk!"

"That's what I was afraid of, Grace. I was afraid you would feel that making love to me was a mistake—that it could only happen because we weren't in our right minds. And yet, I don't think I have ever felt another moment like that since. To me it was a moment that was right in my life, and I let it slip away."

"No regrets, please," said Grace. "We were just kids."

"And now?"

"I can't do this, Jess."

"He has a thing for you, Grace."

"Who?"

"The sergeant. I saw the way he looked at you. Tell me about him. We've always been honest with one another."

"Garret is very nice, Grace explained. "We worked together a while back–briefly. He's been a prince. What can I say? He's doing his job."

"It's more than that. You forget; I have feelings, too."

"What's that supposed to mean?"

"I can relate: wanting someone, not being able to do anything about it."

"I think I know that feeling too, Jess. You were getting married. You never divulged your feelings for me. You never proclaimed your love or even asked me how I felt about you."

"You were determined to remain unscathed," he protested. "Remember? No baggage. No drama. No need for someone to complete you! How the hell could I infiltrate your perfectly designed defense system?"

"You could have tried."

"I was afraid."

"*Afraid?*"

"Having you as my friend was better than not having you at all."

\* \* \*

*"Oh, Grace. So many men, but so little time," mumbled the figure. "You can't have them all." The puncture made a popping sound and continued to hiss until the tire went flat. A man passing by the bent figure didn't notice the glint off the sharp blade as the sun shone through a slit in the blackened sky. When the man turned around and came back to offer assistance, the figure slipped the knife into a leather bag.*

*"Need some help?" asked the man.*

*"No thanks. I called triple A."*

\* \* \*

Jess took his time changing the flat tire. At least his mind was off Grace. After he had placed the tire in his trunk for the dealer to fix the next morning, Jess drove Grace to her car in silence.

"I'll follow you home," he said, when they reached the parking lot. His voice, even toned, masked any emotion left over from their earlier conversation. She studied his eyes. Something's brewing, she thought.

"Would you like to come and meet my new roommate?" she asked.

"I suppose I can stop in for a few minutes."

Jess pulled into the driveway behind Grace. When he got out of the car, he checked for anything unusual. Everything appeared to be fine, except their arrival spurred a series of loud barks from inside the house.

"Sneaky," Grace commanded as she opened the door. "Enough."

"Hey girl," Jess reached to pet the dog but was discouraged by her snarl and low growl.

"Sneaky, that's rude. Jess is my friend."

"Don't worry," he said. "She's here to protect you, not to make friends."

"She shouldn't growl at someone who doesn't pose a threat."

"Maybe she sees me as a threat. I can be threatening you know." Jess grabbed Grace's arm, pretending to twist. His playful gesture received immediate disapproval from both females. Grace gave him a dirty look. Sneaky barked.

"Don't start!" She recalled how they used to rough house when they were in college.

"Ah, that's more like it," he teased. "Your spunk has returned."

Grace's cell phone interrupted Jess's attempt at being cute. After checking the number, she answered. "Hello?"

"Hi, it's Garret. Just wanted to make sure you got home all right."

"Thanks, Sergeant, I'm fine. Jess came home with me. We're going to hang out here for a while; maybe take Sneaky for a walk. She hasn't taken to him yet."

"Gee," he said, "that's too bad."

"I'm sure they'll become friends." *It's not like Garret to behave like sour grapes.* She didn't care for his sulky tone.

"Well, like I said, I called to see how you were."

He sounded distraught. She didn't want the conversation to end on a bitter note. "The funeral service for Carlos this morning was nice. He was well loved."

"Yeah, I hate going to those things." His voiced dropped off.

"Would you like to come by? I still have some spinach salad left."

"Pass!" The invitation barely earned a chuckle. "No, you guys have a good night. I'll give you a call as soon as we come up with news on the envelope."

"Has it been opened yet?"

"Yeah, it's been opened."

"And?"

"It's a card."

"What kind of card?" she wanted to know.

He hesitated before answering, "A condolence card."

Chemical changes in Grace's brain produced a sensation like too much sun. Her stomach pitched. Her bottom lip quivered. *Was she next?* "Why a card?" she asked, trying to control the tremor in her voice.

"Nothing was written inside," he said. "Could be ego. Could be a warning."

It was difficult for her to talk. Her throat tightened. "You buried Carlos this morning. This can't be easy for you."

"No, it's not pleasant, but it's what I do." Silence filled the next few moments. "I'll call you later. Go have a nice evening. You've had a bad day."

"And what about *you*?" she asked

"I'll be in touch. Bye."

The little lights in her peripheral vision turned to black as her body lost its rigidity. Jess rushed with open arms to catch her crumbling form, but he was too late. She landed hard on the kitchen floor. Sneaky whined and tried to lick her hand.

"Grace, you okay?" Jess lifted her up.

"I need to lie down." Her head was throbbing. The room began to swim. "Migraine." She felt as if she were floating.

* * *

When she awoke the next morning, Jess was at her side. "What happened?" she asked. "How did you get me up here?"

"I'm a lawyer, Grace, not a wimp."

"No comment." She fought down a smile.

"Well, you're better, I see!"

"What time is it?" Grace reached for the window shade.

"Nine thirty."

"What?" She lifted a corner of the shade in disbelief. "Why did you let me sleep like that?"

"You were exhausted. You just about fainted in the kitchen."

"God, this is awful, Jess." She began to free herself from layers of twisted bed linens. Have you been here all night?"

"Yes. Sergeant Weston is downstairs. He came over around eleven last night. Nice guy."

"I have to get up," Grace said.

Jess scooped her disheveled body into his lap and hugged her tightly. He kissed her forehead and let her drop back down on the pillow. "I'll go get Dick Tracy."

"Can I get up first?"

"Why? Don't want him to see the real you!" He mimicked her fluffing her hair.

She knew her breath was rank and her hair was smashed on one side.

"Get out of here! I'm too weak to throw something at you."

Half-way out of bed, she heard footsteps on the stairway and threw a pillow, but as Jess side-stepped the pillow, Garret moved right in. The pillow hit his head and ruffled his hair.

"Don't mess with her in the morning, Sergeant." He reached out a hand; they shook, and Jess departed.

"Good morning," he said tossing the pillow on the bed. "How did you sleep?"

"Great, Sergeant. Have you been up all night?"

"No, I caught a couple of winks in the chair here."

He sat down, leaning toward her with his hands positioned in prayer.

"I'm going to have to ask you some questions about your clients, Grace. I realize that you have your code of ethics, but I have a job to do."

"I can't tell—"

The sergeant cut short her objection.

"We need to catch the person who is stalking you and murdered Carlos," he said. "Whatever you tell me will be kept confidential. I'm not interested in Joe Blow who cheated on his wife.

I'm interested in the clients who have violent histories. I need to know who has anger issues, sociopathic behavior. I'll run these people through the system and see if I can come up with anything. If I don't–" Garret shrugged, then pleaded, "God, Grace! Help me catch this freak, please!"

Nobody wanted to end this nightmare more than she did. "Let me get up. I'll meet you downstairs," she said. "I need coffee."

"I'll fix you a cup," Garret said.

"How about if I fix *you* a cup?" she offered. "It's the least I can do."

"I'd like that," he smiled.

Grace shed the rumpled clothes she'd slept in and stepped into the shower. The steamy water felt soothing as she shampooed her hair, massaging her temples and scalp. Inhaling the scent of papaya and white tea blossoms, she pondered her situation.

For the most part she had always lived her life cautiously. *Really?* Images of derelicts shouting obscenities at her while she walked home late at night in Chicago. Loud sirens so frequent they became part of the audioscape. Tough guys in hot cars squealing through intersections, frightening old ladies. Fights breaking out on street corners. Drug dealers being slammed against black and white cars with flashing lights. It was the same when she lived in LA: Stench like rotted potatoes loaded on gurneys. Onlookers that wept as gurneys carried away the forgotten smell, guilt filling their eyes. Large men poking threatening fingers at young girls in doorways. She had witnessed horrific things, but she never felt the kind of fear she felt now, except... *That one time when you thought you were being followed.* Her body shuddered. *This is worse, much worse.*

Refreshed, she brushed her towel-dried hair and her teeth. She dressed in jogging pants and a T-shirt, her wardrobe choice for the time being. She didn't want to keep Garret waiting.

Sneaky wagged her tail and smiled, stealing Grace's heart. The dog waited until she was ready to go downstairs and then followed by her side. Garret was in the kitchen.

"I hope you don't mind me helping myself," Garret said, pouring two cups of coffee. He reached in the refrigerator for cream.

"No, I'm sorry to keep you waiting. I can't function in the morning without a shower and coffee."

"I'll keep that in mind." His eyes grabbed hers in a quick embrace. She hated to let go.

"I've been thinking about my clients," she said. You asked if any of them were capable of murder or carried a vendetta toward me. I have one client that's delusional. I don't think she poses a threat, but I am seeing some erratic behavior that makes me wonder."

Acid churned in Grace's chest, heat crawled up her neck and spread across her face. She hated this feeling of *betrayal*. She took an oath. Client privacy was protected by law. She didn't feel any of her clients posed a threat to themselves or threatened to harm another. Even if they did, any action taken would require protocol. Her voice of reason spoke up: *A man is dead. Someone wants to kill me.* "I have another client. She says she wants to kill everybody, but she's, well, she's disabled. She's been a client for years."

He casually poured cream in his cup. "Names?"

"You know I can't give you names. I'd lose my license."

Garret placed coffee in front of her and squeezed her hand. He understood. "How about the guys?" He sipped his coffee, hiding the fact he was way ahead of the game. Grace didn't know he had stopped by the office earlier. Sal was there picking up a pair of walking shoes she kept under her desk. When he told Sal about the card, she turned pale. Then she saw red. Garret had no idea the woman could swear in three different languages. When he asked her if she thought one of Grace's clients was capable of murder, she pleaded the fifth. And then she turned on her computer. She claimed she needed to check the end of month billing. Sal launched into a dissertation on kids and how they feel the need to whip out their cell phones and take pictures of *everything* they see. When she asked him to come around the desk and retrieve a cup from the top shelf in the cabinet, he knew what to do. All he needed now were a few clues and a way to legally obtain information, so it would be admissible in court.

Grace felt stuck between a rock and a hard place. Could it be one of her male clients? She worked so hard to help these men restore the power that had been taken from them at an early age. Why would they want to hurt her? *Someone wants me dead,* the voice inside her head piped in. She took a breath. "I have a male client who's been diagnosed with borderline personality disorder. He's displayed fits of anger during our sessions, but I feel his destruction is more internal than external." The pressure in her head increased. *This can't go on.* "What more do you need to know?"

"Do you know if he has any priors?" The edge in Garret's voice didn't match his expression. Grace knew he was only trying to do his job.

"When this all began," she said, "I wondered if it was he who was stalking me. He's taller than the person I saw at the restaurant, but then again, maybe that wasn't anything. Maybe the stalking started with the car in the garage. Maybe the person I saw fleeing was just out for a jog."

"Hard to say. Anyone else?"

Grace's mind flashed to Carlos's slit throat. *I could be next.* "One more. He's a triage nurse; he would have access to surgical knives."

"Humph," Garret said. "Spider and I discussed the way the button was removed from the chair." He stopped talking long enough to scribble some words on his pad. "I'd better get going." He put the pad back in his pocket and took another sip of coffee. "What's on your schedule today?" he asked.

"I need to go into the office later."

"Call the station. I'll have a car pick you up. Until then, Sneaky will take great care of you."

Her eyes met his and warmed. "I'll be fine."

Garret rushed forward to give Grace a hug. He intended to make it quick, but she held on to him tight. He caressed her back while he enjoyed the fresh scent of her damp hair.

"I'm sorry, Garret. I don't know what came over me," she said, stepping back. "And look, I've made a wet spot on your shirt."

"It'll dry," he said, wanting so bad to devour her lips. His shirt was the furthest thing from his mind. She stirred his senses and his testosterone. If he didn't leave immediately, his heart would overrule his head. "I've got to go."

"Yes, you do," she flushed. The color in her cheeks was a dead give-away. His mind committed her beautiful face to memory. *One day.* Luckily, the phone rang, dispelling the moment. "Lock the door," he commanded.

Grace saluted and followed his orders. When the tumblers fell into place, she rushed for the phone.

"Hello?"

It was Jess. *Perfect timing,* she thought. Ironically or not, she didn't want to analyze what just happened between her and Garret.

"Hi Grace. I'm at the tire dealer. The guy here told me my tire was slashed. Is Sergeant Weston still there?"

"No, he just left. You're kidding me. Slashed?"

"Yes. He said, gauging the size of the hole. "The puncture came from an object the size of a letter opener."

"Damn, Jess, this isn't good."

"No, it's not. Whoever did this was watching us at the restaurant yesterday." Silence fell on her end of the phone. After a moment, his concerned voice asked, "Hey? How are you feeling?"

"I'm fine," she said, massaging her temple.

"Good. I'll call Weston about the tire. Can I come by?"

"Sure."

"Breakfast?" he asked. His voice held a mischievousness she found hard to resist.

"You win. Bagel?"

"Extra cream cheese."

"You're spoiling me."

"You got it," he said and hung up.

# CHAPTER 19

# Twenty-Second Precinct

Garret called his crew into his office. Spider sat halfway on the desk chewing a toothpick, a nervous habit Garret had come to recognize. Jake Stramski, his best detective, leaned against the wall, his hands shoved deep in his pockets, jingling change. Dave Rabinowitz had been on the team since the get go and had a short report to share with the group.

Carlos had been replaced by Lavern Neilson, a twenty-eight-year beat cop who recently obtained her bachelor's degree in computer science and communications. Garret had faith that she was the right person for the job, and it seemed less painful to fill the position with someone completely different from Carlos. Despite her petite stature, she was a good cop: strong, intelligent, and personable enough to make the transition less painful for the department.

Garret leaned back in his chair, his hands steepled on his chest, "What do we have, Jake?"

"Excuse me, Sergeant," the dispatcher interrupted, poking her head in the door. "Jess Bartell is on line two. Says it's important."

Garret didn't hide the irritation in his voice. "Yeah, Jess, what's up?"

"When Grace and I left the restaurant yesterday, my tire was flat. I changed it. I didn't give it much thought, but I just came from the tire dealer. He said the tire had been slashed. I thought you would want to know."

Garret sat up. His body stiffened, "Is the tire still at the dealer?"

"No, I had them put it in my trunk; I'm on my way to Grace's. Would you like me to drop it off?"

"Yeah. Has it been handled a lot?"

"I'm not sure. I took it off to put the spare on."

"Thanks, Jess. I'll see you in a bit."

Garret shut the world out for a moment while he absorbed the information. He began to think Carlos may have been murdered because he caught the perp off guard. He was found lying by the garbage can next to the garage door. Maybe the perp intended to slash Grace's tires and ended up slashing Carlos' throat instead. *The creep has a screw loose.* His fingertips dug into his palms. *Mistake number one. No one kills a cop and gets away with it.* He inhaled slowly and exhaled his fury. He sat up straight, slapped his hands on his desk and said, "Let's get back to business. You're up, Jake."

Jake removed his hands from his pockets. "We found a broken security camera lens in the garage on Seventh, second floor where Miss Simms parks her car. It looks like it was shot out with a BB gun."

"We're running stats on the break," Spider interjected.

Jake resumed, "The condolence card was purchased from a dollar store in Folsom. The clerk didn't remember anyone unusual. Their security camera tape hasn't been changed since it ran out last month! Asshole kids who work there don't care." Jake shook his head in disbelief and continued. "There's no DNA on the envelope. The glue strip was wet with a sponge, not licked. The handwriting on the envelope is being analyzed. They don't expect to come up with too much. It doesn't match what we have in our database, and the writing on this one doesn't match the first note with *Die Bitch* written on it."

"Spider?" Garret turned to face the man beside him. "You're up next."

"We've dusted the house, office, and parking lot. Geez, this guy is slick." Spider was not easily impressed by most criminal activity. He was usually able to find *something.*

"Stay on it," Garret said, redirecting his attention, "Dave?"

"We've narrowed down the instrument used to cut the button off the chair to a suture remover. It looks like a seam ripper. Do any of you sew?" Dave asked, breaking the tension. They all laughed. "Boys, a seam ripper looks like a snake tongue, sharp of course. A suture remover can be forked or a single-sided blade. I checked with the upholstery shop here in town. The guy told me they don't use suture removers as a rule, but some of their upholsterers *do* have them. You can get one at an ER or at a doctor's office. It's one of those items the insurance companies are charged for, so if you want to take it home once they remove your stitches, they give it to you. Not many people know this. Shit, it's also an instrument used by *seamstresses*, which leaves the field wide open. I have my people checking with the alteration places listed around here. So far we have zip," he sighed. "That's all for me."

"All right, add this to your list," said Sergeant Weston, addressing his men. "Our perp may have slashed Jess Bartell's tire yesterday at the Park Ultra Lounge. He took Miss Simms there for lunch. He's bringing the tire here. We'll check the entry with the weapon used on Carlos and see if we come up with a match. I want surveillance on Miss Simms twenty-four-seven. O'Malley, you're on it. And Dave? I want this guy Jess Bartell checked out too."

"Jess Bartell, the lawyer?" Dave asked, sounding surprised.

"You know him?"

"Yeah, he was involved with a couple of my cases. One pretty recent. One a long time ago. Nice guy."

"Yeah, he seems so," Garret said. "He is also married and has a thing for Miss Simms. Check him out."

Sergeant Weston's crew didn't waste time. They filed out of his office quietly and went to work. Garret pulled a software packet out of his file drawer and downloaded it on his computer. The program was used to cut through security blocks put on private information. It was designed by a hacker they arrested last year and wasn't meant for departmental use. Right now, he needed a break. He'd pull out all the stops to catch the son-of-a-bitch who killed Carlos and was terrorizing Grace. The first name he typed in was Becky Jensen. The computer listed thirty-seven similar names in Sacramento. Garret narrowed the list down to those with Becky's age and address.

"Rebecca Lynn Jensen

"06-08-1991

"Female

"Caucasian"

He scrolled down to her California driver's license, her last known address, phone number, and her Social Security number. Next, her place of birth:

"Norridge, IL

"Born: Northwest Community Hospital, Arlington Heights, IL

"Birth mother: Carole Anne Metcalf

"Birth father: unknown"

Garret scrolled back up to her Social Security number and clicked. From there, he was able to access her bank records, outstanding loans, and educational status. Clicking on any one of the sub-areas would do a search on her credit card, ATM, online activity—the works. Not finding any points of interest, he moved on to personal information. Garret found that she was adopted by Daniel Jerome Jensen the day he turned twenty-three, January 4, 1994. Clicking on Daniel's name picked up some dirt. He was arrested for assault in 1995, twice in 1996, and eight more times between then and 2005 when the assaults stopped. The charges were always dropped.

The complaints came from neighbors in close proximity to the Jensen house. Reports indicated that he was always intoxicated when arrested. Although Mrs. Jenson sustained visible contusions from his violent behavior, she wouldn't press charges.

When arrested, he appeared as gentle as a pussycat; the police had no choice but to let him go each time. Garret almost missed the last report. It explained why Jensen stopped beating up his wife.

The sergeant sat back in his chair to digest autopsy reports for Daniel, Carole, and eleven-year-old George Jensen. The cause of death? Asphyxiation from smoke inhalation, the bodies charred. Garret searched for further information.

According to the Norridge local newspaper, the next-door neighbor came home late and smelled smoke. He heard Becky's screams coming from the basement window when he stood in the breezeway between the houses. He was able to break the window and pull the fourteen-year-old girl out of the basement right before the house burst into a blaze. The neighbor was quoted in the police report, "The girl's hands were bloody from pulling at the ropes that bound her wrists together." The rest of the family perished in the fire.

Garret scrolled through all of the articles searching for clues to what caused the fire. Fire Marshall Aaron Slowik had no comment. Garret wrote his name down on a nearby pad and resumed his search.

Was this girl capable of murder? What would have made her snap? He finished sleuthing through her home town for any medical, dental, or employment info.

There was nothing to be found after her discharge from Lutheran General Hospital two weeks after the fire. There were no family members, so he figured she must have come to California at that time.

He looked for employment records, insurance, and disability. He drew a blank until Becky became employed at Nordstrom and applied for her driver's license in June the same year. He navigated through her employee information and finally found something pertinent that had happened two months ago. There was a medical claim submitted for Rhinehart Ambulance Company and Mercy Hospital. He followed the lead to dispatch records at Rhinehart. A 911 call was placed from the Nordstrom department store: "Caucasian female, age 23, hysterical, violent behavior, public disturbance."

The report stated medication was administered on site, and the female was transported to Mercy. Garret clicked his way to the insurance information. Becky had been seeing Grace since the day of the incident. The diagnosis evidently wasn't serious enough to have the girl admitted to a mental health facility for observation. He wrote down the name of the attending psychiatrist who released her.

Garret loved this stealthy information highway. He was able to connect with the hospital records and read the doctor's report. The report stated paramedics followed procedure sedating her when she became violent. The doctor's exam at Mercy concluded she was delusional.

"But are you dangerous?" Garret whispered. "Are you my killer, Becky? Did something make you angry?"

The sergeant emerged from his office issuing orders. He gave the dispatcher Becky's home address and asked her to get his guys on the radio. "Tell them to meet me there. I don't want anyone to make a move until I arrive. I have to speak with Miss Simms first." He scribbled down the address and phone number and added, "Have Spider call me as soon as he gets any info on the tire. Thanks."

# CHAPTER 20

# Just Friends?

J ess dropped the tire off at the police station and drove to Grace's. When he arrived she was still dressed in a T-shirt and a pair of casual, drawstring, cotton pants that reminded him of their college days. Her hair had dried in ringlets, and she was free of make-up. He couldn't remember her ever looking this gorgeous.

"Hi, come on in."

Sneaky pushed her way between the door and Grace standing rigid. A low growl rumbled in Sneaky's throat.

"Wow, that dog's determined to have you all to herself, isn't she?" he said, drawing back.

"You are as enlightened about animals as I am. Isn't she sweet?"

"Well, it's hard to tell, Grace. I think she wants to bite me!"

Grace crouched eye level with her dog.

"Sneaky, remember, sweetheart? Jess is my friend. He's nice, although he can be a *shit* sometimes, and he can't throw a ball worth a damn. He knows how to use a brush, and I'm sure he will be happy to show you."

"Yeah, right!" Jess muttered.

The shepherd wasn't buying it. She held her position.

"Sneaky, go lie down," she commanded with steel in her voice. "I'm fine. Really."

The dog padded to the rug by the kitchen sink to lie down. Jess hurried inside the house before she changed her mind. "Are you okay?"

"I'm fine, Jess. We *do* need to talk."

They sat down on the sofa. He put his arm around her, drawing her close. She snuggled against him for a moment, enjoying his body against hers. She missed being with him. Many nights they cuddled and talked as friends. She needed him to be that for her now. She was scared, stressed, and he felt safe. *He's not yours.* "Does Jenna know you're here?"

"She called me when she read about the murder in the paper."

"That was last week. I mean *now.* Does she know you're here with me now?"

"No."

His tone made her wonder. "Don't you think you should call and tell her?"

"No." He squeezed her briefly before rising.

"What's going on, Jess?" She saw that wounded look on his face and knew something was wrong.

"Jenna and I are separated," he said, his voice infused with remorse.

"What?" She hated when he held out on her. "Why didn't you tell me before?"

"You've got enough to be concerned about. We're *talking.*" He paced, rubbing his brow. "She moved in with her mom. Like I said, we talk."

"I'm sorry, Jess. What happened?"

"That night you and I went to Bandara's, it was late when I got home. She was upset.

She told me how I come alive when I've been around you. She said she knows technically I've been faithful; it wasn't about that. She said that you breathe life into me. She said she felt bad that she has never been able to do that."

"Jess, I—" His mouth covered hers before she could respond.

He responded to a need he'd denied for ten years. His body molded into the curve of hers. His smoldering eyes melted her words into desire. His mouth searched for acceptance, his kisses light and tender at first. Their tongues played, igniting the old flame. Their lips joined starting the fire.

Jess explored places he'd only dreamed of, retracing each touch with warm kisses. He reached under her T-shirt and inched his way up toward her breasts. He tasted tender flesh he had only dared to think about in private moments throughout the years. She thrust forward, gathering the mounds of pillow softness together and filling his mouth with her womanly charms.

He nibbled his way back to her lips by way of her neck, as her naked peaks pressed hard against his chest. She brought his body closer to hers. Long legs wrapped around his waist. He pressed himself against her gently riveting hips, unable to stop the groan that escaped. Passion boiled below the surface, about to erupt.

"You are *so* beautiful." He brushed the hair from her cheek to study her face, seeking the love he would never find in another.

"Oh God, Jess, what are we doing?"

His kiss smothered any further protest. Her body continued to betray her better judgment. She was so aroused she couldn't help herself. He touched her sweet spot, and the juices flowed just as they did in her fantasy. He knew what she liked. It was instinctive. They had been lovers in their minds since they met, and she knew she wanted to taste him.

She turned and slid down his body, caressing his firm thighs and tight buttocks. She eased his pants down far enough to press her lips on his swollen manhood.

"God, Grace, I love what you do to me." His sultry whisper hungered for more. She took him to the edge, teasing with wet lips. She coaxed him into her warm, juicy orifice with her gentle sucking.

"Let me make love to you, Grace." He pulled her to her feet and gathered her in his arms, eager to continue their lovemaking upstairs in bed.

He undressed her slowly, exploring each curve of her body with his fingertips. Her skin tingled into tiny bumps until the sensation reached her nipples. They ached to be kissed again. He knew her well. He obliged without her having to say a word.

"You are delicious, my Grace, more delicious than I ever imagined." His smile was playful, his eyes adoring. They laughed as they touched and tasted until a kiss fanned the flames into an inferno. It was as if their souls connected at the tip of their tongues, entwining into one force.

"I want to feel you inside me, Jess," she quivered, straddling his muscular form.

"Want no more."

He took her hands and stretched them overhead. Turning her onto the pillow, he parted her legs. Just like in his fantasy, he smiled at her readiness, inserting himself into her wet opening and whispering her name.

Their bodies moved in perfect rhythm; passion verbalized in euphony of moaning endearments. When they reached the crescendo of their lovemaking, their eyes met and held while their love pulsated into waves of pleasure.

Afterward, Jess cuddled Grace in the crook of his arm and stroked her hair. She fell asleep.

The sound of the phone brought the couple out of their sweet after-love. Grace checked the number. It was the Twenty-Second Precinct.

"Grace Simms," she said.

"Miss Simms, this is Officer Belinda Stenberg. Sergeant Weston is on his way to speak with you. His ETA is twelve minutes."

"Thank you for the heads up."

"You're welcome, Miss Simms. Goodbye."

Grace bolted out of bed and quickly showered, rinsing away the moments she had waited years to experience. The thought of Garret walking in on their afterglow made her stomach clench. *Not that it's any of his business.* Grace scrubbed harder. *Why do I feel like I made a very big mistake?* She dried herself in a hurry and got dressed.

Jess was still lounging in bed. "Hey, what's wrong? Who was on the phone?"

"Garret— *Sergeant Weston* is on his way over. Here are some fresh towels if you'd like to shower."

"What? No hug? No kiss? I feel used," he pouted.

"I'm sorry, Jess. This whole thing is so crazy." She stepped into his arms, her lips joining his in a quick exchange. "I don't know what just happened. We stepped back in time to experience something we both yearned for. I don't know what comes next."

"I love you, Grace. I think you know that."

"I had my suspicions!" She whacked his naked flank with a towel and gave him her best flirtatious grin. She wanted to tell him the feelings buried deep inside, how she had loved him from the moment she'd set eyes on him. She wanted to tell him there hadn't been room in her heart for anyone else but him. She couldn't tell him that now because suddenly, *I'm not sure.*

She dismissed her emotions and tended to the bed, now in disarray. She shook the coverlet, smoothing away any evidence of their lovemaking and went downstairs to wait for Garret.

# CHAPTER 21

# Dig Deeper

Hello, this is Sergeant Weston from the Sacramento PD. I'm trying to reach Fire Marshall Aaron Slowik. Is he available?"

"I'm sorry, Sergeant," the receptionist said. "Aaron Slowik retired several years ago. Can I put you through to Fire Marshall Dempsey?"

"I'm calling in regard to a residential fire that happened in 1999."

"One moment, please. I'll put your call through."

"Dempsey," the voice asserted.

Garret identified himself to the fire marshal and explained his reason for the call. In return, the man gave him the particulars: Time, date, address, victims' names, and more.

"Sorry, Sergeant, that's all the information I have on the Jensen fire. Let me give you Slowik's home phone number. He has a memory like a trap. If there were anything unusual about that fire, he would remember."

He thanked the man for his time and dialed Aaron Slowik's number on his cell phone. Just as Garret was about to give up on the call, a man answered, obviously out of breath. Garret apologized for the interruption and stated his business.

"Yeah, I remember the case well. A neighbor saved the girl. The rest of the family died."

"Can you tell me about the fire? Do you remember what started it?"

"Why the interest?"

"We have a homicide we're trying to solve here in Sacramento. Becky Jensen is a suspect."

"Geez, no kidding? Well, she wasn't the cause of the fire. As I recall, her brother was holding a lighter in his hand when he died. We figured the kid started the fire because of his situation. The stepdad had a history of violence. The coroner reported that Mrs. Jenson's face had *sixty-three fractures*, and the girl had been in and out of emergency rooms for broken bones. Daniel Jenson was found with a pair of kids' underwear on his head. His left lung had been punctured by broken ribs. An aluminum baseball bat was found on the floor near the bodies. Broken glass everywhere."

Garret could tell that Slowik was still bothered by the insidious death.

"There was something twisted about that girl—twisted in a sad way. I went to the hospital to see her. Then she was transferred from Lutheran General to a private facility for a week or so. Word was that someone was touched by the tragedy and offered to pay to transfer her to a facility in California for long-term care. The records, I imagine, are sealed because she was a minor." The marshal sounded like he was ready to end the conversation. He put a few seconds of dead air between them before adding, "I can give you the name of the woman who was the facilitator at the time the girl was hospitalized, if that will help."

"Yeah, that would help a great deal."

"Gotta pen?"

"I'm ready when you are."

"Sylvia Sanchez. I think she moved to Bolingbrook some time ago."

Garret thanked the man for his time and ended the call. He dialed directory assistance, spoke the name of the town, and waited for the number. Once he had the information needed, he pressed the key that made the connection.

Unfortunately, he reached an answering machine with a witty message recorded by a retired person who couldn't come to the phone because she was off living life. He left a brief reason for his call with all the pertinent information that Sylvia Sanchez would need to return his call.

On the way to Grace's, Garret let his mind wander. He

warmed to the memory on the staircase when he and Grace collided. He could smell her hair in his mind and wondered if that reality were possible. As much as he wanted to focus on the murder and stalking cases, he had no control over the thoughts that seeped into his mind. They took him to a place where something was beautiful.

* * *

When Sergeant Weston arrived, he was greeted by a friendly bark and wagging tail.

"Obviously she adores you!" Grace watched the interaction between Sneaky and the man who sparked excitement in the dog whenever she saw him. "Come on in." Grace led him into her office. "Coffee?"

"No, thanks. I'm meeting my men in a few minutes," Garret said, moving closer to Grace, "I just wanted to stop by to give you a heads up on Becky Jensen."

"Becky? How did you?"

"Let's just say I stumbled across her name."

"Why? Why her, Garret?"

"I'm sorry, Grace. She's a strong suspect. There are things in her past, things you may not know about."

"Garret, no!" Grace's eyes filled with tears and anger. Her heart filled with angst. She knew Becky was damaged, but she never figured Becky to be violent. She recalled the time Becky wore a bizarre outfit to her appointment. She contemplated that Becky's piercings had begun to heal, and her heavy metal look was totally out of character. Grace wondered if something else besides feelings for her mystery man were brewing. Eventually, Grace passed it off as acting out. The girl had her defiant moments, and Grace knew clients often used anger as a protective shell. Thinking back, she realized the girl dressed the way she did that day as a way to display her anger.

Fear stripped Grace's confidence in her judgment of character. If it were true, if Becky were that demented and Grace hadn't seen disaster coming, what else had she missed? *A man died because you didn't do your job.*

Garret started toward Grace, about to fold her in his arms, but he stopped midstride when he saw Jess appear in the doorway, freshly showered. They both looked at Jess as if he had dropped out of the sky. Grace flushed, embarrassed by the casualness of Jess's appearance—barefoot, bare-chested, and wearing a grin like a man who just got laid.

The awkwardness grew excruciating. Garret gave Grace's arm a comforting squeeze and turned to Jess calmly. "Hi Jess. I stopped by to give Grace a heads up on one of her clients."

Jess's grin expanded into a courtroom closing smile, "Hey, don't mind me."

Garret returned to business. "I'm sorry, Grace. I promise to go easy on—" He glanced over at Jess and stopped himself from divulging Becky's name. His gaze fell on Grace. His eyes softened. "I'll let you know the outcome."

"Thanks, Sergeant." Her words came out crisper than she intended. She knew he had his job to do. He walked the line by warning her. "I appreciate you coming to tell me."

"No problem."

Grace's brow gathered. "Can she call me?"

"She may need a lawyer, Grace; I'll see what I can do."

"Who needs a lawyer?" said Jess, finishing drying his hair and wrapping the towel around his neck. "Who needs a lawyer, Grace? Can I help?"

Garret intervened, "I don't know yet, Jess, but thanks. I'll be in touch." The tenderness in his eyes turned callous as he turned to leave.

"Please, Garret, *please*...don't let them hurt her," said Grace, caught up in conscientious turmoil. Becky was her client; the girl trusted her to keep their conversations private. Yet she was terrified that the Becky could be responsible for murdering a man and may have been the one stalking her. Grace needed to sit. She felt woozy.

Jess led her to the couch where her vulnerability started earlier. He deliberately brushed her breast with his fingertips as she sat down.

Grace bristled. *Does he think this a good time to hit on me?*

Their lovemaking held no significance at the moment. What had transpired in the last few minutes with Garret overshadowed what had taken place earlier. And Jess wasn't included.

"What's going on, Grace?" Jess asked, sensing her aloof. "Tell me, please. Let me in."

"I can't. Not until she's arrested. Then you'll know what everyone else does. Until then, she's my client, and I won't betray her confidence."

"*Bravo,*" Jess said, sarcastically. He was frustrated. He was sure that Sergeant Weston knew all the details that Grace wouldn't share with him. Moreover, he'd seen Grace's discomfort when he walked into the room. *Embarrassed? Or something more?*

"Jess, if I asked you to divulge secret information— stuff that you were sworn to keep confidential—what then? Would you tell me?" She stood up and headed toward the back door. "I need some air. This matter is not up for discussion."

Jess followed. "You're upset. Isn't it natural to want to help?"

She turned to face him. Her eyes flashing, she blurted, "You can't!"

"We just made love. I thought you let me in."

"I let you inside my body, Jess, maybe my heart, but how dare you assume that gives you *carte blanche!*"

"Ouch," he said, watching her form slip from view.

\* \* \*

Jess went upstairs to finish dressing. He wanted to plead his case and tell Grace he felt shut out. She was right. If the situation were reversed, he would be hard pressed to incriminate a client. He wanted to tell her how much he loved her, how he regretted not making his feelings known all those years before. He sat on the edge of the bed unable to move.

Rage burned deep in his soul. This wasn't the way he imagined it. He imagined Grace loving him back. *I'm not happy,* he thought.

# CHAPTER 22

# The Fire

Once in the car, Garret felt like crawling into a hole. His gut rumbled. Acid worked its way to his esophagus. He didn't need to be an investigative police sergeant to know what transpired between Jess and Grace. Any man could sense it. *It should have been me who made love to her this morning.* Instead, he backed her against a wall, urging her to give him information about her clients—all against her will.

Conflicting emotions filled his heart, making it ache. Certainly he saw something special in the way Grace had looked at him. *Didn't she blush on the stairway when our bodies touched by accident?* Her voice had sweetened when she spoke to him. Was he reading too much into the way her hips had swayed while she moved around the kitchen the other night? Damn, she was seductive!

*Bad timing*, claimed the defeatist voice in his head. His turmoil stemmed from bad timing. *That's all.* He had no control over what she had going on with Jess. Until the case was closed, he couldn't make a move. *Let it go*, he convinced himself. *No sense dwelling on it.*

Somehow he didn't feel better.

His thoughts returned to the case and to Becky. He needed to know what happened the night of the fire. *What did that bastard Dan Jensen do to Becky and her brother—to their mom? What kind of monster did they live with?* He was feeling sorry for a girl he hadn't even met, but he knew Becky was important to Grace. Therefore, that made Becky important to him. Besides, he knew Grace wouldn't have reacted the way she did if Becky weren't a tormented soul.

The whole situation made him sick. His investigation would most likely obliterate any trust Becky had established with Grace. Bringing up the past could wreak havoc on the girl's life. Wasn't surviving a fire enough for the girl? *Hurting her is inevitable*, he thought, convinced he couldn't help it. He had no choice but to set a fire of his own.

He pulled up behind Jake and Dave, got out of his car, and stood to look at the third-floor apartment. Beautiful, thriving ferns hung from the girl's balcony. *Hardly characteristic for a killer*, he thought.

"Okay, listen up," Garret talked softly, but sternly to his crew. "This girl is fragile. No rough stuff. I want to talk to her first."

The officers nodded in compliance.

"Lavern, Miss Jensen may feel more comfortable with a female. I want you with me," he said. "Dave, you and Jake hang here. Let's see how this plays out."

Garret's men responded, congruent with their orders. Lavern followed Garret's lead. Creeping up the stairs with his gun drawn, Garret felt as though they were flushing out a sparrow with a bazooka. He stopped at the top of the landing, took a deep breath, and knocked on the door.

The girl who answered the door was visibly confused. Her tousled, short, black hair and baggy clothes made her look like a preteen, not a twenty-three-year-old. She tried to push the door shut, but was stopped by Garret's size-eleven shoe. "Go away! What do you—?" She pushed again, this time harder. "Leave me alone," she screamed.

"Miss Jensen?" Garret inquired through the crack in the door, his voice gentle and patient. "I'm Sergeant Weston with the Twenty-Second Precinct. This is Lieutenant Neilson," he added, displaying his badge. "We just want to talk to you. Can we come in?"

"Why? I didn't do anything," she cried.

"We just want to talk to you about Miss Simms." His voice dropped to almost a whisper. "Please...don't make this hard. Let us come inside."

She peered through the door. Her eyes, now streaked with black, smudged mascara, looked wild. She blinked away tears and eased back, away from the door. Garret stepped in, followed by Lieutenant Neilson.

Becky plopped into a chair that reminded Garret of a big, padded, cereal bowl. She crossed her legs, Indian style, and glared at them when they took a seat on the couch across from her.

"Becky— May I call you Becky? Or would you prefer Miss Jensen?"

"Becky will do," she said flatly.

"We're investigating the murder of Carlos Munoz."

"Who's he? I thought you said you wanted to talk to me about Dr. Grace."

"I spoke with some people in Chicago who told me about the fire, Becky."

"Why? *Why did you do that*? That's none of your business! I didn't do anything!" Becky popped out of the chair and stood inches from Garret's face.

Lieutenant Neilson tensed; her hand reached for her pistol, but Garret grabbed her knee to stymie her pursuit. He softened his grip, a signal to standby. Nielsen remained seated.

"Grace Simms is a friend of mine, Becky."

"Now I'm *really* confused," the girl retorted. "What's Dr. Grace got to do with a dead guy?"

"A policeman was murdered at her house."

Her eyes grew large. "And you think I had something to do with that?" She sat back down and laughed. "I think *you're* crazy," she said, twisting her hair.

"You and your brother had some bad times," Garret said sympathetically. "I heard a neighbor pulled you out of the basement window." He swallowed the bad taste threatening to erupt as he watched the "sparrow" fall to the ground. The girl crumbled into a heap of sobbing pain. He bent down by her side, hating himself for having to pluck her feathers as well. "Who tied you up when you were a girl, Becky? Why? Why would someone tie you up? Were you bad?" He waited for the response that would tell him what he wanted to know.

"I didn't do anything," she sobbed, "I tried to get away! I begged him, but he wouldn't let me go."

"Who wouldn't let you go?"

"Georgie. I knew what he was going to do. I couldn't stop him!" Her words became muffled as she buried her face in Garret's shoulder. He gently held her heaving body. He had never heard anyone cry that hard before. One last question and he promised himself he would quit.

"When you and Grace talked about these things, did she make you feel it was your fault?" He hoped Becky would understand that Grace did not betray her.

"Dr. Grace doesn't know," Becky said. "I told her Georgie was in college somewhere. I never told anyone about the fire." Her voice grew hoarse. She cried even harder.

Garret rose, pulling the sparrow-like figure to her feet. He nodded to Laverne, signaling it was time for damage control. He took Becky by the arm and helped her back into the chair. Laverne sat with the Becky while Garret went downstairs to talk to his men. After explaining the situation to Dave and Jake, he excused himself and dialed Grace's number. "Grace? She didn't do it, but I think she needs you. I opened a can of worms. Sorry. It had to be done." He rubbed his hand over his face trying to wipe away the anguish he felt for creating the ugly mess that Grace would have to clean up.

"What happened?" Grace's voice sounded small.

"While I was digging for information, I found out about a fire at Becky's house in Chicago. She was tied-up in the basement. A neighbor—the guy who heard her screams—pulled her out. Her mom, dad, and little brother were upstairs. They didn't make it out." He hung his head. The words stuck in his throat. He could feel Grace's sadness through the phone. "She said you didn't know."

Grace couldn't speak. She knew Becky had an awful childhood, but she was not prepared for this. Not divulging an atrocity of this magnitude? Something this significant was never shared? Becky told her that Georgie was in college. She lied! Then it occurred to Grace, when Becky described her brother the other day, she was describing him as a boy. *That must've been the last time she saw him.*

"Grace? Are you all right?"

"Yes," she answered, remaining stiff. "I'll have Jess drive me to my office. Bring Becky there.

"I'll have Lieutenant Neilson drive her." He paused, "Grace, I'm—"

"Thank you, Sergeant," she said curtly. She was in no mood to accept his apology. "Thank you for calling me, for not leaving her there alone."

* * *

Grace hurried upstairs to change clothes while Jess shouted questions from the bottom of the stairway.

"What's up, Grace? What happened?"

"I need you to take me to my office," she called down the stairs. "Becky needs me." Grace realized she let the name slip. Right now she didn't care if Jess knew. All she cared about was her client.

* * *

Jess concentrated on traffic while Grace stared out the window, her thoughts reverting to previous sessions with Becky. She remembered being surprised when Becky told her she even had a brother. And now this? What else didn't she know? It seemed Becky survived more horror than Grace had ever imagined. No wonder the girl had developed an imaginary savior. *Tied-up in the basement while her house was burning down! Saved by her neighbor. Was he her "mystery man?"*

When they arrived, Officer O'Malley stood by the curb and waited to escort Grace into the building. Clouds blocked the sun. More than cool air chilled Grace's bones.

"I better go," Jess said. "I have an arraignment at three I need to prepare for. I think I've goofed off enough for one day." His smile filled with sadness. "Good luck with everything," he whispered, touching her cheek. He placed a gentle kiss on the other. "I'm here if you need me."

"We'll talk later," she said, feeling the need to apologize for the interruption to their morning. Instead, she decided to save her apology for a better time, when she could focus on what happened between them.

# CHAPTER 23
# Disturbed

Sergeant Weston sat behind his desk, his head resting in his hands when his phone intercom announced, "I have a Sylvia Sanchez on the line. She's calling from Chicago."

"Thanks, Belinda, put her through."

Garret didn't need to speak with the woman now that he felt Becky was no longer a suspect. Becky was one very disturbed girl, but he didn't think she was a killer. *Merely hiding an ugly past.* Cold killers don't fall apart when confronted. *They lie.*

"Hello, Ms. Sanchez. Thank you for returning my call."

"Glad to do it, Sergeant. Your message sounded disturbing. What's this about a murder investigation?"

"It was resolved this morning."

"Did Becky have anything to do with it?"

"No, but it was an intense situation. She's not doing well at the moment."

"It was touch and go with her to begin with, but I heard she was getting along there at the home. I'm sorry to hear that's not so."

"Can you tell me what happened, Ms. Sanchez?"

"Professional confidentiality would apply here."

"Yes, of course."

"There was a fire."

"Yes, I know about that, I read it in the paper."

"Did you know she was tied—" Garret cut her off.

"I talked to Slowik. Go on."

"She must've been tied up for some time because the rope

was embedded in her flesh—practically to the bone in places from struggling. Luckily the neighbor found her before the upstairs became engulfed in flames and smoke filled the basement."

"Oh my God." Garret's mind pictured the girl in a heap, sobbing her eyes out while he badgered her for answers. His stomach wanted to heave. "How did she end up in California?"

"While she was in the hospital, they x-rayed her from head to toe," said Mrs. Sanchez. "She had some old fractures, some estimated as far back as the age of two that had healed over. Because of her high pain tolerance, doctors needed to rule out a few nasties like CIPA."

"What's that?" Garret asked.

"A rare autosomal recessive disorder that makes one unable to feel pain. Manifests in childhood. Good excuse to send her to Stanford. Her psyche evaluation revealed severe child abuse. The report read like a horror novel."

"Aw, geez," Garret groaned.

"Good news was she didn't have CIPA. The safe house was my idea. A friend of mine owned it. I pulled a few strings to get her in. I took her out there myself. Like I said, last time I heard she was doing fine."

"Do you have access to her files?"

"Nope. Everything was sent to California. Lawyers handled all the paperwork necessary for her medical benefits, money from life insurance policies, even the sale of her parents' property."

"I see."

"The kid went through a lot. I think the only time I saw any life in her was when she was with one of the lawyers. He was a livin' doll, young. Looked like a kid himself. He worked hard to get benefits and a trust set up for her."

"Do you remember his name?"

"Hmmm...Justin? No, that's not it. He used a nickname. I'm sorry, I can't think of it at the moment. If I remember, I'll let you know. Is there anything else I can do for you?"

"No," he said. His voice faded, "I appreciate you getting back to me."

"Sad. Very sad."

"Yes," he agreed. "Thank you for your time, Ms. Sanchez. And if you think of the lawyer's name, please give me a call."

Garret stared at the phone for a few minutes, trying to piece facts together. Why was he still digging? He needed to get the image of the Becky out of his head. He unlocked his drawer, pulled out the software, loaded it, and typed in "Tim Ashton."

# CHAPTER 24

# Breakdown

Lieutenant Nielson escorted Becky into Grace's office. "Hi Becky. C'mon in," Grace said, placing her hand on Becky's shoulder. Becky shrugged it away. The girl plopped onto the couch, her legs beneath her. She glared at Grace through red-rimmed eyes.

"Looks like you're having a rough day," Grace said tenderly, as she closed the door, ready to face Becky's wrath.

"Let's see, the police practically break my door in. I get accused of murdering some guy I've never heard of. Then I get hauled off in a squad car. Now everyone thinks I'm a criminal!"

"Not everyone." Grace waited for her words to settle. "Sergeant Weston called me because he was concerned about you. Do you want to tell me what happened?"

"They came to arrest me, Grace! You must think I'm stupid. You told them something to make them believe I was a murderer!"

"There's an investigation going on, Becky. Someone is stalking me. It's possible this person also killed one of the officers working on my case. All of my clients are suspects. That's the truth. You were not singled out."

"What did that cop tell you?" Becky sneered.

"He mentioned a fire, that your house burned down some years back. Do you want to tell me about it?"

Becky grabbed a pillow and held it to her chest. Tears rested on her lower lids. Her demeanor changed dramatically. "What do you want to know?"

Grace's heart sank. The girl sounded so small. "What happened, Becky? What preceded the fire?"

"I don't know what George was thinking," the girl began. He called me from the basement. He said he wanted me to come downstairs because he had a new trick to show me. He told me to sit in the chair. He tied me up," Becky paused. Then, he told me he was going to kill mom and Dan and set the house on fire." Becky hugged the pillow tighter. "I begged him to untie me. I said we could run away." Becky's gaze hit the floor. "He wouldn't listen."

"Where were your mom and dad? Didn't they hear you scream?"

"Scream?" Becky seemed confused. "I never scream."

Dr. Meltz told Grace that Becky had screamed at the mall; Garret said that Becky's neighbor heard Becky screaming in the basement. It was possible Becky didn't remember screaming. Her mind protected her from the memory and blocked it out. *Typical.*

Grace knew the mind is like a computer. When overloaded, it crashes. Often memories, like files, were misplaced or missing. Emotions were suppressed. Becky's files needed to be restored. "Do you remember the man who saved your life, Becky?"

"John from next door."

"Tell me about him."

"He was a nice man, I guess. I caught him looking at my legs once. It gave me the creeps. I never thought much about it after that."

"Do you remember anything else?"

"I remember…he was the one *crying* when he pulled me out of the window. It was weird."

"What does John look like?"

The cold stare returned.

Grace's heart sped up. She had a hunch. "Do you remember seeing the man from the mall before or after the fire?"

Becky's response held no emotion. "I don't remember."

Grace believed her client. If the neighbor were her mystery man, she would've reacted differently. Becky lit up when they talked about her mystery man. "Tell me what you do remember," Grace said. With her hunch disproven, Grace felt her heart return to its normal rhythm.

Becky recalled the horrors of her childhood apathetically, as if it all had happened to someone else. However, when she finished telling her story, she curled up into a fetal position on the couch and began to shake.

Grace sat beside Becky, no longer able to hold back her own tears. She lifted strands of hair from the girl's wet cheek, pulled her close, and held on tight while the girl shook and broke into pieces.

\* \* \*

Garret reloaded the confiscated software and followed the same procedure researching Tim Ashton, just as he had with Becky. He started with the basics. Ashton had no criminal record. No traffic tickets, no liens of any sort. He owned a home off of Fair Oaks Boulevard. His credit check came up clean, and he held accounts in several banks.

Garret pulled up Ashton's medical history. Coincidentally, like Becky Jensen, he grew up in Illinois. "What the heck? I thought California had the corner on *nuts*," he mumbled. "Here we go. Much better," he whispered as he pointed the cursor and clicked.

"Timothy Allen Ashton, hospitalized for violent behavior–attempted suicide–released after two months in Forest Hospital." Garret clicked the location: Des Plaines, Illinois. The release form read: "Timothy Ashton no longer poses a threat to himself or to others." Dr. Richard Traeger and Abigail Ashton signed the form.

To Garret, Ashton didn't fit his particular profile. The sergeant needed to trust his gut. He erased the screen and typed in another name on Grace's list of clients: James Freeman

"My, my, James! You do have a bit of baggage, my friend." Garret scrolled through court reports, learning James, accused of molesting his daughter, had charges dropped. His file was still active. "God, I love this software," the sergeant whispered to himself.

Next Garret read about a little altercation James had with a Miss Candice Applegate. Miss Applegate placed a 911 call, claiming James assaulted her in the parking lot of the Hunter's Club, a strip joint off of Highway 50. Officers were dispatched to the scene. However, when they arrived, Miss Applegate repudiated the charges. She told officers Mr. Freeman was intoxicated and apologized to her for his behavior. *No arrest.*

*Moving on.* Garret opened Freeman's employment records: Triage nurse, two dependents. Garret checked his bank profile, finding no outlandish debts, just a few late fees here and there. He noticed a lot of credit card activity at The Hunter's Club over the last six months.

"Okay, buddy, let's check out your girlfriend." Garret pulled up Candice Irene Applegate, charged with driving on a suspended license. "Naugh-ty girl." The violation was recent. He checked all of her other information. Employed at the Hunter's Club, she made minimum wage, yet her bank records revealed she was doing better financially than James. Garret concluded Candy was a stripper. They made huge tips performing lap dances, hence the activity on James' credit card. *Are you a stalker, Mr. Freeman?*

He looked a little further into Candice's personal files. She had been arrested eight years ago for petty theft and did community service. She was employed by Sunrise Upholstery at the time. *Interesting.*

Garret checked her medical paper trail. After finding nothing noteworthy, he went back to James. *Bingo!* He found what he was searching for.

# CHAPTER 25

# Questions

It seemed fewer than eighteen hours since Grace called Dr.
Meltz to arrange for Becky to be admitted into the hospital.
She sat with her client until the paramedics arrived. Once they
left, she closed the door and cried. *How did everything get so crazy?*
Her clients would be questioned; they would be thrown into the
wreck she tried so hard to prevent. *What about Jess?* What happened
between them should've been savored. *Still just friends?*

She reached for the phone and dialed the answering service to
retrieve her messages:

9:01 a.m.: "Hey Grace, Bruce here. What's going on? I heard
on the news that a cop got murdered. Your name was mentioned
several times. Are you keeping your appointments? I'm scheduled
to come in tomorrow morning. I don't think I can wait much longer. I need to talk to you."

The next message came from Sal.

"Hi, Grace. I hope you're holding up okay, honey. I feel like
a deserter. You can call me, ya know. We're all wondering about
you, especially the kids. They want to know when I'm going back
to work. They said I'm a pain in the ass! How do you like that?
Anyway, I'm thinking about you, but my thoughts are beginning
to grow horns. You know what a vivid imagination I have. I know,
I'm not your mother, but I worry. Call me! Bye."

When Grace checked the clock, she realized she had less than
a half hour before Chris and Yolanda came in. She got up and
prepared for their session. It wasn't going to be easy to conduct

business as usual under these circumstances, but she cared deeply for her clients and didn't feel it fair to disregard her commitment to them. *Besides, it will take my mind off of myself for a while.*

The phone rang. She glanced at the clock. *Not much time to talk.* "Grace Simms," spoke her voice, unusually raspy and low.

"Hi beautiful," Jess said. "I let your dog out. She didn't bite me. I'm feeling victorious. Do you think we can have dinner tonight? We need to talk."

"Sure, Jess. It will have to be after seven though. Does that work for you?"

"Great. I'll be in court all afternoon. I hope to wrap up this case I've been stressing over. Are you okay?"

"I'm fine. I have clients coming in."

"How's the girl?"

"She was admitted to the hospital. Thanks for asking. Jess. I know I make it difficult for you at times. I'm sorry."

"I understand, babe. And hey, don't forget: I'm here if you need me."

"Thanks." Grace thought his offer to help sounded like a calling card. The phone barely touched its cradle before it rang again.

"Grace, it's Garret Weston. Can I swing by? I need to talk to you about James Freeman."

"My client is due to arrive in a few minutes. We can talk now."

"Sure."

Grace sensed a pang of disappointment in his tone.

"If I tell you what I know," he said, "can you verify my concerns? Would that be crossing the line?"

"Depends."

"I'll take my chances. Here goes: James Freeman, arrested for molesting his daughter. Charges didn't stick. Should I be concerned?"

"No."

"He's a regular at the Hunter's Club. Ever mention it?"

"Be more specific," she said.

"He had an altercation with an employee from there. Has he mentioned a crush?"

"Is this leading somewhere?"

"I'm trying to figure out whether he was stalking one of the strippers."

"Stalking? Doubtful. Dating? Possibly. Why?"

"Thanks."

"Where are you getting your information?"

"That's privileged," he said.

"Touché," Grace admitted. A moment of silence hung between them.

"How are you?" he asked warmly.

"I'm fine." Her answer sounded abrupt. Those two words seemed to fly out of her mouth automatically. *Fine* wasn't how she felt.

"I checked on Becky," Garret said as if he sensed Grace's pain. "She's doing well. The hospital admitted her. The doctor gave her something to sleep."

"Yes, I spoke with the doctor. Thanks."

"Well, I'd love to chat, but I have a murderer to catch."

"Good luck," Grace offered.

"I need more than luck. Any insight you want to share will help."

"I can't recall anything pertinent."

When Garret hung up, Grace's mind began to chatter. She didn't recall James ever mentioning that he *hung out* at the Hunter's Club. *If he did*, she assumed, *it was because Candy worked there*. It was possible they had a fight. From what James revealed in their sessions, it sounded like the stripper had a bit of a temper. Was James capable of being a stalker? *Or a killer? No*, Grace assured herself. He just didn't make good choices when it came to women – *that's all*.

# CHAPTER 26

# Triage

Electronic doors to the emergency room swooshed open. The waiting room overflowed with injured people and their loved ones. Two men approached the thick, sliding-glass window labeled "Patient Check-In." Garret flipped his badge open and introduced himself to the woman behind the desk. When the woman finished her call, she escorted the men through a double door, down a corridor and into a small room marked: "TRIAGE."

"James Freeman? I'm Sergeant Garret Weston. This is Lieutenant Jake Stramski. I would like to ask you some questions."

"Concerning?" James spun to and fro on his chair, attending to the patient before him, barely acknowledging the men's presence.

"Is there somewhere we can talk?"

James held up Mrs. Etta Pearl's chart. "I'm pretty busy at the moment. Mrs. Pearl is in a great deal of pain, and she has been waiting patiently for over an hour." Garret noticed the woman's knee appeared three times the size of the other one. Her stretched skin looked angry.

"We won't take much of your time," Garret told the woman. "I promise to return him in five minutes, Mrs. Pearl, and I thank you for your patience. I hope you're better real soon." Garret patted the old woman's shoulder.

James led the officers to an empty triage room.

"Can we make this quick? I'm the only one here right now."

James closed the door and leaned against the desk with his

arms folded across his chest, his legs crossed at the ankles. Garret saw this cocky pose just about every day for the last twelve years, but he still found it amusing. To him it signified weakness.

"I need to know where you were last Wednesday."

I remember picking up my daughters from school," said James, his tone sharp. His shoulders went back. He straightened his spine.

"Is there anyone who can verify that?"

"Yeah, I also picked up my neighbor's son. The kids got out at two-fifteen. I took them right home. Josh came home with us that day, I think. He and my daughter Charming worked on a science project. I had to be at work at four. Tiffy, my babysitter, showed up at three forty-five. My timecard will verify what time I arrived here. You can talk to Josh's parents. I'm sure they would like to know that I'm being questioned for murder. Especially after charges of being a child molester were dismissed."

"I don't remember disclosing the nature of my visit," Garret insinuated.

"Oooh, you got me. I listen to the news. Why else would you be here? Did Grace tell you where to find me? Because, if I recall, I signed a confidentially agreement."

"Nope. I'm a damn good guesser. Ask your parole officer. Want me to call him for you?"

James uncrossed his arms and stood up straight. His cocky expression faded.

The sergeant took one step closer to James and softened his tone. "I'll need to check your timecard, and if you can give me your neighbor's name and number, it would make my job a whole lot easier."

"I didn't do anything wrong."

"Tell me, James. Do you harass women exclusively when you're intoxicated?"

"What are you insinuating, Sergeant?"

"Your friend at the Hunter's Club. Reputed assault charges. Ring a bell?"

"I wasn't intoxicated, and the friend was my girlfriend.

"I thought the Hunter's Club had rules about dating customers."

"Some rules are made to be broken, I guess."

Sergeant Weston pressed on. "Explain to me why your girl-friend called the police."

"A friend of mine was getting married," James explained. "We had been partying. When I was leaving, I saw Candy in the parking lot. She was coming to work."

"And?"

"She saw me talking to one of the other strippers and attacked me. I grabbed her arms and twisted them behind her back to restrain her. She was trying to claw my face! The woman's a hellion. I would say she was more humiliated than in fear of her life when she made the 911 call," James chuckled. "We made up. End of story."

"You two still an item?"

"No, I broke up with her a couple of weeks ago. I have kids. I need to date a better class of women."

While Garret and James talked, Jake Stramski looked around the room. He didn't see any instruments lying about, nothing that could've been used to remove the button from the red chair.

"I've always wanted one of those stitch removers. Do you have any around?" Jake interjected.

"I haven't removed any stitches today. Check with your doctor," James said, sneering.

"I'll be in touch." Garret flipped a business card at James. "Now, go take care of that sweet Mrs. Pearl and...thanks for your time."

Garret's intuition told him James was being straight up. Nevertheless, he would have one of his guys check out his activities for the next few days, just to make sure.

The sergeant went back to the station to review some of the information he had gathered earlier on James. If not James, then who? His puzzle pieces had too many straight edges that didn't seem to fit anywhere.

# CHAPTER 27

# Recognition

Officer DeMarco knocked lightly. "Miss Simms?"

"Oh gosh," Grace mumbled. "I must've dozed off. What time is it?"

"Ten minutes after five."

"I'm so sorry. Have I made you late?"

"No problem, Miss Simms. Are you ready for me to take you home?"

"Yes, give me a couple of minutes, will you please?"

"Certainly. I'll be right out here."

"Thank you, Officer DeMarco. I just need to make a quick call." Grace gathered her belongings and dialed Jess.

She reached his message center: "Jess, it's Grace. It's about five ten. I'm leaving the office. I'll see you at my house. Don't hurry. I know you've had a busy day."

Grace followed the officer out the door. A woman in her late twenties, early thirties, approached the elevator from the opposite direction. Grace recognized her. It was the same woman Grace talked with by the elevator a week or two ago. Grace recalled how she loved listening to her silky, Southern drawl and how stunning she was with her long, thick, red hair that settled perfectly into place. The cut layers sparkled with highlights. She was tall. Her body appeared toned and athletic. Her breasts showed full and perky in her low-cut blouse. Her plump lips shimmered with tinted gloss. Her eyes, concealed by Harve Bernard sunglasses, didn't hide her shapely brows. Grace was fascinated by her beauty.

"Go ahead," the woman said, letting Grace enter first.

"After you," Officer DeMarco blushed. He seemed fascinated with her as well.

"I've seen you here before," said Grace, trying to engage the woman in conversation.

"Last week maybe?"

"It's possible. My doctor is down the hall,"

Grace expected to hear the woman's southern drawl. Her voice was unmistakable. The low, velvety tone was unique and had stuck in Grace's memory. *What happened to the Southern drawl?* she wondered. The change piqued her curiosity.

"Oh, which doctor is that?"

"Dean or something like that. He's new." The woman didn't offer more information. She kept her eyes glued to the panel of buttons beside the elevator door.

"So many new ones have moved in, I can't keep up with them," Grace persisted.

"May I ask where you get your hair cut? It's beautiful."

The woman didn't speak. Instead, she reached into her purse, pulled a card from one of its pockets, and handed it to Grace.

"Thanks. I'll have to check out this salon." Grace pretended to be interested in the information on the card. Two observations she found contradictory about the woman. First, her hands depicted manual labor with chipped polish, ragged cuticles, and bits of dirt embedded in the corners. Two, she wasn't wearing perfume. Grace wasn't able to pick up any scent on the woman, a fact that seemed unusual for her age, demeanor, and the way she was dressed.

"Is Dr. Dean that good-looking man I see around here occasionally? Tall. Sandy blond hair? Blue eyes?" Grace saw the woman's hand ball into a tight fist, then relax.

"Yes, that's the one." Her words were quick and sharp.

*There is no Dr. Dean in this complex*, Grace thought. *She's lying.*

When the doors opened, the woman darted out. Grace watched her cross the parking lot. The woman was stopped along the way by another woman Grace knew—*Tina.* Tina cleaned Grace's office.

As the two women chatted, Tina's brow furrowed in concern. She rubbed the stunning woman's arm sympathetically while shaking her head. Grace got the impression she was telling Tina a story of woe. When they parted, the stunning woman glanced in Grace's direction and hurried away. Tina headed toward the building with her cleaning cart.

Grace approached Tina while Officer DeMarco waited by his car. "Hi, Tina. How are you?"

"Oh, Miss Simms! I'm fine. How are you? I heard…" Her voiced dropped, implying she knew about the murder.

"I'm fine," said Grace, "although I haven't been working very late. We miss you."

"I miss you too, Miss Simms. Maybe you keep your office and your house too clean?"

"I've had so much going on lately. Sorry, I haven't called you to reschedule my weekly cleaning."

"I understand. You call when you're ready."

"Tina, who was that lovely lady I saw you talking to?"

"Oh, that was Candice, my cousin. She helps me clean sometimes. I brought her to your house once. She's good and she's fast."

Grace's blood ran cold.

"It was nice to see you, Tina," she said, trying to act as though the news had not shaken her.

"You too." The woman squeezed Grace's arm the way she did her cousin's and walked away.

Grace immediately called Garret's cell. When he picked up, she blurted out, "Garret, I think I know who my stalker is."

"I'm listening," he said.

"The woman who cleans my office—she has a cousin, and her name is Candice!"

"Slow down, Grace. Breathe."

"She's about the same height as that suspicious looking person I saw at the Crab Shack. And, I've seen her here, in my office complex. My God, Garret, she cleaned my house!"

"Did you get a last name?"

"No. But I'm pretty sure she's the ex-girlfriend of one of my clients, James Freeman."

"Where are you now?"

"I'm on my way home. I'm with Officer DeMarco."

"Stay with DeMarco. I'm on my way."

Grace heard the stress in his voice. "Yes! Of course."

Within ten minutes, Grace reached home. She unlocked the back door and allowed Officer DeMarco to enter first. Sneaky barked loudly. Grace figured either the dog objected to the intrusion or she needed to go out to do her business. Pam warned Grace it would take time to familiarize herself with the dog's lingo.

"Hi, Sneaky. Everything okay, girl?" When Grace bent down to smooth the dog's fur, she was drawn to shards of glass lying on the kitchen floor.

"Oh!" Grace put her hand over her mouth as her stomach flipped.

Officer DeMarco drew his weapon, motioning to the broken window. His jaw clenched and unclenched while stiff arms held the gun in front of him. Grace noticed his chest wasn't moving. He held his breath as he inched his way toward the sunlit entryway leading into the dining room.

"Stay back," he warned Grace.

Sneaky whimpered as if trying to tell Grace something important. Her fur stood up. A low growl came from deep in the dog's throat.

Grace heard a pop before the thud, and her blood ran cold. She saw Officer DeMarco's body slump to the floor near the entryway. The beautiful woman she had seen earlier stepped into view, sunlight igniting red highlights in her hair like flames. Grace gasped. Her instincts were right: it was *Candy*, now pointing a .22-caliber pistol at her head. Grace held her breath. She watched the woman callously kick the officer's body to check his consciousness before picking up the officer's gun that had slid across the floor. *Remain level-headed*, the voice inside Grace's head instructed, *Breathe!* Candy checked the safety on the .22, pearl-handled pistol and slipped it into the waistband of her slacks. She cocked the .38 special and stepped over the officer's still form.

Grace backed away. She could hear Sneaky's nails click on the tile kitchen floor, but she didn't see where the dog went.

"In the car, Grace," Candy directed in her icy voice. "Come on! You don't want me to shoot your dog, do you?"

The very thought made Grace's heart break. She suddenly realized how attached she had become to her dog. She wouldn't let anything happen to her. But could this woman be reasoned with? *You have to try.*

"Sergeant Weston is on his way, Candy."

"Is he?" Her smile was chilling. "How do you know that he's

not dead already?'"

"I just talked to him. You couldn't have killed him and been *here* at the same time."

"My, aren't we sure of ourselves?"

"I can put two and two together, Candy. You couldn't have had time to do it all. Besides, you left my office just a couple of minutes before I did."

"Oh, you're so smart, aren't you? I'm smart too, Grace, I just wasn't born with a silver spoon up my ass!"

"What?" Now things were beginning to make sense, and it wasn't about her. *This is about James.* "What makes you think I was?"

"James couldn't shut up about how 'classy' you were. We could've been happy," Candy said, bitterly. "He liked being with me, that is, before you stuck your analytical bullshit in his head."

Grace countered, "He came to his own conclusions about what was best for him, Candy."

"He liked the way you crossed your legs, your polished look."

"He felt bad about hurting you when he broke up with you. I assure you, it was never about me, Candy. It was about the kids. He's very protective when it comes to his kids."

"Did he tell you how he fucked me in the kitchen right before he told me he couldn't see me anymore?"

"That must have been humiliating," Grace said with her most compassionate, professional voice.

"He said he needed someone like you in his life—the perfect role model for his little girls. Can you imagine how I felt? We'd make love, and he'd talk about *you*! She mimicked James's tone, 'I wonder what Grace would say about this or that...'"

"Is he worth ruining your life for, Candy?"

"I want him to suffer."

Grace needed to find the woman's conscience in order to reason with her. "I understand, but why Carlos?"

Candy's shrill laughter raised tiny bumps on Grace's skin.

"Carlos Munoz was a regular at the Hunter's Club. Did you know that? He used to bring me gifts, like this little gun here," she said, affectionately stroking the pearl handle of the gun she had tucked in her waistband. "I treated him *real* nice."

"Why did you kill him?"

"I didn't know he was a cop. When he came out of your house

and saw me getting ready to slash your tires, he grabbed my arm to stop me. He recognized me, which surprised me," she sneered, "since I was wearing clothes."

"You killed him because he recognized you? Why didn't you just walk away?"

"I told you! I want James to suffer." Grace sensed the woman was beginning to open up under pressure.

"He's not suffering," Grace pointed out. "He'll find another girlfriend. He'll find another therapist, and he'll get over all of this. What about you? Are you going to be able to get over this, Candy?"

Candy was done with chatting.

"In the car, bitch! I've heard enough of your psycho-babble. Whatever James thought, you don't impress me!"

Grace's heart raced in her chest. Her mind desperately searched for another strategy. "Fine," she said with resignation, "Let's get this over with."

"Shut up!"

Grace moved obediently from the kitchen to the door leading into the garage. Sneaky barked and growled but didn't move. Grace could tell the dog was waiting for the command to rip this intruder's head off. Grace held out hope that Garret would arrive soon. However, hope dissolved when she opened the door and saw Garret lying face down on the garage floor, blood pooled next to his head.

Grace screamed, and Candy whacked her across the face with the gun so hard she split her lip. The pain radiated through her cheek and behind her eye so badly that Grace feared she fractured her skull.

"Wanna try that again?"

"What made you so mean?" Grace couldn't believe she said that out loud.

Candy's laugh was vicious.

"No one has ever asked me that question before. I've been asked about every orifice on my body, but never what makes me tick. Nobody cares about that."

Grace got fragmented images of men stroking her silky hair while their filthy hands wandered up her dress. "Is that what fuels your rage, Candy? Men have been mistreating your whole life?" Grace had to talk fast; her lip was beginning to swell.

"What would you know? Life has been easy for you. When's the last time a guy stuck his dick in *your* mouth when he told you were special?"

Grace's mind flashed to the tiny creature tangled in the spider's web in her neighbor's garage when she was twelve. Releasing the bird was what made her feel special. "You're a hummingbird caught in a spider's web, Candy," she said soothingly. "Let me help you get free." When Candy's eyes began to tear up, Grace felt a glimmer of hope.

"I can't let you do that. I'm beyond help now. I've killed a cop, possibly another. I have to kill you, too…to hurt James."

"No," Grace pleaded, "this is not the way."

"I loved those kids!" the woman cried. "Charming smelled like sweet peas, and Jetta…Jetta reminded me of myself when I was her age. I wanted to do everything like my big sister." A tear rolled down Candy's cheek. "I wanted a baby—little James," she said, rubbing her tummy unconsciously, "handsome like his daddy."

"Are you pregnant?" Grace asked tenderly.

"No! Thanks to *you*! I wanted to be a part of his family! I would've given up stripping. I would have done *anything* to have a future with him. He didn't want me. He wanted you! You! You were all he ever talked about!"

Grace struggled for the right words. "He didn't want *me*," she protested. "He—"

"Shut up!" the woman shouted. "I don't need your lies!"

"He wanted something he couldn't have," Grace tried to explain. "Don't you see? He's broken himself, in many ways. He thought I was whole, just like you do. I'm no different from either one of you. I bleed. I cry. I hope. I dream. I get disappointed. I make bad choices. I dwell on my flaws, on my future. We all have rotten things we go through. You've just had more than your share."

"Shut up! You don't *know* me!"

Desperate, Grace kept talking. She had nothing to lose. "You are *so* beautiful Candy, but you don't let people see what's on the inside. The outside is the part you draw attention to. Packaging may be admired, but it's quickly discarded. You've never learned to love yourself."

"Yeah, now that you mention it, my *packaging* probably wasn't enough for James either. He and that lawyer friend of yours checked out *all* the girls in the club."

"Is he worth ruining your life over?"

"Do you really think you can change my mind, Grace? Do you think your eloquent little speeches will save your life?"

"I was hoping I could save *yours*."

Candy unlocked Grace's car door through the open window on the passenger side. She waved the gun for Grace to move in behind the wheel and then slid next to her. "My life isn't worth saving," she said, reaching towards Grace to jam the key in the ignition.

"My cleaning lady, Tina, thinks so. She spoke highly of you."

"You're a liar." She moved closer and pressed the gun to Grace's temple.

"Truth!" Grace said, knowing she was taking a risk. "When I asked her who you were, her eyes lit up with pride. She said she didn't know what she'd do without you. Aren't you two related?"

"She's a second cousin on my mother's side. She drives a BMW, did you know that?"

"No, I've only seen her at the office." Grace intended to stall her as long as she could.

"Yeah, she makes good money cleaning up after rich bitches like you."

"She said you cleaned my house. Is that when you planted the button from my red chair in my jeans pocket?"

Candy's laughter sounded like nails on a chalkboard. "I can't tell you the pleasure I felt defacing your thrown." She waved the gun in the air. "Now let's go!"

"We're not going to get very far, Candy. You know that, don't you?"

"I said, 'Let's go!'"

Suddenly, her cell phone, still connected to her Bluetooth, rang. The lighted screen showed the call was from Jess. "What do you want me to do?"

"Don't answer it," Candy ordered.

"It's my friend. We were supposed to have dinner together."

"La-dee-da. Drive."

Grace's heart sunk when the line switched over to her message center, but then, suddenly, she had an idea. "I have to clear the call or else my phone will keep beeping."

"Do what you gotta do, Grace. Be smart."

Grace hit number nine, activating the signal linked to the police station and alerting dispatch of a situation. She dropped her phone on the seat, pressed the button for the garage door opener, and put the car in reverse.

The screech the garage door made coming to a halt overhead drowned out the double >click< of the slide retracting on the 9-mm Glock aimed at the back of Candy's head.

"Put the gun down," Garret commanded, between clenched teeth.

"I guess I didn't hit you hard enough," Candy spat, fury distorting her beautiful face.

"Nice and slow." Garret's tone was deadly.

"I'll kill her!" Candy cried.

"And then I'll kill *you*," Garret said, his voice as hard as the metal he held in his hand. His steely expression assured Grace he wouldn't hesitate to blow Candy's brains out. "Put the gun on the seat and get out of the car…now!" He shouted, and Candy flinched.

Grace sat frozen, her eyes pleading with Candy to do as she was told. Candy's face hardened. "Fuck all of you," she said, and before anyone could react, she put the gun in her mouth and pulled the trigger.

Grace screamed as she witnessed blood and dura mater splatter against Garret's chin. It ran down his dark blue jacket.

Within moments, cars squealed into the driveway. Red and blue lights flashed on the garage walls, adding to the surrealism.

Garret spoke, but Grace didn't hear him or notice he had opened her car door. She couldn't take her eyes off Candy's limp body slumped against the passenger door, her lifeless expression accusing.

"Grace!" *Jess?* Grace thought she heard a familiar voice call from a distance. Her head felt as though it had been shoved inside a bell. Sounds echoed all around her. Warmth spread beneath her and her world went black.

\* \* \*

Jess rushed to Grace's side, but of course, Garret got there first. It seemed lately he always got there first. Jess tried to help, but Garret had already scooped Grace into his arms. Jess stepped back. He watched Sergeant Weston carry away his college sweetheart, the girl of his dreams. As Jess turned to close Grace's car door, he caught a glimpse of Candy's bloody wrist dangling at her side. *Awesome.* When he bowed his head to suppress a giggle, he spotted a .22-caliber pistol tucked into Candy's waistband. *Stupid bitch. Should've stuck to something you were good at.* He pulled his shirt sleeve over his hand and lifted the pearl handle. *Careful. Don't want to leave prints.* He casually slipped the pistol into his jacket pocket. What he spied next made him break out in a toothy grin. Lying on the floor was a manila envelope addressed to Grace. *Déja Vu!* He recalled the first time he saw the envelope lying on the seat of Grace's car through the window. He closed his eyes reliving the fear in her voice that day in the parking garage, when Grace called out, "Hello, is anyone there?" He pressed his lips together keeping his merriment contained. *I'll be watching you.*

# CHAPTER 28
# Aftermath

The next morning, Grace's struggled to sit up in her hospital bed. "Jess, the flowers are beautiful. Thank you."

"I didn't send them."

"Oh."

"How are you feeling today?" he asked, eyeing the colorful blooms arranged in the delicate vase.

"Better. The swelling's gone down quite a bit." Grace touched her bruised face gingerly. "It's not as bad as it looks.

"God, Grace, I was so scared," Jess said, sitting on the bed beside her.

"Me too."

"The doctor said he might be sending you home tomorrow. He said another doctor would be stopping by to check on you?"

"Yes. Dr. Meltz."

"He sounds familiar." Jess's eyes squinted, suspiciously.

"He's an old family friend," she said, sweetly. "Speaking of which, when Candy talked about James frequenting the strip club, she mentioned my 'lawyer friend.' Since you're the only lawyer I consider a friend, I have to ask, did you know her?"

Jess's pupils darkened. "Geez, Grace. Do you know how much riff-raff I encounter on a daily basis? Hard to recognize someone with their head blown— Sorry, I didn't mean to bring that up. Anything's possible." Strained lips loosened into a smile. "Can I bring you anything?"

"No, thanks. How are you?"

"Great," Jess said. "I called your mom. Boy, she hasn't changed."

"Did you tell her not to come?" Grace could hear her mother's condescending voice barking orders at the staff.

"Yeah, she said her neighbors saw you on the news. Her phone has been ringing off the hook. I didn't know your dad was in an eldercare home."

"He has dementia. Kind of ironic."

"*Ironic?* In what way?"

"I'm tired, Jess," she said, closing her heavy lids. She had no intention of spilling the beans about her father's indiscretions.

"Okay. Get some rest, I'll see you later." Just as Jess rose to leave, Garret appeared in the doorway. Garret extended his hand. Jess ignored it, blocking the sergeant's entry. "She's tired," he said. "She needs to sleep."

"She's been through a lot," Garret agreed, peering over Jess's shoulder to the petite frame that stirred beneath crisp white sheets.

"Garret?" she called. "I thought that was you." The drugs made her groggy, but Garret's voice stopped her from slipping under.

"I was in the neighborhood." Garret maneuvered past Jess and settled on the edge of the bed, the area still warm from where Jess once sat.

Grace noticed him looking at the flowers. She smiled at him. He smiled back.

No one noticed Jess leave.

"Thank you. They're beautiful. How are you?" she asked.

"I have a headache. Candy walloped me good with that thing hanging in your garage."

"What thing?"

"A spring. Big."

"Oh my God. I meant to get rid of that a long time ago. It was the hydraulic spring from my garage door. It broke last summer. I had the spring replaced. I don't know why I kept the old one. Well, yes I do. I keep everything."

"Me too." Their eyes engaged and held for what seemed like an eternity to Garrett. His heart thumped wildly in his chest. Her lids lowered to his mouth, and she spoke.

"How is Officer DeMarco?"

"He's going to pull through. The doctor said an inch to the left and he would've been gone." He brushed his fingertips across the bruise on Grace's cheek.

"Hurt?"

"Not too bad."

"Doing okay?" he asked, taking her hand.

"Tell me what happened." She let her gaze drop, but didn't withdraw her hand. Her hand belonged in his.

"After I talked to James, I put two and two together. Carlos worked an undercover gig at the Hunter's Club a while back. When I arrived at your place, yesterday afternoon, Candy was already inside."

"She must've had a key." Grace shared her conversation with Tina, her cleaning lady.

"I broke the window to distract her," Garret said. "I knew Sneaky would bark, flush her out. By the time I broke the lock on the garage door, she was waiting behind the door to clobber me with that spring."

"Uh–" she gasped, covering her mouth. "If only I had thrown that darn spring away!"

"It's not your fault," Garret said. "She was clever enough to use anything she found as a weapon."

"She was so troubled." Grace's eyes became misty. "She wanted what everyone wants."

"What's that?"

"Love, family, a *future*."

"Not exactly the way to get started."

"Yeah." Her voice became thick with emotion. "How do you get used to this gruesome stuff?

"Eventually…uh…you toughen up."

"I guess, but when it happens to you, it's different."

Garret squeezed her hand. "You're right. It is different. Life will never be the same. Experiences like this change you. You of all people know that. Can I tell you a little secret?"

"Please do," she said.

"I gauge my life by these kinds of experiences. For instance, today I made it through the day without an incident like Candy's. That made for a very good day." His eyes revealed wounds from days that hadn't been so good, like the sun slipping behind a cloud momentarily and chilling the air before returning its warmth. "You'll be fine," he smiled. "Do me a favor? Take your own advice—talk about it."

"I will. I promise." She choked on her words.

Garret gathered her in his arms and kissed her forehead. He held her close to his heart while she wept.

\* \* \*

Jess returned the next afternoon to pick up Grace from the hospital. She planned to stay with her neighbor, Eli, for a few days until the police finished investigating Candy's suicide and the horror defiling her home was remedied.

"Do you really think you'll be ready to return to work tomorrow?" Jess asked, stroking her arm. Grace pulled away. For some reason, his touch bothered her today.

"What am I going to do? Sit and dwell on what happened?"

"What would you tell a client?"

"I talked to someone; I'll be fine." She stared out the window.

"I stopped by your place this morning on my way to work. The vultures are still swarming."

"You'd think they would get tired of the gore," Grace said.

"Are you kidding me? Reporters thrive on that stuff."

They drove past Grace's house and pulled into Eli's driveway. A van pulled behind him. They heard doors slam. Too late: Cameras loomed and clicked in front of Grace's face. She covered her face, thwarting any chance of a decent shot.

When Jess threatened the TV reporters with lawsuits for trespassing on private property, they scrambled back into the van and sped away. He helped Grace out of the car. She was shaking. She stepped away from his hold.

"I refuse to let this go on," she said. Her tone supported her pure stubbornness. "Garret will take care of these guys. The sooner I get back to my life, the better." She scurried into the house.

"The sooner Garret Weston is out of your life, the better," Jess muttered to himself. Grace stopped in the doorway and turned on him.

"What's that supposed to mean?" She began to see another side of Jess. He had never rivaled for her attention before. Garret posed a threat. The expression on Jess's face struck her at the core of her being. His eyes went flat. His mouth twisted. She had seen that expression during her internship at Folsom prison, working with the criminally insane. *Disturbing.*

# CHAPTER 29

# Back to Work

Sal diligently sorted through papers that had piled up on her desk during her absence. The coffee machine gurgled and spat the last cup of brown liquid into the pot. Grace sat in her office, the door wide open. Garret's men had returned her chair before she arrived that morning. He included a note: "I hope this makes your day more comfortable. —Garret." Today she didn't notice the familiar fit; she didn't care about the heady scent of leather. Today she felt the red chair was bigger than she was, as if she had shrunk.

She looked at the clock. Bruce had arrived precisely at nine. It was now nine ten.

Mentally, she wasn't ready. *One more minute.* She wasn't herself. *Just one more...* At nine-fifteen, she went to collect her client.

"Come on in, Bruce."

"Man, I didn't think you were going to— Wow, who hit you?" Bruce lowered his voice. "There's a mob of reporters downstairs. Did you know that?"

"They were here when I came in," she said with disgust. "I guess they don't have anything better to do."

"Yeah, I guess."

Grace started to scribble the date on her notepad. She hesitated. She didn't know what day it was. *Maybe it's too soon to be back at work.* She checked the calendar. How many days had gone by since Candy blew her brains out? *Focus.* "What's new?" she asked.

"I haven't been to a casino in four days," Bruce announced

proudly. "I decided to quit gambling."

"Why the change of heart?" Grace found it difficult to sound enthusiastic.

"My wife and I talked." Bruce's cheeks colored. He had more zip today than usual.

"What did you talk about?"

"Debra has been riding me for years to go back to school and get my master's in engineering. I looked into it and found I don't have to put in as much time as I thought."

"That's encouraging. What else?"

"We talked about what happened to 'us.' I told her she shoved me into the background all the time; nothing I liked mattered to her." He squared his shoulders. "She actually listened." Bruce seemed more self-assured. "I told her I wanted to buy a sail boat."

"What did she say?"

"Cool. She said, 'cool'!"

Grace made the notation. She waited for him to continue. She wanted to hear the 'terms.' The Debras of this world didn't leave and come back without negotiating. Bruce would be fooling himself to think otherwise.

"We agreed to take things slow," he continued. "She won't move back home, not yet." Bruce's energy dropped. "Maybe when I finish school. There's a job opportunity where her brother works that I'd qualify for. I don't know…it's not in the bag or anything. Anyways, I have to straighten up my act if I'm going to pursue it."

"Is this your solution?"

"It's a start, isn't it?"

"Do you plan to seek marriage counseling?"

"Isn't seeing you enough?" he asked defensively. "Do you think additional counseling is necessary?"

"What do you think?" Her patience wore thin.

"Well, she said she would 'try,' if I got my act together."

"Oh? Did you wreck the marriage all by yourself?" Grace observed the way her words bit through her client's hopeful veneer.

"I'm the one with the gambling problem."

"Why did you start gambling?"

"I won that hundred bucks on a scratch-off lottery ticket. It felt good to win."

"Generally people who need to repeat the feeling that comes

with winning are those who don't feel they're winners in other areas. The high you experienced from winning—how do you plan to replace it?"

"I can live without it."

"There's nothing wrong with wanting to feel good. You need to feel good. Everyone does. Do you see where I'm headed?"

"I'm listening."

"Say you get the job; you get the boat. Will Debra let you smoke your big fat cigars? What happens if she complains about her hair getting blown around? These are issues you need to examine, Bruce."

"I guess you're right." Reality pierced his bubble.

"Perhaps you can focus on the positive aspects, rebuild from there. But the work needs to be done. You mentioned that the two of you like to dance."

"As a matter of fact, I did ask her to go dancing with me this Friday night."

"Who called who?"

"I called her. I wanted to see if she needed anything. That's when we got to talking about me going back to school."

"I guess she did need something after all."

"What do you mean? She didn't ask for anything."

"Control. She needs control over you. Did you miss her having that control, Bruce?"

"That's not fair, Grace!"

"I'm not trying to be unfair. I'm trying to help you take a closer look at your relationship."

"What do you suggest I do?"

"Figure out what you want from the marriage. Find out what she wants. Work from there. You can start clean if you're honest, or you can fall back into the same rut, make-believing everything is fine. Don't mistake control for compromise."

"I thought all I needed to do is stop gambling."

"You need to figure out why you gamble. What's the reward? Is it the money? Does it make you feel better about yourself when you win? Does it make you feel powerful? How about when you lose? Does losing feel so familiar that it almost feels good to you?"

"You're asking all the hard questions today, Grace."

"Think about what you really want," she said. "It's your life we're talking about."

"I will."

"Shall we meet in two weeks?"

"Yeah, sure." He didn't sound convincing.

"So where are you going dancing?"

"The Reunion in El Dorado Hills. Ever hear of it?"

"Yes, a friend of mine mentioned it was a really nice place. I hope you have a wonderful time."

Grace walked Bruce only as far as the door. Once he left, she leaned back in her chair and closed her eyes. Candy's bloody face popped into view. Grace's eyes flashed open. *It wasn't my fault.* The guilt would pass; she needed to keep busy.

"I smell coffee," she sang to Sal as she walked down the hallway.

"I have your cup right here," Sal sang back. Soon, Grace materialized before her, and Sal added, "You don't have anyone until eleven. Do you want to talk?"

"I don't pay you enough for that, Sal."

"We can talk about a raise," Sal replied. "*Or* we can pretend we're *friends.*"

"We are friends. Tell me, what's going on with the boys?"

Sal got the hint: Don't push. Don't pry. "Buns looks too cute with his front tooth bonded. I might have to knock it out again." Grace wanted to laugh, but her lip throbbed. It was so good to have Sal back. Grace missed her company, her jokes, her love.

"How's Sam?"

"I have prom pictures," Sal pulled an envelope from her purse. "Interested?"

"You've been holding out on me!"

Sam, handsome to begin with, looked divine in his tuxedo. The two woman *oohed* and *aahed* over the strapping, six-foot teen and his girlfriend, Alexa, a gorgeous, brunette with hair that cascaded in ringlets over slim, bare shoulders. She wore a midnight-blue, strapless dress that fit snug against her petite form until it reached her hips and flared into a whimsical skirt. Grace tried not to show the ache in her heart. Would she ever have similar pictures to show? "They make an adorable couple." Grace handed the pictures back to Sal.

"Are they serious?"

"Not really. Alexa got a scholarship to SDU; Sam is going to Purdue. I think they've had sex. I heard them whispering about something the day after the prom. Whatever was said was followed with a kiss and a giggle."

"Hmmm," Grace smiled. "You may be on to something there. Sex does make you giggle!"

"Oh?" Sal placed her hands on her hips. "Have you been holding out on *me*?"

Grace donned her most innocent face. "I don't kiss and tell."

"I don't want a kiss; I just want you to share the juicy details!"

"Maybe some other time. We haven't talked about anything yet."

"*We?* Meaning Jess?"

"How do you always manage to pry things out of me so easily?" Grace asked.

"Practice. I have five kids, remember?"

"I missed you."

"I missed you, too. You okay?"

"No, I keep seeing Candy's face. She died so angry."

"I'm sorry, honey."

The phone rang. Sal checked the number on the LED display. "It's James."

"Let the machine get it." They both stared at the phone until the message light lit up. Grace felt a tremor reach her hand.

"I'll be in my office." Grace closed the door. By the time she dialed her message center, her hand literally shook. James' number had appeared on her caller ID every day since the shooting.

Today was the first time he had left a message: "Grace? I don't know if you're at work today," his voice strained. "I've been listening to the news, but I need to know what happened to Candy? They brought her in the ER while I was on duty. Geez...I freaked out. God, Grace, she didn't deserve that." His trembling voice gave way to a few short sobs. "I, uh, I need to talk about this, Grace. Call and let me know when I can come in." He paused. The voice that continued sounded more composed. "And hey, I'm glad you're okay. Bye."

Tears rolled down Grace's cheeks. She shouldn't be at work today. But where else could she go that the horror wouldn't follow? She picked up the phone, started to dial Jess, hung up and dialed

Garret instead. "Sergeant Weston, please."

"I'm sorry. Sergeant Weston isn't in today. May I transfer you to his voicemail?"

"No, that's okay. Thanks." She placed the phone in its cradle, trying to shed the weight of her disappointment. She couldn't sit and wallow. It wasn't in her nature.

To her surprise, when she stepped out from her office, she heard the voice she yearned for. *Garret!*

"Are you flirting with my secretary?" she squealed.

"Uh-oh, you caught me!"

"Go away, Grace. Can't you see he's flirting with me?"

"She's a married woman, Garret."

"I guess I'll have to flirt with you then," he teased.

Sal offered everyone coffee. She was in her glory. Grace took Garret's hand and led him to the waiting area. He looked amazing sitting next to her in the crème-colored chair.

"Pam is looking after Sneaky," he said. "They finished cleaning up your house this morning, but I thought you would need some time before going back home."

"Thank you. I'm going back today. I miss Sneaky. I'm beginning to get attached, you know." Grace hung her head. "She wanted to let loose on Candy. I couldn't let her— Candy would've shot her."

"I'm sure you're right. Have you been sleeping?"

"Not much. I usually cry myself to sleep around three or four o'clock. I know you told me how you go about your business after something of this nature, but I'm not sure I can."

"Well, you can do what I do: count your blessings that you survived it." Garret squeezed her shoulder. "I just stopped by to check on you, make sure you were okay." He moved the curl dangling over Grace's eye.

Sal brought cups of steaming coffee. Garret took a few sips and got up to leave.

"I'm going fishing. Want to join me?"

"I'd love to, but I have clients," she said reluctantly. "James is coming in. It's going to be a messy day."

"Dinner?"

"Rain check?"

"Okay. No pressure." He rose, tall and strong. "Take care. Call if you need anything."

"Thank you, I will." She hugged him tight. He felt more than good. He felt like her future.

***

"Wow!" Sal said, once Garret was gone. "He gets better lookin' all the time!"

"Yeah," Grace sighed. She could still smell his scent on her clothes.

"He's not married?"

"Noooo. Put away your bow, Cupid." Grace raised one brow. "I have enough to deal with right now."

"That's right, the 'we' thing, you were about to share."

"Jess has separated from his wife," Grace paused, waiting for Sal's reaction. Sal wasn't shocked. "I feel responsible in a way."

"Is this the therapist speaking…or the woman?"

"Both. He caught me in a weak moment. It hasn't turned out the way I imagined."

"What were you expecting?"

"I'm not sure. Jess is the only man I've ever had feelings for.

"Until you met Garret?"

"Yes. Now I'm confused."

"They're both gorgeous. I can see your dilemma!"

"There shouldn't be a dilemma," Grace complained.

"Want my two cents?" Sal asked. "Date them both. Get to know them better. Don't feel you have to choose; you don't. It will work out the way it's meant to." Sal placed her hand on Grace's shoulder. "I know you met Jess a long time ago, but do you really *know* him?"

"How can you even ask that? We're best friends!"

"*Friends* are different than *lovers*," Sal said, her words spoken like a seasoned veteran. "Besides, you were a kid then. Kids don't really know shit from shinola, no matter how hard they try to convince themselves and their parents. Think about it."

"I tell my clients to take it slow; become friends first."

"Right, I agree, but that doesn't guarantee the *lovers* part is going to work. If you were to be with Jess now, the rules would change. Trust me!"

Grace knew Sal not only spoke from her heart, but also from experience. Grace could only rely on her gut and what she learned in school. She lacked first-hand experience. "You're right," she agreed. Just then, the phone rang.

Sal popped up to answer the call, leaving Grace time to reflect on when she and Jess made love. This time, when she closed her eyes to relive the experience, Garret came to mind instead.

"Grace, Jess is on line one," Sal announced.

Grace swore his radar picked up her thoughts. It almost felt creepy. She left Sal and closed her office door. "Hey there—"

"Have I told you how beautiful you are, lately?"

"No, as a matter of fact, you haven't." Grace felt her imaginary wings begin to flutter. He was drawing her in.

"Well, you are, which brings me to the reason for my call. I would like to enhance that beauty of yours with a spa day in Calistoga—a mud bath, massage, shopping by the Bay, dinner at North Beach? I have a bottle of Mille Baci. We can walk barefoot in the sand. I hear there's a full moon tonight."

"Sounds tempting. Can I get back to you later?"

"Playing hard to get? God, Grace, my palms are sweaty! How am I going to be able to think! Represent my clients? Poor Mrs. Avonpall could end up serving a life sentence instead of acquiring the homestead left to her by her deceased uncle, Clyde."

"Well, Counselor, that's my answer. Take it or leave it."

"I like a girl with sass. I'll call you later."

She could tell he wasn't going to take no for an answer. "When did you plan to leave?"

"Lunchtime. We can grab a burger on the way. Then again, knowing you, you haven't eaten breakfast. Would you prefer I pick up bagels?"

"So eager to please," she chuckled. "Let me call you later, okay?"

"I'll be checking my messages."

Grace dialed the front desk. "Sal, can you get James for me? I can see him at eleven. What time is my new client coming in?"

"One."

"Thanks."

Grace pulled her Rolodex from her drawer and dialed the hospital. The operator connected her with the psychiatric unit.

"Dr. Meltz, please. Tell him it's Grace Simms." She waited for the doctor to answer his page. A moment later, his voice boomed in her ear.

"Gracey! Good God, woman. You've been making a spectacle of yourself in the news. I always knew you were trouble!" He laughed heartily.

"Next they'll be calling me to appear on Maury Povich. What do you think? Should I accept?"

"I'd hold out for Jerry Springer! Hair pulling, juicy details."

"I'll take your advice into consideration."

"Good, girl, you know I'm always right. Now, what can I do for you?"

"I'm calling about Becky Jensen. How's she doing?"

"She's on twenty-five milligrams of Seroquel, ten milligrams of Lexapro and doing fair. She hasn't said a whole lot in group. She told me a little bit about the fire she was in as a child. She was very angry that Sergeant Weston went snooping into her past. How did he get all that information anyway?"

"I don't know exactly. He has his secret sources—his network of gremlins."

"Well, he broke the bank. I think there is a lot of *dreck* we need to tap into if we're going to help this girl. Are you going to be stopping by anytime soon?"

"I wasn't planning on it, but I suppose I could."

"Good. She likes you. She trusts you. That's important right now."

"Okay. I'll be by later today. Leave me a pass."

"You got it. And hey, come and see me. We'll talk."

"I may do that." She thanked the doctor for his time and hung up the phone. Slumped in her chair, she thought, *no time for a meltdown.* First, she needed to get James out of the muck. Next, she needed to get to the hospital to see Becky. *No time to play either.* She stared out the window. She felt the need to be left alone to lick her wounds. *I'm tired.*

\* \* \*

James Freeman signed in at eleven o'clock. When Grace came to get him he was pale and somber. She followed behind him, closing the door.

"You got your chair back, I see," he said, his voice a notch above a whisper.

"Yes," she replied, running her hand along the smooth red surface. The leather felt cold.

"I'm sorry, Grace. What happened is all my fault."

"You have nothing to be sorry for, James. None of what happened was your fault."

"It was me who pissed her off!"

"Does it feel better to take the blame?"

"I, eh, just wish— God, I wish I could take back the ugly things I did."

Grace listened without remark. James needed to vent his anguish and his remorse. She wondered if berating himself made it easier for him to cry.

"If I hadn't broken up with her, none of this would have happened."

"Breaking up was the right thing to do."

"I pushed her over the edge. I fucked her in the kitchen and then broke her heart!"

"She was troubled, James. You were her quick fix, a BandAid. She needed stitches."

"She needed love."

"She needed help, James. People don't just wake up one day and become homicidal or suicidal. Those kind of feelings fester for a long time."

"Maybe I could have helped her get over some of her problems."

"Maybe, but you have your own issues to resolve first. Relationships—good relationships—start with individuals who know who they are. Two 'whole' people are apt to make a healthier couple."

"That's a little idealistic, don't you think?" James asked.

"Perhaps, but let's say one person has a problem with jealousy. How do you think it will manifest itself in a relationship?"

"I know," he defended, "But I'm more open about that stuff than I used to be."

"Sure, you start out being open, a good sport. Then, say your buddy hits on your girlfriend. At first you don't want her to see that jealous side of you, so you act cool. Maybe the next day it's still eating at you, so you say to something insulting or hurtful. The next time someone looks at her, you react sooner. Hurting becomes easier. Pretty soon it becomes automatic."

"I know I have a problem," he admitted reluctantly. "Candy

and I had a fight in the parking lot of Hunter's because I was jealous. I told that cop it was the other way around." Fresh tears formed. "All those guys stuffing money between her tits, trying to touch that beautiful body of hers—it made me crazy."

"When you met her, you knew that was her livelihood, yet you continued to see her. What changed?"

"The kids. I told you that."

"There was more to it, James. You talked about me; why?" Grace visualized the torment on Candy's face. He talked about her to hurt Candy.

"I don't know. Maybe because when we had sex I was always thinking about where she'd been before."

"She felt she wasn't good enough for you."

"Did she say that?"

Grace was at a loss for words. She stared at the pained expression on her client's face. Her words had cut deep. After a long pause, she took a deep breath and cleared her throat. "Do you see what I'm getting at?" she asked gently. "You both started off with these underlying issues that were bound to escalate in time. Neither one of you knew how to trust."

When James hung his head, wet droplets rolled off his cheeks and stained his jeans. "I liked her, Grace. I didn't mean to hurt her." His body began to shake. He let go and sobbed.

Grace patted his shoulder, her voice soft and consoling. "I know..." Candy appeared in the back of her mind: Candy's caustic words were spewing forth desperation. Grace relived her words: *"All he ever talked about was you!"* In slow motion, Candy pulled the trigger again. Blood splattered everywhere. Grace withdrew her hand from James, swallowed, and tried to blink away the image.

Once James collected himself, he finished the hour with updates on Charming and Jetta. Talking about his daughters lifted his spirits. Grace didn't shift as easily. She felt torn. Part of her smiled and nodded as James told his stories. Another part of her struggled not to blame him for involving her in Candy's death. They made arrangements to meet in two weeks, with an option of meeting sooner. Deep inside, Grace didn't think *sooner* was a good idea.

Deciding to put off the hospital visit until late afternoon, Grace dialed a number on her phone. "Hey, Jess, I'm going to have to take a pass on your lovely offer to go to the coast today. I have a new client coming in, and I need to run over to the hospital. Can I have a rain check? I've always wanted to slosh around in a mud bath. Anyway, we'll talk later." Grace put the phone in its cradle. She stroked the soft, red-leather arms surrounding her. Her chin began to tremble. A tear slipped down her cheek. It was as if she were doing battle with an invisible force. *Myself.*

# CHAPTER 30
# Wilde Defoe

S al knocked lightly once more before entering Grace's office. "Hey, Sleeping Beauty. Your one o'clock is here."

"I must have fallen asleep. Give me a couple of minutes. I was dreaming of Gar– What's his name again?"

"Who?"

"My one o'clock?"

"Wilde Defoe."

"You've got to be kidding!"

"Nope." Sal stepped in and shut the door. Her eyes sparkled with glee. "He's unusual, Grace," she revealed in hushed tones. "I've never seen anyone like him. I'll tell him you'll be right with him."

"Thanks." Grace smoothed her blouse and slacks. She slipped back into her shoes. "Snap out of it," she whispered to herself, fighting a wave of foreboding. She needed to pull herself together. She'd never seen Sal react to any of her clients that way before. If it was worth a closed-door warning, he had to be a real doozy.

"You must be Wilde," Grace said, extending her hand. "Would you like to come into my office?" She knew Sal watched her reaction, but she couldn't keep from staring at the young man. His jet black hair was styled into the longest, stiffest Mohawk she had ever seen. A variety of piercings adorned the young man's chiseled features. His T-shirt fit snug across well-developed pectorals. His arms rippled with definition and colorful tattoos. He walked with a hedonistic swagger, like a runway model strutting his stuff on the catwalk. When he passed, Grace caught a whiff of exotic scents—cinnamon, sandalwood, patchouli, and vanilla. She breathed deeply. He smelled divine. Sal practically hung over the counter fanning herself.

Grace pictured steel doors with bars closing behind her. A wide grin spread across her face as she imagined the snapping sound of a whip. "I have some forms for you to fill out Wilde. Then we'll discuss your reason for coming to see me today, okay?"

"Yeah, sure." Although the young man exuded self-confidence, Grace detected a hint of nervousness beneath the rich timbre in his voice.

When the paperwork was finished, he handed it to Grace and waited for the next step.

"Let's see, you're twenty-eight years old, you're a musician, and your health history looks pretty uneventful. So, what brings you here today, Wilde? What would you like to talk about?"

"I'm not sure I want to live."

"Are you telling me that you're suicidal?"

"Not exactly." Despite his cool demeanor, he struggled with his feelings.

"Have you ever attempted suicide?"

"No."

"Mood swings? Unexplained sadness?"

"I'm not depressed."

"What do think is creating these suicidal thoughts?"

"They don't exactly feel like suicidal thoughts, although I think I've always had a fascination with death." He twisted a ring on each finger of his left hand. When he finished, he began twisting the rings on his right. "I've always wondered what it would be like to die."

An image of a pretty girl in sunglasses floated through Grace's mind. The sound of the gun blast made her bite the inside of her cheek until the image vanished. She hoped her client was too busy fiddling with his rings to notice her wince.

"I have dreams about dying."

"Tell me about your dreams." Grace shifted her weight. Her heart rate increased. *Is it warm in here?* She got up to check the thermostat.

"There's this one dream I keep having over and over. In the

dream, I'm surrounded by dirt, like I'm in a grave or something. I look up, and I see more dirt pouring on me. Pretty soon I can't breathe. I'm being buried alive—or something.

Grace half-listened as the young man talked about dying. Her mind pictured Carlos's coffin being lowered into the ground and loose dirt being shoveled into the hole. She saw Carlos's family standing on one side of the grave, Garret on the other.

"I wake up sweating, gasping for air," said Wilde, stretching his long legs. He laced his hands behind his head and shared another dream.

Grace had to ask him to repeat some of what he said, she couldn't stay focused. Time seemed to be dragging. It wasn't like her to watch the clock. She felt antsy. *I shouldn't be here.*

"I'm going on the road with my band," Wilde said. "Is there something I can do so I don't have these dreams anymore? I have to share a room with another dude. I don't want to freak him out."

Grace explained that fascination with death wasn't abnormal at his age. "Teenagers begin romanticizing about death as part of their growing process." She gave him a few suggestions on how to clear his mind before sleep. She concluded with emphasis on the excitement of performing, his new surroundings, and how a tight schedule would serve as a distraction.

"Our time is up today, Wilde. We can meet when you return from your tour if you want."

"Oh yeah, like definitely." He reached out to shake Grace's hand. "Thanks."

"Before you go, there is something I'd like to ask. She looked up at the young man towering before her.

"Sure, what is it?"

"How do you get your hair to do that?"

"You want to touch it, don't you?" Wilde bent his head down. Grace ran her fingertip along a stiff spike. When their eyes met, his green orbs flickered with amusement. "This stuff called Spike Gel. Lots and lots of it," he said, purring.

After he had left, she noted their session in the fresh binder. She liked Wilde. He was colorful, his persona sensual, yet down to earth. Aside from the reoccurring dreams, he seemed centered. So what was bothering her? She shuddered and smoothed the hair on her arms. *Death.* Talking about death bothered her. Wilde found it fascinating. She found it disturbing. Perhaps a change of scenery would help her clear *her* mind.

\* \* \*

"Sal, I'm going to the hospital to see Becky. Page me if you need me. Grace grabbed her purse from behind the front desk. Sal continued working diligently, nodding her usual "uh-huh" to acknowledge the orders. Grace reached over and gave her a hug.

"I don't know what I would do without you, Sal."

"Don't fluff me, Grace. I was so scared for you."

"I know. Me too, but it's over now," she said bravely. "Business as usual."

"Business as usual." Sal patted Grace's hand, holding back tears. "Go! I'll page if I have any emergencies."

Grace felt a discomfiting presence walking through the garage. She hoped time would lessen her paranoia. At home, she had Sneaky to watch over her. The dog was the one good thing that came from the experience. *And maybe Garret?* What about Jess? Sal's advice came back to her as she slid into her rental car and pressed the door lock.

*Don't choose. Get to know them both,* she repeated in her mind. She didn't know if she could do that. What if she lost them both? She had dreamed of getting close to Jess for so long, yet she couldn't get Garret off her mind. Was she fickle? Now that she had slept with Jess, had the spell been broken? The mystery gone? On to the next acquisition? *No,* she told herself, *I'm not going to be shallow.* Jess wasn't someone to toy with, and Garret was no fool.

\* \* \*

The parking lot at the hospital was under construction. Grace's only option was to park on the street a half-block away, but it gave her more time to clear her mind before she entered the lobby and headed for the psychiatric ward.

"Hi, Ms. Simms. Dr. Meltz left a pass for you. Come on in." The receptionist buzzed Grace through the door and handed her a clipboard to sign in.

"Thanks, Rachel. Is Dr. Meltz still here?"

"Yes, I think so. Check his office. Sometimes he sneaks out without telling me."

"Bad boy!"

"Exactly."

Grace admired the artwork lining the walls on her way down the hallway. Most of the paintings were done by patients. The art varied from watercolors to acrylic, from abstract to land and sea-scapes. "Dr. Meltz?" She knocked politely on the open door frame.

"Hey Gracey! Come in. Lunch?"

"No, no thanks. I just wanted to check in with you before I saw Becky. How is she today?"

"Angry…confused. She hasn't said a whole lot to anyone. I asked her about the fire again; she's not sharing. I increased her medication. I believe I told you that. She seems to be delusion-al. Talks about her angel, some guy she loves. She's not making a whole lot of sense."

"I know what she's talking about."

"Good! Fill me in!"

"When she first came to me, she told me about this man who she thought protected her. She can describe his physical attributes but can't provide me with any details pertaining to his age or where she knows him from. Whoever this man is, he's pivotal. She claims to have approached him at the mall where she worked. I believe it was the day she was brought into the ER and you saw her. Recent-ly, she saw him enter a coffee shop. Although she saw him from a distance, she positively identifies him as the man she refers to as her angel or her savior."

Grace sat in a worn, blue chair and rested an elbow on Dr. Meltz's desk. "Now, in light of the information given to me by Sergeant Weston at the Twenty-Second Precinct—he's the one who found out about Becky's family dying in the fire—there was a man who rescued her from the basement of her home where she was tied up and left to die. I asked Becky about him, but she claims he's not the one. So, I'm still unclear as to who this man is, why she fantasizes about him, or why she considers him her savior. She told me he gave her the ability to hang on all these years."

"Interesting." Dr. Meltz stroked his snow white beard.

"I'm still not clear on how she got into the Briggs shelter," Grace continued. "I thought just extreme abuse cases are accepted, and the waiting list is a mile long."

"A mile?" Dr. Meltz raised an eyebrow as if amused at Grace's over exaggeration.

She blushed. Dr. Meltz was one of the best psychiatrists in California. She felt privileged to be in his company.

"I love to see you blush, Grace. It's refreshing. Now, how are *you?*"

"Tired. Determined to get past this nightmare."

"I was told a woman shot herself in front of you. Is that true?"

"Yes. It happened so fast, I can't tell you much about it. I remember the barrel of the gun pointed at me one moment. When I looked away, I saw Sergeant Weston holding his gun to her head. Suddenly she turned the gun around, stuck it in her mouth, and pulled the trigger. I still see her face. It'll go away, I'm sure, but I met with a client today who talked about death, and it made me uncomfortable to say the least." She lowered her gaze. "When I close my eyes, I see blood spray."

"We can do a little EMDR if you like."

"Do you have time?"

"For you? Of course! Close the door, we'll get started."

The premise of EMDR, Eye Movement Desensitization and Reprocessing, was to have a patient relive a troubling experience while the therapist engaged the client's attention on an external stimulus using rapid eye movement. Doing so reprogrammed the brain's reaction to the incident. EMDR worked well with Dr. Meltz's post-traumatic stress disorder patients.

"Follow my finger with your eyes and tell me what happened."

"Okay." Grace relived the incident over again, giving Dr. Meltz all the details while she followed his finger.

"Now I want you to tell me again, but this time I want to hear about your feelings. Tell me how you felt."

Between Grace's sobbing, they repeated the exercise, each time her emotions becoming less sensitive to the memory. Once she was able to talk about what happened without reacting, Dr. Meltz suggested she remember something pleasant. The first memory that popped into her was head was her birthday at the Crab Shack with Jess. But right behind that memory came the day she met Garret halfway up her stairs and their eyes connected.

"How do you feel? Better?" Dr. Meltz asked.

"Yes, thank you. Maybe I'll get a little sleep tonight."

"You're going to be fine, Grace. And you know we are all here for you. Don't be stubborn. We're all human."

"I promise."

"Okay, let's go see our girl." He reached over and ruffled Grace's hair. When Grace was a little girl, Dr. Meltz would muss her hair; she thought he did it to annoy her. Today, it seemed like something a dad would do.

Dr. Meltz led Grace to the day room to find Becky. She curled up in a chair by the window, twisting her hair. Her thin frame swam in a baggy T-shirt, cut-off sweat pants, and a pair of chenille socks. Her face, void of make-up, looked younger, almost pre-teen instead of twenty-three. She seemed fragile and small.

The girl didn't budge when the couple approached her. She continued to stare out the window, oblivious to her surroundings.

"Hi, Becky." Grace stooped down, cutting off the girl's line of vision.

"Dr. Grace?" she questioned in a foggy voice. Grace sat on the edge of the loveseat and took Becky's hand.

"Hey, how are you?" Grace's heart felt heavy. This was not the same girl who had come to her a short time ago fantasizing about a man she loved.

"Can I go home now?"

"Not now. Maybe soon."

"It smells in here, and I don't like the food."

"I'm sorry, Becky. Maybe I can sneak you in a burger. Would you like that?"

"No. I'm not hungry."

"How are you feeling on the medicine Dr. Meltz prescribed?"

"Like a slug. I have no spit. My mouth feels frozen. I feel like I'm walking on a waterbed," she said, looking around, "but there's no waterbed, is there?"

"It takes time for your body to adjust to the medication," Dr. Meltz interjected.

"Would you like to visit with Dr. Grace privately in the conversation room?"

"I guess."

Dr. Meltz helped Becky rise. Grace followed them to the soundproof room used for therapy sessions.

"I'm sorry things turned out this way," Grace told Becky once they were alone. "Let's talk about what happened, so we can get you thinking clearly...so we get you back home." When Becky responded to Grace's optimistic smile with a blank stare, Grace didn't hedge. "I need you to tell me about the fire."

"We talked about it already," Becky slurred, "the other day, didn't we?"

"A little bit. Let's talk more about Georgie. Did he hurt you?" Grace had to know. *What did her brother do to her?* If she were going to help, she couldn't waste time being delicate.

"No," Becky answered. Grace felt relieved. But if Becky were telling the truth, *who–?*

"The night of the fire your neighbor pulled you out of the basement," Grace's tone became sharper. Inside her temper began to flair. "You were taken to the hospital. The doctors ordered x-rays. Do you remember?"

"Yeah. The doctor kept asking me questions, like you."

"The x-rays showed your ribs and left arm had been broken before the fire." Grace curbed her frustration; her voice softened. She made direct eye contact and proceeded, "How did your bones get broken?"

"I don't know. I didn't know they were broken," the girl replied.

Grace had read about cases of fear-induced hypoalgesia. As with exercise hypoalgesia, the body reduces its response to pain by producing an analgesic response instead. A no-pain, no-gain regimen forces the body into accepting pain as a natural occurrence and adjusts accordingly. In a situation where one's life was at stake, to feel pain would be a hindrance, rather than helpful. Grace's blood ran cold. "Who hurt you Becky?"

"Dan stepped on me."

"What do you mean he stepped on you?"

"One time when I got mad at Georgie for ruining my doll, I hit him. Dan saw me do it, and he threw me on the floor and stepped on me. He told me if I ever hit Georgie again, he'd crush my skull."

Grace wanted to react. "How often did he hurt you?"

"I don't know...a lot I guess. I know he got mad at me once because I didn't cry. I think that's when he hit me in the back with a broom handle. It was hard to breathe, and it left a bruise, but it really didn't hurt."

"Where was your mother?"

"I never saw her when he did stuff like that. I mean, I knew she was there somewhere, I'd hear her crying, but I didn't see her."

"Did you tell anyone he was doing this to you?"

"Who was I going to tell? What would I say? 'My dad steps on me when he's drunk?' He said he wasn't my real dad; he was my stepdad. He felt sorry for Mom; that's why he adopted me." Becky held herself tight, but there were no tears. "He thought he was funny. I was supposed to think he was funny too," she guessed, "except I couldn't breathe." Her eyes looked straight ahead, but Grace knew she was reviewing her past. She didn't blink.

"What else do you remember about Dan?"

"My arm broke the time he pushed me down the stairs. He wrapped it up real tight and made me wear a long-sleeved shirt. It happened during the summer. I didn't have to go to school. Not that it mattered."

"Why do you say that?"

"I went to school with a black eye once. My teacher called my mom. Mom said— She blamed it on Georgie."

"Did your stepdad—?" Grace stopped. She cringed at the word *step*. The bastard deserved to die! She composed herself before she finished the question: "Was Georgie abused too?"

"No, well, my stepdad didn't hit Georgie; he just made fun of him when he'd wet his pants. Dan would put Georgie's wet underwear on Georgie's head and make him wear them." Becky smashed the tiny bug that landed on the table with her thumb. "I tried to clean him up," she said, barely in a whisper.

"You and your brother must have suffered deeply." Grace's throat was beginning to hurt from the strain of holding back her emotions. "Do you want to tell me what happened the day of the fire?"

"No, I'm tired now."

"Tell me about the man. Who is the man with the beautiful eyes?"

"I don't want to talk anymore."

"All right, you get some rest. We'll talk more tomorrow."

"Okay, Dr. Grace." Becky floated out of the room like a little ghost. Grace closed the door and pounded her fists on the table. Dr. Meltz poked his head in the door.

"How did it go?"

"It's a good thing that her stepfather is dead," she seethed, "because if he wasn't, I think I'd kill the son-of-a-bitch myself!"

"Simmer down, Grace," he said and closed the door. "Did she tell you what happened?"

"Yes." Grace broke down in tears.

Dr. Meltz grabbed a tissue and pulled up a chair. He lifted her chin and dabbed her cheeks. "Let's have it then," he said tenderly. Grace couldn't control her sobs as she retold the awful things that happened to Becky and her brother. Drying the last of her tears, she wondered if she were right for this profession. Her heart felt like it was torn and bleeding. Her blank slate, no longer blank, was now scribbled with hatred for the dead man who stepped on a child to exhibit his power. *The weakling!* She felt sick. But who was Becky's angel? Grace still didn't have a clue. Whoever he was, she needed to know, now more than ever. She needed him to give them both hope.

* * *

Grace left the hospital drained. She entertained thoughts of going home, going to bed. It was still early. She didn't want to be alone. She started to dial Garret, but changed her mind. It was too soon. He needed time to heal. She decided to call Jess, instead. "Is your client, Mrs. Avonpall, behind bars yet?"

"Mrs. Avonpall requested new counsel," Jess said. "She wanted a lawyer who didn't have his head in the clouds."

"People can be so demanding." She recalled how Garret issued orders to his men.

*He directed, not demanded.*

"Meet me at the Crab Shack," Jess suggested. "I'll buy you a drink and some fried food. We can talk about how demanding I can be."

Grace laughed half-heartedly. Aside from the crimp in her mood, she sensed he was telling the truth. *He is demanding. Not a good sign.*

* * *

Grace considered leaving her rental car at the office and walking to the restaurant, but quickly changed her mind. *Not ready to leave the protection of my car yet.* She rolled the window down to let sunshine warm her face, to enjoy the remainder of a beautiful day. When she shifted her gaze from her dashboard clock to the lawn area across the street from the Crab Shack, she shuttered. Recalling the fleeting view of the cloaked Candy, she tapped two fingers against her wrist. Like magic, her thoughts were rerouted to the fun she had on her birthday: the pink boa, the fairy dust, the chocolate cake—and Jess. "*Thank you, Dr. Meltz,*" she whispered aloud. The EMDR was working. Her thoughts were redirected automatically to a happy thought.

Jess announced his arrival with a light toot of his horn before navigating a parking space across from Grace. They met half-way to the front door. Jess slipped his arm around her waist. She felt herself stiffen, blaming her reaction on the tension lingering in her subconscious. Hospital visits generally left her blue, but her earlier visit with Becky left her feeling more dismal than usual. Darkness lurked deep inside her soul.

Luckily, they had beat the dinner rush and were seated immediately. Before long, the waitress brought drinks and Grace began to relax, believing it possible the day could end on a positive note after all.

"What kind of greasy food do you want? Without waiting for her response, he said to the waitress, "Onion rings and your calamari—we'll start there." The girl wrote down his order and left. "Get whatever you like, Grace," he said, flipping back and forth between categories of entrees, salads, and sides.

"How do you get away with eating so much grease and not gaining an ounce?" she chided.

"Huh! You should have seen me before, when I put on twenty pounds. Jenna was worried I'd keep gaining. Can't be too fat or too bald—her rules. I thought I looked fine, maybe even more mature."

"You never told me that," she said, sensing herself pull away again. *Not Jenna. Not now.* She concentrated on the menu. It seemed like minutes passed in silence.

"I don't advertise the weight," he said. Grace's mind drifted back in time. "Besides, it's over. Why dredge?"

She peered over the top of the page. She couldn't imagine him heavy. She'd only seen him the way he looked in college, and now—no in-between.

His perception picked up on what she was thinking. He

puffed out his cheeks and crossed his eyes to act silly. She laughed, reminding herself why she called him in the first place. Simple laughter helps one *forget*. Jess was happy to oblige. He was good at it.

"So…were you restricted to celery and carrots?" She wanted to know about the power Jenna held over his self-image.

"Nah. I got more law cases and kept busy. The weight came off eventually. It was one of the most stressful times in my life—the wedding, new career, paying back student loans, trying to fit into a new family. It was not a good time for me."

The waitress brought a plate of calamari, a basket of onion rings, and another round of drinks.

"And," he added, "I missed you. As busy as I was, I always found time to think about you. I'd catch myself reliving old times while driving or puttering around the house. We sure had crazy times, didn't we?"

"Yeah," she sighed. "As I remember, you were a bad influence on me."

"Oh, come on! I think it was the other way around."

"Maybe." Grace donned an innocent smile. The conversation went dry for a moment, each measuring the risk of where the conversation could lead.

"We haven't talked about the other morning yet," Jess started, his hazel eyes darkening to permeate Grace's coy defense.

This time it was she who grabbed for a napkin, wanting something to tear. But she quickly decided her life was messy enough. She opened the napkin and spread it over her lap. She met his eyes. "Let's talk."

"You know how special I think you are," he began seriously, pausing for full effect.

Grace knew his reputation for charming the pants off a snake in a courtroom closing. She prepared herself.

"I think what happened was fantastic," Jess said "I, uh…I just want to know if you still—" He took in a breath. "Do you still respect me?" He held his miserable look until Grace threw a calamari ring at him. She hadn't expected him to joke.

"God, Jess! Get serious!"

"I am serious…about you being fantastic."

That wasn't what she wanted to hear either. *What do you*

*want?* questioned the niggling voice inside her head. "I'm pretty vulnerable right now. I have no regrets about making love with you. Christ, I thought about us for so long, it seemed like it already happened." She held his gaze. "But now that it has, I'm not sure how I feel."

"Are you disappointed?" His tone changed. Now he seemed genuine. His ego was at stake.

"No! On the contrary, everything was the way I imagined it would be—better."

"What's the problem then?"

"Is there a problem?"

"I hope not. I should've married you ten years ago!"

"I wasn't part of your plan. And like it or not, that plan is still a part of your life."

"Don't worry about Jenna. Let me take care of—" His eyes grew darker. "She has nothing to do with us."

"Oh? Suddenly Jenna doesn't exist anymore? We made love; now she disappears from the scene? Out of sight, out of mind? I don't know Jess. I think ten years of marriage deserves a little more attention than that." Grace sounded bitter. How many of her male clients had moved on so quickly. Those who didn't have financial commitments or some sort of dependency issues were good to go before the papers were filed. On the other hand, her female clients seemed to cling to the memories and torment themselves. *Like I have for all these years, like Mom did.*

"Wow. Why does it have to be so complicated? It's not like we're strangers."

"Relationships need to be thought out. We're friends. True, we spent time getting to know one another through the years, but there's still a ten-year gap." She sucked in a short breath. "Sex changes the dynamics." Her parents preached those very words to her when she turned fifteen.

"Of all things, I have to fall in love with a psychotherapist!"

"Well, I have a feeling that if I don't present a solid case, you'll blow holes through it Mr. Lawyer!"

"You're right. This isn't going the way I intended. Let me be plain and simple. I love you. I want you in my life."

"I love you too, Jess. You're my friend, but now it's different, so let's give this change some time. I need to shift gears. I'm not sure how. It's too soon to be your girlfriend. I want you to be sure about your feelings for Jenna. You two have been together a long time. She packed her bags, but she's not out of your life."

"You're right. I need to take care of Jenna, but as far as I'm concerned, it's over."

Grace watched Jess's pupils expand until they reminded her of an eclipse. She was witnessing another side of him. She pressed on. "Trust me, Jess. It takes more than a couple of weeks for a marriage to end."

"Not for me. We've been merely going through the motions."

"Funny thing about feelings: they are so unpredictable," Grace said.

"Maybe you aren't as sure about *us* as I am." His darkening eyes turned cold, but his voice remained even toned. "Is that where this conversation is leading?"

"I have a lot to sort out." Grace clasped her hands under the table and squeezed. "I haven't given myself the chance to let anyone get close to me." The lump was back in her throat, preempting tears that would form if she continued to talk.

Jess relented. "Are you hungry?" he asked, eating the last crumb on the plate. "We can order dinner. Do you want to try the crab legs? We can sword fight?" Once he received a smile, he added, "We'll work it out, babe."

"*Babe* is a term of endearment used to address your wife or your girlfriend, of which I am neither."

She may as well have slapped him across the face. His coolness reached her across the table. Nothing she could say would salvage the moment. It all happened too fast. For years she had yearned for him. Now that he wanted her and wanted a fresh start, she was scared to death. *Of what?* Had fear overtaken her heart? Spoiled the very idea of love? Was it stress? Candy? Becky? Her parents?

No one could be blamed for what prevented her from returning his love. She had held out for a love she thought no one but Jess could give her. Now that he offered his love, she balked. Garret came to mind. *Is he the reason?* Butterflies invaded her stomach…

"I'm sorry, Jess. I'm not in the mood for this discussion. Can we just keep it light for a while?"

"Sure, no problem," he said crisply. "Food will make us both feel better."

They read over their menus in silence. Gone was the playful beginning of their evening.

Grace's appetite diminished, making it hard to decide on an entrée. She settled on a pasta salad. Jess ordered a steak. *Funny how differently men deal with their emotions,* she thought.

"It's good to have Sal back," she said, attempting another topic. "I missed her."

"I can imagine."

"Tell me, what's been going on with you?"

"Not much. I heard about an interesting case today. Kind of unusual."

"What kind of case? Tell me."

"This guy stabbed his wife while asleep. He claims he took medication prescribed by his doctor and can't remember a thing."

"Did the wife die?"

"No, luckily, but she wants a divorce."

"Can you blame her?"

"No, I guess not," he said, matter-of-factly.

"What's the most compelling case you've ever tried?"

"Man, that's a tough question. I think it was when I first passed the Bar and started working for Everett. I think I told you, didn't I?"

"Wasn't that case in Chicago?"

"Yeah, involved a kid." His voice dropped. He grabbed a napkin and began to shred. "I almost quit my job before my career started." He took the small pieces and shoved them aside. "You know how it is when you're the new kid—you get the crap no one else wants."

"Yeah, I know what you mean." Talking about Chicago made her think of Becky and her mood sunk lower. "Did everything turn out all right?"

"It was so long ago. I don't recall the details, but I do remember gaining twenty pounds."

"Where was I?" Grace drew a blank. "Was it when my dad was in that nasty car accident and I had to leave school for a few weeks? I don't think I saw you after that."

"Right, I had just passed the Bar. I was in Chicago preparing for the case. Jenna and I were planning the wedding. I was stressed. I ate Uno's pizza morning, noon, and night."

Grace's didn't care about the past at the moment. Her mind wondered to the young girl she left curled up in a chair with the heel of her sock drooping around her ankle. She felt responsible for the girl's drug-induced state. What were they to do with Becky now? Was her angel with her?

"Earth to Grace."

"Sorry." She moved her elbows to make room for the waiter to set down her salad. They ate in silence.

After dinner, Jess walked Grace to her car. She begged another rain check, too tired for a nightcap. He promised to call in the morning, and they parted ways. Grace pulled out of her parking space oblivious to her surroundings. Suddenly, something caught her eye. She jammed on the brakes and threw the gearshift into park. "What are you doing, Jess? I almost ran you over!"

"I'm sorry. I can't leave without a kiss goodnight." He came around to the driver's door and snatched her out the car and pressed her body against his. She saw desire turn his hazel eyes into dark stones.

"I—" She sputtered and tried to pull away.

His mouth intercepted her protest. His tongue tasted hers with expertise. Relenting, her body molded against his. Holding her tight, he devoured her lips while caressing her lower back.

The blast of a horn brought them back to reality. "Get a room!" the old man shouted, shaking his fist. Embarrassed, Grace got back into her car. Jess followed her home in his.

The moment they arrived at Grace's house it seemed something was missing. *There's no bark.*

Jess stood behind her. His passion hadn't waned. He kissed the back of her neck while she unlocked the door, but once inside, her rigidity signaled him to stop.

"What's wrong?"

"I miss my dog. She's still with Garret."

Jess let out a low whistle, sounding like a tea kettle ready to blow. "Well, good. At least she won't try to bite me." He pressed his pelvis against hers and moaned. "Need help getting out of those clothes?"

"I'm sorry, Jess," she said, backing away. "This isn't working for me tonight."

"I can see you're preoccupied. " He jammed his hands in his

pockets. "Let's hang out for a while, see if maybe later—"

"I don't think so. I need time to—"

Jess stepped in closer. "I can stay and hold you for a while."

"Under other circumstances, I— You— Not tonight. Please understand."

"I do, babe, I do understand, but these magic fingers could be just what you need."

"Babe?"

She asked him not to call her that. *He can't help himself. He needs to feel in control.* Why hadn't she noticed before? Had her heart overruled her head? She knew he felt rejected, but disregarding her wish not to be called *babe* was juvenile, even petty. A bruised ego didn't constitute vindictiveness in her book. "We'll talk, Jess. Thanks for dinner."

"Fine. I get the hint. I'm leaving." His smile fell flat; his eyes turned to steel. "I'll call you tomorrow."

She didn't want to part like this— him angry. She felt a tiny bit guilty for responding to his kisses the way she did. But when she reached for his arm, he shrugged her attempt. She flinched when the door slammed, rattling the glass in its frame.

Grace lay on the bed staring at the ceiling, Luther Vandross's voice wooed in the background. She got up to shut off the music. She wasn't in the mood to be wooed. It felt as though someone had sucked the life out of her. She missed her dog—*and Garret.*

She went through the motions of getting ready for bed in a trance. What was wrong with her? Why did she feel so morose? What happened to the level-headed woman that just turned thirty-one? Miss Independence? The therapist who sat in her red chair giving advice to troubled souls each day? She felt like crying. *Too tired to cry.*

Becky's voice pervaded her thoughts, "*I think about his eyes. I think about the way he looks at me.*" She thought of Jess's eyes, passion filled, wanting her, and pleading with her to want him back. Followed by *coldness.* What had she done? Did she act selfishly? Was she being selfish still— Still thinking about Garret? He moved her. Now she couldn't him off her mind. "Who the hell are you, Grace?" she whispered to herself. Tears didn't come, but sleep did.

# CHAPTER 31

# Torn

Jess pulled in front of his house. He sat in his car, unable to move. He had stuffed his feelings for Grace inside for so long that now it felt like his heart was going to burst. His chin trembled while he reasoned away the years.

He thought back to the day he asked Jenna's father for her hand in marriage. He remembered clutching the small, velvet box in his pocket. His palms were sweaty, his mouth dry. It had been the best day of his life. Engaged a mere six months before he was to leave for Chicago, they had hot sex at her parent's beach house several times a day. They took long walks and made plans. He would finish law school and build their future. Jenna's goal was to plan their wedding and help her dad in the office. He'd make it work. He didn't know about any tingling feelings in the pit of his stomach or what it felt like to love until he met Grace.

He peered out the car window at the monstrosity that stood in the shadows. *Jenna will take everything*. He couldn't let that happen.

*Jenna didn't want to move to Sacramento*. "Why would I want to leave LA for some dead little town?" he recalled her saying. He remembered how hard it was to convince her that it was the best move for his career. He had to bribe her with 4,200 square feet of brick and stone, a gatehouse, and a four-car garage. He also offered an Olympic size pool with landscaping that would dazzle any garden or ladies club. The house kept her busy. A membership to the country club gave her the opportunity to play tennis and socialize in style. He could not care less. He didn't like fake people. They bored the hell out of him. She was content.

He sat motionless in his car, staring at his palatial peace offering. Memories poured into his head.

After he had graduated college, he and Grace talked on the phone two or three times a week. Everything was fine until one day Jenna decided to open the phone bill and went ballistic. "Daddy's not paying the bills, so you can carry on with some *nothing!*" Jess hated when she meddled in their finances, but also hated her guts when she belittled Grace. He finger combed his hair. *So much to lose all the way around.* His head hung low. Brick and mortar can be replaced, but *I can't let her slip away once—*

He turned toward their bedroom window. Dark. *Jenna, Jenna, Jenna.* He envisioned the conversation that took place in that room.

"Do you remember Grace?" he recalled asking Jenna the day after they moved to Sacramento. When Jenna didn't answer, he said, "I heard she lives in around here somewhere. I thought I'd look her up and maybe go for a drink. She may be able to throw some business my way." Jenna glanced over at where he stood, her face unreadable. He scrambled for something to say: "Small world, huh?"

Jenna gave him one of those you're-fucked looks and walked away. *I shouldn't have told her. She went right to her father.* His jaw tightened. He thought about how their marriage had been a farce from the beginning, but Jenna had served his needs. *A stepping stone.* He never imagined meeting someone like Grace.

Jenna had been resentful of his relationship with Grace since they met in college. Jealousy? Hard to tell since Jenna was raised to believe she was better than everyone. But the only time she ever said anything was when she discovered Grace's number on the phone bill and gave Jess the third degree. "Is she married yet? I know you, Jess." Jenna flipped her hair and checked her lipstick. "Grace isn't your type. Why would you want her in your life?" And Jess wanted to wipe the smirk off her face when she added, "Maybe that's what intrigues you. You've always had a thing for the less fortunate."

Jenna's statement couldn't have been further from the truth. Grace came from a fine background. He was the square peg. He's the one who didn't fit in with her family, *and* he was more than intrigued with Grace. He wanted to smell her hair on his pillow and feel her tender lips trail down his stomach, teasing him below the belt. He wanted to sink deep inside her, feel her oscillate against his hips. Jenna never had a prayer.

Grace filled the space behind his closed lids. He was afraid that she didn't feel the same and wanted to let him down easy. He pictured Garret. The man Grace found so easy to talk to. He pounded his fists on the steering wheel. He knew he married the wrong girl, but he had to stick to "the plan."

For the first time in his life, he opened his heart. Loving Grace hurt so bad. He opened his glove-box and stared at the pearl-handled gun that fit snugly inside the black leather pouch. "If things don't change," he whispered, "somebody has to go."

\* \* \*

After a fitful night's sleep, Grace rose to start her day. Her pensive mood from the previous day lingered. She felt like a mannequin, dressed in a grey, silk sheath and flats. She grabbed a sweater and went downstairs.

Her cell phone rang as she was about to drop it into her purse. A smile warmed her face. "Garret?"

"I didn't go fishing after all." Her heart skipped a beat. "Hey, listen, I understand client information is privileged, but I just wanted to pass on some info that might help Becky Jensen." She wanted him near, to see his eyes when he spoke. His voice sounded sad.

"I'm listening," she said.

"I talked to a social worker in Illinois by the name of Sylvia Sanchez. She told me Becky's medical records, along with the court papers that got her transferred to Briggs are here in Sacramento. Maybe your friend Jess can get a hold of them for you. They may help."

"Thank you, Garret. Does this woman have a number?"

"Yes, I can give you her information. It's in the office. Do you need it now?"

"When you get a chance. I can wait until you're able to go back to work."

"I don't feel bad physically. You know the drill. It's procedure to take the time off when a partner dies on the job. My superiors would be thrilled if I were on *your* couch right now, but, under the circumstances—"

"I know. I'm sorry I can't help you, Garret, but please talk to someone. If you need a recommendation, I can give you names of some excellent therapists."

"And what do I do about you?" he blurted.

"What do you mean?"

"Never mind. I was just thinking out loud."

"I'd like to know what you meant," she insisted. She heard rustling and crunching coming from his end of the phone. She smiled knowing, *he's shuffling his feet.*

"I like you," he said. "You must have sensed that by now."

"I like you too," she said, pressing her palm to her cheek. Her words sounded like an understatement. "And we work well together, I might add." It was her turn to feel awkward.

"When this all blows over, will you marry me?"

Grace's stomach dropped to her toes. Her cheeks flushed. The door to her heart flew open. She slammed it shut. His question was overwhelming.

"No." She swallowed, pushing back her fear. "But I'll accept an invitation to dinner."

"Sorry. That slipped," he laughed. "How about dinner with me?"

"Oh? So now you don't want to marry me?" she teased.

"Agree to dinner first; we'll see what happens during dessert." His voice was low and sexy. Grace began to melt.

"I'd love to have dinner with you, Sergeant," she replied.

"I don't eat green stuff. Is that okay?"

"I remember, but that will change once we were married." A giggle escaped her lips. She felt sixteen again.

"Well, you'll have your work cut out for you," he challenged. "I'm one hundred percent carnivorous."

"Hmmm, I think I know where we'll be going for dinner then."

"Good." As though he sensed her time constraint he said, "All right, I better let you go, and I'll call you with that phone number."

"Thank you." She held the phone to her breast. Her heart sang.

# CHAPTER 32
# Indiscretions

Grace listened to Bruce drone on and on. "Debra said she wanted to make it work, and then she stands me up! I waited at the restaurant for an hour! I felt like an asshole, sitting there by myself and making excuses. So I left and went to the casino. What was I supposed to do? Shit, at least the babes at the casino show me more respect!"

"They want the tips, Bruce. Don't lose sight of what they're there for."

"I would've spent that money on Debra. That restaurant wasn't cheap!"

"You have every right to be angry, but let's be realistic here, Bruce. Who did you hurt by blowing the money at the casino? Did you hurt Debra?"

"No." He looked away. "How could I hurt Debra? She didn't show up!"

"Let's start from there then, shall we?"

"You're right," he admitted. Anguish furrowed lines between his brows. "I felt like crap when I lost all that money." He hung his head low and forced a chuckle. "At least I had a little fun doing it."

Grace remained silent.

"I believed the bitch when she said she wanted to talk, work things out." He sighed and shook his head. "You're right," he sneered at Grace. "I'm a chump. Damn her!"

"Something tells me there's more to this story than just the gambling."

"I wouldn't have been there," he moaned, balling his meaty hand into a fist. "I wouldn't have—" He pounded his knee. Then he pinched his lower lip.

"I'm listening," Grace coaxed, cocking her head to one side.

Tears threatened to fill his eyes. "I met a woman at the casino." He paused. His cheeks pooled with deep red. "She was sitting next to me at the slots. She smelled nice." The corner of his mouth twitched involuntarily. "We made eye contact, and she smiled. We talked a little about the machines. I asked her if she was having any luck and she said, 'Now I am,' referring to me." He placed his hand over his heart. "I bought her a drink. We walked around a little bit, and I asked her to dinner."

"More drinks?"

"Yeah," he snarled back. "Oh, so you think a woman has to be drunk to be interested in a guy like me?"

Grace didn't dignify the question. "Go on," she said, doodling on her pad. She had no comment and no opinion. She felt no compassion. In the back of her mind, she pictured her dad and Dr. Meltz's wife giggling in the dark. Grace pulled her skirt tight around her knees and restored eye contact with Bruce, willing the memory to disappear. Bruce hadn't noticed she wasn't listening. He kept on talking.

"Then she sat next to me at the table in the restaurant. Hell, I can't remember Debra ever sitting next to me like that, even when we were dating!" Bruce perched on the edge of the sofa and grinned proudly. "Renita—that's her name. She started rubbing my leg, and when she talked to me, she leaned forward. Her—" Bruce started to hold his hands away from his chest, but when he caught Grace's cold stare, he reconsidered. "Her breast kept brushing against my arm." He began to squirm. "Need I say more?"

He wiggled his eyebrows and flashed Grace the knowing smile people sometimes gave when referring to sex.

Grace tapped her pen under her chin. "Is there more to say?"

Bruce practically frothed at the mouth. He was dying to tell someone about his escapade. *It's my job to listen; let him brag.*

"She—Renita—is from Virginia," he went on to say. His sweaty palms rubbed his tan, perma-pleats. "She's staying at the Best Western in Sacramento."

Grace tuned in and out. Her disgust jostled a memory of when she was a little girl. Her dad's friends sat around in lawn chairs drinking beer and scotch while they bragged about the babes they picked up at bars during the medical conventions. Meanwhile her mother and the other wives gathered in the kitchen exchanging recipes and information on the best schools.

"Her job brings her this way twice a year," Bruce said. "She gets lonely. We hit it off, and like I said. She 'encouraged' me."

*Here we go again with the blame game,* Grace thought. Bruce couldn't take responsibility for having sex with Renita. She led him to it. She seduced him. There was always a good enough reason; it was always someone else's fault. She decided to let him hang before putting the mirror in front of his face. She looked at him dead on. She saw a glimmer of herself. Sometimes people fall into bed with the wrong person. Why? Because they're lonely? Scared? *This isn't about me.*

Grace waited for Bruce to speak. The sound of the ticking clock grew louder as the silence continued. When her client wiped moisture from his forehead with his sleeve, Grace figured he had reached his breaking point, so she proceeded. "Did you go back to the motel with her?"

"Why not? My wife stood me up! But you think it was wrong, don't you?"

"Do you think it was wrong?" Grace asked.

"No!"

Grace wasn't convinced. Locking eyes again, she forced him to confront his behavior.

"I know," he whined. "Technically, I'm still married to Debra." He thumbed the gold band back and forth on his finger as his mood darkened. "Hell, *she's* the one who walked out on me, dammit! She stood me up," he cried, hammering his fist into the air.

Beet-red color faded from his face, returning him to his uni-beige self. "It's clear she doesn't give a shit about me," he stated flatly. "So no, I don't feel guilty!"

Grace didn't feel triumphant. He still wasn't taking responsibility. She glanced at the clock. *Ten more minutes.* "Renita knew you were married?" she asked, gesturing to his gold band. "And she was okay with that?"

"Yeah, more than okay. She mentioned it right away."

"What did she say?"

"We were at the restaurant. She picked up my hand, looked at my ring, and asked me if I was a happily married man—or a married man she could make happy?"

Bruce smiled. His knees knocked together. He wanted so badly to share his evening. A knot formed in Grace's stomach. Her concentration unraveled further as Bruce described his sexual escapade with a woman he'd known for less time than it took to do a load of wash. She remembered her mom and dad arguing in the kitchen. Her mom crying, *"Did she make you happy?"* The bitter accusation hung in the air before her father stormed out the back door and her mother cried after him, *"Did she?"*

Grace hadn't thought of the implication until now.

After Bruce left her office, Grace stared out the window, sorting her past. Sal interrupted to say, "Jess called. He wants you to call him. Garret Weston called twice. He said he has a phone number for you. Check your cell."

For the first time, Grace noticed Sal wasn't her usual vivacious self.

"You okay, Sal?"

"Fine, why?"

"I've known you forever. I can tell when something is bothering you. Want to talk?"

"No."

"Now you have me worried."

"Maybe later."

Grace closed the door. There was no need to add Sal's problems to her plate. Instead, she checked for messages on her cell phone. While listening for options to retrieve her voice mail, her mind wandered back to Sal. She started feeling selfish for being consumed with her own problems of late. "To listen to your messages," the recorded voice prompted. Grace pressed one. The voice she heard next was a welcome relief.

"It's Garret. I have that number for you. I have something else for you, too," he teased. "Call me."

Grace was about to dial Garret when the flashing red light caught her attention.

She didn't wait for Sal to answer the call. She recognized the number. It was Yolanda.

"Hey, Yolanda, what's up?"

"Grace, can I come in and see you…by myself?" Yolanda's voice sounded raspy, as if she'd been crying.

"Sure, it sounds like you need to talk. Let me check with Sal to see if I have any openings this afternoon."

Grace put Yolanda on hold while she arranged an appointment for one o'clock. There wasn't much time for lunch. Grace's stomach growled. She wished she could reconsider the doughnut she passed up this morning. She willed the vision to reach her taste buds. The light tap on the door came before she had a chance to salivate.

Sal poked her head in the door. "I'm ready to talk," she said, rolling her eyes. "Do you have a minute?"

"Absolutely."

Sal refused Grace's offer to sit. "I got the results of my mammogram," she said, as she paced the length of the room. "I have another tumor. My doctor set me up for a needle biopsy. I need Friday off."

"Oh, Sal. I'm *so* sorry you have to go through that again. Would you like me to go with you?"

"No, thanks. John's taking the day off. He wants to be with me."

Grace rose and closed the gap between them and hugged Sal tight. "We're all here for you. Everything is going to be all right." Grace wanted so bad to believe it would be. She held her friend in loving arms and let her cry.

By noon, Grace's head began to ache. The weight of the world on her shoulders pinched a nerve in her neck. She swallowed two aspirin with cold coffee on her way out to pick up a sandwich before Yolanda was due to arrive. She started to dial Jess on her cell phone but stopped. She wasn't in the mood to be cheered up. She wanted to be alone to think about Sal. *What can I do?* Sal didn't want her pity. *I'm feeling sorry for myself because of the possibility of losing Sal.* She held back tears. *If anything happens to her—*

Grace sat near the window at the deli to wait for her order. A woman walking by stopped and put her face to the window. She was startled by Grace on the other side of the glass. When the woman left, another person took her place. She saw Grace, and jumped back. Grace didn't hear her name being called to pick up her food. *That's what I do. I'm an outsider looking into windows. I peer into the hearts and souls of other humans, just as these people are looking inside this shop. I know something is on the other side, and yet...I'm surprised when that something stares back at me.* She had known Sal was concerned about something. Why was she so shocked to find out it was true? Grace picked up her order and headed back to work. Her appetite waned; her heart felt heavy.

Grace turned the corner in time to spot Garret leading Sneaky on a leash into the lobby to her building. Her mood lifted.

"Garret!" she called. He smiled and waited while Grace greeted Sneaky with enthusiasm. The dog stuck her tongue out, ready to lick, but resorted to nudging Grace's hand with her snout instead. "She remembered the rules. Did you see that?" Grace asked.

"She missed you. Didn't you, girl?" Garret fluffed the dog's fur, dodging the whip of her tail. "Is that lunch?" He pointed to the bag tucked under Grace's arm.

"Yes. I have a client in fifteen minutes."

"How about dinner later? I'll bring Sneaky by."

"I'd love to have her home. I'm not sure about dinner though."

"Okay, no problem. Another time." Garret turned his attention to the dog.

Grace sensed his disappointment.

"Yes, I would like that," she said, her eyes connecting with his. "No green stuff, right?"

"You got it." He smiled. His eyes devoured hers in small, tender bites.

"What time should I bring her by?"

"Can I get back to you? I have a late schedule tonight."

"Okay," he said, touching her wrist. "Call me then."

"Thank you for bringing her by. That was thoughtful."

Grace hugged Sneaky and then turned to Garret. He pulled her close, his arms wrapped around her like a cloak. His body, pressed against hers, felt warm and safe. He felt *good*.

# CHAPTER 33
# Confessions

Grace emerged from her office, still chewing her lunch. At one o'clock, Yolanda walked through the outer office door. Her big, dark glasses looked out of character on her small round face. Her long hair, worn up on warm days such as today, clung to her face and neck.

"Hi guys! Did I miss anything?" Sal asked, following behind Yolanda. Sal bee-lined for her file drawer to pull Yolanda's chart.

"You're timing is perfect. Yolanda just got here." With file in hand, Grace escorted the young woman to her office.

Yolanda removed her dark glasses, revealing red, swollen eyes. *No bruising.*

That was a good sign.

"What's going on, Yolanda? Tell me."

"Chris would kill me if he knew I was here."

"What happened?"

Yolanda didn't answer. Tears flooded her eyes. Grace suspected fear pushed her words back into her mind, but when Yolanda's shoulders began to shake, Grace knew Yolanda's emotions needed to speak first.

Grace impulsively reached out and tucked her client's thick hair behind one ear. Yolanda tilted her head to one side, confirming Grace's suspicions. Grace examined the marks on her neck. When she finished, Grace handed Yolanda a box of tissues and lowered her voice to a soothing tone. "What's going on?"

"When I first got pregnant, I was having problems getting

aroused," she explained. "Chris brought home some porn movies, thinking it might help." Yolanda dabbed her eyes and waited for Grace's approval before continuing with her explanation.

"It's okay. Go on," the therapist reassured.

"They were all pretty stupid, but this one got us both turned on," she said, staring at her lap. "The guy tied this woman to the bed, something Chris and I had joked about but had never tried. Then he slipped this silk scarf around her neck as he kissed her. I'm sure you can guess the rest."

"I get the picture."

"Anyway, Chris wanted to try it, so we did."

"Was it consensual?"

"At first it was," Yolanda sniffed. "Chris likes to experiment."

"It's called erotic asphyxia. Did you enjoy it?"

"It's kind of...adventurous," Yolanda said.

"It's also very dangerous."

"We, uh...we did it up until the baby was—" Yolanda's tears spilled before she completed her sentence. Grace waited patiently until Yolanda was ready to purge her tormented heart. "I feel so guilty! It was selfish! I shouldn't have let him do that to me. I didn't mean to hurt my baby!" she sobbed.

"What do you mean?" Grace's blood ran cold.

"Chris wanted to do it when I took off of work that last week. I said no, but he hounded me. I should've—" Her head fell into her hands. She fell apart.

Inside, Grace was numb, fully aware that erotic asphyxia, the act of choking a partner at the point of orgasm, was life threatening, but there were always people who liked living on the edge. "Did you tell your doctor?"

"No!"

"He didn't see the marks?" Grace suppressed the ire, about to reach its peak.

"We were always careful not to leave any."

*But not careful enough to consider the life inside you.* Grace fought to keep her cool. "You have marks now. What changed?

"Chris has changed."

"In what way?" Grace thought the guy was a jerk from the get-go.

"He wants me to suffer," Yolanda cried.

"Does he say that?" Grace was pitching for any excuse to lock his ass up.

"I see it in his eyes."

"Words are better proof."

"You don't believe me?" Yolanda asked.

"I believe you. I'm just saying that unless you're a mind reader, you can't be sure of what he's thinking unless he says it."

Yolanda stared at her shoes while she stroked her bruised neck.

"Yolanda, is Chris getting rougher?"

"Yes."

"And you've told him to stop."

"Yes."

"Do you still get aroused?"

"Yes."

"Okay, so there are some mixed signals here."

"Yes."

"Are you afraid of him?"

"Yes."

"What do you want to do to stop him from hurting you?"

"I don't know, Grace. I love him; he loves me."

"No, Yolanda. Deliberately hurting someone is not love. It's cruelty."

\* \* \*

Grace didn't plan to go straight home after work. She walked to Capitol Park to meet Jess. She sat on a park bench, opened a white paper bag, and threw the remainder of her lunch to the squirrels. Jess joined her minutes later.

"Hi, beautiful," he said, planting a light kiss on her cheek

"Hey," she responded. Her focus remained on two squirrels fighting over the same hunk of bread.

"What's up? You look sad."

"It's been a crummy day."

"Talk to me, Grace. I'm here for you."

"Somehow those words feel like they're biting me in the ass."

"What's wrong?"

"Everything."

"Tell me about *everything*," he proceeded tenderly.

"I can't Jess, I don't— I don't know how." Her face twisted with pain. Tears began to flow. She couldn't say what hurt or why. All she knew is that it wouldn't go away. And whatever *it* was, consumed her.

Jess felt helpless. He wrapped Grace in his arms and held her while she cried.

He wanted to say and do the right thing, but he knew Grace had a problem he couldn't fix.

His problem was he needed to be needed. He couldn't expect that to happen with her.

She was self-reliant and independent. Her problems were hers to solve. She wasn't going to let him in without a fight.

He wiped her tears away. He had to try.

"Do you want to talk about it?"

"No," she sniffled

"Oh, I see. You're the only one who can fix things."

"Is that what you think?"

"Why would I think any different? You never share what's bothering you, except maybe with Sergeant Wonderful. When it comes to me, everything is privileged information!"

"That's not true!" She stood, dumping the bag of crumbs on the ground. The squirrels bolted and hid behind a tree.

Jesses voice rose with sarcasm. "Maybe you should give yourself *and* everyone else around you a break!"

"What's that supposed to mean?" she huffed, arms akimbo.

"Getting angry? Good! That makes you human like the rest of us!"

"I don't need this." She turned to leave.

"Fine. Go," he conceded. "Go home and be miserable. Don't let me in. Why should today be any different?"

"What are you talking about?"

"You've had a shield around you since the day we met."

"First off," she fumed, "I am *not* miserable. I'm troubled at the moment."

"Well, I'm sure you'll find a logical explanation for it."

"Why are you attacking me like this?"

"I'm frustrated. I can't get close to you, no matter how hard I try. You just won't let me in."

"How can you say that?"

"Do you remember the night we went skinny dipping in Lake Michigan?"

"As I recall, I went skinny dipping. You were still dressed."

"I *felt* naked. I told you I loved you that night. Do you remember?"

"We had been drinking!"

"See, there you go, a logical explanation." Jess shoved his hands in his pocket and turned away.

"You were getting married. We were drunk. What was I supposed to think?"

"You're right." His eyes flashed her way. "You're always right."

"No, I'm not. I wanted you so bad that night. I was afraid!" She reached for him. He pushed her away. Grace flashed on Becky's face. *"He pushed me away, Grace."*

Grace took a deep breath and exhaled a sigh. "I'm sorry, Jess. I didn't want to lose you. You were my best friend."

"And now?"

She answered him with a kiss.

He took her home.

* * *

The phone rang, interrupting their lovemaking.

"The machine will get it," Grace said, ignoring the ring.

Jess leaned on one elbow, "Are you sure? I can start all over again," he said nibbling her neck.

"I'm sure," she sighed. "It's probably my mom. I haven't called her in a while."

"In that case I think you should answer it. You two can have a stimulating conversation while I stimulate something else."

"You are so bad."

"That's not what you were saying a moment ago." He teased her earlobe with his tongue, and she giggled. When the voice came over the answering machine, they stopped playing to listen.

"Hi, Grace. It's Garret. I had planned on bringing Sneaky over tonight, but something came up. I hope you'll forgive me. I know Sneaky won't," he added. "She misses you." When Garret's voice paused, Grace's heart reached her throat. *He sounds so melancholy.* "Well, I'll give you a call tomorrow," he finally said. "Again, I'm sorry for canceling. I promise to make it up to you when we have dinner. Take care, bye."

The answering machine clicked, rewound the greeting tape, and beeped once announcing that a message had been left. Grace and Jess remained quiet.

Grace suspected Jess knew the police sergeant was interested in her, but what he didn't know was how she felt about him. "Sorry, I forgot to tell you Garret was supposed to bring Sneaky home later tonight. I've been so wrapped up in *me.*"

"You agreed to have dinner with him?" Jess's voice was crisp.

"I like him. He's nice." The knot tightened in the pit of her stomach.

"Wow, why do I feel like I'm in fifth grade all of a sudden?"

"You don't look like you're in fifth grade," she said stroking his leg.

"That's not going to work, Slick." He pushed her hand away.

"Did you just call me *Slick?*"

He glared at her.

"Oh, Jess." She rolled over, pulling the top sheet with her.

He grabbed her arm. "Can we talk?"

"Now?" she said pulling away.

"Yes, now."

She propped the pillows up against the headboard. "Do you want some coffee?"

"No, I want to know why you can't talk to me."

"Isn't that what we're doing?" She adjusted the pillow behind her back.

"No, you're avoiding me."

"In what way?" she asked, picking fuzz off the blanket.

"I asked you a question," he said. "You didn't answer me."

"Okay Counselor, what is it you want to know?"

"How do you feel about this guy?"

She rolled her eyes. "Don't tell me you're jealous?"

"Are you going to analyze me or answer the question?"

Grace got out of bed, pulling the sheet with her. She wrapped the sheet around her body, stalling for time. Although Jess was right that she was attracted to Garret, she didn't like Jess's tone. He sounded overly possessive. "Do I ask you about Jenna?"

"What do you want to know?" he challenged.

"I don't want to end up like some of my clients, Jess. Can't you understand that?"

"So what am I now, your occasional bed buddy?"

"Aren't you forgetting one tiny detail? You're married! Separated doesn't count; technically you're still married!" She tightened the sheet around her, yet she still felt naked and ashamed. "I have broken every vow I have made to myself by being with you right now!" The clarity of what she had gotten herself into hit her hard. "You're married. That makes me the other woman, and that's not who I want to be."

"Do you want me to leave?"

"That's probably a good idea." Her eyes pleaded with his. "We're not in college anymore, Jess. I'm not the same Grace you knew back then, and you're not the same—"

His eyes darkened. His words turned frigid. "This is about Weston, isn't it?"

"Please don't do this, Jess. We've known each other a long time. Don't make it ugly."

"I see. You can talk to Weston about everything, and I'm left in the dark."

"Because I don't talk to you about what? My clients? About Becky?"

"Well, well, that's the first time you've mentioned a client's name, do you know that?"

"God, Jess! Do you talk about your clients?"

"Not by name, no. But I've shared cases with you, stories about some of my clients."

"I can't talk about Becky! Her case upsets me too much."

"Okay, *that* I can understand." He reached for his pants lying at the bottom of the bed and slid into them. "It must be the name," he muttered.

"What's that supposed to mean?"

"I had a client a long time ago who upset me. Her name was Becky, too. She was barely fourteen years old. It was that case I worked on in Chicago, you know, my first real litigation case."

Grace sat down on the bed, her heart beat wildly. Her suspicions grew.

"How long ago, Jess?"

"It's been about nine years, I guess."

"I need to know what happened."

"Why?"

"Please, Jess, this is important."

"It was an unusual case. The girl's family died in a fire. She inherited the property. She was under age, and the circumstances were pretty nasty. There's an organization that houses abused women here in Sacramento, and the woman who runs the organization was a friend of the woman handling Becky's placement at the time. Anyway, long story short, I filed the necessary papers to get the property settled and get her in the home."

"Did you ever meet the girl?"

"Yes."

"What happened when you met her?"

"Why?"

"Please, Jess," she begged.

"Well, after we finished with everything, she hugged me."

"What did you do?"

"After I pried her off of me, I reassured we'd get through everything together."

Grace got goose bumps.

"Do you shop at Nordstrom?" she wanted to know. There was an urgent edge to her voice.

"What's with the questions?"

"Do you shop at Nordstrom?" she pressed.

"Sometimes."

"Has anything *strange* ever happened to you there?"

"Why the hell are you—?" He studied Grace's face for a moment before it clicked. "Yes, there was this girl–" Jess's jaw dropped. "She— Oh no."

Grace froze.

"It's you— You're *him*!"

# CHAPTER 34

# Reunion

Evening visiting hours had just begun when Grace and Jess arrived at the hospital. Becky was not in her room. She was slouched in a chair in the dayroom when Grace and Jess walked in.

"Becky?" Grace called excitedly, "I've brought someone with me."

Becky didn't look up. "I don't want to talk today, Grace. I'm tired. My tongue feels like it's moldy."

"Maybe we can do something about your medication, but right now, I want you to meet someone." Tears glistened in Grace's eyes as she beckoned for Jess to come closer.

Becky blinked several times in disbelief. "*Ohhh*," she groaned, "I knew you were *real.*" Her body heaved with emotion as she leaped up and buried her face against Jess's chest and sobbed.

Jess rested his chin on the top of Becky's head. "It's okay," he whispered. "Everything's going to be all right now."

"I knew you'd come back to me," Becky cried. "I knew you loved me."

"Wait a minute—" Jess unclasped Becky's arms from his waist and stepped back. "No one said anything about *love.*"

Becky's eyes grew large, her mouth moved, but no sound came out as her clenched fists beat on Jess's chest. Jess looked to Grace for support. She, too, was stunned by the girl's transformation.

"Becky?" Grace pulled the girl away from Jess, her voice calm and soothing, "Jess is the lawyer who helped you after the fire. He *is* a real person, just like you said, just like you tried to tell everyone. He's human, not an angel. He was kind to you. Maybe that's why you have such strong feelings for him."

"What do you know, Dr. Grace!"

"I know that—" Words caught in her throat with a truth they both shared. "You were a young girl then." *So was I*, Grace thought to herself. "The love we feel at a young age is different from the love we feel once we're grown up." She glanced at Jess, who had stuffed his hands in his pockets and stood staring out the window. "You don't *know* Jess, Becky. Your young mind created a fantasy about him. You're holding onto feelings from when you were fourteen, and that's not you anymore. You're an adult. Love can be different for you now. It can be *real.*"

Grace saw herself in Becky at that moment. She too had been under Jess's spell. She thought about Garret and the love growing between them, weeding out and leaving behind what she once felt for Jess.

***

The next morning Grace reached into the box for the morning paper and folded it under her arm. Her eyes became misty thinking about the night before, the reunion at the hospital with Jess and Becky. She felt that with Dr. Meltz's help and continued therapy Becky would be able to heal from her broken heart. She could resolve issues from her childhood and work on living a better life. Jess was helpful filling in details pertaining to Becky's family and the fire, but didn't have much to say on the ride home. He said he was scheduled to be court in the morning and needed to get some sleep. But Grace had a feeling he had other things on his mind, *like his bruised ego?* Perhaps he would focus more on his wife, Jenna.

*Funny how life comes full circle.* Fresh blooms on her rose bush reminded her of how fragile and beautiful life could be. Her lips spread into a smile. *I can't wait to tell Garret.* She was eager to share her news about Becky and make arrangements to get Sneaky back. *What about dinner plans?* She touched the pink rose petals and a thrill charged through her body. *I have no say in how I feel. Strange, but I like it.* She closed her eyes to summon Garret's face. She had never felt this way before. He affected her in a way she couldn't explain. *I'm falling in love with him*, she thought dreamily.

Grace took the newspaper to the back of the house, where she sat on the deck overlooking her lush green lawn and fragrant trees. She sipped hot brew out of her favorite ceramic cup, enjoying the cool summer breeze. *I wonder what my horoscope has to say about my love life today.* She spread the paper out on the table and began searching for the puzzles and game section of the Sacramento Bee. Turning the pages, a headline caught her eye, and she stopped. A warrior's drum beat in her chest. She gasped for air. Coffee sloshed over the rim of her cup and seemed suspended in mid-air before the cup crashed to the deck and shattered on redwood planks. The headline read:

### Police Sergeant Shot

"An undercover drug bust went bad Wednesday at 52nd and X streets when suspected gang members shot Sergeant Garret Weston of the Twenty Second Precinct in the head, leaving the policeman in critical condition."

Grace couldn't believe her eyes. Her body trembled. She re-read the bold print over and over until her brain was convinced her eyes weren't playing tricks on her. Tears fell like rain. Her heart fractured into tiny pieces.

* * *

Grace hurried through new construction in the hospital until she reached her destination, the intensive care unit. *Breathe.* She swiped her badge, waited for the buzz, and pushed through double doors.

Monitors beeped like sentinels in Garret's sterile environment. She hoped her red-rimmed eyes would be less obvious in the room's dim lighting. *He needs positive energy, not tears.* Would he know who she was in her yellow, hospital gown and cap?

She took his hand. *"Hi,"* she said softly. "It's Grace."

"I owe you a steak," he mumbled through dry lips, trying to smile.

"Shhhh. Don't talk. We have plenty of time," she said, caressing his face.

"Remember, I don't like green stuff," he said weakly.

"I know," she smiled. "No green stuff, I promise."

"Grace," he whispered. His green eyes glistened with emotion. She bent closer. His voice strained, becoming barely audible: "I love—" Suddenly his words were drowned out by frantic beeps coming from the machine. When the beeping stopped, a high pitched hum filled the room.

Seconds felt like eternity to Grace, shoved into the corner while a team of medical personnel pounded on Garret's chest, injected needles in his IV bag, and called his name. Paddles thumped after someone shouted "clear," again and again. The even tone coming from the monitor pierced her heart, staring at the straight line on the screen, willing it to move. Doctors and nurses clad in colorful scrubs scurried around the bed, speaking a language only they understood. Grace couldn't move, she couldn't breathe.

# CHAPTER 35
# Full Circle

Grace's hands lay limply in her lap. Her stringy hair matted beneath the yellow cap didn't faze her. She was wearing the same clothes she put on two days ago. Or was it three? How much time had passed since Garret was shot? Days? A week? She couldn't remember. It seemed like yesterday. His body, kept alive on ventilators, *the rest of him gone.* Grace felt as though a part of her had gone with him.

Detective Spiderelli stopped by with an update: the person who shot Garret was still not found. Doctors didn't expect Garret to pull through…yet, another day would go by and then another. She prayed. What was the use? It seemed God already made His decision.

Who could she turn to? She was angry, *afraid.* Not Sal. Sal had problems of her own, undergoing tests to detect if her cancer had returned. Jess? He would try to fix things. Besides, she hadn't heard from him since he dropped her off the night they visited Becky. Too much had happened. She was no longer herself. *I need help.*

Grace stepped outside the hospital to get some air. She looked up at the stars and took a deep breath. She tried to hum a comforting tune, yet the sinking feeling returned. She walked to a nearby bench but didn't sit down. Her scalp tingled; chills zipped up and down her spine. *Someone is watching me.* She quickly dug in her purse for her phone, but what she really wanted was a weapon. No use. An emery board and a stick of gum wouldn't suffice. She stood still, listening, and waiting. Suddenly, a shadow emerged from the dark.

"Jess! You scared me half to death! What are you doing here?"

"You weren't at home. I figured you'd be here." His eyes, dark and brooding, settled on hers.

"Why? How did you—" He placed his hand on her shoulder.

"I read about it in the paper. Any change?"

"No, Garret's still in a coma." Tears pooled in her eyes.

Jess stepped in closer. "It's okay," he said, stroking her arms. "We'll get through this together."

Grace flashed on Becky sharing in her session. Her angel spoke the very same words. *Jess's words.* Grace shivered. She had told Becky that angels didn't wield that kind of power, that the man who spoke those words sounded evil. She looked deep into Jess's eyes and wondered.

*** 

"It's been two weeks since Sergeant Weston was shot. I heard there hasn't been any change." Dr. Meltz's voice penetrated her thoughts, and Grace vaguely realized he was patting her hand, but she didn't respond. Dr. Meltz leaned forward. "You keep drifting off, Gracie. Where do you go? What do you think about?" he asked, his tone tender.

She smiled as the video played behind her closed lids, reliving the moment she fell in love—that day on her stairway when they met half-way and their eyes found each other. "I think about his eyes," she said, her voice raw, almost a whisper. Tears rolled down her cheeks as the beautiful green eyes etched in her mind pierced her heart. Suddenly, a chill came over her, and she shivered. Another pair of eyes, dark and brooding, materialized behind her closed lids. *Those* eyes wouldn't let her go.

"His eyes?" The psychiatrist leaned forward in his chair.

Grace's mind ventured back to the day when Becky first came to her office for help and her heart filled with fear. Life had, indeed, come full circle. She turned to Dr. Meltz and said, "Yes, I think about his eyes, I think about—" *The way he looked at me.*

# Epilogue

Jess sat in his car outside the old Victorian with the grey door. A brass shingle hung from the eave: Dr. Marcus F. Meltz, Psychiatrist, M.D.

The attorney checked his watch. Grace had been inside for forty minutes. He wondered what she was talking about. *Me?* He chuckled to himself. *Loverboy?* Of course. *Coma.*

He hadn't anticipated Weston surviving a bullet to the head. He hadn't expected Grace to react the way she did, hitting the skids, falling down the rabbit hole, and needing a shrink. He peeked inside the glove compartment at the pearl-handled pistol he lifted from the dead stripper. He reassured himself that Grace would eventually come to her senses and, like himself, realize... *no one else can have you. You're mine.*

Other Books in the Grace Simms Trilogy

## *The Grey Door*
## *The Black Dress*

If you enjoyed
## *The Red Chair*
sign up for news and information
about future book releases at...

www.RedChairTheBook.com

# For Discussion Groups

Filled with complex relationships and distinctive characters, *The Red Chair* is an engrossing novel for book groups and reading circles that want to decipher the feelings, pain, and growth of everyday people while delving into the struggles of a percentage of eccentrics.

Grace Simms often learns truths about herself when she counsels her own clients. Is she more like each of them than she cares to admit? Is that why she is so protective of their secrets – or is she merely toeing the legal line of confidentiality?

It's easy to generate discussion around these kinds of questions by using an Observe-Analyze-Relate discussion strategy, or *OAR* for short. While reviewing each chapter, take time to *observe* the narrative and dialog a degree deeper. By observing closely, you'll soon discover, for example, that Candy is way too eager to go home with James Freeman. As you *analyze*, ask the *why* question. What's motivating Candy to start a long-term relationship with a man she just met? Before moving on to a new chapter or section, complete the circle of discussion with a conversation about how you personally *relate* to your observations and analysis. For example, do you personally know women who attach themselves to men too quickly? If you were in a similar situation as Candy, would you do anything to "get out?"

Readers can apply the OAR discussion strategy to characters, symbols, chapters, scenes, and plot points. For example, what are your observations about the potential symbolism of Grace's red chair? How did Grace feel when she touched it? What feelings erupted inside her when the chair was taken away as evidence? How did her feelings toward Garret change? What else in her life was red? In analyzing your observations, what kind of symbol do you perceive the red chair was for Grace? To her clients? To the overall theme of the book? What's your evidence for interpreting the symbol? Do you have similar symbols in your own life? Are they conscious symbols or subconscious?

It always best for a discussion leader to have some observation questions ready for the group, but a healthy book group always ends up generating its own set of prominent observations based on dominant characters or plot twists. To give book discussion groups a head start, we present ten question-sets of discussion prompts. We provide even more at the book's website: www. RedChairTheBook.com. On the website, we also encourage you to add your own questions or discuss ones that have been posted – all of which will keep us plenty busy in anticipation of *The Grey Door*.

—The Editors

**1.** What are the circumstances affecting the behavior of each of Grace's clients? Which of their behaviors are common to Grace's own situation? How do you shape you own life by observing others around you?

**2.** Grace has her own wandering eye for handsome men. When does it manifest itself and under what circumstances? Why can she channel her lust for some men, but not for Jess? What strategies do you employ to resist temptation? When is it right to surrender to your passions?

**3.** How do James's features change when Grace asks about his parents? What behaviors contradict his desire to be a good father and husband? Grace says he has "trust issues." Why? Will James end up bring a good parent? A good husband? Have you ever had a relationship with a person like James?

**4.** How is Becky like Grace? Does Grace have her own angel? Her own demons? Her own secrets? Compare and contrast how each woman handles her own hurts. How unique are your own struggles? Do you share your hurts, joys, and strategies with others?

**5.** On a bench in Capitol Park, Jess blows up at Grace. What was his complaint? Were his outbursts justified? Did Grace learn anything? Is he a controlling person or merely a concerned person? How does he deal with his jealousies? By the end of the book, how have your feeling toward Jess changed? If you were Grace, would you have gone home with him or broken up?

**6.** Sal is both a friend and an employee to Grace. What conflicts does this create? Does Sal ever violate Grace's trust? Is Grace ever condescending toward Sal? What is the source of their bond? What threatens their relationship? Do you ever have to treat your best friend differently because of a work role or outside influence?

**7.** Who are the flirts in this book? How does flirtation manifest itself? When Jess and Garret flirt with Grace, are their intentions well received? Or are they inappropriate? How do flirtations build or retard their relationships? When someone flirts with you, what circumstances make it uncomfortable? How do you react or correct the situation?

**8.** Wilde Defoe arrives late on the scene with a concern over dying. What coping mechanisms does Grace give him? What feelings does he invoke in Grace? How does Grace cope with the death of Candy? How did Becky deal with death? Why might Grace, who is a trained professional, have more to learn about coping with life and death herself? Have you experienced a loss or tragedy? More than once? How have you learned to cope? Was there more to learn the second time around?

**9.** A well-developed character in a work of fiction has to have a vulnerability to be true-to-life. What is Garret's vulnerability? When confronted with conflict, how does he react? When facing a decision, what path does he take? Does he become a better person or worse? How do his choices affect Grace? How do you react when a person is forced to take a path that affects you negatively?

**10.** Grace appears to like coffee. Who makes a better cup: Sal, Grace, or Garret? Does Jess ever drink coffee? When does Grace take cream and sugar? Why? How does coffee facilitate the development of relationships in this story? How is coffee a metaphor? How does coffee connect and enhance your own friendships and relationships?

# About the Author

Dänna Wilberg is a multi-award-winning, short-film maker who produces and hosts two television programs in Sacramento, California.

*Paranormal Connection* covers topics such as communicating with the spirit world, UFOs, astral projection, remote viewing, self-healing, past lives, astrology, spirit guides, tarot cards, and alternative health. *Story Connection* focuses on the "story" behind the story and includes interviews from a variety of artists and ordinary people doing extraordinary things.

Dänna has been writing romantic suspense and paranormal fiction for more than ten years. Her novel, *The Red Chair* is the first release in her Grace Simms Trilogy published by Pretty Road Press. *The Grey Door* and *The Black Dress* are scheduled for release in 2015. Dänna weaves *messages from the universe* in her story telling and attributes her success to hard work and a *persistent muse*.

To give readers additional insight to Dänna Wilberg as an author, Pretty Road Press (PRP) asked her for some short answers to some of the most common questions from fans:

**PRP:** What is your writing routine like? How did you stay disciplined to write the Grace Simms Trilogy?

**Dänna:** I try to write every day. When I am not writing, I am creating stories and plots in my head.

**PRP:** How does being a television producer help or influence you in creating a novel series?

**Dänna:** Being the producer of a show about the paranormal and another one that focuses on storytelling, I meet a lot of interesting people who supply me with endless ideas for character development.

**PRP:** What challenges did you have to overcome after your accident? What happened? How did it affect your writing and creative work?

**Dänna:** My car accident left me with a brain-stem injury that presents cognitive issues and limited short-term memory, all of which make it difficult to learn and express myself at times. Writing provided an outlet for my pain and frustration.

**PRP:** What hint can you give us about what will happen in *The Grey Door*? Are there hints hidden in *The Red Chair* that we should be looking for?

**Dänna:** Life doesn't always turn out the way we want it to. *The Grey Door* allows the reader to experience how Grace deals with disappointment and healing when faced with tragedy.

**PRP:** What qualities did the Northern California counties of Sacramento and El Dorado possess that helped you choose them as a setting for your story?

**Dänna:** Sacramento and El Dorado counties are filled with fun places to eat and drink, and they provide interesting backdrops for all my characters.

**PRP:** What other authors influence you as a writer and why?

**Dänna:** Dean Koontz for his incredible imagination and Anne Rice for her dark romantic characterization.

**PRP:** How are you and Grace Simms alike?

**Dänna:** Grace and I love cake and red chairs.

**PRP:** What special qualities about your native Chicago delight you? Do you have a connection to Northwestern?

**Dänna:** Chicago is where I first fell in love. It seemed a natural place to start. Northwestern is a beautiful college and provided a perfect setting for romance.

**PRP:** What other personal experiences had an influence in the scenes you have written for *The Red Chair*?

**Dänna:** The story about Sugar is partially true. She was my neighbor and made great lemon meringue pie. I have been fooled by people many times; perhaps it's because I was meant to write this book.

Made in the USA
Columbia, SC
31 March 2019